The Flapper, the Impostor, and the Stalker

THE
FLAPPER,
THE
IMPOSTOR,
AND THE
STALKER

a novel

Charlene Bell Dietz

QUILL MARK PRESS . ALBUQUERQUE

LIBRARY OF CONGRESS CONTROL NUMBER: 2017955505

Dietz, Charlene Bell
The flapper, the impostor, and the stalker: An Inkydance book-club mystery /
Charlene Bell Dietz.—First Edition.
ISBN 978-1-9452-1265-9 (hardcover)
ISBN 978-1-9452-1266-6 (paperback)
ISBN 978-1-9452-1267-3 (electronic)

1. Roaring Twenties—Fiction 2. Science Institute—Fiction 3. Murder—Fiction
4. Economic Espionage—Fiction 5. Multigenerational—Fiction 6. Mystery—
Fiction

Quill Mark Press
933 San Mateo NE, Suite 500–159
Albuquerque, NM 87108

AUTHOR'S NOTE: The characters in this book live only in my imagination. I've strived to adequately portray the mood and social mores of 1923 in Minneapolis and during the Roaring Twenties in Chicago. Many of the national events, public figures, and local places are factual but used fictitiously. I hope my readers will forgive my extended use of artistic license in creating the placement of a pier on Lake Michigan.

BOOK DESIGN Lila Romero
BOOK COVER Cityscape by American Studio, N.Y. [Public domain], via Wikimedia Commons. Flapper photograph courtesy of M. G. Cassidy.

DEDICATION

Mike, you always stand beside me.

ACKNOWLEDGEMENTS

Thank you to my writers' group: Patricia Wood, Margaret Tessler, Joan Taitte, Mary Blanchard, Dianne Flaherty, Linda Tregal, and Annie Kyle.

My gratefulness extends to my Beta Readers for their critical judgement and honesty:

Haley Dietz
Mary Ann Domina
Sue Hettema
Marleen Kurban
Margaret Tessler

A special appreciation goes to my three brothers: Graham, Donald, and Bruce Bell. You kept the memories of our whispered family stories fresh.

Be sure to live your life, because you are a long time dead.
—SCOTTISH PROVERB

1

Minneapolis, 1923

Malum non sustinuit, Kathleen wrote. *Evil must not be . . .* The night wind billowed the bedroom draperies into the room. A sound caught her attention—a fragment of a cry. She stood and stared out into the darkness.

Silence. The noise had come from Lyndale Park, just across the side street from her home. *No one went there on a school night.*

Confused, she slipped back onto her chair and dipped the nib of her pen into the bottle of India Black. She wrote her last translated word: *endured.*

Another burst of spring wind snapped the bedroom draperies, slapping the back of her hand. She jerked, spoiling the last word. An ominous ink splat landed on the cover of her *Theater Magazine.*

Dammit.

"To hell with Latin." Only her ears heard the cuss word because her parents were enjoying their nightly cocktails downstairs. "And a walloping double go-to-hell for college."

She should have told them sooner.

Kathleen grabbed her linen hanky and dabbed at the mess.

Ink smeared across the magazine's lemon-yellow and peach colors. The illustration of an alluring actress exemplifying a Mardi Gras masquerade portrait—ruined. She threw the square of linen into the wastebasket and slammed her Latin book shut.

She rose to close the window, but the strange noise niggled at her.

The lamplight on the street corner cast a buttery glow. Mr. Field's Boston terrier began to bark.

It quieted. He must have shushed it.

The night breeze brushed against her face. She analyzed and reconstructed the haunting sound, a sound of distress—a gurgle with an abbreviated, swallowed yowl—like from a cat.

Miss Folly—oh, no! She caught her breath. Some malevolent carnivore had attacked her neighbor's cat.

Please, one more sound, Miss Folly. She fought a sinking coldness. *Come on—let me know you're still there.*

More silence.

She snatched one shoe. Hopping, she slipped it on. She did the same with the other, burst out of her room, and scurried down the circular staircase, skipping steps. Her parents called to her, but she ignored their questions. Her father grabbed her by the arm as she dashed past him. He twirled her about and demanded to know where she was going.

She pulled and begged but couldn't get her brain and tongue to work together. Too many seconds passed. She threw them some words about Miss Folly in the park and the soulful, twisted meowing.

Her mother scoffed. "It's impossible to hear anything so far away."

Her father released her. Kathleen burst into the kitchen and out the door, hearing him say, "With low clouds, sounds are amplified."

She stumbled down the porch stairs and scrambled along the darkened back path that led to the side of the park. A gust of wind lifted locks of her hair and then let them fall, just as her mother had after she had come home with her new bob.

Voices caught on the breeze. They swirled and faded, leaving no trace of meaning in the words. *Who on Earth would be in the park after nine?* Then again, she had slipped out and met Chester once. It had been around ten o'clock. But she had never seen anyone else, at least not on a weeknight.

Kathleen sprinted across the dirt road into the park, pushed past limbs and bushes, and called, "Kitty, Kitty, Miss Folly."

She strained to change visible forms into recognizable shapes. Tonight the electrified air in the park felt foreign.

[2]

When she skirted around an evergreen, she halted and caught her breath. A man with a flashlight stood near the rose garden. Holding a dog close on a leash, he gestured to a police officer. *It must be Mr. Field. His dog killed Miss Folly.*

Yet it made no sense to call a policeman about a cat.

Someone slipped an arm around her shoulders, and she squealed. Her father—warmth and comfort.

Poor Miss Folly. She laid her head on his shoulder.

He pointed to the street in front of their home, where other neighbors hurried to the park. The officer escorted Mr. Field and his dog from the rose garden toward the street and insisted the others stay back, then he strode over to the police call box next to the lamppost. Kathleen swept her gaze over the grounds, still hoping Miss Folly survived. She wished she had a flashlight too.

"Pops, look over in the grass. It's too big to be a cat." She nodded toward the rose garden. A gust of wind caught something next to the larger object and tumbled it toward them. The wind stopped and so did the object. She couldn't make out what it was. Then the wind hit hard and blew it across the ground almost to Kathleen. She lunged forward, stooped, and retrieved it. A hat—a cloche—one like a young lady would wear. Her fingers felt damp and sticky—

She gasped and dropped it.

"It's bloody."

She focused on the object by the rose garden. Her eyes adjusted to the darkness. The lump on the ground looked like a heap of mulch. Then moonlight broke through an opening in the clouds and illuminated a whiteness extending from the pile. A leg—a body, not a pile of leaves—lay sprawled next to one of the many winter-pruned rose bushes.

This can't be. Cold crawled up her spine.

Her father shoved her behind him, but Kathleen nudged back around for a better look.

The leaded weight of the night moved through her, smothering her voice. She managed a soft, "This is real, isn't it?"

He didn't answer. She ignored a vague awareness of movement close by and studied her father's face.

"Pops?"

He continued to stare at the scene in front of them. She wiggled her foot to rid it of an insect or—something—her ankle—

"Aaah—yikes!"

She jerked and clutched at her father. Electricity charged through her body. Her muscles froze until she recognized the warm, silky fur as it moved against her leg.

Miss Folly. Awful heaviness floated away.

The cat continued to weave in and out and around Kathleen's legs. She scooped the cat into her arms, snuggled it, and refused to look at whatever lay in the grass. Her father reached over and rubbed Miss Folly's ear.

"I doubt if we'll learn anything." He nodded toward the officer. "The constable's making people leave. I suspect you know more than they do because you've got the hat."

"I should give it to him." Kathleen, trembling more from the experience than the chill in the air, held Miss Folly's warm body close.

"You should." He took her elbow to guide her. She picked the hat up with two fingers.

When the officer saw them he flailed his arms, shooing them back.

Kathleen's father called out, "Sir, here's something you should have."

The officer held his palms out for them to stay put and strode over.

Kathleen spoke before her father could. "The wind carried it across the lawn. What's happened? It's a girl over there, isn't it?"

"Can't talk about it, young lady."

He took their names and address and listened to them say what brought them to the park. He finished writing. "Everyone needs to leave. Go on home now."

"Who's the girl?" Kathleen took renewed energy from the purring cat. "You can tell us that, certainly."

He refused, saying there were procedures as well as a family to be notified.

"Then she's *dead.*" Kathleen couldn't breathe. "What killed her? Why?"

Her father put his arm around her and steered her toward their home.

"Pops, how could this happen?"

Miss Folly continued to purr. Kathleen held her tighter.

"Kathleen, you know as much as I do about this."

But Pops, tell me something. Make a guess. You're supposed to know more than anyone.

[4]

He that lives on hope has a slim diet.
—SCOTTISH PROVERB

2

Kathleen kept pace beside her father. When they reached the dark path behind their home, he insisted she lead. The back porch light cut a swath down the steps to the path, and her mother stood with her eyes shielded, searching for them.

"You found Miss Folly. What a relief. Mrs. Lewis would fall apart if anything happened to that cat."

"Mother, it's a girl over there." Kathleen pointed back to the park. "I'm sure she's quite dead."

"Dear, that sounds so disrespectful. Angus, she can't be correct."

Her father strode up the porch stairs and into the house. "We'll discuss this inside." He escorted her mother through the kitchen door.

Kathleen hung back. She sank down, sat on the step, and stroked Miss Folly.

She shuddered to think of what the event in the park meant. *Pops always has answers.* She'd spent her life dependent on his knowledge. She didn't like the thought of him not knowing anything.

The cat squirmed and set her sharp teeth firmly on Kathleen's wrist. She let the feline go and watched Miss Folly scurry toward home.

When Kathleen entered the kitchen, she heard her mother's voice coming from the living room. She watched from the doorway. Her nine-year-old sister, Mary, wide-eyed with fright, stood on the landing.

"But I don't understand." Mary pulled at the high neck on her long nightie. "What's happening?"

"Nothing to worry you." Her mother moved to escort Mary up the stairs. "Here you go, back to bed."

"But now I can't sleep." Mary looked back toward Kathleen.

She's too young to know about these things. Kathleen gave her a reassuring smile.

"Let me tuck you in again," her mother cooed to the child. "You'll be fine."

"Mary, do as your mother says." Her father stared out the large window.

Kathleen recognized his *I'm troubled* behavior. She had figured out years ago he couldn't see anything out there at night. The darkness outside reflected the living-room lights. He wouldn't be able to see Lake Harriet at all. He kept silent, unlike her mother.

She came back down the steps, talking. "When I looked out the front door and saw neighbors heading over there, I knew we had trouble. Kathleen, did you recognize who might have owned the hat?"

Pops must have talked to her while I was sitting with Miss Folly.

"We couldn't see much of anything. I'm sure Father told you the officer wouldn't let us close, and he told us nothing."

"Surely someone must know something. Angus, can't you call someone?"

"At this point," he said, "this is none of our business."

"It may be none of our business, dear, but I find it terribly upsetting." She sat on the couch, patting her pockets.

He raised his glass of bourbon and took a sip.

Mother still doesn't get it. Pops has no intention of discussing anything about this.

Kathleen went to the hallway table and picked up the telephone. She imagined the cool warmth of his bourbon slipping down her throat. He must have caught her reflection because he called to her without turning around.

"Kathleen, you're not to talk about this with your friends. Stay off the telephone tonight."

The telephone operator came on the line and asked, "Number please."

"Sorry, Operator. Never mind." Kathleen hung up. "Sophie and I

[6]

tell each other everything." She moved into the living room. "She'll hear about it at school tomorrow anyway."

"Dear, you don't have to be the one to tell Sophie everything. Angus, what do you think happened out there?" Her mother pushed her hand down between the sofa cushions.

Kathleen heard her father say something in a low voice she couldn't understand.

"What's the harm in telling Sophie?" Kathleen stood with her hands on her hips. Her parents held everything too tight, kept everything too private. They made categories of things one must never discuss—religion, money, politics, sex, and now death.

He glared at her. "Anything said at this point can only be counted as gossip. Gossip harms. Now finish your studies. It's late." He put his bourbon down and picked up his pipe, lit it, and settled into his dark-leather club chair.

"It's not that late." She set her jaw and decided she wouldn't go upstairs for a few more minutes. She hated being bossed.

Her mother reached over the arm of the couch and opened the drawer in the end table. "I'm surprised to see those papers from Stephens College still on the hallway table. You need to attend to them." She directed her words to Kathleen while her fingers searched inside the drawer.

"She still hasn't filled those out?" Her father tapped his pipe in the ashtray. "They came two weeks ago."

Whatever hid in the drawer seemed lost to the older woman. She leaned over the arm of the sofa and peered in.

Heat prickled Kathleen's cheeks. "Stephens Female College appears to be a fine institution, but . . . I suspect neither of you has even bothered to go to Missouri."

Her mother spoke. "Of course we have. You're being impertinent." She pulled out a crumpled Pall Mall pack and shook the remaining cigarette out. "My goodness, I must be smoking more than I realized."

Kathleen glanced at the pack and her pulse accelerated, but she kept her voice steady. "I apologize if I sound disrespectful, but I do have a right to be a bit off put about this, Mother. Missouri feels synonymous with drab."

"What the—?" Her father relit his pipe. "Your apology is *not* accepted. Elizabeth, her insolence is out of hand."

Kathleen's mother crossed her ankles, moved the ashtray closer, and lit a cigarette. She inhaled, then swept her gaze around the room, as if ignoring them both.

Kathleen stood rigid. "I do appreciate your generosity in picking out such an expensive college." She wanted to look down but didn't. "I've been quiet about your plans for me, but I can't pretend any longer. I've taken acting and dancing lessons and practiced for years, and now you tell me to stop and do something different. I don't see how this makes sense."

"Your argument doesn't do it, young lady." Her father leaned forward. "You've also spent years going to school and studying. Focus on those scholarships."

"Now you've made acting and dancing useless skills for me, just like you never let me drive after all those driving lessons. How can you expect me to go to some academic institution out in the middle of nowhere?" She gave her mother a pleading look. "I'll wither away under a pile of books."

Her mother shook her head. "Columbia is between Kansas City and St. Louis. Only you would consider that nowhere. And if you cared to read the information, you would see drama and dancing classes are taught at Stephens. Now off to your room and finish your studies. It's late."

Kathleen huffed. *What a bunch of poppycock.* "For the love of—I'm seventeen. Shouldn't I be allowed to make decisions concerning my life?" Her throat closed. The words now struggled out. "All I want is to dance and act—be an entertainer. I'm capable of learning everything on my own. I don't need teachers, and I don't need a close-minded committee of family members telling me what to do."

Her father sat back in his chair and studied her. She detested the way her erratic breathing betrayed her inner turmoil.

"Mother." She looked at her father. "Pops, who knows what will happen? Think of the dead girl over in the park. Please let me follow my passion."

He rubbed his thumb against his pipe. "Don't throw everything away on your dreams, Kathleen. Becoming an entertainer would bring disgrace on you and this family, and one day you'll need your family." Her father waved his finger toward the hallway. "Fill out those papers and place them on my desk by tomorrow evening."

Learn young, learn fair; learn old, learn more.
—SCOTTISH PROVERB

3

"Kathleen, wake up. You'll be late if you don't hurry." Her mother shook her.

Who could have slept last night? First the paddy wagon came with extra policemen. Next, other cars pulled up. Flashlights flickered between trees and bushes and swept back and forth across the park. She'd missed the removal of the body.

Before daylight, when everyone had left the park, she had fallen across her bed fully clothed and slept hard until her mother woke her sometime after six o'clock.

She freshened up, changed, and anticipated a grouchy day ahead.

At breakfast, Kathleen devoured a piece of buttered toast while standing next to the stove, reading the article in the morning's paper. It said Mr. Field's dog had found a young woman dead in the park. *Young woman—how young?*

Kathleen picked up her books, left the house, and closed their front door—with a finality, imagining she'd never return. Her father would find those damned scholarship papers on his desk even before his morning coffee.

She hopped off the bottom porch step and looked around for Mr. Field and his dog. Mr. Field hadn't recognized the woman, and the police refused to discuss the case until family members were notified.

Today no one puttered about their lawns. Morning newspapers, usually ignored until later, were missing. Everyone must be at their kitchen tables, drinking coffee, smoking, and hunting for details about last night's incident.

Several blocks from her home, she heard footsteps behind her. She turned to wave but found the sidewalk empty.

How silly—

Still, she quickened her step.

Even before the murder, she had sensed someone following her when she walked home for lunch yesterday. Sporadic sounds of dead winter grass crunched under someone's feet. It creeped her out.

She'd have been safer driving the automobile to school, but her mother shrugged her fears off, saying, "Dear, this whole thing has you shaken up, that's all."

Why bother to learn to drive if they won't ever let me use their automobile?

The sidewalk, lined with overgrown bushes and hardwood trees, appeared vacant, except for a stray dog peeing on everything vertical. Branch and leaf shadows looked spooky because they didn't move in predictable patterns.

Kathleen entered the school building and saw Dolly and Sophie down the hallway. Dolly, fussing with that ridiculous red bow on her frilly dress, chattered away—probably about the dead girl.

How annoying. Some girl died last night, and they act like it's a game. She leaned against the wall outside their English class and closed her eyes. She concentrated on calming her jitters. The longer her two friends huddled together, discussing last night's incident, the more it grated on her nerves.

"This is plain baloney." Dolly sliced the air with her hand. "Why won't they tell us? If she did go to this school, they know who got murdered."

Kathleen sighed. "They need to notify the family before they release the victim's name. Give it a break, will you? You're both giving me the heebie-jeebies."

Their English teacher opened the classroom door.

Kathleen pushed away from the wall and followed the girls into the room.

"Pay attention when the teachers call roll," Dolly whispered. "Then we'll know."

Kathleen slid into her desk seat. This time she gave Dolly credit. *A dead classmate wouldn't answer roll call.*

A good tale never tires in the telling.
—SCOTTISH PROVERB

4

Kathleen stared at the blank spaces next to most of the questions on the test. Perspiration collected on her forehead and neck. A superior grade in Latin meant she'd get that scholarship her parents harped about, propelling her into a life of hideous boredom.

The clock hands inched closer to the three o'clock dismissal time. She drew some little circles in the margins.

Twelve minutes left. She sighed. She expected more from herself. A lump grew in her throat. She gripped her pencil and scribbled in answers, filling in every blank. At three o'clock, the teacher signaled for them to stop. She signed her name at the top of the first page with so much force the lead point broke.

Nothing better than happy goddamned parents.

Kathleen stood, gathered her books, and tucked them under her arm. She swiped the cursed exam off the desk, marched to the front of the room, and placed the test on the to-be-graded stack.

Defeat washed over her. *Missouri.*

She trudged down the stairway, jostled through the throng of students, and passed the principal's office. The secretary called to her and motioned for her to wait until she finished her telephone conversation.

Mrs. Howe smiled at her, then flipped through some notes, put her finger on one, and said, "Someone called and asked questions about you yesterday."

"Who?"

"The person wanted to know what time you got out of school."

"Was it a man or a woman?"

Mrs. Howe tapped the pencil on her chin. "You know—I can't say. The voice sounded strange. Do you know anything about this?"

Kathleen assured her she didn't.

"Your parents need to know, but today has been horrid. I've had to answer at least a hundred telephone calls."

Her parents would lecture her. "Don't bother, I'll tell them."

"It's my job, Kathleen. I'll call your mother right now."

"Swell. I have a streetcar to catch." Kathleen glanced at the door and back. Mrs. Howe, telephone to her ear, made a shooing motion with her hand.

Kathleen navigated past other students in the corridors and spied Sophie and Dolly waiting for her in front of the announcement board, their heads bent close in conversation.

Dolly waved the air with her right hand, directing the symphony of her words.

Kathleen shifted her books to her other arm. An irritated wave of exclusion swept over her. "Let's go do those stretches."

She steeled herself for Dolly's nonsense, but Sophie spoke first.

"I wish my mother would let me drop out of dance. It's pure torture."

"Don't make an art of whining." Instantly, Kathleen regretted her remark. Sophie walked a tight edge in the sensitivity department.

Dance class was Kathleen's salvation. When she danced, her worries disappeared. Concentration on the exactness of movement while the music flowed through and swirled around her became everything.

"I don't have long legs like you." Sophie's face twisted into envy. "My body can't take it. It's not designed for stretching." Sophie's figure packed all the right curves into a short, solid box. She grabbed Dolly's arm. "And look at you. You're a stick."

"Tell your mother you want to sing." Dolly nodded at some guy. "My mother knows I'm going to be an actress, so I have to study it all."

Kathleen found Dolly's remarks irksome. "Our mothers know ladies must be well rounded."

"Then your mothers are you-know-whats if they don't care what you want." Dolly flipped one of her long, blonde curls and pivoted her eyes side to side, watching boys like she was watching a tennis match. She might look like a Gibson girl or Little Bo Peep, but Kathleen knew who earned the title for the real *Miss B.* Flounces and frills caused the guys to follow Dolly like puppies. Rumors suggested she adequately rewarded select young men for their efforts.

Dolly should read about flappers and learn about something useful—such as vinegar sponges.

Kathleen strode ahead until she came to the place where they waited for the streetcar. Younger girls stood near a husky boy, who enjoyed their attention by saying, "You know what happens when the heart is punctured? Well, it's a pump, so blood squirts out all over the place. My dad heard blood was splattered everywhere 'cause he went over there last night when he saw all the flashlights."

Kathleen moved farther down the wall. No one would let it go. Her stomach churned. She rarely felt sick from nerves.

Kathleen had wanted to confide in Sophie about being followed, but after last night's murder, Sophie would fall apart. Going home for lunch today, the spooky feeling had happened again. Yet the kids riding bicycles down her street had seemed unconcerned.

"Bernice, Rita, and Thelma were absent from class today." Dolly hurried to catch up. "Who was missing from yours?"

"Lillian." Kathleen looked away. She wished she had one of her mother's cigarettes.

"That's all?" Dolly screwed her face up in disbelief. "I don't know Lillian."

Kathleen shrugged. Lillian kept to herself, seemed kind and rather smart. Kathleen didn't know much more, except for gossip—girls whispered about Lillian being crazy in love with an older man.

Dolly's continuous chatter drove Kathleen mad, but Sophie enjoyed it. In a few months they would graduate together from high school and separate. Then all they needed to do was figure out the rest of their lives.

"Certainly the parents know by now." Dolly smiled at a passing man.

Sophie moved next to Kathleen. "How do they know this girl went to our school?"

"They found her body in Lyndale Park," Dolly said, "so she probably did. Heavens, Kathleen, you live right next to that park." Dolly's big, blue eyes grew even larger.

"Our streetcar's almost here." Kathleen stepped to the curb. She didn't know why she hadn't told them about last night. All this chatter did sound like childish gossip.

When her little sister got on her nerves, Kathleen went for long walks in the park, through the gardens and along the paths. She felt safe, even when she slipped out into the dark. Now her parents would make it off-limits. She and Chester would need to find another meeting place.

She wanted to talk to Chester, but he had said he wouldn't be back until tomorrow night.

The streetcar pulled to a stop. When they boarded and settled in their seats, Kathleen fixed her gaze on the passing scenery. After four years of traveling this route, she still watched for the old man who grew more spindly over the months. He'd sit on the bench on his front porch and throw sticks for his scraggly dog to retrieve. There was the young mother pulling weeds out by their roots from her tiny garden. She'd bounce her new baby on her hip or walk down the block with her little bundle cradled in her arms. Now the child, a girl, played nearby while the mother continued gardening.

All three looked lonely. Kathleen wondered who they were. What were their problems and their passions? For that matter, what was her passion other than dancing and acting? An empty ache of loneliness crept through her too.

Sophie took her arm and leaned in toward Kathleen's ear. "It's scary having this happen so close to your home."

Kathleen nodded. They were about to go across the bridge. She wondered about the depth of the water.

"All the nights we've spent together at your house, and all those times we went for a walk—" Sophie's voice cracked. "We even walked down to the bandstand."

Kathleen moved her arm around her friend's shoulders. At least Sophie understood how this would change their lives. Chester's insight would be worthless because he lived in a different world—an older, stodgier world. Kathleen promised herself to never underestimate the value of Sophie's friendship.

Dolly pulled the cord, and the streetcar stopped three blocks from the dance studio. The girls scuttled off, checking behind to be sure they hadn't left anything, and fell into a harmonious stride down the sidewalk. Kathleen jerked to a stop, pulled out a coin, and slipped it to the boy selling the evening edition of the newspaper. The three stared at the black-and-white photo of their classmate.

Lillian Bluet would not be graduating with them.

Sophie lost control. "How horrid, simply horrid . . ." Muffled sounds took over.

Kathleen's hands quivered when she passed the paper to Dolly and led Sophie to a doorway. She held Sophie until she quieted. When Kathleen turned, Dolly was standing there, watching.

"It's not like she was your best friend, Soph." Dolly folded the paper. "We all feel terrible, but still it's not doing you any good to be center stage and all grummy over this. Sure, it might have been one of us, but carrying on isn't going to change things."

"What did the paper say?" Kathleen took the newspaper from her.

"Oh, they never tell you anything much." Dolly pointed to a paragraph. "There's information about her family. She was murdered around nine or ten last night. Her mother said Lillian had gone to the library to study—as if we all haven't used that excuse before."

"How did she get from the library to the park?" Sophie sniffed and peered at the paper from over Kathleen's shoulder.

Obviously, at least one of them had never used the library excuse. Kathleen decided not to answer Sophie's question, but Dolly did.

"She met someone in the park who killed her. Whoever she dated will be the first person they question. Or maybe a stranger killed her while she was waiting for her boyfriend. Do strangers wander through Lyndale Park at night?"

"Dolly, dry up. We're going to be late." Kathleen folded the paper and tucked it between her books.

Sophie stood inert, gulping air.

"Sophie?"

Sophie grabbed Kathleen's arm. "What if the murderer is one of the guys who sits next to us in class?"

Be watchful. The shadows you've cast are imminent.
—CHINESE FORTUNE COOKIE

5

The next afternoon, Kathleen entered the Chinese restaurant, stopped, and stared. Chester sat at a table in the corner, the one partially screened by a large potted plant. He saw her, stood, glanced around, and checked his pocket watch. Replacing it, he rushed over, grabbed her elbow, escorted her to his table, and pulled out the other chair.

"I'm surprised to see you here." Kathleen sat and placed her books on the floor. "You're supposed to be out of town on business until tonight."

"Finished the assignment early." He shrugged. "Vivian's expecting me home later this afternoon. She's unhappy when I'm gone."

He stood to catch the waiter. While he was telling the waiter to bring another special and a second glass of water, Kathleen spied Dolly coming through the entrance way. Their eyes met, but Kathleen wasn't about to invite Miss Flounce and Fluff over. Dolly glanced at Chester's back, scowled, and left.

Chester checked his pocket watch again, then walked to his side of the table and scanned the room before he sat.

He touched Kathleen's cheek with the back of his hand. "Can't believe my good fortune. You appear out of nowhere."

"My little sister again . . ." Kathleen tucked a short strand of her dark hair back. "I need a quiet lunch."

He fell silent while the waiter poured the water. Kathleen picked up the Chinese-red napkin and smoothed it over her lap. She noticed how Chester's wavy, blond hair never stayed slicked back.

"Why are you dining alone?" She wished he weren't so private about his life.

"Vivian hates Chinese food." He leaned back then slid his hand over Kathleen's. "Your skin's as soft as an angel's. Let's meet at the bandstand tonight."

"Haven't you read the newspaper?" His puzzled look told her he hadn't. "The other night in Lyndale Park someone stabbed one of my classmates."

"My word." Chester pulled his hand back. He flipped his napkin several times before placing it in his lap. "You can't be serious."

Kathleen remained silent.

"That's ghastly. Have they caught the killer? I'm assuming she died." He cracked his knuckles.

"Do you know how annoying that is?" Kathleen surprised herself with her boldness. Before he responded, the waiter approached, served their food, and moved on.

Kathleen's face grew warm. "You worry about the sweet Mrs. Davidson becoming unhappy when you aren't home, but you suggested leaving her tonight." She stifled her other questions and poked at her food.

"She's anything but sweet." Chester picked up his chopsticks. "Did you know this particular young woman, the one who was stabbed?"

"Lillian Bluet. She sits behind me in—Kathleen caught her breath. "She *was* in my Latin class."

The bronze color drained from his face. His army-brown eyes opened wide.

"You knew her?" Her appetite disappeared.

"Her father." He gave a tiny cough before adding, "An investor at our bank—I know him well. What a damned shame, a damned shame."

There was something he wasn't telling her. She could feel it. He started to eat, but one of his chopsticks slipped, and a touch of the spicy Szechuan beef spotted his expensive blue silk necktie. Kathleen pointed at the spot, and he swiped at it with his napkin.

Kathleen sighed then said, "She's rather a canceled stamp, unless you go for that boringly pale Edwardian look. I found her a touch standoffish. I haven't a clue why she would be in the park after dark, and on a school night too."

She'd met Chester in the park a few times—once last week on a school night. Chester looked at her. She suspected he was thinking the same thing.

His eyes darkened. "I'd never forgive myself if something happened to you." He nudged his plate aside and set his chopsticks on it. Most of his Szechuan beef remained untouched.

All their stolen smiles, discreet touches, and whispered secrets stirred up feelings she never knew existed. For the first time in her life someone thought of her as a person—not a child, a daughter, a friend, or a student, but a companion with emotions and desires.

Again, he pulled his pocket watch out and checked it. Did he want to leave? She needed to do something.

"We could meet someplace else." Kathleen slipped his watch from his hand, turned it over, and examined the engraved initials. She traced her finger over the letters and chuckled. "Chester Andrew Davidson, your initials spell CAD."

She started to open it, but he snatched it back and replaced it in his vest pocket, as if he'd heard that joke a thousand times. He signaled the waiter for their check. "My father gave this to me when I graduated from high school. I don't appreciate your making fun of it."

Would he now tell her he was leaving and wouldn't be seeing her again? Under the table, she crumpled her napkin in her fist and held her breath.

He said, "Mr. Bluet must be beside himself with grief."

Kathleen wanted to go somewhere with him and forget about school.

"And you, young lady, need to get to class." He cracked his knuckles again.

She stiffened. The waiter hurried over.

"Ah, the fun part." Chester slipped the check off the small, gold-rimmed dish and left the two fortune cookies on it. "You first. Pick which one holds your fortune."

She ignored him—a tiny punishment for matters he had no control over, like Vivian. Or rather, matters he didn't care to control, like sending her to class instead of taking her for a ride. She hated those bent, half-moon cookies with their cutesy paper messages. The fun part—all he ever cared about seemed frivolous. If she brought up

[19]

anything serious, he wouldn't care, or even pay attention for that matter.

"Kathleen, your fortune waits." He lifted the little plate with the two cookies and held it toward her, then he winked and waited.

She selected the closest one, broke it open, and pulled out the thin strip of paper. *Happiness only lives in the heart.*

"What does it say?" His eyes twinkled, showing creases at the corners.

Kathleen flipped her fortune cookie back on top of the other crisp pastry and crumbled the fortune tight in her fist. "Will you talk to Mr. Bluet?"

"I suppose." He took the remaining cookie.

She twisted the corner of her napkin and studied the other luncheon diners sitting at their linen-covered tables in the dimly lit, red-and-gold room. *Why did Lillian have to be found in Lyndale Park?* She tied the napkin into a knot and tossed it next to her water glass.

"Tell me." His gaze swept over the room, then came back to her. He lit a cigarette, leaned over, and offered her a drag.

"They found her near the rose garden, back by those trees." She inhaled and slowly blew out a perfect smoke ring, fixing her eyes on his.

"Not that. What's your fortune?" He took his cigarette back and touched the corner of her lips.

"It's stupid." Something softened inside when he took care of her. She let the paper slip from her hand onto the floor.

He held up his little strip of paper. "Mine says, *Prepare for a great change.*"

"Excuse me for interrupting, Mr. Davidson." The maître d' appeared at his elbow. "Miss McPherson, it's best if you leave—by the back door. Your father called and made reservations. He's on his way."

Kathleen scooped up her handbag and books and rushed through the restaurant into the kitchen. She nodded at the skinny cook and the plump old woman washing dishes, opened the screen door— letting it bang behind her—and stepped into the dusty alley. She glanced at the clock tower. Her Culture and Society class had started ten minutes ago. The teacher would bawl her out . . . again.

Sounds of the screen door opening startled her. *Chester.*

"I thought it was Pops." She smoothed down her plaid woolen skirt.

[20]

Chester took her books and tucked her arm under his. "I'll walk with you."

"I'm not going back to school." She didn't care if she sounded harsh. She pulled free and leaned against the brick building. "If Pops is coming here, then who's minding the bank?" Her father controlled his bank the way he did his home.

"He doesn't expect me until tomorrow morning."

"Tomorrow? Why does your wife expect you this afternoon?" She ran her hand up his lapel and rested it on his shoulders.

"You're a naughty one." He put on his hat and took her arm again. "Miss too much school and you won't get into that fancy college."

She spied his maroon Lincoln half a block away and picked up her pace.

"Whoa, young lady." He stopped.

"Take me for a ride." She skipped once, turned, and took a little hop backward toward his motorcar. "We could drive out into the countryside. You could let me drive."

He pulled her in close, tilted her chin up, and brushed her lips with a furtive kiss before he said, "Your education awaits."

"You could educate me." She smiled, ignoring the cold lump that crept inside. "No one knows you're in town."

He remained silent.

The lump became a heavy rock and rolled around. She couldn't figure out what went on behind his smiles. She hated him too. He took charge all the goddamned time.

"Vivian expects me to be home shortly." He patted her hand. "Let's cancel tonight, too. I'm tired, and you do need to study."

Kathleen jerked away. "I expected you to be with me tonight, and you don't care about that?" Everything inside her hurt. She breathed short little breaths, her hands curling into fists.

"Easy, calm down. Vivian said she's planned something special." He walked along the sidewalk as he talked. "Besides, if you don't hurry, you'll miss your next class too."

He sounded phony, like a shoe salesman. Or did he worry she'd tell her father about him? He knew she wouldn't. She'd die before she'd let her father know the truth.

Now they were beside his automobile. He looked around, then gave her another quick kiss on her cheek. Chester handed her books back before he positioned himself behind the steering wheel and waved good-bye. His sleek automobile sped down the street and disappeared around the far corner.

What in Heaven's name was happening? All those little children at her home, her late lunch, Dolly checking out the restaurant for whatever purpose, and Chester's evasiveness . . .

Mrs. Vivian Davidson wasn't the problem. She hadn't planned anything special. The problem was he'd found someone else. The muscles in Kathleen's jaw tightened.

Her problem was Dolly.

Few things are harder to put up with than the annoyance of a good example.

—MARK TWAIN

6

Kathleen's mother picked up her Pall Malls. "You're being melodramatic, dear. No one's following you." She tapped out a cigarette. "I told the school secretary your ballet teacher probably made that call. She's been pestering me to change your class time."

"I bet it was the murderer." Mary plopped down on the couch. "Everyone's talking about it."

"Nonsense, Mary. Run upstairs and get my silver lighter. It's in the sitting room next to the bay window. And for Heaven's sake, Kathleen, slip your shoes on. Ladies do not run around barefoot."

Kathleen settled more deeply in the chair and tucked her stockinged feet under her.

Mary scampered up the stairs, her long, dark sausage curls bobbing with every step. Kathleen waited until Mary was out of hearing range.

"Mary's turned our home into the school luncheonette."

"Does it bother you?"

"Do you know how many Peckenpaw children there are?"

Mary came down the stairway and glanced at Kathleen on her way to her mother with the lighter.

Her mother took it. "So the Peckenpaw children came for lunch."

"Louisa fixed us chicken sandwiches with slices of apples."

Kathleen reached down between the chair and the seat cushion and retrieved her nail file.

Her mother signaled Mary to sit next to her. "Only one is in your class."

"Constance said she didn't feel right about coming to our house for a fine lunch." Mary looked over at Kathleen. "She's worried about her brothers and sisters. They're always hungry." Mary examined her shoes and rubbed a spot of dirt off the shiny black surface with her thumb.

Kathleen lowered her file. *How did a little girl like Mary end up with such a huge heart?*

Her mother took a long puff, then let the smoke escape from her lips. "How many Peckenpaw children are there?"

"Eight, Mother, but there are babies at home. Only five came for lunch." Mary pulled a dark curl from in front of her left ear and began twisting it around her finger. "They weren't noisy, and they didn't touch anything either . . . they even thanked Louisa."

"Sounds like a charity case for your guild, Mother." Kathleen filed another nail.

"A splendid solution." Her mother held her hand up. "Now, as far as inviting them for lunch, let Louisa know first. We can't be running out of milk."

"Mother, she's always dragging some poor ragamuffin home with her." Kathleen set her nail file down on the table. "Next she'll have them sleeping over here."

"Dear, there's no harm done." Her mother's eyes twinkled.

"Be warned, Mary, feed them all you want, but I'm not sharing my bed."

Mary giggled.

Kathleen untangled her legs and kicked her shoes aside. She scooted past Mary, giving her little sister's silky curls a quick tousle. Then she charged up the stairs, but the front door opened before she reached the first landing.

"I'm home." Her father hung his hat on the hook.

"Angus, dear." Her mother rushed to give him a peck on his cheek.

He cleared his throat and said, "Kathleen, come back down here. I need to talk to you."

She squeezed the banister, fighting for an excuse.

"Kathleen, you heard me. Don't just stand there."

When she reached the bottom step, he motioned her into the living room and pointed to a chair. She held her head high and marched to her designated seat.

He paced over to the large windows and, with his back to his family, he looked out on the view of Lake Harriet below. No one moved. After a minute, he faced them. Kathleen saw a sadness in his eyes she'd never seen before. His eyes were damp, and his lips drawn thin.

Good Lord, what have I done to him?

She fought back tears. Her vision changed, as if she looked through the wrong end of a telescope. *A few stolen moments, delicious forbidden kisses—of course it was exciting, but it wasn't worth destroying Pops.*

"Dear, what's troubling you?"

Kathleen flinched, but her mother had directed the question to her father. Then she rose and went to him. He drew her in with one arm and held her tight against his side.

"Kathleen," he said, "I'll have no arguments from you. From now on you'll do all your studying at home, not the library. If you need library books, then check them out at school and bring them home."

His words came from Lillian's death, not because of Chester.

"You don't care if my grades suffer?" Her voice was strong but not loud. "If you insist I go to college, I'll need reference books. They won't let anyone check them out."

"Hell, my library is full of reference books, if you ever cared to spend time there. I'll have no excuses for poor grades."

Kathleen eased back into her chair. She had expected this.

"I won't have either of you girls going to the park. Mary, do you understand? The park is strictly off-limits, as is the band shell, and the lake."

"But Daddy, our end-of-the-school-year picnic—" Mary jumped up, and now her fingers twisted the hem of her pinafore.

"A month away, we'll see what happens then. Elizabeth, I'm fine. Let's sit."

"I'm in charge of the games and we need to—"

"Mary, this is not a discussion."

Mary ducked her head and sank back into her seat. Their parents settled on the couch. Her father picked up a pack of Camels and fumbled around for his lighter.

[25]

"Excuse me, please. I have something I need to do." Kathleen stood and headed toward the stairs.

"You're not excused."

Drats. Kathleen plopped back down.

"Elizabeth, may I borrow your lighter?"

He lit his cigarette, took a deep inhale, and let the smoke slide out. "I have more to say, and it involves Kathleen."

Kathleen set her jaw and waited for his admonition.

"I've spent the afternoon with someone whom I consider an ethical businessman and a close friend." The sadness returned to his eyes and his jawline sagged.

Kathleen braced herself. He did know about Chester.

"Mr. Bluet's situation reminded me of how very dear you two young ladies are to your mother and me." He rested his elbows on his knees. "How Mr. Bluet manages is a mystery. He's a broken man."

"Dear, did he mention if the police know who killed his daughter?"

Her father glanced at Mary. "They believe Lillian went to the park to meet someone, but we won't discuss those matters now."

Kathleen's face grew warm. She glanced away.

"I'm proud of you, Angus, for being with him. What a difficult time." Her mother clutched his arm. "I'll fix you a bourbon. I could use a glass of brandy, myself."

"Mary, you're too young to go, but . . ." He looked toward the ceiling and shook his head.

No one spoke. After a few seconds, Angus cleared his throat and stared at all of them.

"Dear, are you all right?" Her mother gently touched his cheek. He nodded toward Kathleen.

"Since young Miss Bluet was a classmate of Kathleen's, the three of us will attend her service."

"Pops, please." Kathleen's heart raced. "She sat behind me in Latin class . . . that's all. I won't know anyone or what to say or do. I can't go." She shouldn't be expected to face death at seventeen.

"Mrs. Dagget will be there. When I told her you'd be coming, she said she'd bring Sophie." He leaned back. "Besides, the bank officers are going. You'll meet the new vice-president, and Chester Davidson and his wife will be there. You remember them."

Custom meets us at the cradle and leaves us only at the tomb.
—ROBERT GREEN INGERSOLL

7

When the choir sang, Kathleen willed them not to stop. With the pipe music of the organ flooding every nook and cranny of her being, and the choir's angelic voices climbing high above the rafters of the massive church, Kathleen closed her eyes and listened to *hallelujahs*—over and over and over. The harmony, the resonating, the beauty of it, left no room for sadness.

If the choir put their hearts into it, felt it with all their being, their message might pierce that elusive other place where spirits go, that other world Kathleen knew nothing about. She wanted each note and every word to reach deep into the soul of Lillian. But the sounds faded and stopped.

Moisture rose in Kathleen's eyes. How could someone as young as Lillian be gone forever? Where did she go? She had to be somewhere, didn't she? Kathleen knew what the church said, the Bible words, but in all seriousness, how was anyone to understand this type of leaving without being filled to the brim with fear?

At the cemetery numbness took over. Kathleen went through the motions and words expected of her. Heads were bent in reverence, the minister murmured, and birds chirped their choir from the budding branches above. Seconds later, pairs of dark, polished shoes shuffled their mourners toward the line of empty cars waiting to depart for the Bluets' home. Kathleen watched her own shiny-black shoes struggle to keep up with the crowd.

In the back seat of the car, she played with her gloved fingers and stared at the passing neighborhoods, but her ears were filled with nothing. Her father parked in the sweeping circle drive and opened the door for her mother. Kathleen pushed the seat forward and stepped out onto the gravel. They made their way up the walk.

A doorman greeted them, and a maid took their coats and the men's hats. Someone directed them into a spacious room filled with bouquets of sweet-smelling lilies. At the far end stood tables set with every imaginable little savory. Kathleen stood at the edge of the lush carpet, taking it all in.

Off to the side, her parents talked with another couple. Seeing he'd caught her attention, her father beckoned to her. She wound through a maze of people and stood next to her mother.

"Kathleen, this is Mr. and Mrs. Bluet." He held his palm out. "Kathleen and Lillian had classes together."

Mrs. Bluet, a slim woman with silver hair and eyes that seemed to want everyone to go away, held out her hand. Kathleen took it. She wasn't sure what she should do next. Mrs. Bluet held on fast, as if she might fall if she let go. Mr. Bluet held his wife's other arm, apparently to anchor himself as much as to be supportive of his wife.

"Kathleen, is it?" Mrs. Bluet studied Kathleen's face. "I'm comforted to know you were a friend of Lillian's." She paused, still squeezing Kathleen's hand. "We worried she was alone too much. Perhaps if she'd had someone to study with that night—" Tears now streamed down her face.

She let go of Kathleen's hand and dabbed her cheeks with a linen handkerchief. A maid Kathleen hadn't noticed before handed Mrs. Bluet a glass of water.

"Mr. and Mrs. Bluet." Kathleen's voice sounded thin, but she was expected to say something. "I didn't know Lillian well, but I liked her." Kathleen's throat closed. She wanted to say she wished they were closer friends, that Lillian had a wonderful ability to conjugate Latin verbs, that she and Lillian should have talked to each other more, but she couldn't get the words out.

Another couple waited nearby to pay their respects. Kathleen's father said something to them and ushered her mother and Kathleen to the side, telling them maybe they should eat a little.

Her mother caught a glimpse of a friend and disappeared. Kathleen stood and watched the crowd gather. She didn't see Sophie.

But she saw Chester. He was visiting with a small group only a few feet away. He had to have seen her, but now he faced the fireplace. What would happen if she marched over and greeted him and his wife? She should. After the lunch fiasco with Dolly poking her head into the restaurant, he deserved to be uncomfortable.

A thin, brown-haired woman in his group let out a high-pitched laugh. She stood out from all the dark-suited women in the room. She wore a coral tweed dress, a yellow feathered hat, and orange shoes that sported lime-green bows. *How brave of her . . . and how disrespectful.*

Kathleen took a deep breath. If she intruded on Chester's group then she would be disrespectful, too. She made her way to the table, picked up a small china plate from the stack, and fingered the Egyptian design of gold and blue encircling the edge.

Still, she couldn't keep checking on Chester. She selected a few items. The only things she recognized were thinly sliced cucumbers with curls of something fancy on top and some finger sandwiches. She moved down the table to the sweets and the miniature chocolate éclairs.

"Did you meet them yet?" Sophie's voice. Kathleen looked around and gave her friend a smile of relief.

"You mean the Bluets?" Kathleen surveyed the room. Many couples stood in line to offer condolences. "It was agonizing."

"I didn't know what to say." Sophie picked up a napkin. "I didn't even know Lillian, but still my mother insisted." Sophie took a plate and filled it. They moved toward the windows, looking for a place to sit away from everyone. All the chairs were filled, so they stood next to one of the tall windows, where Kathleen listened to every detail of Sophie's conversation with the Bluets.

Kathleen glanced several times at Chester. He kept his back toward her. How could he be so attentive and sweet one moment, then give her no more regard than if she were a clerk at the five and dime?

The loud, garish woman moved away from his group and walked in a path directly toward Sophie and Kathleen. In one of her lime-green gloved hands she clutched an orange handbag. Kathleen poked Sophie. Sophie stopped talking and stared.

"Who's that?" Sophie held a finger sandwich near her mouth.

"I'd say trouble. She's someone my mother knows."

The woman stopped in front of them. Her glance slid past Sophie and landed hard on Kathleen. Kathleen returned an icy glare. The woman didn't move. Kathleen shrugged and glanced beyond her.

The woman looked Kathleen up and down and twisted her lips into what she must have thought was a smile.

"You're rather gangly," she said. "I'm going to complain to your father. He told me you were exceptionally bright and pretty."

"That's because he's exceptionally handsome, brilliant, and truthful." Kathleen grinned. She heard a choking sound from Sophie.

"You obviously don't remember me." The woman touched a gloved finger to her lips. "Let me see. I sent a sterling silver baby cup to your parents when you were born."

"We've never been introduced, Mrs. Schrader, but I've seen you at one of my mother's guild meetings. We celebrated your generosity in purchasing new, warm coats for the men living near the railroad tracks."

A flood of heat washed over Kathleen. She wanted to move away from this woman.

"I had that cup engraved—back in 1905. You must be about eighteen now. I'm sure they never mentioned who gave you that expensive cup, did they?"

"When father started the bank, he mentioned he didn't know what he'd do without your husband on the board. My father seemed rather lost after your husband died." Kathleen glanced over and saw Chester staring at them. "It's a pleasure to be able to thank you myself."

Had Mrs. Schrader recognized her, or had Chester pointed her out? But why?

"You're graduating in a few weeks. What will you do then?"

"This is my best friend." Kathleen motioned toward Sophie. "Sophie, this is Mrs. Schrader. Mrs. Schrader—Sophie Dagget."

"Will you live at home?" The woman ignored Sophie. "Do you plan to work at your father's bank?"

"My mother's a college graduate. They expect the same of me." She tugged on Sophie's sleeve. "Sophie's mother is looking for her. Please excuse us." She took her plate and Sophie's, set them on the small occasional table, then ushered Sophie away.

When they neared the sideboard where the coffee, tea, and drinks were served, Kathleen caught sight of Mrs. Schrader in its large mirror. She now occupied herself with the task of selecting savories.

"For crying out loud," Sophie whispered. "I've never heard you talk like that to an adult. I can't believe how you were so—so copacetic. And I don't see my mother."

"Pops once told me," Kathleen surveyed the room before saying, "if someone's acting nuts, they often don't realize if you act just as crazy. Being off the trolley is part of their nature. Besides, Mother says to stay away from her."

"Because she's balled-up weird?"

"Because when Mrs. Schrader's around, bad things happen."

Sophie stared wide-eyed at Kathleen.

Kathleen helped herself to some punch. Sophie grabbed Kathleen's hand and shoved her face close to Kathleen's.

"All right, already." Kathleen moved Sophie closer to the window with their backs toward the room and lowered her voice. "Mrs. Schrader had a little boy who drowned in the bathtub, and then Mr. Schrader died when he fell off some ladder. It all seemed suspicious, but they couldn't pin it on Mrs. Schrader."

"But why would she—"

"I heard my parents talking about how Mr. Schrader couldn't take his wife's craziness anymore. He decided to divorce her, but before the divorce, she arranged to become a rich widow."

"Not only rich, but often annoying," a soft voice whispered close to Kathleen's ear.

Kathleen whirled around. Some of her punch sloshed out and onto Vivian Davidson's black suit jacket.

But Chester Davidson's wife ignored the sticky liquid and continued, "They should put her away."

"Oh no, I'm sorry, Mrs. Davidson." Kathleen's brain flitted from one thought to another. She handed Sophie her punch and looked for something, she didn't know what. "I need a towel to—" She grabbed a napkin and started dabbing at Mrs. Davidson's sleeve.

"It's not a problem." Mrs. Davidson took the napkin from Kathleen and placed a firm hand over Kathleen's arm. "I find pink punch doesn't show on black. Please don't give it another thought." With her grip on Kathleen, Mrs. Davidson guided Kathleen an arm's length away, cocked her head, and said, "You've grown into an attractive young woman since I last saw you. When was that?"

Sophie took a sip of Kathleen's punch.

"A few months ago at the bank's Christmas party." The party was the only time Kathleen ever socialized with the spouses of bank employees. How could Mrs. Davidson forget?

Sophie set Kathleen's punch down and headed toward the punch bowl.

"Chester told me you were friends with Lillian. Is he right?"

Why would he tell her that?

Kathleen glanced around. Sophie was now ladling punch into a cup. Kathleen's mother came up and started talking to Sophie.

Drats, Sophie, don't leave me alone.

"Well, were you?" Vivian, still holding Kathleen's arm, squeezed tighter. Kathleen looked down at it, then up into Vivian's eyes. Vivian's serious face softened. She smiled, let go of Kathleen, picked up Kathleen's punch, and handed it back to her.

"We were classmates." Kathleen nodded a thank-you and glanced toward Chester. Her stomach stoked tiny embers into flames. Chester and her father were talking.

When she looked back, Mrs. Davidson's narrowed eyes stared at her. Kathleen slid her gaze around the massive room and sipped the punch.

"You weren't close, you and Lillian?" Mrs. Davidson's voice rang harsh. "Your friendship wasn't the type where you young ladies would sit around in your nighties and chat about silly girl things?"

"Your question confuses me, Mrs. Davidson." Kathleen worked to keep a steady voice.

"If she *was* one of your friends, close friends," Mrs. Davidson's soft words morphed into a hiss when she said, "I would expect you to be quite sad and full of questions."

Kathleen blinked and stepped back. *What had happened here?*

"Honestly, Mrs. Davidson, I barely knew Lillian, and I don't know what to say. I *am* sad. I *do* have questions."

Mrs. Davidson worked her jaw back and forth. After a moment, her face relaxed, and she said, "This is all such a tragedy for the Bluets." She touched Kathleen's arm again. "I must say hello to your mother. But ask yourself why Miss Bluet died so young."

"Golly." Sophie, now with her own punch, watched Mrs. Davidson talk to Kathleen's mother, then head back to her group.

"What?" Kathleen caught a short breath. "Why did you say that?"

"Well, your mother is so . . . both of those women are—"

"Don't worry about it, Sophie. Neither is a friend of my mother's. One is a guild member and the other is the wife of the bank's loan officer. Come on, I'm starving."

They headed to the desserts and loaded their tiny plates. Kathleen pushed open one of the veranda doors and strode out into the weak sunlight. Gray stone stairs led down to the gardens. Kathleen sat on the top one. Sophie scooted up next to her.

"All those dreary adults—" Sophie nibbled on a chocolate-dipped coconut cookie.

Kathleen ate something coated in sugar.

Sophie finished her cookie, wiped her hands on her napkin, and said, "I heard the police are coming to school tomorrow to ask questions. They want to know who Lillian was meeting."

"Who told you?" Kathleen bit into an apricot tart.

"Mom. She talked with the school secretary about clothing donations. Mrs. Howe tells her lots of things."

"Wonder who they'll question." Kathleen didn't care.

"They think Lillian was waiting in the park to meet some guy." Sophie put a tiny cookie in her mouth. After she swallowed, she said, "I can't figure out why they'd want to talk to any of us girls if they think one of the guys murdered her."

"I don't know what to believe." Kathleen caught the honey-sweet smell of forsythia on the breeze.

"When mom took the clothing-collection box to school, she said Mrs. Howe told her that the day of the . . . well, you know . . . someone left a message for Lillian. The person left it on Mrs. Howe's reception desk that morning."

Kathleen waited.

"Mrs. Howe said she didn't know what the note said, it was sealed and all, but when she handed it to Lillian, Lillian seemed all excited. Naturally, Mrs. Howe asked her about it. Lillian said it was from an uncle she hadn't seen in a long time."

"Why is this important?" Kathleen finished off her punch. "A note is a note. Uncles can leave notes, can't they?"

"After Lillian was . . . you know . . . Mrs. Howe felt something wasn't right about that note. She called Mr. Bluet and told him. Guess what? He has no brothers, and Mrs. Bluet's only brother lives three blocks away. Lillian babysits for their little girl."

Kathleen smirked.

"Kath, I'm on the level here. Truth."

Kathleen felt an uneasiness. Who had told her Lillian loved an older man? The muscles in her stomach gripped. *Was Chester really out of town that night?*

"Kath . . . I'm going to be lost when you leave for college. I sure wish I could go to Stephens with you."

"I wish I didn't have to go." She gazed off in the distance. "Have you ever been tempted to flunk a test on purpose?"

"You wouldn't—"

"I've thought about it."

"Golly, Kath, we study so hard."

"Don't I have a right to be happy?" Kathleen checked out the French doors. "Look at us, today, right here in the middle of sadness."

"You'll love college."

Kathleen shifted her gaze to beyond the garden hedges. What she loved didn't come from books and classrooms. When she performed she lived in a different world.

"Think of it, Sophie. Poor Lillian led an uninformed life, devoid of experience. What's life if you haven't created a masterpiece, felt the agony of extreme despair, or experienced a great love?"

Sophie studied her. "I'd give anything to go to college."

"You sound like all those blasted adults. I want to dance my heart out. At least you'll play the piano and get to sing."

"Horsefeathers. Just think about giving lessons to a bunch of little kids. I hate being stuck at home."

"You could apply for a secretarial job. You're good at typing and numbers."

Sophie slung a pebble off the steps. "I'd rather jump off the Cappelen Bridge."

Kathleen silently agreed. She couldn't imagine anything more boring. She listened to murmurs coming from the funeral reception. *Had Lillian planned on college?*

She brushed crumbs off her skirt. "What's Dolly going to do after graduation?"

"Stuff."

"What does that mean?"

"She has plans." Sophie didn't meet Kathleen's eyes.

"Are we playing a game here?"

"No game." Sophie looked away.

"Dolly told you not to tell me." Kathleen wanted to shake Dolly until her curls frizzed.

"She doesn't have to worry about the future." Sophie chewed a fingernail. "That's all."

Kathleen grabbed Sophie's hand away from her mouth. "What's the story? We're best friends, right?"

"But she doesn't want anyone to know." Sophie's face screwed up in imaginary pain.

"But you know. She told you an earful." Kathleen looked away. "You're better friends with her than me."

"Baloney, and you know it." Sophie jumped up. "You're mad because I can keep a secret."

"I'm mad because you don't trust me anymore." Kathleen scooped up her plate and cup.

"You don't like Dolly. If I tell you, you'll like her even less."

"Why do you care what I think?"

Sophie looked around and whispered into Kathleen's ear. "Dolly thinks she has a sugar daddy to take care of her."

"Who?" Kathleen's heart quivered. She knew who.

"She won't tell me. Someone she's been seeing these last few weeks—an older man."

Dammit, Chester.

"Tell her to stay away from me." Kathleen headed across the veranda toward the doors.

"See. I knew this would make you mad." Sophie picked up her cup and plate and followed after her. "I shouldn't have told you."

Outside the French veranda doors, Kathleen stopped. Mrs. Davidson stood watching them.

"What's the matter?" Sophie stopped too.

"Her." Kathleen swept a quick look toward Vivian Davidson. "I'm tired of talking."

Sophie shook her head, walked up, and pushed through. Kathleen followed.

"Young Miss McPherson?" Mrs. Davidson wagged her finger in the air. With a throaty laugh, she said, "Vivian, oh, Vivian, your memory . . . We do remember you at the Christmas party. You wore a red-and-green tartan dress with golden threads."

Kathleen introduced Sophie, but she just wanted to go home.

Mrs. Davidson studied them both before saying, "Mrs. McPherson mentioned you ladies take fine-art lessons after school. Acting, dancing, singing. When do you study? You have to study quite diligently if you're going to Stephens College."

"I seem to have a knack for absorbing textbooks." Kathleen sighed.

"I attended Stephens." Mrs. Davidson scrutinized Sophie. "You must be a friend of Lillian's."

"Golly, I didn't even know her." Sophie shrugged. "My mom made me come."

Mrs. Davidson's eyes narrowed. She looked from Kathleen to Sophie and back again. "Where *are* all of Lillian's friends?"

From the body of one guilty deed a thousand ghostly fears and haunting thoughts proceed.

—WILLIAM WORDSWORTH

8

The next morning, Kathleen slipped into her first-period English class seconds before the teacher closed the door. She hated the walk to school. She'd find a different route tomorrow. She strolled past Sophie and Dolly without acknowledging them. Their desks were in the first row and next to each other. Kathleen's assigned seat was in the row behind.

Throughout the class period Kathleen fumed as Dolly and Sophie slipped notes to each other.

After class the students filed out, but Kathleen took her time collecting her books. She didn't know how to hide the bruising and rawness from the rage building inside her. *Dolly and Chester.* If she moved with purpose, kept her mind on her goals, and remembered to breathe—

"Kathleen."

She jerked around and saw Dolly staring at her. Dolly, her face red, darted around the desks and stood inches from Kathleen's face.

"Something bothering you, Dolly?" Kathleen stepped aside and headed toward the door.

"You stay away from him." Dolly raised her voice. "You understand? He's mine."

Kathleen took a deep breath and faced Dolly.

"Yeah? Yours and who else's?"

Dolly jutted her chin out and started over. "You had no business being in that restaurant. I hate you. I hate you. I hate you, Kathleen McPherson."

"It's a free country."

Kathleen walked out the door and down the hallway to her second-period class with a smile on her face. Her insides burned.

She cringed at how she and Dolly would handle the streetcar ride to theater class after school.

Kathleen turned the corner and found two police officers standing outside the principal's office. Mrs. Howe, a hanky knotted in her hand, nodded in agreement to some request. The officers studied a map of the school.

Kathleen entered her math class on time, but the teacher was late. Students, some sitting on each other's desktops, gossiped. Some figured the police would question Lillian's teachers, one by one, in the conference room.

A substitute teacher rushed in and took over.

With teachers being shuffled around and students worrying about who would be interrogated next, no one could concentrate on learning. *They should have canceled school.*

Kathleen relaxed when Latin class ended. She didn't care to be interviewed, but now, heading down the hallway, she needed to face Dolly and their streetcar ride.

Sophie stood alone by the front door. When she saw Kathleen, she waved.

Kathleen pushed past Sophie and said, "Where's little Miss Gold Digger?"

"You're mean." Sophie followed her out the door. "You said you'd keep it a secret."

"All that note passing in English class . . ." Kathleen stopped and faced Sophie. "She knew you told me, and I know who her sugar daddy is."

"How could you know? I don't even know." Sophie started walking.

"Why isn't she here?" Kathleen matched her stride.

"She's sick—went home."

Kathleen slowed her pace. She'd overlooked something—something bad. A shiver shot through her. If Dolly started spreading rumors, her father would find out.

She caught up with Sophie and walked beside her until they arrived at their waiting place.

Sophie ignored Kathleen.

"You're not speaking to me?" Kathleen swatted at Sophie's arm.

She grinned and swatted back. "This Lillian thing makes all of us grummy."

The streetcar arrived. They took the usual route up to Franklin Avenue, where traffic slowed then inched along. Finally the streetcar crossed the bridge. Kathleen nudged Sophie and pointed out the window.

"What do you think that's about?"

Police cars and people were milling about near the muddy bank of the swollen Mississippi. Kathleen and Sophie spent the last few minutes of their ride speculating about river drownings and being late for class. They hopped off the streetcar, bolted down the walk to the brick building, pulled the door open, and charged through the hall to their theater class.

Mr. Russin stopped speaking and stared when the girls entered. The other students turned to look. Sophie and Kathleen trotted down the aisle and up the steps to the stage. They slipped into two of the three empty chairs.

He looked over all the students and focused on Sophie. "Miss Dagget, describe to us the evolution of emotions before one commits a cold-blooded murder?"

Sophie reddened and cleared her throat. "Anger? Maybe fear comes first?"

Kathleen held her breath. Had the class discussed this earlier?

"Miss Dagget, if you claim your inadequate answer is the result of your never having murdered, your claim is equally inadequate."

Kathleen knew this was a setup.

"Mr. Russin." Kathleen waved her hand. "I assure you there is no one more kindhearted than my friend sitting next to me."

He stood and pointed one finger high above his head. "I assert that each and every one of you is a murderer. Hence, the excuse of not being able to feel the part of a murderer when asked to play one on stage is moot. Close your eyes. Think back to when you killed an annoying fly. Slow the moment down so you can dissect your emotions—the annoyance, the rage, the determination—did you hesitate? What raw emotion was experienced before and up to the moment you smashed its tiny, little brain into a bloody speck?"

During the remainder of the class, they paired off and recited murderous lines. Kathleen's anger toward Dolly fueled her motivation.

Even during their ride home the image of Dolly with Chester continued to make Kathleen burn.

She left Sophie at her front door and strode down the block. Long afternoon shadows made everything spooky. Dinner, her new theater magazine, and a bubble bath might ease her mood.

A twig snap. Her muscles tightened. She looked around and, seeing nothing, dashed down the sidewalk and up the porch steps.

Her mother greeted her at the front door.

"Don't take off your coat, dear. Louisa's made an apple cobbler, scalloped potatoes, and cooked a ham. Come help me take these to the Davidsons' home. Your father's over there now."

"What's happening?"

"Oh, sweetie, someone saw Mr. Davidson's automobile plunge into the river early this morning, and now there's no sign of him."

Chester? Oh my—

"The woman is distraught." Her mother started to button Kathleen's coat.

Kathleen brushed her hand aside. "Is he alive?"

"We'll talk in the car."

"Mother, I can't go."

"Mrs. Davidson specifically asked for you to come."

Mrs. Davidson barely remembered her at Lillian's service. She couldn't talk to Mrs. Davidson.

"I have homework—I need to—"

"I won't listen to excuses. It's time you learn adult social graces. No matter how ugly, if you're of a certain caliber, you face them."

Swell. Mother, you don't even know me. Empathy isn't the problem.

Believe nothing and be on guard against everything.
—LATIN PROVERB

9

A gourd-shaped woman with a dour face, wearing a blue-gingham dress and a crisp, white apron, opened the Davidsons' etched-glass front door. She helped Kathleen and her mother remove their coats and gestured toward the parlor before scooting into the dining room with the potatoes, ham, and cobbler.

A steel tightness wound around Kathleen's head.

How could Chester be missing?

She edged to the doorway. Her mother moved into the parlor to join the others who had come to comfort Mrs. Davidson. Kathleen heard her father's deep, but quiet, voice.

"The bank will take care of everything." Her father, seated in a soft cushioned chair, leaned forward as he talked to Vivian Davidson. He had aged this week—his usual angular face looked worn-out and beaten. "You won't have to deal with the details."

Details? What did he mean?

Kathleen's eyes blurred. Those nights after the Christmas party, when she couldn't sleep, she'd curl up in her bed and envision the tenderness of their conversations and dream of when she and Chester would finally become lovers.

He couldn't be missing.

She blinked and wiped her eyes with the side of her cuff, working to make sense of why these people around her were even here. These people either discussed what they thought had happened to Chester, or they talked about other things.

We're supposed to be consoling Mrs. Davidson.

"I heard the Bluet girl didn't die right away."

A male voice: "It's not in the newspapers, but the murderer cut . . ." His voice disappeared into the drone of other conversations.

A squeaky woman's voice caught Kathleen's attention. "What a bunch of hooey. How could anyone stab someone in the heart? Would any of you let someone stand in front of you, pull out a knife, and stab you? No, you'd fight or run . . ."

"I want to know how a knife stabs a heart when there's a rib cage protecting it."

"Heard the constable couldn't understand why there wasn't a struggle."

This all sounded akin to high-school gibberish. Didn't they care about Chester?

Her throat tightened. It hurt. Here in the hallway of his home, the hallway where he hung his hat, where he came and went every day—she stood on the same hardwood floor he stood on and walked through the same doors. Kathleen swallowed and looked over at Mrs. Davidson.

She couldn't do this. She couldn't comfort his wife.

Most of the visitors were eating and chatting with each other. This looked like a social tea.

Food and gossip didn't appeal to her. In the far corner of the parlor, next to the piano, an elderly, prune-faced woman wearing a black woolen dress with a white-lace ruffled collar and buttoned-up black shoes sat in a rocking chair and shot dark glances around the room. When her eyes met Kathleen's, she hesitated, then let her gaze landed on someone behind Kathleen.

The woman twisted her mouth into a sneer. Kathleen turned to see who might deserve this unfriendly welcome.

Mrs. Schrader stood by the front door, slipping off her coat and giving it to the maid. She linked arms with a dapper gentleman and whispered something in his ear. He handed the maid his fedora hat. He looked old like Mrs. Davidson—at least thirty-five.

His jade window-pane suit, matching vest, yellow-striped shirt, and lavender bow tie, though stylish, announced high drama. Her father's dark woolen suit spoke of business and possibilities.

His fedora now hung on the rack next to her father's homburg.

Kathleen slipped further from the entrance and into the drawing room. Mrs. Schrader's conversations were equivalent to standing in a miasma of decay.

Kathleen wandered to the far end of the room near the piano and examined a group of photos. Her heart quickened. She hunted for Chester's photo.

The first photo showed three young girls about Mary's age at tea—with obligatory smiles. She studied another of a girl in her early teens, wearing a gypsy costume. Kathleen moved to the next photo—the same girl with a small dog. The dog wore a ruffled collar. Kathleen felt a tug on her sleeve and looked down.

"Sit here with me," the old woman in the rocking chair rasped. "I don't want that Schrader woman to take this empty chair."

"You know her?" Kathleen slid into the seat. Mrs. Schrader, wearing a pink satin dress and a matching hat with peacock plumes, clucked and bobbed her way around the room.

"Unfortunately." The woman snapped her tongue. "Mrs. Schrader used to be one of Mr. Temple's favorites. Lordy, look at who she's dragging around. The three of them stick together like fleas. I'd say Mrs. Schrader is way too free with her favors to suit me."

Kathleen's mouth went dry. *Three?* And she didn't know anyone named Temple or the man with Mrs. Schrader now. She couldn't find a suitable response.

The woman hummed the melody "Daisy, Daisy, give me your answer, do." She abruptly stopped, looked over at Kathleen, and cleared her throat.

"I do suppose Mr. Temple had many favorites. But, mind you, I always suspected Vivian was his main one. She received the best of his affections for many years. He never could keep his hands off her, but neither of them would admit it. Rightly so . . . And that Ivy, he taught her tricks, how to slip in and out of everywhere and read minds. Who knows what he taught the other two. Vile . . . scandalous." She did more tongue clicking. "They've kept their mouths shut tight, and I'd say rightly so, rightly so, but I know they'll burn in hell for it."

Kathleen should have taken her chances with Mrs. Schrader.

"Vivian, the silly goose, gets tangled up with too much stuff and nonsense . . . turns her life over to a man who's no better. I know what goes on with Chester Davidson, I do. Chester Davidson is just another Mr. Temple, mind you that."

Until Dolly had stepped into the restaurant, Kathleen had no idea Chester might have flirted with others. He'd said he was miserable because he'd married the wrong woman, a woman who constantly whined and complained and never listened to anything he might say. Her cheeks grew warm.

Chester must be a philanderer.

She swallowed hard and waited for the woman to speak again. When she didn't, Kathleen hunted for something neutral to say.

"Where is Mr. Temple?" Any man willing to take on Mrs. Schrader and Mrs. Davidson must be nuts.

"Where he needs to be." The woman squinted at Kathleen. "His undoing happened when he left all his clothes scattered around the living room of Mr. and Mrs. Granger. Of course he didn't know the Grangers, none of us did, but it did cause quite a stir."

"Do you mean *all* his clothes?"

"Indeed I do. The Grangers called the police, and everyone searched the Grangers' house and yard and even their boathouse for a dead body. They shoveled and hoed up the vegetable garden, too. Too bad he wasn't there."

"Did they find him?" Kathleen hated being like the other chatty people who said they had come to console Mrs. Davidson.

"Some trolley driver had the good sense to call headquarters and let them know a naked man was riding around in his car." The woman nodded to herself.

Kathleen knew her mouth was open.

"Mr. Temple told the police he didn't know where his clothes were. He had to get home, and the fastest way was to take the trolley. He argued with the trolley driver over the fare. He'd told the trolley driver he had no pockets, so he had to go home to get money. He'd promised to give him double what he owed. Mr. Temple never did pay attention to the value of a hard-earned nickel. Throw it away, all away, he did."

"I can't imagine anyone taking off their clothes in public." A tiny shiver spread through Kathleen.

"I chalked that public display of nakedness up to the best day of *my* life." The woman grinned a mouth full of yellow, crooked teeth. "They hauled Mr. Temple off to that crazy house up north in Fergus Falls."

Kathleen, with her parents, had seen the imposing campus of Fergus Falls State Hospital. Until she read the sign, she thought it was a university.

"Lord knows I'd had it with him even before he started forgetting where he was or talking to all those people that weren't there. You can bet I was plum tired of keeping my mouth shut about all his chasing after pretty faces because he wanted to play with what was under their skirts."

Kathleen's face grew unbelievably hot. She searched the room. Her mother, talking to someone, glanced at her.

"Excuse me." Kathleen lurched forward, stood, and signaled with her finger, indicating she had to leave. "My mother—"

The old woman reached out and clutched Kathleen's hand, then squinted across the room. She pulled her gaze away from Kathleen's mother and studied Kathleen with her icy-blue eyes.

"You're that McPherson girl." She nodded to herself. "I've been told things about you." The woman dropped Kathleen's hand and touched the pink cameo brooch fastened to the lace at her neck. "How-de-do. I am Mrs. Temple, Vivian's mother."

Kathleen's lungs fought for air. She made her rubbery legs move away.

Good Lord. Where are they—all the happy and sane people?

"Dear." Her mother approached and slipped her arm around Kathleen's shoulders. She whispered, "You mustn't spend too much time with Mrs. Temple. She may not be emotionally well. One can never believe much of what she says these days."

"Will we be going home now?"

Kathleen's father seemed to be wrapping up an involved conversation with one of his employees. They were shaking hands.

"Not yet." Her mother lifted a wisp of hair from Kathleen's cheek and tucked it behind her ear. "Mrs. Davidson insists on speaking with you before we go."

Oh swell. Her head ached and the ringing in her ears grew louder. When her feet moved, she felt like she was walking in wet cement—never mind she couldn't breathe. This house had to be cursed. Why else would there be this many lunatics in one place? And it was a trap, too, because it held her hostage. She'd never be allowed to go home.

Her mother nudged her forward and continued talking.

"She's alone now. This would be a good time."

Kathleen forced herself to do as her mother asked, but when she stood in front of Mrs. Davidson she couldn't find any words. No longer was she a high-school student, or her parents' daughter. She stood there, a hollow shell, with nothing left inside.

"I needed you to be here, Kathleen." Mrs. Davidson stared into her eyes. "This night is a horrible night for both of us." She took Kathleen's hand. "You're far too young for all this grieving. First Lillian, and now you must comfort me. Please sit." Tugging Kathleen's hand, she guided her over to a chair next to hers. "We'll continue our talk."

"What talk?" They'd said only niceties at Lillian's house. There had been no real discussion. She perched on the edge of the chair. Her heart jittered.

"About college. You can't let anything stop you from going. We're similar in many ways. Look at us—tall, dark, and slender. We're both academics—cerebral, one might say."

Alike? Mrs. Davidson and everyone else here looked old—thirty or more. Kathleen bristled. True, they both were tall and slender, with dark hair. But they weren't similar.

Mrs. Davidson's eyes filled with tears. "You remind me of myself. Now my life is full of regrets, and this thing with Chester . . ." Her handkerchief trembled in her hand, and she slid a packet of papers over it. "I married Chester when I didn't know what I wanted from life. We are all silly girls. Did we talk about that?"

Kathleen shook her head.

"We girls fill our days and nights with giggles and secrets and stupid choices, but all of us long for some mysterious missing part of our lives . . ."

The older woman choked back a soft sound, and her hand jerked from under the packet. Her face filled with pain. Then Mrs. Davidson poked Kathleen hard with her finger.

"She received a scholarship to Stephens Women's College, but, fool that she was, she threw her education away, never used it. She married that Chester Davidson instead."

She? Kathleen kept silent. Mrs. Davidson seemed more preoccupied with Kathleen's future than Chester's disappearance.

"You're a young woman." Mrs. Davidson, her voice softer, leaned in close. "Make choices based on your intellect, not your emotions."

Mrs. Davidson's eyes filled with apparent disdain when she

looked at the corner of the room where her mother sat, rocking. She turned her gaze back.

"Kathleen, you are me. We can't squander our one chance for happiness. I'm writing a letter to Stephens Women's College. This takes preparation, but we'll work together."

Mrs. Davidson's words confused her, and a heat of shame washed over her. She shouldn't have flirted with Chester.

"Mrs. Davidson, they'll find Ches—Mr. Davidson. His automobile may be in the river, but I'm sure he's alive."

"He's gone." She struggled with soft, throaty sounds before saying, "You read the newspapers. How many cars get swept away in the Mississippi each year?"

Mrs. Davidson pulled her hanky up to her eyes and dabbed at them. Kathleen searched for something reassuring to say.

"I think maybe in his case—"

"They're never found." Mrs. Davidson lowered the hanky and opened her eyes, then gave Kathleen a hard look that pierced through her. "He's *dead.*"

"But how can you be certain?" She hadn't meant to upset Mrs. Davidson.

The guttural sounds started up, and tears spilled down Mrs. Davidson's cheeks. She used the hanky before she covered her trembling hand again with the packet of papers.

"He didn't even leave a note. Wouldn't you think he'd at least tell *her* why?"

Kathleen wanted to go home.

It requires more courage to suffer than to die.
—NAPOLEON BONAPARTE

10

Elizabeth McPherson told Angus they'd see him at home. Kathleen reclaimed their coats from the maid, anticipating the cold night air. Before she could escape, Mrs. Schrader slipped in front of her mother.

"Elizabeth." She held her hand out, palm forward. "I can't let you go until I show off Pritchard. I'm sure you've been dying to meet him after all these years of my bragging about his work."

Her mother pulled Kathleen next to her and said, "Another time, Ivy. I must get Kathleen home. Her books are waiting. It's a school night."

"Horsefeathers, two more minutes won't matter." Mrs. Schrader squinted at Kathleen. "Your gangly daughter convinced me she's intelligent. Why would she need to study?" Mrs. Schrader clamped her hand over Elizabeth's arm.

Kathleen knew her mother would never cause a scene, so she followed them both into the dining room, certain she'd never get home. Pritchard and another couple carried on an animated conversation at the far end of the table.

He wore a gold watch chain draped across his vest as Chester did. He glanced at the watch and then tucked it back into the small vest pocket.

"Pritchard," Mrs. Schrader called, "I want you to meet Mrs. McPherson. She knows some very influential people like the Bluets."

[48]

He glowered at Mrs. Schrader from underneath his brow. Then he examined Kathleen's mother as if she had applied for some inferior job. His lips were pulled back in a carefully rationed smile of acknowledgement until he saw Kathleen. Then wide-eyed interest spread across his face.

"Mr. Pritchard, we finally meet." Kathleen's mother extended her hand for him to take.

"Pritchard." He clasped only the tips of her fingers in his handshake. "Pritchard is what I'm to be called—Please do not call me mister as I have no intentions of ever being one. I do recall seeing the young woman standing behind you. Kathleen, isn't it?"

What the—? Kathleen's mind searched as goose bumps rose on her arms.

"You know my daughter?"

"I said I've seen her . . . she rides the streetcar after school with her friends to Mr. Russin's theater class. Mr. Russin and I are . . . close acquaintances. Excuse us, I find the hour too late for any more chitchat." He gripped Mrs. Schrader's arm and hustled her into the hall, where he retrieved their coats and ushered Mrs. Schrader out.

Kathleen watched Pritchard and Mrs. Schrader leave. When they were out the door, her mother mumbled a solemn farewell to the other couple and silently directed Kathleen to the door, down the walk, and into their automobile.

Her mother leaned over and rubbed Kathleen's shoulder. "Are you all right?"

Kathleen nodded, hating that ever-present lump in her throat. She felt her mother's soft hand touch her cheek. The spot glowed warm for a moment. Kathleen wished she were young enough to snuggle again, but the moment ended almost before it happened.

Her mother navigated the car around the others parked in front of the Davidson house. "These last few days . . ." She drove the automobile up the street. "I disliked asking you to come with me tonight . . . but Mrs. Davidson insisted, and your father thought . . ."

"Mother?" She shouldn't ask, but she had to know. "What did Mrs. Davidson tell you and Pops?"

"I was about to ask you the same."

Kathleen sorted back through the conversation.

"Do you think Mrs. Davidson and I are alike?"

"Good Heavens, why would you ask that?"

"She said we have features in common, and our brains and emotions are similar." Kathleen rested her head on the side window. It was damp and cold and felt lovely.

Her mother didn't say anything until she pulled into the driveway leading to the back of their property.

"Besides the obvious similarities of height and coloring, I see nothing even close to being alike. She's aloof, harsh, and demanding. You're exuberant about whatever strikes your fancy, you're kindhearted, and—oh dear—I guess I *would* have to say you are demanding."

"Mother—"

"Your father's home."

Her mother's description of Mrs. Davidson didn't fit. Kathleen couldn't let it pass.

"I felt sorry for her," Kathleen said, then added, "I thought she seemed fragile and vulnerable and not at all what you said. She told me she regretted getting married instead of putting her college education to use, and she doesn't believe Ches—her husband—is alive."

The back of her throat ached, causing the bridge of her nose to tingle.

"She's right about Mr. Davidson," her mother said. "Seems he took his own life." The cold night air slipped into the car around their feet. "Be extra sweet to your father because he's in quite a state about all of this. He wonders if he's to blame."

"Why?"

"Because of Mr. Davidson depression. He'd disappear for hours and even days, then when he returned he'd be inconsolable." Her mother squeezed her hand. "It's getting cold. We need to go in."

Her mother left the automobile and headed toward the kitchen porch. Kathleen followed. She needed to correct her mother, but how? She stopped to watch a few reflected lights dancing on the night-water of the lake.

A few seconds later Kathleen entered the bright yellow kitchen. Her mother, cleaning up cookie crumbs from the marble tabletop, urged Mary to finish her milk and go to bed.

Louisa, buttoning her sweater, bid everyone good-night. Kathleen's father must have gone into the other room. Kathleen took a glass from the cupboard, picked up the milk bottle, and poured some before placing the bottle back inside the ice box. She carried it into the darkened living room where her father sat in his chair, sipping what was probably bourbon-on-ice.

He acknowledged her presence with a slight lift of his tumbler. She sat on the couch close to him and sipped her milk. He stared out the window—probably watching those same lights down on the lake.

"Why are you two sitting the dark?" her mother said as she entered the room and began bustling around turning on lamps. "Such an exhausting week . . . Kathleen, I'm proud of the way you've handled these deaths."

"But Chester isn't dead, Mother. I'm sure."

Her father scowled and looked at his wife. He expected her to say something.

When she didn't, he said, "Young lady, whether he's dead or not, it's disrespectful for you to refer to him other than using his surname. You have no right to be so casual."

"The point isn't his name, Pops. The point is he's alive. Seeing his car go into the river doesn't prove he drowned. Why is everyone acting this way?" Kathleen set her jaw and stared straight at her father. "Does everyone want the man dead?"

Having said it, maybe she'd struck a truth. Still, his being missing seemed far better than being dead.

"Elizabeth, control your daughter." He stood and strode to the window. "Her mouth is far too loose."

"Dear, your father's right. I know this has been horrid for you, but a little self-restraint goes a long way."

Why did everyone let her father, even when wrong, be right all the time? She seethed. Loose mouth or not, she would not keep still.

"He's not dead." She spewed out the words.

"He killed himself," her father's voice boomed. "That makes him quite dead."

Elizabeth darted to his side. He urged her away. Kathleen stood now, shaking with anger.

"And why would anyone think he committed suicide?" She caught herself waving her hands like Dolly. "It makes no sense."

"Dear, we discussed this in the automobile—"

"We didn't discuss it, Mother. You told me what you heard, what you thought. You left the car without hearing what I thought. That's *not* a discussion."

"Elizabeth, I told you she'd get out of hand with her impertinence." Her father cut from the window to stand inches from Kathleen's face. "I will not have you talking to your mother in that tone."

"Swell, everyone will be sticky sweet and ignore what's happened because it's unpleasant." She forced herself to quiet her waving hand and lower her voice. "I can't believe the two of you. A man's motorcar is in the river, he's missing, and his wife is devastated." She glared at her parents. "What do we do? We argue about how we talk to one another."

Elizabeth sat and patted the couch cushion next to her. "Sit, we'll discuss this until you feel better." She nodded at her husband. He slumped into his chair and downed his bourbon.

Kathleen sat.

"Now, where do we start?" Her mother smoothed her skirt down. Her father studied the ice shards in his glass.

He cleared his throat and said, "Kathleen, most people struggle to overcome their disappointments in life." He leaned forward, putting his elbows on his knees, holding his glass with both hands. "Mr. Davidson thought he would become the new vice-president of the bank, but he didn't have the people skills to be effective. I couldn't award him that position. Instead, I made him my top loan officer for businesses." He leaned back and put his glass down. "I found him more than competent in his ability to appraise the true value of different companies. When a large firm needed more capital, I'd send Mr. Davidson to find out what else might be going on behind the scene—what the company might not want the public to know."

Kathleen listened, but she still couldn't make the connection from this to Chester being dead. She struggled not to interrupt and to let her father finish his story.

"Mr. Davidson seemed fine with this new position. Actually, he appeared to enjoy it. We had no idea he was putting on a big act for us." Her father went to the bar and poured more bourbon into his glass. "Mrs. Davidson saw a different man, a broken man who couldn't rise above the disappointment of not achieving his goal of being vice-president."

"Kathleen, dear," her mother said, "Mrs. Davidson told us the whole tragic story. After he lost the vice-president promotion he drank heavily, and he'd rant about being a dismal failure. Mrs. Davidson said these last few weeks he'd disappear for days, or just sit, stare, and drink."

"She's lying." Kathleen stood. "He wasn't that way at all." *Why would Vivian say those things?*

"But he was, dear. Poor Mrs. Davidson."

"Mother, that's not true." Her voice came out too loud. "Pops, you knew him better than that. Tell her."

He glowered at her. "Kathleen, you need to calm down." He took a sip of his drink. "I hate that my decision caused his downward spiral."

"It didn't, Pops. Think about it. You never saw him depressed—you didn't—I'm sure you can't remember a single time when he wasn't smiling." She stood and moved closer to him. "Doesn't he always seem happy? Depressed people aren't cheerful."

Her father turned and busied himself, putting fresh chunks of ice in his drink.

"Pops, he loves life . . . He must, because he's so silly all the time."

Her father paused, his drink halfway to his lips. She knew she had his attention.

"You know how excited he gets over the most insignificant things." She could convince him. "Just last week, we—" Her mind screeched to a halt. She froze.

Her mother jumped up and shouldered next to her father. She clasped his arm. They stood, staring at her wide-eyed.

"I mean—I'm only saying—"

Her mother's hand covered her mouth. She sank back onto the sofa, one hand resting on her chest. Her father's eyes darkened. He set his glass down and gripped Kathleen's shoulder. She winced.

"Tell us. What are you *only* saying?"

Kathleen tilted her head away and bit her lip. She needed to find a way to fix this.

Her father's words, tight from anger, came at her hard. "Mr. Davidson's reputation with women reached far beyond our city limits. Knowing this helped me decide he shouldn't be our vice-president." He kept his grip on her shoulder, but with his other hand he tilted her chin up to face him. "I refused to listen to the stories about him and young girls."

Her mother made a short, muffled, sobbing sound.

Kathleen closed her eyes.

His voice bellowed out, making her flinch. "I demand you tell me what happened between the two of you!"

"Nothing—I bumped into him one day at lunch. We talked."

"You're not even eighteen. Goddamn it." His voice quivered. "What was he thinking?"

Her voice and words came out, but the sounds made no sense. She couldn't find any of the right words, and her father's gray, colorless face frightened her.

"How far did this—this relationship—go?" His eyes narrowed. "Don't you even think of holding back. I demand the truth."

"We only talked, Pops. We found things to laugh about, and we'd just talk."

"Bullshit." His voice filled the room.

"We only met a few times these last couple of weeks. Believe me, nothing happened. "Chester—Mr. Davidson—was always a gentleman."

Her father pounded his fist into his palm. "What in the hell—a couple of weeks? Why don't I believe you?"

"Honestly—"

"Don't say *honestly* to me. You're not honest, you're a sneak, and you're a cheat—a married man, for God's sake—"

"Pops, you don't understand . . . we were only friends."

"Elizabeth, did you know about this? No, of course you didn't. We need to make a plan. We can't have this."

"But, Angus, maybe she's telling the truth." Her mother folded and unfolded her hands.

"Don't argue with me. This is shameful and totally inappropriate." He paced the room, rubbing his face. "I've never felt this disappointed in my entire life. Those stories about Chester and those young girls—"

Kathleen shivered, watching the storm brewing on her father's face.

"People will talk about you and about his philandering. We can't have our daughter connected to this." He slammed his hands down on the mahogany bar. "Elizabeth, Kathleen must leave."

We must be willing to get rid of the life we've planned,
so as to have the life that is waiting for us.

—JOSEPH CAMPBELL

11

Early morning sun splattered off the new leaves, making light and shadows dance on the sidewalk in front of Kathleen's home. Clouds moved in, promising rain. She shifted her books, strode off toward school, and shoved her father's angry words out of her mind.

Last night her mother had convinced him to let Kathleen stay and finish school. Kathleen swore she wouldn't tell anyone about Chester and her. Still, her father wanted to ship her off to an aunt in Kansas or someplace. Her mother insisted that when young ladies dropped out of school and left home it fueled worse gossip.

Kathleen didn't care about any of this; except for the emotional pain she'd caused her parents, and her shame for the hurt she might have caused Mrs. Davidson.

She lengthened her stride, looked behind her, and checked out the shadows. Everything appeared normal, but electricity filled the air like it did the night Lillian died.

Darn these creepy feelings. If her parents would only let her drive to school and to her after-school classes . . .

Breezes carrying smells of damp earth and rotted vegetation rose from the wooded area next to the lake. She decided to take an alternate route where she didn't feel so exposed. She trotted down between the houses closer to the water and found the well-worn path of compacted black dirt. Kathleen seldom came this way because she hated bugs.

Again, she quickened her pace.

Mulch on soft damp earth squished under her feet. Kathleen stopped. She heard another squish, but this time not from her foot. She jerked around, examined the darkened vegetation, and stopped breathing to listen.

Crap, this wasn't a good idea.

The hairs on her neck bristled. Someone must be watching.

A scuttling through dead leaves nearby made her start. A raccoon scurried across the path and up a tree.

She needed to hurry or she'd be late. Another older track sloped back to the sidewalk above. Kathleen darted up it, snagging her toe on a gnarled root. She went sprawling with her books flying. Something zinged through the air above her hair. It thudded in a tree.

Sunlight glinted off metal—*a knife?* Its blade stuck deep in the bark. Kathleen, her heart pounding against her ribs, turned and looked behind her.

A cackle-like laughter mixed with the sound of crackling brush. She saw nothing.

Drenched in sweat, too fearful to move, Kathleen listened as seconds passed. Still nothing.

She grabbed her belongings, sprinted up the rest of the slope, and burst out into the open. She gasped for air and scanned the street in both directions.

Brakes squeaked. A school bus pulled up. Children, waiting in a row, boarded. Whining sounds. A shaggy dog loped after a child and into the bus. The driver shoved it out.

Kathleen dashed up to them. She needed the nearness of others. She studied the sidewalk and the areas behind her as the bus pulled away.

The sensible thing to do would be to tell someone.

But if she told anyone there'd be a fuss, the police would be called. Besides, after last night, she couldn't tell her parents.

Kathleen sprinted down the sidewalk, her face hot. Perspiration dripped from her underarms. When she arrived at school only the latecomers were slinking through the halls.

Kathleen pulled opened the classroom door but didn't see the teacher. Sophie and Dolly sat at their desks deep in conversation.

Dolly's long sausage curls were transformed into blonde braids encircling her head. She wore a charcoal-gray dress and matching stockings with black shoes. The silly, melodramatic girl wiped her swollen eyes and peered up at Kathleen.

Sophie looked over at Kathleen, got up, and joined her.

"Golly, what happened to you?" Sophie escorted Kathleen to her desk. "Your skirt's covered in mud."

Dolly stared too. Kathleen, out of breath and sweating, shrugged away from Sophie and plopped down in her seat. Sophie stood over her.

"You're not getting away with this, Kathleen. Tell me."

Kathleen shook her head.

Dammit. She'd left some of her books behind.

The teacher entered and told them to get out their Shakespeare books. Sophie scooted back to her desk, and all eyes faced the front.

Kathleen swiped at mud caked on her skirt and knee with her handkerchief, tucked her blouse back in, and straightened her stockings. She willed her breathing to calm. She had no idea what the teacher was prattling about. She no longer cared about Shakespeare.

When class ended Sophie grabbed her arm. "I'm worried. What's going on?"

Kathleen drew in her lips, darted down the hall, and headed up the stairs to her next class. She needed time to think.

If she told her parents, they'd definitely ship her off to Ohio or Kansas or wherever, not because of Chester, but for her own safety. And Sophie fell apart over the least little upset.

The knife—Lillian stabbed dead with a knife . . . Saliva filled Kathleen's mouth. She dashed to the bathroom, dropped her books, and banged open the door to an empty stall.

When she'd finished, she wiped her face with a wet paper towel, collected her belongings, and headed to her next class, weak and shaky.

Classwork and teachers muddled her mind. Her thoughts flitted from Lillian to the knife in the tree, to the crazy people at the Davidson house, and to her father's irate temper. Her classwork papers remained unfinished.

She slipped away to the school's library during lunch hour. She couldn't eat and didn't have the energy to retrieve her books or to walk home.

No one enjoyed their life anymore, not even her parents. Perhaps

Mary—but she didn't count. Yet Mary found sadness too. *The Pecken-paw family. What happened to happiness?*

A few months ago Kathleen had spent twenty-five cents of her babysitting money to purchase a small, scandalous, social-justice book sarcastically named *Gloom.*

She had hid it under her mattress because it addressed all sorts of inappropriate topics and jokes. But even in jest, she found truth, especially about how women should be entitled to the same privileges as men. And why shouldn't they? Why must her father always be right?

She spent her afternoon classes wondering, while looking out the windows at the sun peaking between gray clouds full of drizzle. When school ended, she made her way down the hallway to the front doors. The secretary called out to her, beckoning her into the office.

"Someone found your books and delivered them to the school earlier. I'm surprised at your leaving them scattered all over, and they're damp. You know they cost your parents money."

After mumbling an apology, she found Sophie waiting for her out front.

Kathleen asked, "Where's your friend?" and thumbed through her Shakespeare book.

"You're my friend."

Kathleen found her homework where she'd placed it, neatly folded in the center of the book. It was wet, and written on it in bold letters were the words, *Next time.*

Kathleen slammed the book shut and started walking.

"Golly, Kathleen. We had this same conversation at Lillian's about Dolly and me. You know how it hurts."

Kathleen watched for anything unusual. She glanced at Sophie. Guilt flooded her at seeing Sophie's scowl.

"We'll talk on the bus." She wouldn't let there be a *Next Time.*

When the streetcar pulled up, Kathleen and Sophie scuttled to the back. Sophie slid in next to Kathleen and said, "Dolly's not going to go anywhere until they find out what's happened to that guy whose motorcar went in the river—except of course to school. Her parents won't let her stay home. She's in mourning, but she doesn't even know for sure he's dead. She's got it bad." Sophie scowled. "Tell me about this morning."

"Last night I had a fight with my parents over something stupid."

Inside, Kathleen groaned. She'd carefully planned what she'd say, and now it came out all jumbled. "But that's not the point. I spent last evening at the home of one of my parents' friends. Have you ever been around a group of crazy, depressed people?"

Sophie didn't say anything.

"Right, you don't know what to say because you don't understand what I'm talking about."

Sophie spoke softly. "Dolly's depressed, and at the Bluets they all looked depressed. I think those women went off their trolleys, too." Sophie's face screwed up like she wanted to know if she passed the test.

"Do you remember," Kathleen continued, "when we were at the Bluets, sitting out back talking? You said you wished you could go to college with me. What if we could go somewhere together, not to college, but someplace where we could dance and act and you could sing? I have to be around happy people. I bet with our talents, we could turn this horrid world into something much more joyful—help make it one big party."

"How?" Sophie's eyes opened wide.

"We'll go where you won't have to teach kids piano, or act or dance, unless you want. You'll be able to sing your heart out and, who knows, maybe even write your own songs."

"My mother would never let me." Sophie tugged at her sleeve and looked off into the near distance. Her wistful look seemed encouraging.

"Sophie, we'll get to wear sparkly dresses. And wouldn't you love to wear those modern, classy clothes? We'd bob our hair even shorter, wear lipstick, and be around people who know how to have fun and not have a care in the world."

Sophie should see the photos in Kathleen's collection of theater magazines again. Then she'd be excited too.

"I'm sick of funerals and consoling others," Kathleen continued. "Look at how miserable Dolly is. Aren't you tired of that too? We'd be around progressive people, thinking people, people who know how to make the most out of life. They're searching for talent, Sophie. We'll fit right in."

"Where, Kathleen? No one much appreciates our abilities here."

"Chicago. There are all sorts of openings for attractive young ladies with well-turned ankles and voices like canaries. That's what the advertisements say."

Sophie seemed to hang on these words. Kathleen ramped up her enthusiasm.

"Let's get paid for doing what we love. Sophie, wait until you hear them clap and cheer. They'll shower us with applause until our ears hurt. They may even throw us bouquets."

Sophie stared at her.

Perspiration had soaked through Kathleen's shirt again. Would Sophie tell her mother or Dolly about this? She couldn't let that happen.

"We're best friends, aren't we? After class, I'll tell you about my great plan."

*Action may not always bring happiness; but there is no
happiness without action.*

—BENJAMIN DISRAELI

12

At the fine-arts school both girls went
their separate ways. Sophie dashed up the stairs to her private voice
session, and Kathleen hurried down the hall for her advanced soft-
shoe lesson. An hour and a half later, with Kathleen hot and sweaty,
they met in the hallway and headed out to catch the streetcar for
home.

"Whew, Kath, the air around you is a bit strong."

Kathleen gave Sophie her squinty-eyed look. "I deserve a little
respect here. It's been a rough day." Her mile dash to school that
morning with her nervous system about to short circuit would make
anyone's glands overwork. She looked forward to the soaking bubble
bath she didn't get the night before.

Kathleen pulled opened the door to the street, blocking Sophie,
and checked the sidewalk in both directions. Everything seemed
normal. She nudged Sophie out and double stepped to the streetcar
stop.

"Golly," Sophie said, "I couldn't concentrate on anything my voice
teacher told me. Going to Chicago kept rolling in and out of my
thoughts." She stopped, fumbled around in her bag until she found
her streetcar token, then rushed to catch up. "But you know my
mother, and I can't believe your parents will you let go you either."

Kathleen climbed onto the streetcar and headed to the back.

Sophie settled in beside her. When the doors closed and it started to move, Kathleen inhaled and studied the other passengers.

Sophie narrowed her eyes. "Something's very wrong. There's a bigger reason you're talking about going to Chicago."

Kathleen peered out the window and shrugged.

"Tell me." Sophie punched her friend's arm. "I'm not saying one more thing until you do."

Kathleen bit her lip and said, "I've never seen my parents as angry as they were last night. They might not let me go to the university." She swallowed back the taste of bile. If she told Sophie, the girl would fall apart from worry.

"Why? What did you fight about?" Sophie gave Kathleen her full attention.

Kathleen fiddled with the strap on her bag. "They said something about sending me away to Kansas. If I don't have my own plan they'll take over my entire future." She touched Sophie's wrist. "Please help me. We can test my idea—nothing permanent—and then we can make up our own minds. Our parents won't even know."

"Are you bonkers?" Sophie pulled free and looked away for a moment. "You said Chicago—Chicago. Do you know how far away it is? How can we test out any *plan* in Chicago without our parents knowing?"

"I've figured it all out." Kathleen sucked in a lung full of air. "We tell our parents we're going to spend tomorrow night—and Saturday night—at Nella's grandmother's cabin with some other girls because . . . because we need to practice for the Shakespeare audition." She found herself taking short little breaths. "Your mom knows what a big thing that is, and my parents will be delighted at our earnestness."

"Seriously?"

Kathleen talked fast, hoping to hold Sophie's interest. "We pack a bag, go to school, go to our theater class, then take the streetcar to the train station."

"Wait a minute. We lie? Then we leave town for two nights?" Sophie grabbed Kathleen by the arm and shoved her face close to Kathleen's. "You're not serious."

Kathleen peeled Sophie's hands off of her and smiled. "We take the Great Western Limited that leaves at eight o'clock Friday night, and we'll be in Chicago Saturday morning at eight forty-five. We'll audition for some plays I've seen advertised. If we aren't accepted, we get back on the train that evening, and we're home on Sunday. No one will ever know."

"Holy crackers—you are serious." Sophie sat back against the seat and stared ahead.

Kathleen's stomach tightened. She had to get out of Minneapolis. Even without Sophie, she couldn't let someone track her—hunt her down—like Lillian.

Sophie interrupted her thoughts with a voice that was almost a whisper. "If I don't leave my mother will ruin my life, and worse, I'll be living at home when I'm thirty. I'll still be sleeping in the same bed I slept in when I was six. She'll see to it I never marry. This may be my only chance."

"You can't tell anyone." Kathleen didn't know if she was overcome with excitement or happiness, but her insides went all jittery.

"What should we pack?" Sophie's voice cracked. Kathleen gave her hand a reassuring squeeze.

"Certainly not school clothes. We need an older look." Kathleen's mind sorted through advertisements she'd seen in glamor magazines. "And take all the money you have. We'll need to buy meals and maybe taxi fare."

"Jeez, Kathleen, I don't have much . . . some piano-lesson money I've earned this month and my allowance. I have a savings book for my bank account.

Kathleen worked her jaw back and forth. "I have a problem. I can't go to the bank for any of my savings account money because my father would know. I do have cash in my room from my allowance and babysitting." She sat forward. "But you could go to the bank during lunch tomorrow. Don't take it all out. Leave a little in so they don't close out your account."

"Let's pick some of our mothers' clothes." Sophie grinned and said, "Bet you we'll look at least twenty."

"And don't forget rehearsal clothes."

They planned all the way to their stop.

When they left the streetcar, Kathleen grabbed Sophie's hand. "I didn't think you were brave enough to do this. I'm so excited. This could be our chance of a lifetime."

Kathleen hugged Sophie.

"I do have a favor to ask." Kathleen looked up and down the street. "Would you mind walking halfway home with me? It would give us more time to talk about everything."

Those three extra blocks would put Kathleen's house in sight. She could see if anyone was lurking about her neighborhood.

Adventure is not outside a man; it is within.

—DAVID GRAYSON

13

Kathleen needed to wash up for dinner. She tossed her books on her bed. Her Latin book tumbled to the floor and a note fell out. She picked it up and studied the bold letters.

Only fools tolerate the actions of deceit.

She fingered the note, wondering who wrote it. Dolly? The wording sounded far too sophisticated. Her father? He would never leave her a note. Chester? If Chester wrote it he's still alive. But if he wrote it, the message made no sense. The knife thrower had to have written both of them. Tomorrow she'd ask the school secretary to identify who returned her books.

At dinner Mary carried on about wishing she had a brother. Some boy in her class didn't have socks and got mad when she took him two pairs of hers. Kathleen didn't join in. She couldn't stop thinking about her stalker and Chicago. Once in bed, she didn't fall asleep until the early morning sunlight slanted through the trees.

A knock on her door woke her, and her father entered. He sat on the edge of her bed, brushed her hair from her eyes, and took in a huge breath.

Kathleen froze. *He knew about Chicago,* she thought. He'd interfere with her plans.

"You're going to be late for school. I have to leave for the bank in a few minutes. I've been thinking about the other night." He cleared his throat. "I'm sorry for my harshness. We've all been through a miserable few weeks." His forehead wrinkled. "I must say, you've handled yourself well in front of the Bluets and again with Mrs. Davidson."

He never came in her room before school. He'd call to her from the doorway to tell her it was time to get up, but he never sat on her bed. Ever.

Her muscles tightened. He would say more.

He paused and in a soft voice said, "I detest thinking about Mr. Davidson's bad behavior around attractive young women. But . . . you're more sophisticated than most girls your age. I've given this nasty business much thought. If you had a conversation or two with Mr. Davidson, and if he was up to anything untoward, you would be wise enough to recognize his shady side. You're far too intelligent." The lines around his mouth turned into a grin. "I trust that you told me the truth, and I'm proud you're my daughter."

Kathleen's throat ached and her eyes filled with moisture. Her father stood and quietly left the bedroom. He'd made her dreams of Chicago seem further away.

She suspected her mother had persuaded him to talk to her and probably even suggested what he should say. But in his stubbornness he wouldn't have bent to her mother's wishes if he hadn't meant those words.

~

When Kathleen and Sophie arrived at school, their classmates questioned them about their valises. Kathleen told them they were off to study at a relative's cabin for the weekend.

"Come on, Sophie." Kathleen motioned for her to follow.

She asked the secretary if they could leave their valises in the school office until the end of the day.

While Sophie, she, and Mrs. Howe stowed the bags in a closet behind Mrs. Howe's desk, Kathleen asked, "Who returned my books? I want to thank them."

Mrs. Howe closed the closet door. "I didn't get their names."

"There was more than one?"

"Three ninth-grade girls."

Kathleen thanked her and hurried off to English class. Maybe the girls left the notes as a joke. Magical thinking. They wouldn't write words such as *actions of deceit*.

Again, she couldn't concentrate on any of the lessons in her classes. But it didn't matter. She wouldn't be returning.

After school, Kathleen and Sophie retrieved their valises and secretly stuffed their school materials in the closet behind big rolls of paper. They kept their books of Shakespearian plays. Dolly followed both Kathleen and Sophie out to wait for the streetcar. Her relentless whining made Kathleen want to tie the girl's blonde braids in knots.

"Why won't you tell me?" Dolly stood with her hands on her hips. Sophie glanced at Kathleen.

Drats. Sophie refuses to lie.

Kathleen said, "Because it isn't any of your damned business."

"Stay out of this, Kathleen. You're a foul-mouthed troublemaker." Dolly folded her hands in front of her and smiled at Sophie. "I can't believe you'd go somewhere for a weekend and not invite me."

Sophie rolled her eyes. "You aren't going to go anywhere but school until your so-called sugar daddy surfaces."

Kathleen almost giggled at Sophie's tasteless choice words, referring to a man who might have drowned.

Dolly's face reddened. She whirled around and marched back toward the school building.

Sophie winked at Kathleen.

～

They didn't dare be late this afternoon, because Madam Leah Carlinski monitored their class's progress on the last Friday of the month. Sophie pushed through the theater's double doors, mumbling about how Madam's presence always put Mr. Russin in a foul mood.

The two of them scurried down the aisle, but before they darted up the steps onto the stage, Kathleen grabbed Sophie's arm. Something made her skin crawl. She needed an excuse to look around the theater.

"Wait. You have a smudge on your forehead." Kathleen took out her clean hanky and wiped above Sophie's brow. Someone sat in the far back corner, in the shadows. Kathleen couldn't tell if it was a man or woman. She hated being on guard all the time.

Sophie jerked away. "You about took my skin off."

"Don't worry, you're still beautiful."

They sat and waited for the other students to settle.

The tapping of her cane on the wooden floor announced Madam Carlinski's presence even before she marched out from the side wing. Mr. Russin followed, carrying a sturdy chair. He placed it center stage, facing the students and the auditorium. He disappeared and returned with a pitcher of water and a glass. He seemed flummoxed.

"Mr. Alexander," he said to a student, "fetch a small table and set it here for Madam's water."

Satisfied he'd taken care of her needs, he clapped his hands. The students stood.

"From the diaphragm, eight count now. Start with one count. Breathe in, one, hold, one, and breathe out, one. Two count, breathe in, one-two, hold, one-two, breathe out . . ."

They continued the breathing exercise until they finished their eight count. Mr. Russin reviewed their last week's lesson, then looked at each student.

"Miss Llewellyn, today we delve into the next level of portraying emotions. Demonstrate for us how an actress might show the audience her deep grief when learning of some significant loss—say perhaps a lover who's died. I'll give you one minute to compose and execute your performance. The rest of you use the minute to prepare your performances."

The red-haired young woman with flashing eyes strode to center stage, faced the auditorium, pulled her handkerchief up to muffle some sobs, then let out an agonizing wail.

"Enough," Mr. Russin interrupted. "Mr. Carter, you are next."

Mr. Carter, pimples and all, sauntered center stage and stared out at the darkened theater. He took several deep breaths before he let loose with gasping sounds punctuated with some thigh and chest poundings.

Mr. Russin gripped Mr. Carter's shoulder and pointed at his empty chair. He shook his head and glanced up at the catwalk above. After a few seconds he studied his charges.

Madam Carlinski might as well been given a hot cinnamon stick to suck.

"Miss McPherson."

No one moved.

"We're waiting, Miss McPherson."

She heard feet scuff, a student shifting in his chair, and a nervous cough. None of them wanted to do this.

She rose. This performance belonged to her.

Kathleen breathed deeply, held it a moment, and made her face go blank. She stared out over her shoulder beyond the students into the darkened theater. Keeping her torso tight, she made a quarter turn, and with her chin up, she let her gaze fall and slide past each seated classmate before she moved. As if in a dream, and partly facing the audience, she moved toward center stage.

Kathleen stopped at the table where they'd placed the water. She raised the pitcher in one hand, the glass in the other, and started to pour. Her hands trembled slightly, then more. She promptly replaced the pitcher and gave a soft choking sob. The glass dropped, water spilled, the glass rolled away.

Kathleen quieted, stared at it for three counts, then crumpled in a heap on the floor and buried her head in Madam Carlinski's lap.

Silence.

Mr. Russin said, "Thank you, Miss McPherson, you may return to your seat." Then Mr. Russin continued, "Never make obnoxious sounds that push the audience mentally away from your realities on the stage. During excruciating scenes, draw them to your bosom; bring them up close so they can live deep within your raw emotions."

Mr. Russin didn't ask for questions. Instead he shielded his eyes and looked out into the theater.

"My friend Pritchard is here to work with us today. Pritchard, please come up on stage. Pritchard teaches actors in several New York and Chicago theaters about how to find and cultivate their inner emotions."

Kathleen shivered. Did Sophie know anything about Pritchard? Sophie's uninterested face said she didn't.

Pritchard strode up the steps and presented himself to the group on the stage. He saw Kathleen, and an insinuation of a smile crossed his lips. Kathleen stared at him, unresponsive. Her insides quivered. Pritchard's leering gave Kathleen another compelling reason to flee to Chicago.

At the end of the session Sophie and Kathleen collected their books and valises and left to catch the streetcar. Kathleen glanced back several times to be sure Pritchard or someone else didn't follow them.

Sophie chattered on about everything. When they climbed on the streetcar, they both sat rigid as it rumbled down the way, taking them to the train station. Kathleen's thoughts kept playing an endless loop of her father's early morning contrition. She looked at Sophie's pale face. Sophie stared straight ahead and chewed on a fingernail.

This whole escapade could turn into a disaster.

Pleasure is the beginning and the end of living happily.
—EPICURUS

14

In the train station Sophie clutched her valise as if it would disappear. They paid for their tickets and sat on the bench, watching the large-faced clock. Neither girl talked. Kathleen studied more than the clock. She scrutinized everyone entering the station lobby and all the people waiting for trains. After checking out each person who entered, she waited for the next. No one looked like a homicidal knife thrower, and no one looked like anyone she might know.

The speaker finally announced the arrival of their train. They jumped up, gathered their belongings, and followed the crowd to the platform. When the conductor looked at their tickets, he pointed to the car on his left. The girls searched for their seat numbers and sat. Kathleen hoped they would be by themselves, but an older couple sat opposite them.

She looked around then pulled out her Shakespeare book and pretended to read. Sophie followed her lead.

The train jerked, and something underneath screeched and turned into a short squeal. They lowered their books to watch the train next to them slip by. After a few seconds Kathleen realized it wasn't the other train moving. It was their train pulling out of the station. She looked at Sophie and grinned.

They were leaving the city. Its lights twinkled on, a few at a time, in the faded glow of the day.

Sophie darted a look at the couple, then quietly said, "I have so many questions to ask. I can barely stand it."

Kathleen rose. "Let's go see if the dining car is open." She left her Shakespeare book on the seat and nodded to the couple as she moved out into the aisle. Sophie followed.

When Kathleen pulled open the heavy door at the end of their car, a blast of cold wind hit her. She couldn't hear anything but the loud clacking noise of the wheels on the track. The open-air metal platform slid back and forth. She forced herself to step on it, sprang over to the next car's step, and yanked the door open. Light, warmth, and a wave of safety washed over her.

Sophie grabbed Kathleen's arm. "I hated that. Didn't it scare you?"

"It's way too exposed." Kathleen weaved along down the aisle, past other passengers, to the dining car.

In the dining car, tables for four were on one side with tables for two on the other. Kathleen slipped into the nearest empty table for two and placed the white linen napkin in her lap. Sophie did the same.

"Golly, I'm hungry." Sophie looked around to see what the other diners were eating.

A waiter came, told them their choices, and took their orders.

Sophie whispered, "Did you notice? Almost everyone in here is a man."

Kathleen found herself staring at one in particular. She leaned over to Sophie and nodded. "There's a woman at the other end of this car, sitting with a tall man who seems familiar, but don't look—too obvious." There was something about the back of his head, the way he held it, and his awful, blue window-pane suit. She sucked in her breath.

"Eternal crap."

"What?" Sophie studied Kathleen's face. "What's wrong?"

"It's Pritchard." She wanted to get up and leave, to hide somewhere.

"Should we say hello to him?" Sophie turned to look.

"Don't look. I dislike the man. Let's get out of here." How did he get on the train without her spotting him?

"What's eating you?" Sophie scowled. "I'm starving. I'm not going anywhere." She picked up a bread stick and nibbled on it.

"He knows my mother, Soph. He'll want to know where we're going and why."

Kathleen could ignore the pounding in her head but not the grumbling in her stomach. For two days in a row, she'd not eaten breakfast or lunch. She watched Sophie chew on a buttery breadstick.

She snatched one, devoured it, took another, and said, "Maybe they'll leave by the door down at their end."

"Did you bring the advertisement?"

"Which one, the *Herald Tribune* or the *On Stage Theater* magazine?"

Pritchard must have been one of the last ones on the train. He'd probably come through the lobby while they waited on the platform to board.

Sophie shrugged. "I don't know. Whichever one tells us where to audition."

The waiter brought them beef tenderloins, potatoes, green beans, and cloverleaf rolls.

When he left, Kathleen picked up her fork and said, "We'll be going to the theater district in the Loop. We're trying out for parts in *Ladies' Night Out*. I don't think we'll have any problems finding the audition hall because it's near the Auditorium and the Congress Hotel."

Sophie scowled again. "You said they were only hiring standbys for that play. Don't we want full-time jobs?"

Kathleen checked back on Pritchard. The waiter was setting his food on his table. Some of her tension melted. Maybe she and Sophie could finish and get out of there while he ate.

"Kathleen." Sophie's eyes narrowed, demanding a better explanation.

"Think about it, Sophie. The competition for a full-time job is fierce. Wouldn't you rather have a part-time one than none at all?"

"Yes, but—"

Kathleen set her fork down and held up her finger. "Tickets for *Ladies Night Out* sell for a dollar-fifty. Lots of other theater tickets only sell for fifty cents." She picked up her fork. "Figure out the arithmetic. You'll see which one pays the best, even if the part is a standby."

Kathleen took a bite of potato. She could see only darkness outside, but the windows reflected the interior of the dining car. She saw herself, and there was Sophie, the two of them sitting in the dining car, having a deep conversation, without their parents. They looked like grown-ups—like adults. Prickles of warmth and wonderment spread over her.

Sophie took a few more bites and paused. "Do you know what happens tonight? I don't understand this Pullman thing, especially since we have to share our seats with that other couple. I don't want to sleep sitting up."

The reality of their escapade energized her. "The porters are making up our beds right now. The other couple will have the lower berth, and we'll sleep together in the pulldown, upper berth. They even give us a little ladder. We'll have privacy because each bed's opening has a heavy, green curtain that buttons closed."

Sophie tore her roll in half and buttered it. "I'm so tired I could sleep on the floor. But I'm too excited to sleep."

"Me too. I've had jitters all day. I want to leave before Pritchard sees us."

"The waiter said ice cream comes with our dinner, with fudge sauce and nuts." Sophie paused with her piece of roll halfway to her mouth. "Did you give your parents a telephone number where you could be reached?"

"Good Lord, there's no telephone number."

"Mother said I couldn't go if she didn't have a way to reach me in an emergency."

Kathleen cocked her head and waited.

Sophie grinned. "I made one up. Now isn't that evil?"

They couldn't help it. With their heads held close together, they erupted into giggles.

When she caught her breath, Kathleen said, "I can't believe you actually lied. You are *most* wicked."

Wait. Where was Pritchard? The lady was sitting alone now.

"Who's most wicked?" Pritchard's whisky voice came from behind her. Kathleen jerked up straight. He stepped over beside Sophie and faced Kathleen. "I've been watching you, Miss McPherson, in the mirror at the other end of this car. After watching your mannerisms, I knew it was you. I'm surprised to see two such young ladies off on an unescorted weekend adventure. Especially since this adventure takes you into the heart of Chicago."

Sophie's face turned the color of cranberries. Kathleen suspected her face matched.

"One thing," he said. "If you were talking about Chicago, you are dead right. It is quite the wicked city. I'd even say it's abnormally wicked but, oh, so delightful." He looked from Kathleen to Sophie. "Do your parents think you're spending the weekend somewhere a little more, should we say, quiet? Miss McPherson, if your mother knew about this, wouldn't it ruffle her prim and proper feathers beyond repair?"

Kathleen burned hot. This wasn't any of his business. She sorted through some unpleasant responses, but the dryness of her throat wouldn't let any words out.

He lowered his face until it was level with Kathleen's. "When we play games, and we don't know the rules, who knows what might happen?" He straightened and chuckled. "But that's what makes the pleasure—or the pain—so exquisite."

He strolled down the aisle to his table. Sophie half stood then sat. She squirmed in her chair, looking back at him.

"Kath, what do we do? He'll tell. We've got to leave." She started to stand again. Kathleen grabbed her wrist and held tight.

"Sit. Besides, we have nowhere to go. We'll eat our ice cream like we don't have a care in the world." She couldn't let Sophie become hysterical. "If we act like we don't give a whit, then he won't bother to contact our parents." Kathleen, her vision on fire, held up a finger, signaling the waiter to clear their plates and bring dessert.

Pritchard's stalking me. Is he the knife thrower? She hated being paranoid.

By the time the waiter placed the ice cream in front of them, the topic of what would happen in Chicago filled their conversation.

"Eat slowly." Kathleen raised her spoon. "I want Pritchard and his lady friend to leave first."

Sophie turned in her chair to look, but Kathleen touched her arm.

"I have a clear view of him. You don't need to look." Kathleen took a bite. "If he doesn't head to the smoking car, then we will."

"What for?" Sophie nibbled the tiny sugar biscuit that came with the ice cream.

Kathleen pulled a half pack of Pall Malls from her purse and grinned.

Sophie gasped. "You took those from your mother?"

"We can't look like high-school girls. Is there a better way to convince everyone we're older?"

Sophie's eyes grew large. "I've never smoked."

Kathleen slipped them back into her purse. "That's why we go to the smoking car. We need to practice."

"But isn't the smoking car mostly for men?"

Kathleen bit her lip. "You're right. We'd be too conspicuous. Let's practice in the ladies' powder room."

"My dear, dear friend." Sophie touched Kathleen's hand. "You mean I'll practice. You've already mastered this fine art."

A life spent making mistakes is not only more honorable,
but more useful than a life spent doing nothing.

—GEORGE BERNARD SHAW

15

The swaying of the darkened coach along with the clacking of wheels on the rails lulled Kathleen away from their late-night chattering. She descended into a few hours of fitful sleep.

Children arguing, parents nagging, and people bumping up and down the narrow aisle jarred her awake. Sophie rolled over, yawned, and stretched.

Since their nervousness made them care more about their appearance than lumps of breakfast settling hard in their stomachs, they ignored the dining car.

The porter transformed their beds back into seats for the remainder of the short trip to Chicago. The couple who sat across from them yesterday evening had disappeared to the dining car.

"I hate this dress." Kathleen looked down at the two-piece frock she'd selected.

"You should've borrowed your mother's corset." Sophie tugged at her own ruffled neckline. "You look too flat chested."

"It's the flapper style. But this damned awful belt . . . We both look frumpy." Kathleen screwed up the left side of her face.

"We don't look *that* terrible. Here, you first." Sophie handed her a tube of lipstick.

Kathleen whistled low. "Gal, you surprise me. I bet your mother doesn't know about this."

"When I went to the bank yesterday noon, I saw it advertised in a store window. It said to wear the dark color for day and the light for night." Sophie pulled out another from her pocketbook. "I bought one of each. Don't use too much. They cost me a dollar apiece."

Kathleen slipped the cap off and twisted the tube. The lipstick rose. She twisted it again the other way and it retracted. She laughed.

"I've only seen sliders you push up with your fingernail. These are the newest." She sniffed it . . . a hint of something sweet. "Mirror, give me a mirror." She couldn't sit still.

Sophie placed her mirror in Kathleen's hand. Both girls were giggling.

"Now stop it." Kathleen made her voice serious. "I don't want any of it to smear."

She quit breathing, held the mirror up, and carefully outlined her lips and then filled them in like she'd seen in the movies. She smacked them a couple of times on a tissue.

"What do you think? Is it too much?" She handed the lipstick back to Sophie.

"You're beautiful. You could be the next Clara Bow." Sophie took the mirror, held it a bit higher, and applied the coveted cosmetic to her lips. "Remember Clara in *Down to the Ships*?"

"All the magazines predict she's going places," Kathleen said. "She's only a year or two older than we are. Could be us. You should see what she's doing to her eyebrows."

"Eyebrows? No thanks—my mother would choke if she knew about this lipstick." Sophie blotted her lips on a tissue and looked expectantly at Kathleen.

"Cat's pajamas." She pinched up a fold of Sophie's floral dress. "But this—"

"What's wrong with you?" Sophie swatted at her hand. "You're the one who's always saying everything will be okay. Just stop. We look great."

Kathleen frowned. "I read a satirical article called 'Rules and Regulations of the Indignant Order of Flappers.' It encouraged girls to think and do as they pleased. One of the rules said flappers should wear their skirts just above their knees so when they sit, others will get a thrill. It said, 'Remember that without thrills life is a bore. Do your duty.' With these clothes, we'll hardly be doing our duty."

When the train pulled into the station, Kathleen and Sophie

gathered their belongings and scampered down the metal steps onto the main platform. They scooted around the other passengers reclaiming luggage from the bins in the side of the train. As the girls' pumps clicked on the marble-tiled concourse floor, Sophie slowed to gawk.

"Come—hurry, let's catch a taxi before they're all taken." Kathleen headed toward the lobby and the front entrance.

"Such a pretty place," Sophie called from somewhere behind Kathleen. "All the white with the shiny brass, green tile, and dark wood—"

"Sure. Now get a move on." Kathleen burst through the front doors out onto the large covered entrance with its white columns.

"Look—streetcars," Sophie said.

Kathleen pulled her mother's wool coat tighter against the breeze. "Let's spring for a taxi." Kathleen looked around and pointed to the corner. "I bet they pick up and drop off around at the side entrance." She should have looked for signs.

She rounded the corner of the terminal and saw several yellow taxis loaded with passengers pull away from the curb.

"Drats. We've missed them." She looked up and down the street.

"Here comes one." Sophie pointed out a Checker Cab way down the street, making its way through traffic. It headed toward the terminal. Other passengers were coming out of the terminal's side door.

"Taxi!" Kathleen held her arm up and waved. She and Sophie would need to run a goodly distance to get to the curb in time.

"Don't." Someone grabbed her arm and pulled it down to her side. She jerked and turned.

Pritchard.

"You don't want that cab."

"Excuse me?" Kathleen bristled and stepped away. "We certainly do. We saw it first." She started out toward the curb again—with her arm raised.

"That's right," Sophie chimed in, waving her hand too. "It's ours."

The cab swerved across lanes and zipped into the passengers' loading zone.

Tires squealing caused Kathleen to look around. A black sedan sped up the street, weaving through traffic.

The taxi driver parked, rushed around the cab, and opened the back door. He motioned for them to hurry.

"See. It's ours." Kathleen laughed and sprinted toward the waiting taxi.

"No!" Pritchard snatched them by the backs of their coats, wrenching them backward.

Kathleen stumbled, landing on Sophie. She heard more brake or tire squealing. Some urgency compelled her to untangle herself. Pritchard threw himself over them. Furious, she doubled her fist and landed a wallop on his jaw.

Kathleen struggled, wanting to heave him away. Rapid sounds of gunfire filled the air. Pritchard groaned.

Her breath stopped. *My God! Did someone shoot him?*

She wiggled out and prop herself up. He rolled off and got to his feet. Everyone else had vanished.

Then she saw the taxi driver next to the open car door—sprawled on the cement. His blood pooled on the pavement.

Sophie screeched. She clutched at Kathleen's arm. Kathleen scrambled to her feet and helped Sophie up. Kathleen's mind replayed the sounds of tires skidding and shots firing.

Why?

Sirens approached from the east. Pedestrians reappeared, chattering and pointing.

"This way." Pritchard nodded to the south. "Let's get out of here before the police tie up traffic." He loped off.

Sophie looked at Kathleen. Kathleen glanced around, then shrugged. They snatched up their belongings and dashed after him.

When they reached the next taxi stand a block away, Kathleen caught her breath and said, "Pritchard, what happened back there?"

"Taxi wars. The cab with the green and white checkers painted on top pulled into a Yellow Cab's stand. Yellow taxis aren't going to give up any of their business to a newcomer. All we can do is stand back and watch the bloodshed." He pulled his gold pocket watch out of his vest. "I'm going to be late. We're going to the same district. We'll share a taxi."

Kathleen set her jaw. "How could you even guess where we're headed?" She hated knowing he was stalking her. But if he were the knife thrower, why would he save her from death by taxi?

Pritchard looked them up and down then gave a little snort.

There is always a secret irritation about a laugh we cannot join.
—AGNES REPPLIER

16

She hated the man.

Pritchard could laugh all he wanted. She'd not listen. They should have taken a streetcar.

"My elbow and knee are killing me." Sophie hunched her shoulder and moved her arm around. "Were you hurt when you fell?"

"I didn't fall. I was yanked down by some bastard."

"My ankle doesn't feel right either."

Pritchard patted Sophie's shoulder. "Maybe you'll have to give up dancing and make your fame from acting and singing. That won't break your tender heart."

Kathleen scowled at him. *Pompous know-it-all.*

A Yellow Cab swerved to the curb. Both girls scurried back.

"Ladies, ladies, here you are in the most fabulous city imaginable, off seeking a grand adventure. A tiny round of gunfire and you want to hide under your covers." He climbed into the back seat of the taxi and, with a long pointed finger, motioned for them to join him.

They scrunched in while the driver hefted the bags into the trunk. When he put the taxi in gear, Pritchard reached over and tapped the driver's shoulder.

"I believe we are all going to the theater district. You must hustle because I've used much of my time persuading these lovelies that what I have to say is essential for their well-being."

Several minutes later he said, "Driver, let me off at the next corner. The young ladies will go on to somewhere around Dearborn and Randolph Street. This should cover it all. He peeled off some bills. Good day, young sweets. Perhaps we'll be delighted by another unexpected encounter."

He tipped his hat and strolled down the sidewalk.

Their taxi blended with the flow of cars. It pulled to the curb a few blocks down and stopped.

He opened the door, got their bags, and drove off into the teeming traffic.

Someone bumped Kathleen's shoulder. She jostled Sophie over next to a store window to let three men in business suits pass. Sophie chattered on about the crowds and pointed at the buildings, not looking where she walked. Everyone rushed, colors dazzled, signs flashed, and streets vibrated with horns honking, people yelling, and cars whizzing in and out of traffic.

"This way, Sophie, come on." Smells of warmed cinnamon-sugar made her mouth water.

"Wait, Kath. See the sign on the building over there—"

"We can't poke. Help me look for the audition hall." Kathleen checked the street names and then the names of the stores and theaters.

"Holy Moly," Sophie said, pulling Kathleen's arm, "look at the clothes in this window."

"Not now. See the wooden doorway with the opaque glass?" Kathleen weaved her way through oncoming pedestrians. When she got to the door, she read the ornate black-and-gold lettering. *Live Stage Company & Audition Hall, Hours 8:00 a.m. to 5:00 p.m.* She looked around for Sophie.

Sophie stood in front of a window display featuring beaded evening dresses. Each skinny mannequin wore an eye-catching jeweled headband.

"Sophie—come on." Kathleen motioned for her to hurry. "We can't sink this." She pulled the handle down and stepped inside.

"Oh creepers." Sophie followed her through the door into a narrow hallway.

Kathleen gave her the squint-eye. Sophie instantly shut her mouth. Kathleen took Sophie by the shoulders and stared at her. "We're twenty-years old, we've finished high school, we live on our own, and we need no parent permission. Got it?"

Sophie jutted her chin out. It quivered.

"I don't mean to be bossy, but we can't mess this up. I say this as much for my own benefit, all right?"

The two started down a long hallway lined with photos, playbills, and doors with darkened windows. Sophie tugged at Kathleen's sleeve.

"Look at this picture. Their dance costumes are terribly skimpy."

"Well, they *are* actors and dancers." Kathleen hoped her words explained the near-nude photos. Lights were on behind one door's smoked-glass window. Kathleen read the lettering on the window, nodded at Sophie, took a deep breath, and knocked.

"Yeah, come in."

Kathleen pushed the door open. Cigar and coffee smells reminded her of home. The gnawing ache grew in her empty stomach.

"Good morning." Kathleen's voice chirped too much.

The man tilted back in his chair. Even with his cigar in his mouth, he managed a smirk.

Relax. He's just a grown-up bully.

"Suppose you're looking for work."

Kathleen raised one eyebrow and hinted at a smile. "However did you guess?"

"Missy, I know lots of things. More than you ever will. Let's get on with it. Your names, please." He took two forms from his drawer, put his cigar in the ashtray, and pulled a pen out of another drawer along with his inkwell.

"I'm Miss Kathleen McPherson, and this is Miss Sophie Dagget." Kathleen moved closer to his desk, placing one foot directly in the path of the other.

"Where're ya from?" He didn't look up.

"We're from Minnesota—Minneapolis, actually." Kathleen slipped out of her mother's lambs-wool coat and then, like she'd seen in some movie, draped it over one shoulder.

"And what talents do you profess?" He picked up his cigar and leaned back. Did he expect them to take a while to tell him some story?

"May we sit?" Kathleen didn't want to stand in front of him like an errant schoolgirl.

He nodded to the chairs opposite the desk.

She put the coat over the back of the chair and sat. She kept her back straight and held her head high, her knees together, and her legs demurely positioned with one foot in front of the other—as taught.

He looked unimpressed.

Kathleen tilted her head back, then slowly reached in her purse, keeping her eyes on him. She pulled out her cigarettes, placed one between her lips, and leaned forward for him to light it.

He snorted and tossed her a matchbook.

"Thanks." She smiled to hide her embarrassment and lit her own cigarette.

He waited.

She heard Sophie shift her weight and felt her lean in close. Kathleen ignored her and blew a smoke ring.

Sophie tugged at Kathleen's sleeve. She shot her a questioning glance. Sophie held out her hand for a cigarette.

Geesh. Kathleen took one, lit it with her own, and handed it back to her. She turned away from Sophie and smiled at the man.

He looked bored.

"We've both studied extensively at the Minneapolis School of Performing Arts." Kathleen let the smoke slide out between her lips. "We've obtained the highest levels in ballet, tap, soft shoe, and acrobatics." Kathleen looked at her fingernail and said, "Madam Leah Carlinski, I'm certain you know who *she* is, has been our mentor in the division of stage performance and acting. Miss Dagget, after six years of voice lessons, received the coveted Golden Bell award last year for her excellent vocal performance of Gilda in Rigoletto."

Sophie brushed ash from her dress and let an ill-stifled cough slip out.

"Doesn't she talk?" He nodded at Sophie.

"I certainly do." Sophie flushed.

"How old are you?"

"Twenty," they said in unison.

"Yep, just what I thought."

He set his pen back in the holder, leaned forward, and stared into their faces.

Kathleen kept her gaze on him and took another puff.

"You lying little high-school bitches. You think you can waltz in here, wearing your God-awful clothes—clothes you've stolen from your mothers—and fool me? Sweeties, I've seen it all. We get fifty like you every week, and guess what?" He sucked on his cigar, and with it still between his teeth, said, "Only about five out of fifty get to audition. Get it?"

Kathleen nodded but broke out in a chilling sweat. She couldn't take the train back home. For Pete's sake—what could she do? Someone was determined to murder her. She'd have to tell her parents. Her throat ached. *Missouri of all places—good grief.*

Sophie coughed a couple of times.

He leaned back and chewed on the end of his cigar and stared at the ceiling. He seemed to be talking to himself, then he said, "Can't let just anyone through here." He stared at Kathleen. "Understand?"

Kathleen didn't.

He studied Sophie, then his brow lowered over his dark eyes, and he watched Kathleen for a few moments. He folded his arms and glared at them.

"Are you two teenage runaways?"

Kathleen shook her head. She didn't dare look at Sophie.

Sophie's chair made a scrunching sound as she shifted positions.

He poked his cigar toward them. "Mayor's hot on my ass. No more teenage runaways in the business—kicking up their heels, getting into trouble."

"Sir, please don't send us away." Kathleen's insides fluttered and her heart beat wildly, but she kept her voice soft.

He put his cigar in the ashtray and stared at her for several never-ending seconds.

His voice rumbled. "Geez, how in the hell am I supposed to handle all those demands from the Southside . . . Dammit." He shut his eyes and, with his elbows on the desk, he rubbed his temples.

The man sounded trapped—caught between things Kathleen didn't understand. But if she slipped something of substance between his indecisions, she might win this. Kathleen lowered her lashes and smiled as sweetly as she could.

"Neither of us can afford to finish our college education. We're desperate for a decent paying job, sir. We'll even agree to work part time, if needed."

She'd caught his attention. His eyes narrowed, he picked up his cigar, and he studied them some more.

"Listen, girlies." His words came out low, but he jabbed at them with his cigar. "If you're serious about this show business stuff—take off those clothes."

Kathleen jerked back. She heard Sophie gasp.

He lit his cigar again and puffed a few times. "Come on, come on, I don't have all day. Get out of those dresses so I can see."

Dark, shadowy edges closed around Kathleen's vision. Somewhere way back in a far corner of her light-headed brain she could hear her father's voice. "You're not nearly as smart as you think, young lady. You've disgraced us."

The man slid his chair back. "How am I to know where to send you for your auditions if I don't even know what you look like under all that yardage? Now, stand up and take off those goddamned ugly dresses. Leave your undies on. But I have to see what figure types you are. Okay?" He took another puff.

Kathleen didn't move, and she couldn't hear Sophie.

Red-faced now, he shouted at them. "Well, do you want to audition or not? I'm busy, get a move on or get out."

Kathleen jolted back to the moment. This wasn't the time to play coy. She stood, started unbuttoning her mother's blouse, and glanced at Sophie. Sophie, even though covered in beet-red hives, fumbled with her buttons and belt. They both dropped their clothes to the floor and stood rigid.

The man rose from behind his desk, walked slowly around each of them, and returned to his chair.

"Good enough. Get dressed." He picked up his pen and started to write.

Kathleen snatched up her blouse and tossed Sophie's belt to her. He wrote more on each of the forms in front of him while they finished dressing.

He nodded to Kathleen. "You, you're tall, long gams, they like that, especially with a good figure." He wrote something on a small paper and handed it to her. "Go up the stairs and straight down the long hall to studio 3C. Do you sing?"

Heavens—Kathleen shook her head.

"You'll get your assignments in that studio."

"Thank you." Kathleen wanted to gush out her profound gratitude but instead stood quiet. She couldn't keep from grinning.

He wrote something more on another piece of paper and handed it to Sophie. "Round, fully packed, and a sunshine smile. They like that too. Go up the stairs to studio 1B. It's a large music studio to the left off the stairway balcony. And you'll both be expected to dance and read part of a script. Be prepared with a short dance routine. And you," he said with a nod to Sophie, "you sing something of your choice. Keep it short—less than a minute. Consider yourselves fortunate. Most don't make it this far. Now for God's sake wear clothes you can move in and be prompt for the auditions. If you're even one minute late, you'll be disqualified. They'll expect you right on the dot at eight, Monday morning. Got it?"

"Monday?" Kathleen swallowed. Her ears buzzed—did she hear right? *He couldn't mean Monday.*

"Wait." Sophie's voice came out loud and high-pitched. "We can't on Monday."

Kathleen shook her head at Sophie. Sophie bit her lip and waited. Kathleen looked at her fingernail, took a deep breath, and slowly looked up at the man. He didn't smile. She grinned at him anyway. And for good measure, she gave him a wink.

"Sir, why not let us audition today? It's a perfectly fine day for discovering talent, don't you agree?"

"Naw, Saturdays are rehearsal time. No auditions today. Now shake a leg. Get out of here. Show up on Monday—on time."

"But, Kathleen, we can't—"

Kathleen furrowed her brows, gripped Sophie's arm, and guided her to the door.

When she opened it, an elfin, freckled-faced girl stood on the other side, about to knock. The girl blinked and moved aside to look around them. Then she wiggled some fingers at the man behind the desk.

"Is this the place where I sign up to audition?"

They are able because they think they are able.
—VIRGIL

17

"Oh my goodness. This can't be." In the hallway, Sophie burst into tears.

Kathleen pulled Sophie's hands down from her eyes. "Stop. Now." She held Sophie's hands.

"But he said Monday." Sophie wiped her eyes on her sleeve between muffled sobs.

"Sophie, hush."

The hallway had become a major gathering spot.

Somewhere, someone plinked out jazz on a piano. Three chatty flapper girls in short skirts and bobbed hair swept by them and trotted up the stairs.

Kathleen nudged Sophie over to the wall. She stood in front of her, hoping no one could see.

"Sophie, we'll be all right. We'll figure this out. Quit crying, for Pete's sake."

"May I help?" A man's voice came from behind. Kathleen glanced at him over her shoulder. A thirtyish man of average build in a brown wool suit and a green-checked bowtie with a brown fedora in his hand nodded at Sophie.

"We're fine, thank you."

"Listen, kid," he said, "lots of you babes come to Chicago hoping to get the big break. Most never get to audition. Heartbreaker, I see it every week."

He took out a starched, white handkerchief and handed it to Sophie.

"Missy, don't you worry. You both are real lookers, and with those long gams . . ." He nodded at Kathleen and winked.

"Please, sir, leave us alone." Kathleen glanced back at Sophie.

"Seriously, I know this guy who owns a club. He's looking for new talent—"

"Mister." She gave him her full attention. "I've read about guys like you. Get lost." Kathleen pulled the handkerchief away from Sophie and shoved it at him. "Come on, Sophie. He's one of those old men preying on young girls. Pick up your valise. We've got things to do."

Kathleen jerked Sophie's arm and pushed past him toward the exit.

"Hey—no offense. Ladies, I know people who can—"

Kathleen glowered. "What in the living hell are you up to?" She waved him away with the back of her hand. "We're respectable women."

Sophie sniffed, tilted her nose up, and strutted out into the cold sunlight and city noise.

Kathleen followed. She grabbed Sophie by her elbow and kept a brisk stride down the sidewalk.

Swell. A pimp, and Sophie is hysterical. What in the heck do we do now?

A trolley rumbled by. They continued walking, as if they knew where they were going, weaving in and out of a crush of people. Sophie no longer paused to window-shop.

"I'm hungry. We have no place to go." Sophie blew her nose. "Let's take the train home tonight."

"We've got to stay." Kathleen's stomach twisted into a knot. "We'll find a room."

"You can stay, but I'm going home."

"Would you really go without me? Come on, we'll figure something out."

They left the area of big department stores, businesses, and small shops advertising bargains in their windows. This neighborhood blended with a mixture of stores, hawkers selling wares from carts on sidewalks, and old men talking. Children and dogs scampered around.

An older, well-dressed woman in a doorway reached out and touched Kathleen's arm.

"You girls look lost." Her wrinkled, tanned face showed a missing tooth when she smiled. "May I be of help?" It all conflicted with her stylish heels, plaid ankle-length dress, bell-shaped jacket, and carefully coifed hair. She took a drag on her cigarette.

Sophie's chin trembled, but she kept her mouth shut and looked at Kathleen.

Kathleen checked the sidewalk behind them. No sign of the pimp. "We've had a change of plans. We're sorting it out. That's all."

"I see." The woman blew out a smoke ring. "You don't have a place to stay, do you?"

Sophie spoke before Kathleen could answer. "We'll probably take the train home tonight. Thank you for asking."

We can't go home. Kathleen nudged Sophie and said, "But we're not sure. Why do you ask?"

"Unfortunately for me, I'm left with two empty bedrooms here in my apartment. Why don't you check them out?" She pushed open the door behind her. "But first, my cook baked some fresh biscuits. Let's have some with strawberry jam and coffee. Come on in."

Kathleen sensed more than hunger. Tiny fingers of ice sent shivers through her.

"I don't know . . ." Sophie looked at Kathleen. "We should go home." The sidewalk mix of people flowed around the three of them. "Those biscuits smell good. I suppose it wouldn't hurt to take a look."

At least Sophie no longer talked about going home. Kathleen took a deep breath.

"What do you think, Kath?"

"How much do you charge a night for your rooms?" Kathleen wanted to see into the apartment, but the woman blocked her view.

"Why not come in, and we'll talk. My name is Crystal Everstone." Mrs. Everstone stepped aside and held the door open for Kathleen and Sophie.

Sophie stepped through the door. "I'm Sophie Dagget, and this is Kathleen McPherson."

Kathleen followed, and the woman closed the door behind them A worn, wooden staircase rose directly in front of them, and behind the stairs and down the hallway there appeared to be a door opening to a kitchen. Kathleen doubted a person living in a place like this could afford a cook, but the smell of the right-out-of-the-oven biscuits made her mouth water.

Mrs. Everstone slipped a key from her pocket and locked the door. Her eyes met Kathleen's, and she smiled. "This is a rough city and, being on a busy sidewalk, we don't want just anyone coming in."

She took Kathleen's arm and escorted the girls into the parlor on the right. Something about this woman, not just the locked door, put Kathleen's senses on alert.

Sophie set her valise down by the parlor doorway, took her coat off, and went to sit on the floral-covered divan. Her eyes seemed brighter. Kathleen put her valise next to Sophie's, removed her coat, and perched on a tufted chair. Mrs. Everstone settled into a rather bedraggled armchair. By the looks of it, Kathleen guessed there must be a cat with sharp claws nearby.

All this time, Mrs. Everstone was chatting about her previous boarders. "Off they run without even a fare-thee-well. Seems they came up with some silly notion to try their luck in New York."

She picked up a silver bell off the side table, rang it, and set it back down.

"You see, they left me quite shorthanded, this being Saturday night."

"In what way, Mrs. Everstone?" Kathleen suspected the bell ringing summoned hired help. "Did they work for you?"

A clatter of pottery ware sliding to the floor sounded in the hallway.

"Oh for holy hell." Mrs. Everstone jumped to her feet and rounded the corner.

Sophie and Kathleen's eyes met. Kathleen hunched her shoulders.

"Jesus on a Ferris wheel, girl," Mrs. Everstone yelled. "Look what you've done. Bring us some glasses and clean up that mess."

Mrs. Everstone strode back into the parlor. "Seems we have another change of plans. The biscuits and coffee are all over the floor. Well, never mind. We'll have something more festive to celebrate our new friendship, and I insist you call me Crystal."

Friendship?

Kathleen watched as Crystal went to the sideboard and pulled out a bottle and a slotted silver spoon. A girl, about fifteen with blonde, dirty hair hanging straight around her ears, came in with three glasses. She handed each of them a glass and left the room. Kathleen guessed the girl would now clean up the mess in the hall.

Crystal poured a couple of inches of green liquid into Sophie's glass, put the spoon over it, placed a sugar cube on top, and poured water over the sugar until it dissolved in the glass.

She moved on to Kathleen's rather smudged glass and did the same. Then Crystal poured herself some but didn't use the spoon or sugar. She held her glass toward them.

"Enjoy." Crystal smiled and took a large swallow. Sophie copied her, then immediately gasped and choked. Kathleen took a sip and listened to Sophie cough.

If she hadn't watched Crystal drink the liquid from the same bottle, Kathleen would have sworn they were being poisoned. After it quit burning, she recognized the licorice flavor. She cleared her throat and asked, "Is this absinthe?"

"I prefer to call it my little green fairies. Do you like it?"

Kathleen smiled and took another sip. What the hell were she and Sophie doing?

Sophie stopped coughing, wiped her mouth with the back of her hand, and downed more of her drink. She tilted the glass, looked down into the bottom, then said to Kathleen, "Zats purty good. I've always liked licorish."

They should leave. Kathleen took another sip. It bothered her that Crystal had locked the door.

Kathleen swept her gaze around the room. With the drapes pulled against the prying eyes of the street out front, the colors seemed to glow. She sipped, while studying a sliver of light that pierced the crack between the drapery and the wall. The ray illuminated lazily floating dust motes—they all danced a slow spiral fairy dance. Kathleen forced herself back to the moment.

"Mrs. Crystal, why are we drinking alcohol at this time of day? Sophie's never had a drink before, and neither of us has eaten."

Crystal poured herself another and started to refill Sophie's glass, but Kathleen moved her hand over the opening to stop her. The moving of her hand took more effort than she expected.

"Goldie will bring you biscuits and jam as soon as she cleans up her mess. Drink up, because we do have things to discuss."

Without thought, Kathleen took another sip and knew she shouldn't have. Her tongue thickened. "When will you show us the bedroom?"

Sophie slumped into the arm of the couch, giving the world a silly grin.

"After our biscuits and we chat. No need to hurry." She stood and went to the hall. "Here we are." She helped Goldie pass around plates, biscuits, and jam. A spoon stuck out of the jam dish.

Sophie devoured a biscuit plain. Kathleen put a spoonful of jam on her plate. She struggled to break off a piece of the biscuit and dab it in the strawberry goo. A familiar taste from memories of home helped her relax.

"Your clothes . . . I can tell the two of you are from out of town." Crystal poured herself a little more of her green fairy.

Our clothes? Oh, that's a good one. Not that our valises told you anything.

"I'll show you your rooms, but I insist you let me give you some more up-to-date dresses. Honestly, those look terrible."

"We don't need charity, thank you." Kathleen ignored the rest of her drink. "We'll be fine with what we have."

"Are the dresses sparkly?" Sophie took another biscuit. "Kath, you said we'd wear sparkly stuff."

"The dresses I have will make you each look like a hundred bucks."

"Did you bring us in here to sell clothes?" Kathleen glanced at Sophie. Sophie seemed to be picking at the flowers in the fabric of the couch. "Are you all right, Sophie?"

"I am. I am very good, thank you very, very much. I like these colors."

"Then you'll adore these dresses. I plan to give them to you."

"Why?" Little green moths—not fairies—cluttered Kathleen's mind.

"Because we're friends."

Kathleen's muscles tightened. *Something's missing—something logical.*

"What do you want Sophie and me to—?"

Crystal laughed. "You're the clever one. I need your help. We'll play this little game on some men. They can be such bastards, can't they? That's why I'm giving you expensive, beautiful dresses. You'll look enticing."

She giggled, rang the bell again, and Goldie appeared.

"Goldie, are the dresses ready? I think it's time for us to go upstairs now."

When one door sticks another may open.
—SCOTTISH PROVERB

18

Crystal stood and moved her hand toward the hall stairway. Sophie and Kathleen set their plates down and followed. Before they left the parlor Kathleen picked up her pocketbook and valise and nodded for Sophie to do the same. She didn't want Crystal to rummage through their things while they were upstairs trying on dresses—or whatever they were to do.

When they reached the top of the stairs, a door stood open at the far end of the long hall. A single hanging lightbulb illuminated a rack of dresses with shoes lined up underneath, and at the back stood a large chest of drawers.

"Goldie, I've told you—keep that door closed and locked. Now hurry." The girl lunged down the hallway. Crystal guided Kathleen and Sophie into the first door on the right.

"This is one of the bedrooms. The other is right next to this. Down the hall next to the closet you'll find the bathroom. We don't have hot water, but I'm sure that's not a problem when you consider your rent is free."

"Free rent and free dresses?" Kathleen congratulated herself. Even with moths batting around in her brain, she knew a ploy when she heard it.

Crystal pushed open the door into a small bedroom. The room contained a table, a chair, and a bed. With the shade pulled down, the cleanliness remained questionable, and the room smelled funny, maybe from sweat or body odor. Kathleen couldn't identify it. Maybe Crystal kept the cat's litter box in here.

The licorice taste from the absinthe still covered her tongue, and she didn't like the confined feeling of this room. She went over to raise the shade. She'd open the window and let in fresh air.

"Mustn't do that, Kathleen." Crystal put her hand on Kathleen's arm. "We can't have neighbors spying on us." She picked up a scarlet dress spread out on the bed and held it up in front of Kathleen. "Goldie does have an eye for size. This one should do you nicely. Tell her what size shoe you wear. Now, let's go next door and see what Goldie has for Sophie. Isn't this fun?"

"Crystal." Kathleen glanced around. "There's no mirror in here. Where will we get dressed?" She shouldn't ask *this* question, but she couldn't think of the other one.

"In the bathroom—I have cosmetics there for you, too. Kohl for your eyes, powders, little pots of color. You can put your makeup on in there."

Sophie leaned against the doorjamb and didn't seem to have any questions, just a goofy grin on her placid face.

"Sophie, here's your room, and see the beautiful dress Goldie found for you?"

Crystal held up a shimmering, silver-beaded dress. Sophie gasped and fingered the material. Crystal smiled and winked at Kathleen.

"Goldie, find shoes in their sizes, then go downstairs and help clean things up while I fix lunch. When you two are finished, come down and give us a proper style show. We'll have lunch, and you can get comfortable in your new attire. Then I'll tell you how our little plan works."

Goldie brought shoes and disappeared down the stairs while Sophie peeled off her mother's dress. She dropped it to the floor and squeezed into the new silver one.

"Wait, Sophie, we can't do this." Her moths slowed and settled.

"Aw, Kath, don't spoil the fun." Sophie listed to one side, then caught her balance. "Look at dis dress." Sophie smoothed the front down. "Perrfect. Put on yours."

"There's something about that closet."

"You gonna snoop?" Sophie's eyes widened.

"If I can get in."

[95]

"Hook me first. My fingers don't work good."

Kathleen connected the hook to the clasp at the back of Sophie's neck. She left Sophie to put on her shoes while she scurried to the end of the hallway.

The door handle wouldn't turn. *Dammit.*

She opened the bathroom door, flicked on the light, and squealed at cockroaches scattering off surfaces. She clasped both hands over her mouth and watched the insects disappear into dark hiding places.

Sophie pranced up the hall, weaving side to side, with a goofy, quizzical look. Kathleen stepped into the bathroom and forced herself to do a quick check. She found an assortment of cosmetics, hairbrushes, and bobby pins.

She'd seen hairpins used to unlock a door in a movie. She took two, bent them the way she remembered, and left Sophie to primp in the bathroom.

Kathleen squatted in front of the closet lock and cleared her head of all moths.

After several minutes, her hands steadied, and her attempts brought promising clicks. The distraction of constantly checking for someone coming up the stairs kept her from being successful. She blocked all thoughts from her mind and concentrated only on the feel and sound of the lock pins as each one slipped into place.

She opened the door and glanced at the dresses. They looked ratty, and the shoes didn't look much better. On the floor next to the chest of drawers she saw three small boxes. The top one was open and filled to the brim with cufflinks, men's rings, and watches.

Valuables in here—so that's why Crystal locked the door.

She started to back out but stopped. *Men's jewelry?*

Kathleen studied the different gold, diamond, and silver pieces. She picked up a familiar-looking pocket watch and turned it over. *CAD* was engraved on the back. The hair on her neck rose.

Chester Andrew Davidson.

Crystal knows Chester. She's seen him. Kathleen dashed out of the closet and started down the hall, the pocket watch still in her hand. Sophie, primping in the bathroom, crooned, "Who's Sorry Now?"

Kathleen stopped. She couldn't let Crystal know she'd found the watch. Whatever game Crystal played on men, she stole their valuables and probably their money.

Chester would never leave his watch behind, nor would he give it to anyone. He valued it too much. Perhaps it's someone else's. She studied it. It definitely belonged to him. She glanced toward the stairs and listened.

Crystal must work some sort of operation here, not some game. And she wanted the two of them to be a part of it. *Think, Kathleen, think.* Maybe she runs a gambling house and rigs everything so they lose.

But Chester wouldn't bet with his watch. He said his father gave it to him.

Kathleen slid the watch into her pocket. Maybe Crystal robbed them at gunpoint. No, he'd call the police. How could she fill boxes full of men's jewelry?

Crystal controlled everything, including Goldie. She wouldn't even let Kathleen look out the bedroom window.

Kathleen ran over and pulled the shade aside. The window, an egress to the fire escape, looked out onto the brick wall of the next building. She bet Crystal had nailed the window shut. Kathleen pushed up. The window opened a crack.

She sprinted to the bathroom, grabbed Sophie's arm, and pulled Sophie down the hallway. Sophie started to sputter something, but Kathleen moved her finger over Sophie's lips to quiet her. She stepped over Sophie's clothes on the floor, handed Sophie her valise and pocketbook, and took her back into the first room so Kathleen could pick up her own belongings. Then Kathleen motioned Sophie over to the window and showed her the fire escape.

Sophie mouthed, "Why?"

Kathleen whispered, "It's still morning, the front door's locked, and Crystal's plied us with liquor. She hasn't told us anything except that she wants us to play a mean game on some man—or men. The bedrooms stink, the place is crawling with cockroaches, and there's no hot water."

She shoved the window all the way open. A blur of yowling, dirty fur with claws sliced through the open window, darted across the bedroom, careened through the doorway, and plunged down the stairs.

A misty morning may become a clear day.
—SCOTTISH PROVERB

19

Damned cat. "Hurry, Sophie. Go!"

Sophie clambered through the window, tugged down her dress, and removed her shoes. Juggling her purse, valise, and shoes between her hands, she wobbled down the metal steps.

"Kath, it's cold. Where's my coat?"

"Move." Kathleen feared Crystal might tote a gun. She'd read many women hid knives and small guns in their garters.

"Which way?" Sophie called.

"Through the alley." The cold air helped clear her head.

Sophie slipped her silver shoes on and wiggled as best she could down the alley in the shimmering dress. Kathleen followed. When they came to the end of the alley, Kathleen pulled Sophie around the corner.

"Bet she's looking for us right now. Let's head toward the lake and big hotels."

"You better know where you're going, Kathleen McPherson. I'm cold, my head hurts, and I'm feeling pretty silly."

A woman with a child turned and looked at them. Several business men stopped talking as the girls hurried past.

Kathleen stole a look at their reflection in a store window and snickered. "You make me look frumpy."

"Not funny." Sophie scowled.

"At least you look like you belong in Chicago. Me, I might as well be in Missouri." Kathleen pointed. "Up this way to the Congress Hotel."

Sophie wrapped her arms around her waist. "I can't believe how hungry I am."

"We'll eat after we make a telephone call." Kathleen guided Sophie down the sidewalk and picked up the pace. She nudged Sophie out of the paths of oncoming pedestrians.

Sophie stopped. "I'm not going any farther until you tell me what telephone call."

Kathleen ignored her and strode up to the doors of the Congress Hotel. She gave the doorman a knowing nod. With their luggage in hand, he wouldn't ask questions. He touched his hat, and his smile seemed to wish them a good day.

Sophie spoke into her hand, "We can't afford to stay here. At least I can't."

"We aren't staying here. We're only using their telephone." Kathleen took in the expansive lobby. "Look for one."

"To call our parents?" Sophie stopped.

"Not yet."

Sophie jerked Kathleen's sleeve and pointed to the registration counter.

"The house telephone, it's for guests . . ." Kathleen spied one across the lobby. She strolled across the expanse with her head held high and a dispassionate smile fixed on her face. Her tenseness melted when she noticed a newspaper on the long table next to the telephone.

Sophie plopped down in the chair and said, "Golly, Kath, my brain hurts. I can't think."

Kathleen handed Sophie the newspaper.

"What am I supposed to do with this?"

"We have to stay in Chicago for at least two nights."

Kathleen read a small card next to the telephone. It gave instructions for making local calls and requested, when finished, that the caller pay the required cents at the registration desk.

"Yes, but . . ." Sophie flushed. "What about our parents?"

Kathleen leaned down and looked into her face. She kept her voice low. "I've got it figured out. We'll discuss our parents over lunch. Now, help me."

Sophie held up the newspaper. "You want me to find someplace to stay?"

"I'll look in the telephone book for boardinghouses, and you scan the advertisements in the paper. We need something close by so we can walk."

Sophie turned to the back section. "Here are rooms to let, but how would I know how far away they are?"

"How much?" Kathleen asked.

"No price listed. I'll check the boardinghouses."

Kathleen skimmed the telephone book.

"Wait, Kath. Here's one for women only. What do you think?" Sophie read the small print out loud. "Clean. Modern facilities. Two hot meals a day. No men."

Kathleen took the paper from her. "It's about five blocks from here. I'll call and see if they have a room we can share—two fifty a night."

"At that price it must be good." Sophie sighed.

"It's a bargain if there's hot water and it doesn't have cockroaches."

Kathleen scheduled a time for them to see the room, then went to the front desk and paid. The desk clerk told them about a lunchroom café down the street.

Sophie sashayed out the front door, smoothing down her tight dress. "Food, a room, and now all we have to worry about are our parents."

Kathleen followed, stomach churning not from hunger but from a much bigger worry. She slipped her hand in her pocket and clutched Chester's watch.

Doubt is the beginning, not the end, of wisdom.
—GEORGE ILES

20

Once at their table, Sophie fussed over the menu. "I adore tomato soup on lettuce-leaf sandwiches, but they aren't at all filling. Guess I'll take the roast beef."

Kathleen glanced at the menu board and ordered a ham and cheese with a lemonade for each of them.

The waitress brought their drinks.

"What'll we do about our parents?"

"Promise you'll keep the waterworks off."

Sophie chewed her lip and said, "My heart about leaped out of my chest when that man wouldn't let us audition today. I thought I'd faint. Hunger does that to me. My head gets all funny and everything goes fuzzy."

"Blame Crystal's green fairies."

"Our parents will kill us."

"We'll go back to the Congress Sunday night and call." She'd tell them about Chester's watch.

"Let's not wait. Let's just go home. They'd never guess what we've done. Why even let them know?"

"Come on, Sophie, the man said only a few ever get to audition. We have a monumental chance." Kathleen hoped her words were soaking in. She couldn't go home—not back to Minneapolis. Chicago felt safe.

No crazy knife thrower would track her down here. But what about Pritchard? He knew they were here.

This Chester thing . . . maybe *he* killed Lillian. Maybe he lied about Kathleen's father sending him out of town. Lillian's older man might have been Chester. Shivers skidded through her. If Chester had murdered Lillian, faked his drowning, and come to Chicago . . .

He would have to have been in Chicago after they lunched at the Chinese restaurant because she had held his watch—had seen his initials. Maybe someone stole it and left for Chicago. Someone could have murdered him, robbed him, and pushed his automobile into the river.

"I thought of something." Sophie touched her lip. "That awful audition man didn't even see us dance, or act, or listen to me sing. He doesn't know if we're any good or not."

"He knows we've studied under the best, and that you've won an award. If we wait and call our parents tomorrow night, at the last minute, they won't have time to worry or stop us."

Sophie lowered her chin and gazed at the tabletop.

Kathleen sighed.

"May I join you?" A baritone voice interrupted Kathleen's thoughts.

She shot a look over her shoulder. The voice belonged to the pimp from the audition hall.

Sophie studied him. "I remember you. I'm Sophie Dagget, and this is Kathleen McPherson."

Kathleen poked Sophie. "We're just leaving." She nodded her head toward the door. They didn't need any older men in their lives.

The waitress materialized at their table with sandwiches. She stood there, holding out the plates, not sure where they belonged.

The man reached over, took the plates from the waitress, and set them down in front of Sophie. The waitress thanked him and rushed off.

Sophie grabbed a half sandwich and started eating, ignoring both the man and Kathleen. She would never leave now. The man stared at Sophie way too long.

"Leave us alone." Kathleen set her jaw.

"Sophie, how did your audition go?" He pulled a chair out and sat.

"Who, me? Oh, this dress." She laughed. "I didn't audition." Sophie wiped her lips with the napkin. "You wouldn't believe what happened to us this morning. Some crazy woman locked us in her apartment, got us drunk on absinthe, and gave me this beautiful dress."

[102]

Kathleen put her head in her hands. "Enough, Sophie."

"Well, it's the truth. We had to crawl out the upstairs window to escape and hike all the way over here looking pretty darn silly—in the cold. We'd left our coats downstairs."

"Sophie, shush."

The man continued staring at Sophie, pulled out a notepad and pencil, and leaned in. "Did the woman tell you why she gave you this dress?"

Sophie took another bite. "Oh, she did, but I didn't get it. Something about some game. She said all men are—never mind. Kathleen knows."

He looked at Kathleen. Kathleen groaned.

"Come on, tell me." He sat poised with his notepad and pencil. "Where did this happen?"

"Holy cow." Kathleen grabbed his pencil. "What type of pimp takes notes?"

"I'm not a pimp. I'm a newspaper reporter."

"You're not going to print this in the newspaper, are you?"

"Note-taking's a habit of mine. May I please have my pencil back? Want to be sure I get all the facts down." He looked at Kathleen with sincerity. "Can you tell me the address?"

She handed him his pencil. "I heard trains close by. I think we were over on Clark Street somewhere."

"You could be a lot of help here." He wrote something. "What about this game?"

She glared at him.

"We got off to a bad start," the man said. "Let me formally introduce myself. I'm Ed Thornton, a writer for the *Herald Tribune*." He flashed a toothy smile and motioned for Kathleen to eat.

She jutted out her jaw and refused.

He signaled the waitress. She whipped by, arms loaded with dirty dishes, acknowledged him with a wink, and disappeared behind the swinging kitchen door.

Ed made Kathleen uncomfortable, like wearing scratchy wool. Memories flared of her last disastrous lunch with an older man. She glanced around the room.

"You're right to be cautious." He closed his notebook. "Chicago can be a dangerous place for young ladies who don't have someone to protect them. Many think of it as a mean city."

"Don't lecture us." She'd not be tricked by any man ever again.

Sophie focused on her sandwich without pausing, and she would stay until she'd devoured every last crumb. Kathleen slid her hand into her pocket and wrapped the watch chain around one of her fingers. She couldn't tell her parents. They'd want to know how she knew it was Chester's. They'd tell Mrs. Davidson, or the police, or both.

But she *should* tell someone.

Ed's face softened. "I mostly write about sports, but there's a high-profile investigation going on right now, and the officer in charge, along with my editor, would be quite indebted to me if I cracked this case."

Kathleen shrugged.

"We're talking about important, influential people here. A debutante turned up in the river a few nights ago, and I believe you two may have some answers."

Chills crept through Kathleen. *This must have to do with Crystal Everstone.*

"We questioned the young woman's best friend. The two of them conspired to slip out and take one of their parents' cars last Saturday night. Somehow they finagled their way into a speakeasy. Most speakeasies aren't keen on local teenage girls being their customers." Ed pulled out a cigarette and lit it.

She waited for him to say exactly how this young girl got into the speakeasy.

"According to the best friend, the debutante had met an older woman earlier that day who told her how to get into a particular speakeasy. Seems the debutante had to promise to do something in return. These young high-school girls get huge bragging rights from flitting around in speakeasies. Once inside, the debutante bought her friend a drink, then started talking to some guy, and told her friend to take the motorcar and go on home."

The waitress appeared and handed Ed a steak sandwich and a cup of coffee. She pulled a bottle of catsup from her apron pocket and set it on the table. He stubbed out his fresh cigarette.

"Thanks, Ruby."

He pulled a news clipping out of his wallet, unfolded it, and smoothed it. "Here's a picture of the debutante in a gown she'd bought a couple of weeks ago. The friend verified that the debutante wore this to the speakeasy. When the police pulled her out of the river, she was only wearing her undies."

Kathleen snatched the clipping. She looked at Sophie and studied the silver dress. She checked the photo again.

"Good God!"

Ed pigged down part of his sandwich with a wash of coffee. Sophie reached over and plucked the photo out of Kathleen's hand.

"She's wearing *my* dress."

"Here's how this works." He wiped his mouth and put the clipping back in his billfold. "Lots of young dames come to Chicago hoping to make the big time. Their parents don't know where they are. The girls flop at show business, run out of money, get hungry, and become scared. We know what comes next. Many of these gals try going it on the streets by themselves. Often a madam takes them in, or they end up with a pimp taking a cut. Once in this racket, they rarely make enough money to break free."

He finished his sandwich and held up his cup for a refill. Kathleen attempted a few bites and gave up. She and Sophie would definitely hang on to enough money for return train fare, no matter what.

"There's another level to this street-walking business," Ed said. "It's the badger game and requires at least two to set it up. One walks the streets, or hangs out in speakeasies, often dressed as a respectable young woman. When she snags a guy, she takes him back to some apartment or hotel, or wherever. They hop into bed, and when he's about to—well, when he isn't capable of rational thought—the other badger sneaks in and steals his money. In the so-called Mrs. Everstone's case, she probably sneaks back out and bangs on the bedroom door, making threats. The guy's scared silly—can't think straight. He skedaddles out of there and goes down the fire escape, minus his money."

Ed took out another cigarette and placed the pack next to his cup. Kathleen mulled over an alarming thought.

"This doesn't make sense." *Chester wouldn't have let Crystal have his watch. He'd have done something.* "When the guy discovered he'd been robbed, he'd go back or call the cops."

"You'd think so, but for some reason, only a few of them do. The whole thing is set up to make him feel he's done something wrong. The other player assumes the role of a mother, a husband, or a father.

The guy is usually happy to get out with his life. Even if he does go to the cops, not much happens to badgers."

"So you don't know who the girl took back to Mrs. Everstone's?"

"They questioned everyone at the speakeasy. No one remembered seeing her leave."

If I tell Pops about the watch, he'll know what to do.

Sophie touched the bodice of her gown. "I don't understand about Mrs. Everstone giving me this dress."

"My bet," Ed said, "is Everstone didn't know about the girl's family. Everstone hadn't seen the expensive dress until the girl came to her apartment with some guy from the speakeasy. If Everstone corrupts two runaways from another state no one notices, but a local debutante arouses too much attention. She had to get rid of the girl."

Sophie's face took on a split-pea hue. "And she's greedy, so she kept the expensive dress." Sophie, shaking, stood and picked up her valise. "I'll be in the powder room changing into something much less sparkly."

Ed touched her hand as she passed by. "Hey, kid, bring me back the one you're wearing. I'll need it as evidence and to get confirmation from the parents."

Kathleen watched Sophie trudge away. *How would Crystal have forced Sophie and her to cooperate? Maybe she'd threaten to harm one if the other didn't return with a guy.*

Ed said, "This is more than badger stuff. It's murder. We'll have her cold if there aren't twenty thousand of those dresses out there."

"Wear warm earmuffs. I checked the label when I helped Sophie put it on. It's a Paris designer."

"Hot dog. You name whatever you want. It's yours, Miss Kathleen McPherson."

Kathleen looked at Ed's cigarettes, took one, lit it, and blew out a smoke ring. "For starters."

He straightened, watched her, and said, "I'll need the parents to confirm the dress, but first you show me the location of Everstone's apartment."

"We've got a one o'clock appointment at a boardinghouse."

"Eat up. You and Sophie show me where Everstone lives, and I'll drop you off wherever you want."

It is not easy to find happiness in ourselves, and it is not possible to find it elsewhere.

—AGNES REPPLIER

21

Ed drove them around, searching, until Kathleen pointed out Crystal Everstone's apartment.

"Thanks, dolls. I'll drop you off at your boardinghouse and call the authorities."

Kathleen fingered the gold chain in her pocket. "Did her friend say which speakeasy they went to that night?"

"The one in the basement of the Rex."

"Where's that?" Sophie asked.

"A hotel in the red-light district—several miles from here."

Kathleen squeezed the watch. *Good heavens, Chester. High-class banker, slumming.*

When Ed pulled to the curb, he said, "Remember, if they crack this case, we're all indebted to you."

"Then get crackin'." Kathleen smiled and stepped out.

He took out their valises, and she and Sophie flipped him good-bye waves.

"I'll let you gals know what happens." He tipped his hat, climbed back into his car, and whizzed down the street.

"Aw, Kath, I loved that sparkly dress." Sophie slipped her arm around Kathleen's, and they went up the walk to the front door.

Mrs. Taylor showed them her vacant room. They'd need to share the bed, but the size and cleanliness made up for it. The quilt and sheets smelled freshly laundered, and the wooden floor reflected the late afternoon sunlight, pouring through the spotless windowpane.

Kathleen and Sophie agreed, and Mrs. Taylor guided them into her parlor of dark velvets and brocades. She sat at the mahogany drop-front desk, filling out the rooming form for their signatures, and emphasized the rules: no men allowed, no long-distance telephone calls, and breakfast and evening meals would be served in the dining room at seven and six, respectively. She recorded their money for the next two nights. If the girls desired to stay longer and paid up front, they could.

Kathleen picked up her valise and trudged up the stairs with Sophie following behind. They tucked their unmentionables in the drawers and hung their clothes in the closet. Sophie chattered all the while about Mrs. Everstone, their parents, and her fears, while Kathleen silently rehearsed what she'd tell her father about Chester's watch.

～

Sunday afternoon it rained. Kathleen wished she had an automobile or could afford a taxi. She wanted to go check out the Rex Hotel, but now they needed to call their parents.

"Okay, kiddo." Kathleen nodded toward the door. "Let's get it over with."

"Wish the stores were open. We need coats." Sophie stood looking out at the rain.

"Warmer weather's coming. Promise me something."

Sophie shrugged and walked down the porch steps.

"No matter what, we'll always have money saved for two train tickets home."

"Golly." Sophie lagged behind on the sidewalk. "This feels strange." Sophie gripped Kathleen's arm and stopped. "We're here in this big city, on our own, we have our own room, and no one tells us what to do." Her face wrinkled up.

"It's a great feeling. Like we're adults." Kathleen's stomach jittered too. She didn't dare let Sophie see anything but exuberance.

"Look at us." Sophie stood in the rain and tears pooled in her eyes. Kathleen's jitters changed into overcooked noodles.

Sophie managed a soft, "Let's go."

"Feel better?"

She shrugged.

"I'm doing the best I can."

"I know." Sophie blew her nose. "Where are we going?"

"Congress Hotel."

"Guessed as much."

When they reached the hotel, Kathleen went to the front desk and told them they needed to place long-distance telephone calls. The clerk handed them a form.

Kathleen asked for two. She handed one to Sophie, and they made their way over to the telephone.

Palms sweaty, Kathleen picked up the telephone receiver and held it to her ear. After she placed the call with the operator, she imagined the telephone ringing on their hallway table.

Mary would be pretending to read a book nearby. She always liked to nose in on adult conversations. Her parents, sipping a late-afternoon cocktail in the living room, would stop to stare at it. One would set their drink down and go to answer.

Her father answered. *Dang.*

After his second "Hello," she found her voice.

"Father, it's me, Kathleen."

A pause, then he said, "Is everything all right?"

"We're fine. I'm calling to let you know . . ." She'd planned to say something different. She started again. "I have something to tell you."

He waited.

She couldn't say anything about the watch until she told him where they were.

"We're safe and everything is going well, except—we aren't at the lake—and we won't be home tonight."

Silence.

"Pops?"

She heard him sigh before he said, "I'm afraid to ask where you are."

Kathleen couldn't get any words to come out. She tightened her stomach and cleared her throat, but her mind went blank. This would be ugly.

"Kathleen?" His voice came out low. "Where in the hell are you?"

She swallowed and breathed in deeply and said, "We're staying in an all-women's boardinghouse—in Chicago." Kathleen glanced at Sophie, who was chewing her fingernail and kept her ear close to Kathleen and the telephone.

"Who's we? Who's with you?" Those few spoken words commanded more than he said.

"Sophie." Ten years ago, she'd spilled shoe polish on the Oriental rug. This felt the same.

Silence.

"Pops, we didn't want to worry any of you, but the auditions—"

"Do you understand the magnitude of your folly in this search for fame?" His words on the other end sounded unusually calm.

"Folly?" She bristled. "What folly?" Didn't he believe in her talent?

"Fools' names and fools' faces are often seen in public places." His voice turned to harshness. "I fear more than your name and face will be paraded in the most public of places. My God, Kathleen, think about your heritage. The blue blood of kings flows through your veins. Haven't you any shame?"

She heard the telephone clunk on the hall table. She trembled, waiting. Should she hang up? She heard her mother's footsteps click on the marble floor. Then her mother's strong voice traveled through the line into her ear.

"Kathleen, where are you?" She sounded frightened and worried.

"Sophie and I thought we should put all those millions of lessons you paid for to use."

"I'm not a fool, dear. The money for those lessons didn't motivate this irresponsible behavior."

"I'm not being irresponsible. I have this all figured out." Her heart's rapid beating reminded her she didn't have a clue what to do if they failed those auditions.

"What about your grades? And there's poor Mrs. Davidson? She wanted to know why you didn't show up for your meeting yesterday."

Mrs. Davidson? What meeting?

"Why would I want to meet with Mrs. Davidson?"

"She said to talk about college and scholarships." Kathleen's mother stopped for a moment before she said, "I saw your teacher at the store. They expect you to win the lead part in the Shakespeare tryouts."

"Mother." Kathleen sighed. "That play is small-time compared to what I can do here, and I don't want to go to college, any college. Please let me do what I love."

"Young lady, do you enjoy letting everyone down who loves or cares about you?" Her mother's voice now hissed. "You can't throw away your education. If you do, you're throwing away your future. Use your brain."

Heat spread up Kathleen's neck and flooded her face. "We've been given audition times, Mother. Do you know how special that is? No one, well, only a few, ever get to audition. Sophie and I are going to be stars. Why don't you believe in me?"

She expected her mother to think for a moment. She anticipated a moment of silence. Then her mother would wish her well. Even though disappointed in her, she'd say to let her know how the auditions turned out.

Instead, her mother shot back with a response more forceful than her father's.

"Child, if you aren't home by tomorrow morning, don't bother to come home at all."

Kathleen heard the telephone go dead.

She couldn't move. She didn't want to move. She continued to hold the receiver to her ear, waiting for her mother to return. Kathleen's mouth must have fallen open with a stupid look on her face because Sophie kept asking her what happened.

The operator's voice came through, telling her the time and charges. Kathleen waited for a sense of composure to return, but it didn't. Her hand shook as she filled out the billing form and mumbled to Sophie it was nothing she couldn't handle.

She pushed the telephone toward Sophie. She knew her mother's stubbornness far outweighed her father's. But this . . . If she had mentioned anything about Chester's watch to them—she shuddered.

Beads of sweat appeared on Sophie's face and neck. They turned into her usual nervous rash. She stared at the telephone so long Kathleen took it away from her and placed the number with the long-distance operator. When the telephone rang on the other end, Kathleen shoved the telephone to Sophie's ear.

"Hi, Mom." Sophie wrapped her fingers around it. "Guess what? I'm in Chicago." Sophie grinned. Now the rash moved from her neck to her cheeks.

Kathleen could hear Sophie's mother's voice talking fast and loud.

"Yeah. Chicago. Isn't that great? I'm with Kathleen." She no longer grinned.

Sophie turned away and ducked her head. Kathleen could barely hear.

"Mom, listen . . . we're staying in Mrs. Taylor's boarding home . . . No, it's only for women. We're here to audition . . . Some place called the *Live Stage Company & Audition Hall* near Dearborn and Randolph Street, somewhere . . . At eight tomorrow morning. They want me to sing, act, and do some dancing, too . . . Mom, you don't understand . . . I can't—I do know what you expect of me. I'm sorry . . . I'll call tomorrow."

Sophie hung up and sank into the nearest chair. She covered her eyes. The telephone rang. Kathleen answered. The operator gave her the time and charges. She wrote it on Sophie's bill and swallowed as her throat closed against an acrid taste.

"Golly, I've never talked to my mom that way before." Sophie looked around the lobby. "I think I need to go home now."

"What about the auditions? You heard what that man said. Most don't even get this far."

She couldn't tell if Sophie was even listening. Kathleen sat on the arm of the chair and brushed Sophie's hair out of her eyes.

"Listen to me. We have a chance. We could be on stage by the end of this week. We can't give up on our dreams."

"My mom's hysterical because she's worried I *will* get that chance. Don't you see?" Sophie chewed her lip. "She says Chicago's a dangerous place full of gangsters who prey on young girls who don't know anything."

"You're going to give up your one big chance, go home, and spend the rest of your life teaching piano lessons and sleeping alone in the same bed you've always slept in?"

Sophie stared at Kathleen. Kathleen stared back.

A few seconds later, Kathleen said, "We'll be okay, kiddo." She needed to hear those words, too. "Let's go get dinner."

One cannot and must not try to erase the past merely because it does not fit the present.

—GOLDA MEIR

22

On Monday morning, Kathleen leaned against the fire-escape doorway at the end of the hall and looked at her watch. Sophie's voice would wow them, but Kathleen's telephone call to her parents had killed her appetite and kept her awake. All night she kept checking the time, terrified about being late to the auditions.

The door to Studio A popped open. A skinny kid and two girls yelled at someone inside the studio to hurry up. They disappeared down the stairs, giggling.

The door to Studio A banged open again, and another scrawny guy hustled down the stairway, yelling, "Hey, wait for me."

This morning, Sophie and Kathleen had arrived before eight o'clock. Kathleen's dance audition came first. She opened the door to Studio C at exactly eight, signed in, and took a number. Chairs lined the wall. She found an empty one, removed her outer layer of clothes, and put on her ballet slippers. She stood at the back of the room wearing her black leotard with black tights and a colorful silk scarf tied around her waist. She watched the others perform.

Last night, when she couldn't sleep, she'd planned her performance. The different steps were second nature to her. She decided to start bold and simple then build into something complex.

When they called her number, she began with several quick jetés leading into a pas de bourrée, followed by two double pirouettes. A quick chassé took her into a series of high-turning tour jetés, only to quickly pull out of the formal ballet steps. After sailing through the air with these leaps and turns and high kicks, her lightness almost made her think physical flight was possible.

She adroitly fingered the multicolored scarf roped around her waist. She slowed her movements and changed her steps into a jazzy soft-shoe act, all the while transforming the scarf into a calf-length skirt. Her muscles, with the quickness of birds, tingled with warmth. She forgot to hide her grin.

Now standing out in the hallway, she glanced again at the wall clock. She had hoped she and Sophie would have a moment to compare notes.

Soulful moans of a tenor saxophone came from one of the audition rooms. Kathleen lit a cigarette and stood with one leg crossed over the other as she continued to lean against the doorway. *Being here— unbelievable.*

Then she remembered. Sophie had an extra audition—a singing one.

She tensed again. *What if one of us makes it and the other doesn't? Sophie wouldn't stay here by herself, and I can't go home.*

Kathleen tossed her cigarette butt into the provided bucket. She people-watched for a few minutes and pulled out another cigarette. Her vow to stop lighting up one cigarette after another failed.

Doors opened. Eager young men and women crowded into the hall. Their voices bubbled with enthusiasm, and their faces all carried hopeful expressions.

Sleeping in a strange bed in an unfamiliar environment had fueled insomnia. In the dark, she told herself she didn't care what her parents thought. She had to convince them this wasn't a disreputable way to make a living.

There was no sign of Sophie.

Her parents couldn't be serious. They loved her after all, didn't they? If only her mother could have seen her performance this morning . . .

Sophie emerged from one of the doors down the hallway. She looked flushed with excitement. She stood and looked around.

"Over here." Kathleen waved her arm high.

"Guess what?" Sophie was out of breath. "They told me they had a spot for me singing in the chorus at the . . . darn. I can't remember the name. But I don't have to make a decision until all the results are in and I see what else might be open. Isn't that great? Aren't you excited?"

"Heavens, I'm not the least bit surprised."

"They had me sing one complete song by myself, and they asked me to sing a duet with another girl. And they called a guy in and asked me to sing with him. They gave me a Coca-Cola to drink while we waited for the guy to get there. He had this tenor voice, and everyone knew him." Sophie took a deep breath. "Wasn't that fun? What happened with you? What did they tell you?"

"Nothing."

"Surely they said something."

"They filled out a form rating my performance with numbers. I don't know."

"What do you mean?"

"What I said. I need some water. I have to go read a script in a minute." Kathleen started down the stairs.

Sophie stopped. "They didn't tell you anything?"

"What do you want from me—a lie?" Kathleen scurried down the rest of the stairs.

She heard Sophie's voice call from above, "You know you have more talent than I do."

~

"Thank you, Miss McPherson," Mr. Mann continued. "You may find your name on lists posted for employment opportunities in the lower hall after one o'clock. Please give the script back to Mrs. Peat and ask the next person in line to come in. If you have your results from the dance audition leave it with Mrs. Peat also."

Mr. Mann didn't look up as he spoke. He kept writing. She made her way to the table.

She murmured a thank-you to Mrs. Peat and handed her the script with the dance audition report. Kathleen picked up her purse from the chair at the back of the room and opened the door. The hall waiting area held a dozen anxious faces.

"Mr. Mann said the next in line may go in now." She needed lunch.

Kathleen squeezed through the gathering and looked around for Sophie. No luck. She went to the balcony railing and looked down into the lower hall. Sophie was talking with someone near the front door. Kathleen couldn't see who because of the crowd. She scampered down the stairs and made her way through the crush of people.

When she saw the blonde curls bobbing and the hands waving, she clenched her fists, charged over, and moved Sophie aside.

"What in the hell are you doing here?"

Dolly, her face red and wet, let out a whimper. Sophie pushed Kathleen away and cooed something reassuring to the distraught girl. She shot Kathleen the squint-eye.

"I can't believe this." Kathleen leaned in close. "Why in God's name—? How in the hell did she know where to find us?"

"Stop yelling at us." Sophie tugged at Kathleen's arm. "You don't know what's happened."

Kathleen moved from Dolly's face to Sophie's.

Every inch of Kathleen burned. "How dare you betray our secret?"

"I didn't."

"I'm gone." Kathleen shoved open the outside door. Dolly's presence deflated all of Kathleen's well-being and exuberance. She glanced up and down the street and shuddered.

How foolish to think no one could find them.

She spied a drugstore across the street and strode to the curb.

"Don't do that, young lady." Pritchard's sharp voice stopped her.

She scowled at him. "Will someone shoot me?"

"You can encounter death in many ways." He acknowledged the meaning of his statement with a precise nod down the block toward the street corner. "Cross there. Chicago is well known for its pedestrian murders." He tipped his hat and strode off through the crowd.

Kathleen set her jaw and stepped off the curb. A truck slammed on the brakes, honking. Another automobile swerved around the truck.

She sprang back. Someone yelled obscenities at her. With her chin up and grinding her teeth, she wound through the throng on the sidewalk—all the way down to the corner.

Fame is proof that people are gullible

—RALPH WALDO EMMERSON

23

Sophie and Dolly caught up with Kathleen, and Sophie said, "I saw you talking to Pritchard."

Kathleen walked faster.

Dolly babbled about her difficult train ride. She told in detail how she couldn't find the audition hall and feared someone might be following her.

Sophie kept saying not to worry. She said it at least a hundred times, and she added that she and Kathleen would protect her.

Kathleen huffed and lengthened her stride.

A few doors away from the drugstore, Dolly jabbered about Chicago being huge. But maybe she should be afraid, because it shocked her when she saw Pritchard.

"What?" Kathleen stopped. "How in the hell do you know him?"

Dolly flipped one of her curls. "Everyone who's anyone knows Pritchard."

"Kath, tell me what he said." Sophie now stood in front of Dolly.

"Leave me alone." Kathleen pushed around her, marched to the drugstore, and went inside.

Kathleen spotted empty stools at the counter's far corner and slid onto one. Sophie climbed up on one next to Kathleen. Dolly sat next to Sophie. Kathleen picked up a handwritten menu. The leftover food smudges on it made words unnecessary. She put it down. *What's Dolly's connection with Pritchard?*

"I know what's wrong. Relax." Sophie patted Kathleen's hand.

The soda jerk came up and touched his white paper hat with two fingers. "Ladies?"

Dolly opened her purse and counted out some change, then she counted it again. When finished, she looked up and said, "Please, may I have a cheese sandwich and a Coca-Cola?"

"Bring me a chocolate malted." Kathleen didn't feel nice and didn't care to pretend. Her stomach growled.

"I'll take the same." Sophie smiled. "With a cheese sandwich too, please."

Kathleen dug in her purse and found a flattened cigarette pack. She crushed it and looked around. Stacks of cigarettes, many brands, covered a long table. She selected a pack of Pall Malls, paid for it, and when she got back to the counter her malted milk was waiting. Dolly fidgeted with her Coca-Cola straw and frowned. Sophie carried on an animated conversation with the soda jerk.

"I couldn't believe it. They asked me to sing with this guy. It made me nervous."

"Yeah, a lot of you pretty faces come in here after your auditions. Some real happy and some in tears. We know why, don't we?" He gave this stupid, yucky laugh that went on and on.

Kathleen lit up one of her new cigarettes and blew smoke in his face. "Don't you have dishes to do or something?"

He glanced at Kathleen, shrugged his shoulders, winked at Sophie, and ambled to the other end of the counter to pick up dirty dishes.

"You're just plain rude," Sophie said.

Kathleen took her time puffing, blowing out smoke rings, and staring at the other two girls in the mirror.

Dolly whispered something to Sophie. She sounded panicky. When she saw Kathleen's reflection staring back, she cut it off.

Kathleen stubbed out her cigarette and sipped her malted in silence. The other two didn't say much. When she'd finished, she lit another cigarette.

"I hate it when you're upset." Sophie reached to touch Kathleen, but stopped. "Dolly's in real trouble. I didn't tell her anything about us being here. She found out from my mom. See, you can't be mad at me. And, Kath, if you're worried about the auditions, don't be. You know how good you are."

Kathleen took a few quiet puffs, letting the smoke slip out between her teeth.

"Aw, come on, Kath. Don't hold it against me. This is serious. Dolly needs our help."

"Not mine."

Dolly leaned over and said, "I do, Kathleen. I'm sorry about everything, okay? Can't we forget our quarrels?"

Kathleen smirked.

"Please, let's be friends? Sophie and you have to help me."

Little Miss Fluff's chin quivered and pinkish blotches covered her fair skin. The girl truly looked miserable. Kathleen would be kicked in the teeth before she'd ask why. Yet something disturbing within her wouldn't go away . . . Dolly's desperation felt real, familiar. Kathleen struggled with twinges of empathy. The girl did need help.

"Kath," Sophie said, "she has to find a place to hide."

"Give Dolly my side of the bed. I'll find another place." This burst of charity smoothed some of her residual guilt.

Kathleen slid off the stool and trudged out. *Sheesh, now I don't even have half a bed.* She pieced together similarities in Dolly's plight and her own. *The girl left Minneapolis, fled to somewhere safe, and Dolly knows Pritchard.*

On her way back to the audition hall, she remembered the image of Mrs. Schrader hanging on Pritchard's arm in the Davidson's foyer. But Dolly wasn't there. Had Dolly met him in the theater class? Well, he knew the horrid Mrs. Schrader and the Davidsons, and he wasn't nice to her mother. Pritchard's deviousness made him a man not to be trusted.

Worse yet, Kathleen's knife thrower might now be following Dolly, all the way to Chicago.

I may be compelled to face danger, but never fear it.
—CLARA BARTON

24

When Kathleen arrived back at the live theater studio, clusters of hopeful entertainers filled the hallway, reading lists pinned to the walls. Everyone chattered at once.

Kathleen squeezed her way into the first group, counting on her height to help her see the list. Someone whooped in her ear and broke away from the crush. She filled the void.

The constant excitement coming from exuberant warm bodies used all her air.

She heard Sophie from somewhere behind, asking if Kathleen found their names yet. She shook her head and took inventory of the hallway. Dolly, leaning against the radiator by the front door, waited. Kathleen navigated to the next posting.

Keep Your Skirt Down Maryann—a musical farce showed a triple list, one for musicians, one for singers, and one for actors. *Sophie Dagget* written in bold, block letters took the first line under the singers' column. New energy surged through Kathleen. She waved her arm high above her head.

"Sophie, over here. For you."

Kathleen scooted over to the next listing. Out of the corner of her eye she saw Sophie pushing to the front of the previous crowd to see her name.

This next sheet contained names of musicians and singers.

Kathleen swept her gaze over the hallway. The crowd had now dispersed into small groups comparing notes and congratulating each other. She bit her lip and glanced around. She'd die if she ended up not being selected for even one position. A sinking in the pit of her stomach made her doubt if she had any talent. She'd certainly fooled herself before about other things, mainly Chester. And those thoughts still burned.

Sophie pushed up close and squinted at the paper. A second later she squealed, "Kathleen, my name's on this list too." Then more quietly she asked, "What about you?"

Kathleen couldn't bring herself to answer. She looked away, and there he stood—the news reporter.

Between reporter guy and little Miss Fluff over there, leaning on the radiator—

But Dolly's golden hair didn't bounce and glisten any longer. The oily locks lay stringy around her cheeks and neck. Dolly glanced up at the door, then down again at the floor. Her face looked puffy with pallor around her mouth, and her eyes were red and swollen.

Kathleen should question her, but . . . Kathleen gave an audible huff.

Sophie cocked her head. "What's making your socks all hot?"

Kathleen looked around for something to say. "It's that news guy again. Over there."

He stood at the bottom of the stairway reading a list. Several people stopped to talk with him. He pointed to one of the sheets while he talked to two young men and a woman. They all broke out in laughter and strode off in different directions. He headed toward the back of the stairway and into an office marked *Private*.

Sophie shrugged. "I rather like him. Besides, he says he owes us big time."

"I suppose." Kathleen sauntered over to the lists he'd been reading.

Sophie followed. The first sheet, a short one, called for singers at a cabaret on Wabash and Van Buren. Kathleen glanced at the list and moved over to read the one for dancers. Her breath caught. At the top of the column of names, carefully penned, she saw *Kathleen McPherson*. She read her name over and over to be sure she wasn't seeing things. *Kathleen McPherson* stood out in black ink on stark white paper.

"There's your name." Sophie grabbed Kathleen's arm and jumped up and down, pointing like a little girl. "And look, your name's on this one too. It's for actors."

"Easy, there." But Kathleen's stomach was doing flip-flops. "We don't know much about any of this. Let's make certain there's truly something to jump up and down about."

"You'll find it is," a male voice said.

Kathleen whirled around.

Ed stood there, grinning. "Working there is worth jumping up and down."

"I'm starting to suspect that you're a pervert who uses your newspaper line as a cover."

"Sorry to wipe out your fantasies, doll. I'm only an overworked reporter."

"Oh, Ed." An auburn-haired, green-eyed, twentyish beauty waved to him from the top of the stairs. Backlighting from the sunny upstairs windows gave her an ethereal appearance, along with her wispy, rust-colored dance dress and gold-satin dancing heels.

"Brandy." Ed waved back. "Come down. Let me get a closer look."

Brandy sashayed down the stairs and gave Ed a big hug. "Eddie, look at this list." She jabbed a long-manicured nail at the paper with Kathleen's name. "My name's not on it. You know how much I want to work for Fritzel. This has to be a mistake." She pouted and snuggled up to Ed, playing with his necktie.

"Brandy, Brandy." Ed untangled himself and stepped back a few steps.

"But Ed, I *am* good. I'm one of the better singers in this whole studio. It has to be a mistake. Talk to him, okay? Please?"

Kathleen winked at Sophie. "Brandy, you might be the best singer, but you're obviously the worst reader."

"Who's that bitch?" Brandy ignored Kathleen.

He chuckled. "I'm greatly indebted to her. Make nice."

"Me nice? She insulted my reading skills."

Kathleen sighed, examined her nails, and said, "Check the list for singers, not actors."

Brandy snatched the other sheet off the wall, examined it, and looked up with a gleaming Pepsodent smile.

"I'm Kathleen McPherson—my friend, Sophie Dagget."

"You know them, Ed?" Brandy extended her hand.

"They did me a huge favor on Saturday." Ed grinned. Kathleen noticed he did a lot of grinning. "Brandy, you're on this list over here, too."

Ed steered her down the hallway.

Sophie tugged on Kathleen's sleeve and pointed. *Ladies Night*, scrawled in red at the top of a list, made Kathleen's heart pound. Both their names were there, but *Ladies Night* didn't seem terribly important anymore.

Another tug, and Sophie said, "You're on another acting list over there, but we need to talk—in private."

"Go back to your despondent friend. Her behind must be sizzling by now on that radiator. I'll catch up with you this evening and pick up my stuff." *Then what?* She had to find someplace far away from Dolly, but where would she spend the night?

Several other young people moved in and cornered Ed.

"Aw, come on." Sophie's brow furrowed. "You can't be running around this city full of Crystal Everstones. You're plain nuts if you do. We can all squish in together, or I'll sleep on the floor. "

"I can't sleep there." She should tell Sophie why Dolly made the place dangerous, but this wasn't the time. "Don't worry, I'll be okay."

Sophie would never tell Dolly to find someplace else to hide. Still, if Kathleen didn't say something, Sophie would think her a bitch.

"Dolly doesn't have much money." Sophie glanced around. "I don't know what she'll do."

Kathleen draped her arm over Sophie's shoulder. "Tell Dolly to take my place at the dinner table. Do you know which gig you're taking?"

"The guy who sang the duet with me said I'd make lots if I took the offer on south Wabash Street. But others said not to even consider going there. Maybe I should consider the musical comedy up the street here. But the more permanent one is the south Wabash Street gig."

"You'll need to extend your room rent until you get your first paycheck." Kathleen looked over at Dolly. She'd never seen anyone so pathetic. Twinges of uncertainty darted through her. She said, "I'll see you later, kiddo. Don't worry. Besides . . . my being totally on my own feels rather exhilarating."

"But where—?"

"Maybe I'll party all night, you know, it's that *life without thrills* stuff."

Kathleen pointed Sophie toward Dolly.

Sophie refused to move. "Sometimes you scare me. And I honestly don't know which job to take." Sophie screwed her face up in a most unbecoming manner. "And what about our parents?"

A return-home ticket doesn't matter for me—only success.

"Ask around. Be glad you have choices. Enjoy your dinner. We'll talk later tonight."

"Promise?"

"Of course."

Sophie threw her arms around Kathleen in a hug then scurried down the hallway. Dolly looked over at Kathleen and gave a little wave. Kathleen nodded back. The girls disappeared out into the street.

Brandy and Ed were huddled in their own conversation. Brandy glanced up and beckoned to Kathleen.

"I've wanted to sing at Friar's Inn so much I couldn't see straight. Usually I only say that when I'm tipsy."

"Sing? Why are you're wearing dance clothes?"

"I dance and sing. Mr. Mann asked me to come give a demonstration for those auditioning for a musical."

"What's special about Friar's Inn?"

"Oh, my goodness, they're the jumpiest place in town. Why, Fritzel has three bands, permanent entertainers, and a rhythm section for dining." Brandy took a deep breath before continuing. "Everyone who is anyone hangs out there. You've heard of Merritt Brunie and his brother? Well, they're part of the orchestra, and Bea Palmer, you know her, *The Shimmy Queen*, she even sang there a few months ago. Actually, if you get a gig with Fritzel, you might be able to stay permanently." Brandy sought Ed's full attention with a wistful gaze. "Did you pull strings?"

"He mentioned he'd keep a spot open for you," he said. "Miss McPherson, your name's over here, too. Mike—Mr. Fritzel—doesn't do fly-by-night revues. His entertainers work hard."

The glowing praise of Mr. Fritzel and his cabaret helped her mood. She slipped over to see the other list. The Cort Theater needed standby actors for a July production, *Dangerous People*, but she needed a paying job now. At least she wouldn't lose sleep over her job prospects. Sleep? Crap, she didn't have a bed.

"You're no pervert, Ed." Kathleen shrugged. "You're an agent."

Ed looked down at his hat, grinning. "Your information and the dress on Saturday gave us what we needed. Mrs. Everstone's locked up, pending trial, and we found a home for the twelve-year-old runaway she was holding captive."

"Captive? I thought she was fifteen and the hired maid."

"You probably saved her life, and my whole newspaper is celebrating. Of course it isn't over yet, but the heartbroken parents of the debutante can't praise our news staff enough. I might even get a raise."

Kathleen took a deep breath and shut out her father's lectures.

"Are you okay?" Ed stared at her.

She watched Brandy. Brandy's bright eyes and expressive face told Kathleen she knew things—knew her way around this theater life. And people knew Brandy.

"Tell me more about Friar's."

Ed straightened his bow tie. "Mike Fritzel put his heart and soul into making his place work. Influential people and prominent athletes hang out there, and it's important for Mike to keep them happy. I write stories that involve these people . . . being a news reporter and all."

Kathleen gazed up at him from under her heavy eyelashes.

"Mr. Newspaper guy, I'm starving. Bet you know a fine little place where you can spend some of your new salary. You may treat me to something tasty."

He grinned. "I owe you much more than a meal."

"I won't let you forget." She checked out her left ankle strap while she said, "Oh, invite Brandy. We must cheer her up. Not being able to read would depress anyone."

"Who can't read?" Brandy hustled over.

"Hey there, gal." Kathleen wrapped her arm around Brandy. "Since we'll be working together, you'll need to tell me all about Mr. Agent here." She winked at Ed and headed toward the street. "Brandy, your name reminds me—I've been dying to try one of those Brandy Alexanders. Now, tell me about all those people Reporter Guy takes such good care of, especially the influential ones."

A great social success is a pretty girl who plays her cards as carefully as if she was plain.

—F. SCOTT FITZGERALD

25

"Golly, Kath, you smell of liquor." Sophie, wearing her robe, stepped aside so Kathleen could enter the bedroom. "Where are you staying?"

"Hi." Dolly lowered her gaze. "Thanks for giving up your side of the bed." She sat on top of the coverlet, wearing a pink nightgown abundant with white rickrack. Her brushed-out curls resembled soft, golden straw. She glanced up at Kathleen and tucked her bare feet under her, probably because all their mothers scolded them for running around barefoot.

Kathleen ignored them, moved to the closet, and began grabbing clothes off the floor. She started stuffing them into her valise. The alcohol made her mind fuzzy. She didn't want Sophie to guess.

"Please, stop." Sophie put her hand on Kathleen's. Sophie set her jaw and stared into Kathleen's eyes. "I mean it. The three of us have to talk."

Kathleen shook her head. She cringed inside. Had she hurt Sophie's feelings? She owed Sophie an explanation, but what could she tell her? Did Sophie know Kathleen and Dolly were in love with the same married man? If Sophie knew someone had thrown a knife at her, the dear girl would fly into one of her unending tizzies.

But Dolly had found both of them here in Chicago. Had someone followed Dolly? And what about Chester's watch?

Kathleen picked up a skirt and started to fold it, but now her hands refused to cooperate any better than her mind. She jabbed the skirt into a corner of the suitcase.

Her big, brave idea of sleeping somewhere else tonight—she must be going nuts. If Brandy hadn't stepped in, where in the world would she be?

"Quit packing." Sophie grabbed Kathleen's wrist. "Dolly needs to talk to you."

Sophie could talk all she wanted with Dolly, but Kathleen didn't want to be included with her in anything.

Dammit.

Kathleen knew she needed to face her fears and not hide from them.

The hopeless look on Dolly's Little Bo Peep face said it all. Kathleen's thoughts churned like tumbling cockleburs.

Someone might have thrown a knife at Dolly, too.

Kathleen's energy slipped away. She slid down and sat on the floor.

Dolly's going to get us both murdered.

"Listen to us." Sophie let go of her wrist. "This *is* important."

Kathleen forced herself to face the girls.

"That's a little better, Kath, but come—sit on the bed with us. Dolly, tell your story."

"I'm fine here." Kathleen opened her purse and took out her cigarettes. No one spoke.

"Brandy's expecting me." Kathleen's tongue moved too slowly. "I'm going to her apartment tonight." She and Brandy had carried on, practically ignoring poor Ed. Her sides still hurt from laughing.

Brandy, four years older than Kathleen, knew the ropes, and her flapper stories helped Kathleen forget about the knife thrower. Naturally, having Brandy Alexanders with Brandy made everything funnier.

"I can't sit here forever." Kathleen took a puff.

"Dolly?" Sophie tossed her a pleading look.

Dolly shook her head, shutting her eyes.

"The school called Dolly's parents Friday evening." Sophie stared directly at Kathleen. "They accused Dolly of defacing property and wanted her parents to do something about it."

Kathleen had no idea where this bizarre story would lead. She looked from Sophie to Dolly and back.

Dolly gazed at the window, twisted a lock of hair around her fingers, and mumbled something.

"Why'd they think you'd . . . ?" Kathleen feared she'd had too many Brandy Alexanders. Her words were scrambled. Dolly never damaged anything, even in anger. The silly girl always used her voice and words as weapons—not effective in content, but effective in loudness, and if she waved her arms and hands, it made all of her demands imperative.

Dolly answered, "I'd never been called into the office for anything bad." She stopped talking and slid her hand from her hair.

"It's okay." Kathleen kept her words to Dolly soft. "I'm not mad."

Sophie spoke. "On Friday, the school showed Dolly's parents last year's photo book. Someone had cut Dolly's eleventh grade photo out—there was nothing left but a cleanly cut square hole."

"One of your many boyfriends defaces a book, you get blamed, so you run away and become all hot-headed and dramatic." Kathleen, her head clearer, put her cigarette in the ashtray and shoved more unfolded clothes into her bag.

Dolly sniffed and studied the coverlet spread across the bed.

"When Dolly's father flipped through the book, he found another photo cut out." Sophie raised her voice to an irritating level. "Bet you can't guess whose?"

Kathleen stopped packing, stood, and waited.

Sophie scowled. "Lillian's."

Dolly said, "The school secretary figured it out. Lillian and I both received notes from uncles."

"Uncles? Bet your parents went off their trolley on that one." Kathleen wanted to laugh, but chills quieted the impulse. She suspected these two girls and their clandestine meetings with Chester went well beyond her own sweet kisses and hugs. *Chester, what a bastard!*

Dolly covered her face with her hands.

This seemed clearer now. Kathleen would be safe in Brandy's apartment because the knife thrower must be some other female who coveted Chester's love, took her jealous rage out on Lillian, then went after Kathleen, and now Dolly. Kathleen needed distance between Dolly and herself. She touched the cold hardness of the gold watch in her pocket. *Maybe he's still alive.*

Sophie continued, "The school also received some unidentified telephone calls asking questions, like what time seniors get out of class on a certain day."

"It's not an unusual question. Who cares?" Kathleen scooped up a few of her unmentionables from the back of the closet floor.

"Don't be a snot, Kath. The secretary didn't see any reason not to give out the information. A caller, probably the same one, called and asked questions about Dolly—like where she went on the trolley every day after school."

Kathleen's knees became marshmallows. She tossed a wrinkled blouse toward her valise. She moved over and sat at the foot of the bed.

"Dolly," Kathleen had to ask, "did the secretary ever tell your parents?"

"She called my mom, but I said I didn't know why anyone cared where I went. Guess Mom sort of forgot about it."

"Sophie, your mom's a friend of the secretary. Why didn't Mrs. Howe do something? Didn't these telephone calls alarm her?"

"Someone makes a strange call—what's she supposed to do?"

"She received more than one strange call." Dolly picked up the hairbrush and started brushing her hair. "Mrs. Howe told my dad that the mystery voice always called just as the morning classes were starting or right at the end of the school day—you know, when all the kids and parents tromp in and out of the office. She admitted to being frazzled. She barely remembered the calls."

"Hey," Kathleen stood and snatched the hairbrush from Dolly, "that's mine."

Sophie picked up her own brush, glowered at Kathleen, and handed it to Dolly. "Now you're being stingy. What's wrong with you?"

The truth of it spread heat up Kathleen's throat and into her cheeks. She put her own hairbrush into her valise. She quieted her voice. "Something else must have happened to cause you to run away."

"Someone's been following me, probably waiting for me to be somewhere alone. I can't go on this way. I can't always be in a crowd."

Sophie touched Kathleen on the arm. "Her parents don't know where she is. We have to keep her hidden or she might end up like . . ."

Dolly shoved Sophie's arm away from Kathleen. "Oh, just say it, Sophie. I might end up dead like Lillian with my guts splattered all over." Dolly burst into sobs.

"Dolly, calm down." Kathleen's voice came out soft again. "You're not the only one in danger. Maybe the stalker followed you here. What about us?"

"Don't tell me to stop. You stop. You always think you're so great, Kathleen McPherson. But this time it isn't you. It's me. You're not in danger. Your and Sophie's photos weren't cut out. I checked."

Kathleen's inner muscles relaxed. This didn't involve her. Or did it? Why would someone cut photos out of the book? Were they checking out photos of someone they wanted to know about? Maybe they wanted to have photos of someone they were in love with—or maybe someone only wanted to see what Lillian and Dolly looked like. She snapped her valise shut.

Chills rippled through her. If someone cut photos out to learn what Dolly or Lillian looked like, but didn't cut out Kathleen's photo . . . Her valise slipped and dropped to the floor.

The murderer *already knew* what she looked like.

Cold spread through her. Maybe this person knows Kathleen's father and also knows her.

Sophie touched her again, but gently this time. "Kath, what's wrong?"

Kathleen's mouth went dry. She looked at Dolly, then toward the pulled-down shade.

"How do you know you weren't followed by some homicidal knife thrower?"

Dolly flipped her hair back over her shoulders. "Where do you come up with knife thrower? Someone stabbed Lillian—carved a hole in her chest. No one *threw* any knives."

"Golly, Kath." Sophie sat back on the edge of the bed. "Since you got here, you've been worse than wild kittens in a gunnysack."

"I need to get out of here." Kathleen looked around. "Don't we have any paper? I need a pencil too." She fumbled in her purse and tore a piece from an empty cigarette pack. "Have you picked the place where you'll be singing?"

Sophie handed her a pencil. "Not yet. They gave me addresses and telephone numbers. I'm supposed to talk to them tomorrow morning."

Dolly hung her head forward and brushed the back of her hair hard, like she wanted to rid it of bugs.

Kathleen wrote down a telephone number. "I'm starting at Friar's

Inn tomorrow. I'll be staying with Brandy. Her apartment's over a store near the Inn. Here's her number." She handed Sophie the scrap of paper and nodded toward Dolly. "What about her?"

Dolly glanced at the pulled-down shade.

"You think you're being followed, don't you?" Kathleen sighed, picked up her purse, and decided she'd leave by the back door. "Crap, Dolly. Now we're all in danger."

"Stop it, will you?" Sophie's eyes flared. "No one's after me or you, so you just shush."

Kathleen sucked in a large breath and sat down at the foot of the bed. Maybe it was Sophie's anger, or the relaxing effects of the Brandy Alexanders, but something settled much of the mayhem deep within her.

"Sophie, you're wrong. I ran away to Chicago because someone threw a knife at me." She didn't want to say it, but she did. "Dolly and I and probably Lillian were seeing the same married man—Chester. Lillian's dead, and Dolly thinks someone's following her."

Kathleen hated the shocked look on poor Sophie's face.

"There's more. Sophie, we escaped Crystal's nasty little place only because I found something of his in her closet. Maybe Chester didn't drown in the river, Dolly. He might be the murderer. If he is, I'm also in danger."

Dolly's mouth opened.

Kathleen checked her purse and counted her money.

"What'd you find?" Dolly held her hand out. "Show me."

"I can't. If you two know, you'll tell."

"I have to know." Dolly set her jaw.

Sophie stood wide-eyed. "You didn't tell me—"

"Because you only need to know he may still be alive."

Dolly burst into tears.

Kathleen asked, "How's your money holding out?"

Sophie sighed. "I keep counting it. I've enough to get me through next Sunday. Maybe wherever I work, they'll give me an advance."

"Have you told anyone else about Chester?" Dolly sniffed and dabbed her eyes.

"I haven't decided what to do. Any suggestions?"

Dolly shrugged. "Since Kathleen bailed out, I can pay half the boardinghouse charges. I have enough for several days."

"Crackers." Sophie grinned. "I won't have to ask for an advance."

"One thing you forgot, Dolly." Kathleen picked up her valise. "You need money for food."

"I'm okay with boardinghouse breakfasts and dinners. I won't eat lunch." She nodded toward the window. "Anyone in my situation would be a fool to go out there."

Sometimes it is harder to deprive oneself of a pain than of a pleasure.

—F. SCOTT FITZGERALD

26

By mid-morning their dance practice session had caused a heavy layer of sweat to plaster Kathleen's hair against her forehead. Irene leaped off the stage and faced them. She held up both hands.

"Enough."

All of the girls' faces glistened as if coated in olive oil.

The piano player stopped. Irene bent over at the waist, breathed for a few seconds, and then stood straight.

"Jesus, Freddy." Irene wiped her forehead with her hand. "Open a goddamned window or turn on a fan, will you? We're dying of heat in here." She turned to the five dancers and said, "Take fifteen. Get something cold to drink."

Kathleen grimaced. An open window wouldn't do much good. Friar's Inn, located below street level, trapped the heat. The place had great decor, but during the daylight hours you couldn't call it more than a hot cellar. The girls grabbed bar towels and took turns wiping their necks and faces. Kathleen held a glass out while Freddy dropped in a chunk of ice and filled it with water. She rested it on her forehead, her eyes closed.

"Miss McPherson." Pritchard's voice.

"Sheesh." She snapped her eyes open and glowered.

"You should be flattered to know I've given up a piece of my afternoon to see how you've progressed this last week. Come." He took her elbow and guided her to a table in the corner. "I need to give you some information to pass along to one of your young friends."

He always threw her off—she never knew which direction to take with him.

"You need to leave." She'd not sit or play his little game. "No one is allowed in here during practice."

He tossed her words away with a laugh. She jutted her chin out and stood silent.

"Miss McPherson, no one is allowed in here—you're correct. But what if I happen to be no one? Wouldn't I be allowed in here?" He shook his head. "Yet I am actually someone, and I am someone Mr. Fritzel values."

"Don't treat me as if I'm stupid, Pritchard." She sat. If he knew her boss, it changed everything. She sipped her water and stared.

"From what I hear from my friend Mrs. Taylor," he said, "there's a certain young lady in her boardinghouse who's unemployed."

He knows Mrs. Taylor, too? Kathleen continued to sip without answering.

"This young lady is a friend of your friend. I've seen the three of you in Mr. Russin's drama class in Minneapolis. She and I have conversed about trivial subjects. She seemed to find time for this nonsense between her lessons. Your friend is a precocious little thing . . . a sort of goldfinch with desires more grand than a cockatiel's, I might add."

Kathleen set her glass on the table and crossed her arms. This stupid little girl must have thrown herself at him between classes.

Pritchard went on, "According to Mrs. Taylor, the young lady stays in her room—constantly—all the time—except for meals. Would you know why?"

"Perhaps you'd care to tell me." She tensed.

"I haven't the foggiest, but I believe you do."

"It's none of anyone's business, Pritchard. I won't betray confidences." Her voice sounded prickly. She didn't care. He'd laughed at her too many times.

"Does she want a job? Certainly she must need money. One cannot hide out and not pay for her room and board."

A moment of mental math told Kathleen that Dolly's budget must be about bankrupt.

"She needs work. Why didn't you talk to Mrs. Taylor about this?"

"I have. Mrs. Taylor told me whenever she talks to the young lady ... she cries and runs to her room." Pritchard looked at his pocket watch. "I believe the child is terrified of something. Maybe she had a row with her parents, ran away, and believes they are looking for her. If you engage her in a conversation, tell her the Kimble Club on Randolph is struggling to remain viable."

Irene, standing at the back of the dance area, whistled. "Come on, ladies, let's shake a leg."

Kathleen stood. Pritchard did also.

"Kimble's needs an eclectic entertainer and house organizer—stocking shelves, cleaning some rooms, a little dancing and singing. The hours will be odd—nothing regular. She must say Pritchard sent her. The pay will be tight, but the job will be hers. If she's afraid of someone, she'll be safe there. No one gets into the Kimble unless they've been vouched for. You will give her the message, won't you?"

Kathleen found herself nodding. She was worried about Dolly.

"Good day." He placed his hat on his head, and Kathleen watched him walk to the doorway.

Irene called out, "Miss McPherson, do you care to join us?"

Kathleen started to hustle toward the stage but heard Pritchard's voice again.

"Oh, Miss McPherson."

She glanced back and stopped.

Pritchard stood looking at Kathleen. "Your friend with the angelic voice—she shouldn't be working in the Southside. She must find a way to flee from there—leave that place at once."

"Why would you say that?" Kathleen moved closer to him.

"I had an encounter with Miss Dagget this morning, and I'm concerned. She appears to have fallen in with the wrong crowd, and I fear for her safety. She's distraught about her mother and mentioned you're at odds with your parents. Is that correct?"

Kathleen sensed a wave of heat flooding over her. He'd poked his nose into her business too many times.

"You seem uncomfortable discussing this. I assure you, Miss Dagget said little about the actual situation, but I can guess your parents are under considerable distress about your chosen profession. Regardless, get the girl away from the Southside. Now, excuse me, I must catch my train."

It is the loose ends with which men hang themselves.
—ZELDA FITZGERALD

27

Dance practice ended at four.

On her walk home Kathleen slipped her hand into her pocket to assure herself she still had Chester's watch. She couldn't keep her fingers from worrying over it, but she'd not bothered to inspect it since she'd found it. Indecision tortured her. She needed to take some sort of action.

She pulled the watch out and examined it in the sunshine. *Looks like a Hamilton—not cheap.* She flipped it open and stared. A photograph of a young Chester slipped into the inside cavity of the cover stared back at her. *What kind of bull pizzle keeps a photograph of himself?*

She snapped it shut and shoved it down into her pocket. *What an ass.* He probably played around in the red-light district at the Rex Hotel where he picked up the young debutant in the speakeasy. He got robbed while having a go at her at Crystal Everstone's house, and the girl ended up floating in the river in her unmentionables.

I'm an idiot. Kathleen's blood simmered. *I fell for this worthless bastard.*

A few minutes later Kathleen loped up the stairway and eased the door open to Brandy's apartment. Brandy slept most of the day—understandable because she worked late, then spent the rest of the night partying with friends. Kathleen wanted to party too, but she

[136]

had to be sensible about her own hours. Unlike Brandy's work, Kathleen's required long practice sessions every day. She would gain Irene's confidence by learning the routines, and then she'd find time for a taste of Chicago night life.

"Hey, kid, it's okay." Brandy sat in the broken-down armchair near the window. "I've been up for several hours. Some jerk keeps calling here. When I answer, the bastard hangs up. I figure he wants to talk to you." Brandy lit up and puffed on her cigarette.

Kathleen couldn't imagine what guy would call her.

"Then I got an idea. About the third time it happened I stayed on the line until the operator came on. When she did, I asked her to check the number she'd connected to my number. I told her I needed to call the person back tomorrow, but I forgot to write the number down. She said the call came from Mrs. Taylor's boardinghouse and gave me the number. I'm shocked. He must be a she. What the hell's going on?"

Kathleen shrugged.

The telephone rang. Both of them stared at it.

Brandy waved her hand at Kathleen. "You answer it."

Kathleen didn't want to. She'd feared if the stalker knew what she looked like, he might also know what her voice sounded like. But the stalker wouldn't be at Mrs. Taylor's house. She kept her eyes fixed on the telephone.

"Go on, kid, answer the goddamned telephone. Then maybe I can get some sleep."

Kathleen picked up the receiver and held the mouthpiece close. "Hello?"

"It's you, Kathleen, isn't it?"

Dolly. "Are you the one who keeps calling and hanging up?" Kathleen's face grew warm.

"I can't speak to anyone else. You know. What if it's the wrong person who—well—"

"Criminetly, Dolly, you're the one calling here? You know it's Brandy's number. What makes you think it's someone else?" She watched Brandy stand and stretch.

Brandy slipped her mules on and shuffled into the kitchen area and did something with two glasses.

"I guess I'm not thinking straight," Dolly sniffed. "I got this note from someone. I'm not sure if it really is that person."

Brandy handed a glass to Kathleen.

"Who gave you the note?" Kathleen sipped the drink. *Zowie, a gin Rickey.* She heard Brandy making another drink.

"Mrs. Taylor. She said it's from Pritchard."

"When did you get this note?" Why would Pritchard bother to tell Kathleen to contact Dolly if he'd already written her a note?

"Four days ago. He's found a job for me."

Kathleen looked at the receiver, then took a long swig of her drink. Dolly lived in some terrible craziness in that head of hers. She waited for Dolly to speak.

"How do I know he isn't the one who's after me? Sophie said you know him pretty well. She also said you don't like him. I don't know what to do." The sniffing changed into a thin whine. "Sophie said I needed to talk to you about him."

Kathleen set her drink down. She didn't need any of Dolly's spooks running around in her brain. What if Pritchard *was* the murderer? If he told Dolly about this job it would lure her from Mrs. Taylor's boardinghouse. Besides, he knew way too much about everything.

But *he* wouldn't need to cut Dolly's photo out. He knew what both she and Kathleen looked like. And, again, he had saved Kathleen from the taxi death.

"Kathleen, are you still there?"

"I'm thinking. Give me a minute." She sighed. "All right, this is what you need to do. Call the Kimble Club. See if they know Pritchard and ask if they want you to interview for the job. If they do know him, and if they want you to interview, then do it. You need money, right?"

"Desperately. But I can't leave this house. If I go out—if I'm working somewhere in public—I'm too exposed."

Now what? Kathleen took another long sip of her drink.

"Kathleen?"

"Don't rush me. Maybe one of the other boarders works near the Kimble Club. Ask them what time they go and walk with them. Maybe you can set up your interview then."

Dolly grumbled something, thanked her, and said she would. Kathleen hung up. She slumped down on the couch and stared into her gin Rickey.

"What's happening?" Brandy took out a cigarette and tossed the pack to Kathleen.

The telephone rang.

"Damn." Kathleen answered. "Okay, Dolly, what now?"

The telephone went dead.

Kathleen looked over at Brandy and put the telephone back on the receiver. Brandy cocked her head and waited. Kathleen shrugged. She picked up the telephone and called Mrs. Taylor.

When the woman answered, Kathleen said, "Mrs. Taylor, this is Kathleen McPherson. I lived there until a few nights ago when I gave up my room to another young lady. She just called me. Is she still there?" Kathleen waited until Mrs. Taylor asked Dolly to come downstairs and take the call.

"Dolly, did you call me back after we hung up?"

"Why would I do that?"

"I'm asking because the telephone rang, and when I answered, someone hung up. You did the same thing with Brandy. Are you sure you didn't call me back?"

"Oh, crumb, Kathleen. Mrs. Taylor told Sophie someone kept calling for you the other day."

Kathleen held her breath and waited.

"They finally asked what time you'd be home. Mrs. Taylor doesn't like giving out information, but their calls annoyed her. She decided to tell them you'd moved out and had given your room to another person."

Kathleen moved to the window and scanned the street below for anyone who might look suspicious. How on earth could someone get Brandy's number?

"I'll talk to you later, Dolly." Kathleen hung up and returned the telephone to the table.

"You don't look well." Brandy sat up straight. "What's the matter?"

"I have to move out—now." Kathleen started gathering her things. "Do you know of an available apartment that isn't too expensive?"

"Why?"

"I have to hurry. You must know of some place." The desperation in her own voice surprised her. She'd never sounded like that before.

Brandy furrowed her brow. Kathleen began snatching up articles of clothing from around the apartment.

"You're being melodramatic."

Kathleen didn't bother to look up. She shook her head and continued to stuff clothes into her valise. Brandy moved to the telephone and made some telephone calls, then wrote something down and shoved it into Kathleen's hand.

Kathleen looked at the written address of an apartment a couple of blocks away. She set the paper on the table, clicked her valise shut, and slammed it down on the floor by the front door. She straightened and went to the bedroom to see if she might have forgotten anything.

Brandy watched. Kathleen ignored her. Brandy followed, sat on the bed, lit another cigarette, and rolled over on her stomach, propping herself up on her elbows.

After checking the bathroom and looking under the bed, Kathleen said, "How in the hell would anyone know I'm living with you?"

"They probably found out the same way I learned about the calls coming from Mrs. Taylor's boarding home. Telephone operators won't give out information, but if someone is clever enough in the way they ask, you'd be shocked at how much you can find out."

Kathleen crumpled onto Brandy's vanity chair.

"I fucking hate this."

"Kid, tell me what's going on."

"Later. I need to get out of here."

"Hey, we're friends, remember?" Brandy sat up, swinging her legs over the edge of the bed. "Friends look out for each other."

"Appreciate it, too." Kathleen darted into the living room and stopped in front of the window. She studied the street and sidewalk below. Cars, trucks, and trolleys exchanged places. A jumble of people hurried by. Several women strolled along. Some man stopped to look at a window display.

Kathleen took a ragged breath.

"For God's sake—what's going on?" Brandy stood in the doorway, watching.

Another man leaned against the doorway across the street. *Maybe it's Chester.* He stood so his face stayed in the shadows.

"It churns me up to see you in such a fit, kid."

"Come look." Kathleen waved Brandy to the window. "Do you see a man in the doorway across the street, checking out your building?"

Brandy sauntered over and shrugged. "He's waiting for someone."

"For me." Kathleen grabbed her valise. "I'm going out the back way." She jerked to a stop and set her lips. *Damn him. I'm not running anymore. I'm going to march right down and tell him what's what.*

Brandy grabbed her arm and pointed out the window. A perky

woman, wearing a floral dress with long pearls, came dashing up the sidewalk toward the man. He tipped his hat, took her arm, and they went inside.

"Will you relax? Tell me why your bowels are in such an uproar?" Brandy tossed Kathleen the pack of cigarettes and slid down into her chair.

Kathleen lit one, sat, and inhaled. *Chester's such a bastard. He probably did murder Lillian.* She set the cigarette in the ashtray and picked up her gin Rickey. The ice had melted. She let the liquid warm her tongue while she sorted through what she knew. Then she took a deep breath, steadied her voice, and started at the beginning with Lillian's murder.

Brandy, Kathleen noticed, refilled their glasses without interrupting.

"I love Sophie. She's like a sister—and she's puppy-dog loyal. But Dolly and I will never be friends." Kathleen stubbed out her cigarette. She shouldn't smoke so much, but she found herself lighting up another one without even thinking. Maybe she could blame it on the gin.

Neither spoke for a few minutes. Brandy finally broke their silence.

"You need protection. Ed owes you big, and his friend Mac owes Ed. Mac's a retired police officer. You'll like him. We'll all help get you settled safe in your new place."

"Blast it, Brandy, I don't need protection, and I don't want Ed to know. Don't tell anyone. The fewer who know, the safer I am." Her words stumbled out over her tongue. It felt thick.

"Faulty thinking, girl, and here's why—if Ed and Mac know, they'll help watch out for you. Ed knows hundreds of good people, and Mac knows hundreds of bad people. Know what I mean?"

Kathleen closed her eyes. She couldn't concentrate. Brandy jiggled Kathleen's knee.

"Search the kitchen for snacks while I call them. These guys do anything for food." Before Kathleen could protest again, Brandy had the telephone to her ear, reciting a number to the operator.

If Chester watched this building and saw two big men entering, he probably wouldn't do anything. To hell with Chester. She could deal with him.

Brandy, still on the telephone, laughed about something. If she wanted snacks, that's what she'd get. Kathleen pulled the cherry pie—half of it gone—out of the cupboard, found some olives to put in a bowl, and set a chunk of Roquefort cheese on a plate with some crackers.

Brandy leaned over Kathleen's shoulder. "Looks good, but they'll want more. Why don't you run down to the deli—"

Kathleen shot Brandy a piercing glare.

"Sorry, sugar cups, I forgot." Brandy whipped around and called back over her shoulder, "That'll have to do. I'm going to change before they get here."

Kathleen looked at the meager offering, then plopped a gob of butter in a skillet. While it melted, she stirred in their last six eggs with a dab of milk.

What the devil? She needed to hide—not cook.

Gin Rickeys muddled her brain.

Brandy came prancing out of the bedroom in a green chiffon drop-waist dress, carrying her high heels. She sank down on the couch to put her shoes on. Someone knocked on the door.

She slipped her feet in. "They're here. Quick, go change. I'll make drinks and tell them your story."

Kathleen finished shoveling the eggs onto a large plate, then grabbed her valise and dashed into the bedroom.

She heard Brandy at the door call, "Hi, boys, come on in. Kathleen will be out in a minute."

Now Kathleen couldn't leave, and she didn't want Brandy blabbing her story to everyone.

Glasses clinked. Voices mumbled. Brandy's voice sounded out above them all. Kathleen heard someone else knock on the apartment door. *Crap.* Maybe the murderer had decided to join them. Laughter, more glass clinking, louder talking, and then the bedroom door opened. Brandy stuck her head in.

"You're not dressed? Don't just sit there, come on, honeybun. We're waiting." She closed the door.

Kathleen didn't have anything party-like to wear, and how did this turn into a party anyway? All of her clothes looked frumpy. She'd march out and down the back stairway and go to the apartment Brandy found her. She searched her pocket, her valise, and her purse. No address. It was still out there on the table.

Crap. Heat spread up her neck. Going out there wearing what she'd worn to dance practice sent a wave of insecurity through her.

Kathleen couldn't show herself and meet new people in these old dance clothes—certainly not with Brandy looking like a model.

She slid her gaze around the room. She pulled off her skirt and top, kicked her shoes aside, and helped herself to Brandy's body powder—patting clouds of it under her arms. Next, she rummaged through Brandy's drawers. She found black garters and silk hose. She ignored the rest of Brandy's undies. Her own would do.

Brandy's closet held a rainbow of jewel-toned and pastel-colored dresses. Kathleen selected a low-cut, short-length one. It mirrored a deep-rose sunset reflecting off Lake Harriet after a snowstorm.

When she opened the bedroom door, everyone stopped talking and gawked at her. She looked at Brandy and winced. Would Brandy treat her the way she treated Dolly with the hairbrush?

Brandy's eyes opened wide, then she grinned, rushed over, and pulled Kathleen into the room.

"Everyone, this is Kathleen. Kathleen this is Mac, the ex-flatfoot I told you about. And this is his friend Roy. And this is Franny. I've been telling them your story—"

"Young lady," Mac held up his drink and said, "we're not going to let nothin' happen to you. Consider us all your personal bodyguards. Right, everyone?"

A chorus of agreements and glass clinking filled the room.

Ed moved next to Kathleen and said, "You look lovely in rose with all those sparkly things."

Brandy handed Kathleen a drink. "These sparkly things are sequins, Ed. And I have to admit, this gal has excellent taste in clothes."

Someone knocked on the door. Brandy glided over and opened it. Squeals of delight and sounds of more strange voices filtered through the open doorway. Brandy waved them in.

Her small apartment shrank in size. Someone in this group handed Brandy containers of Chinese food. Brandy handed them to Kathleen. Someone else dialed the music on the radio up to loud.

Kathleen opened each carton and stuck spoons in them. Since she couldn't find any more plates, she set out saucers with forks. The egg plate, now empty, sat on the counter next to the empty pie tin. She retrieved her drink and marveled at the number of people squeezed into this tiny apartment.

More pounding on Brandy's door quieted everyone. When Brandy opened it the squeals ensued. Three big guys and one dainty flapper, wearing a kaleidoscope of colors and carrying a small wooden stool above her head, squeezed into the apartment. The partiers resumed their festivities.

The biggest brute held up his hands for quiet while one of his friends let out a piercing whistle. The room instantly hushed except for King Oliver's Jazz Band on the radio blaring out his new "Dipper Mouth Blues".

"What's going on, Keith?" Brandy asked.

"Candy here needs to practice a new dance. We borrowed a piano from the bar down the street. We need some help bringing it upstairs."

"Hot potatoes—a piano—always wanted one." Brandy wiggled her rear and danced her fingers over an imaginary keyboard.

"I'll help." Mac grabbed a couple fellows, and Kathleen heard them trot down the stairwell.

Everyone went back to what they were doing, but Kathleen wandered to the stair railing and leaned over. She watched these guys huff and shove the piano up the stairs. This piano didn't have all the octaves of a normal piano. It definitely belonged in a bar.

They borrowed it—I doubt it.

Once they got the piano into the apartment, they shoved it into the far corner. Candy plopped down the stool, and Keith sat his large frame on the tiny seat. He began plinking out tunes.

"Black Bottom!" A woman's voice yelled from the other side of the room. She grabbed a partner and they started dancing.

"Teach me—please." Candy, now in the kitchen, promptly ignored her saucer of food. "I've been dying to know this one."

She pushed between the men to get to her dance lesson. Brandy and Roy stood in the corner discussing something obviously funny. Ed squeezed his way around the Black Bottom dancers and headed toward Kathleen.

"You look smashing." He took her hand. She pulled her lips in and lowered her eyes. He let go of her hand and put both hands on her shoulders. "Don't worry. You're safe."

"I don't need anyone to protect me. Besides, you and Mac can't be with me every day, everywhere." Kathleen stared into her drink. She liked the warmth of his hands resting heavy on her, but she didn't much like him. Men his age had no business flirting with someone her age.

"Tell her, Mac." Ed took a drag from his cigarette. She hadn't seen Mac come over.

"It works this way. I've got friends, so to speak, who are everywhere. We two don't have to be on twenty-four hours. You work at Friar's—one of my friends plays the piano there. See? They're all over the place. I put the word out, and you've got nothing to fear."

If she relied on Freddy to keep her safe, she'd be dead by lunch. Freddy weighed all of ninety pounds. If he gave up the piano, he could be a jockey.

Ed slipped his arm around her and bent down close to her ear. "Kathleen, it's okay. Trust us."

"It's not okay. I'll take care of myself."

"Hell! You gotta be kidding me," someone yelled from the kitchen. "We're outta gin."

I believe in low light and trick mirrors.

—ANDY WARHOL

28

"Hey, let's shuffle off to Frenchie's."

Kathleen didn't recognize the voice, but Ed guided her into the hallway, and all of them trooped down the stairwell, out the front door, and up the sidewalk.

"Stop, Ed." Kathleen slowed, but someone bumped into her from behind. She stumbled forward. Ed caught her and continued a loud conversation with another guy without missing a step. Kathleen gave up. She drifted along in the middle of the group. Ed wouldn't let go of her.

The noise level in Frenchie's increased after their party entered. They found a corner table where she, Ed, and Brandy squeezed in with someone else. Roy pulled a table close, and others found empty chairs to bring over. No one could hear any conversation. Kathleen certainly couldn't keep up with it. Marshmallows wrapped around her thoughts.

Ed tugged her hand. "Come on, sweetlips, we're headed out."

She pulled back with sluggish fingers. "We just got here." Her head hurt.

Brandy stood and leaned over Kathleen. "The night isn't getting any younger. We haven't been to the Lion's Den or Colosimo's yet."

They all clamored out the door into the crowded street. Automobile horns blared, music spilled out of doorways, and people laughed and argued and shouted and charged around to someplace important. Colored lights flashed everywhere. Kathleen's pounding head threw her off center.

She didn't remember entering this new place. Ed guided her to a table. She sat where he indicated.

The New Orleans–style band stuffed the room from corner to corner with ear-throbbing vibrations of big, brassy sounds.

Mac shoved a gin Rickey in Kathleen's direction—cold, wet, but not thirst quenching. She sipped and watched as the smokers filled the large room with a thick, blue haze. She saw someone who looked familiar, but a few seconds later she couldn't remember who. More joined their party. She didn't catch any names in the din.

Ed said something to her, jumped up, and greeted an unusually tall, square-cut man with deep-set eyes. The man glanced at the floor and nodded his head. Sadness seemed to permeate him. Kathleen's interest spiked. He shook Ed's hand and moved toward the other side of the room.

Her ears gave up recognizing any sense of conversation. She closed her eyes, taking in the rhythm from the jazz quartet now center stage. Another gin Rickey, Brandy's deep laughter, and now Ed's hand resting on her bare knee snapped her back to the crowded table and their raucous stories.

She scanned the room for the handsome, sad man. He stood by the bar sipping a drink. She watched. He, for the most part, ignored or dismissed the young women who attempted to start conversations. He stood apart from everyone.

Why did he look so sad? His thick hair—she imagined the feel of it, of running her fingers through it. Warmth spread deep into her middle. She swallowed the last of her gin Rickey, pulled out the small chunk of ice, and popped it into her mouth. Maybe she should walk over there. Ed's hand on her knee had moved a bit higher.

Hell, Ed doesn't own me.

The man turned his back to the bar and leaned against it, watching the crowd. His eyes met hers. He didn't look away.

Her face grew warm. She looked down. There sat a fresh gin Rickey.

The music of the saxophone, clarinet, and trombone crept into her bones. The table, her chair, and the floor soaked in rhythm from vibrations. Melodies filled her head with ups and downs and the turning sounds of bass, alto, and tenor notes, creating moods she'd never felt before.

The band slipped into mellow dance music.

Ed pulled her out onto the dance floor. She tugged him back, snuffed her lit cigarette out in the ashtray, then glided out into the crowd of dancers. Her feet hurt in Brandy's shoes, but the wobbliness and gyrating brain came from the gin Rickeys.

Saliva filled her mouth. A wave of heat swept through her, followed by intermittent chills.

Bile crept up her throat. She shoved away from Ed and darted past the bar. She pushed and wiggled between the other dancers and drinkers, found the powder room, moved aside, and stood to let a clutch of women out.

She dashed into a sitting area and willed herself to hold everything until she found an empty stall. She glanced sideways at the full-length mirror in time to see her own rose-colored image move out through the door.

Nothing made sense. Waves of chills and saliva—

Rushing into a stall, she emptied the contents of her stomach. Kathleen's head throbbed. If she could only lie down in her own bed in her own bedroom . . . Even the floor wasn't where it should be.

She moved into the sitting area, took a towel, and washed her face. The person in the mirror staring back didn't belong here in this loud, chaotic place. She missed those after-school trolley rides to dancing and acting lessons. Kathleen's eyes filled with moisture. She'd left her bed unmade the day she and Sophie ran off.

A shriek jerked her back into the reality of the powder room. The sound shocked her, but the following silence caused her to hold her breath.

Before she could understand what she didn't hear, yelling and crying started. Someone shouted orders. Curiosity about the scuffling noises took her to the door. She pushed. The door didn't budge.

Trapped. She pushed harder. It opened a crack.

She heard people on the other side. Kathleen peaked out. Someone's leg—a girl's. She must be sprawled on the floor with her body smashed against it. The nylon hose had a crooked black seam running up the calf.

Kathleen's narrow slice of view showed Mac's large form approaching. He elbowed his way in, shouting to the world, "Move back. Come away. Give her room to breathe."

"Mac, let me out!" She pushed the door with more force.

A stern voice said, "No need for breathing room. This lady has no pulse."

Then a sobbing female voice said, "I came to check the powder room because she hadn't returned."

Voices of authority now stood out against the background of chatter. "Here's the police."

"Stop those people from going out that door."

Officers' shrill whistles sounded. Someone called, "No one leaves."

"Mac—let me out." Kathleen put her mouth up to the opening in the doorway and shouted, "Mac—please."

A constable pulled the door open a bit wider, grabbed Kathleen by her arm, and yanked her through, then shoved her into the crowd of onlookers. She steadied herself and stood there looking, mouth open, at a fallen young flapper.

The girl matched Kathleen in height and wore a stunning rose and sequined dress similar to the one borrowed from Brandy's closet. The brunette's bobbed hair and dress evoked the crazy look-a-like image in the mirror, confusing Kathleen when she entered the powder room.

A police officer rolled the girl onto her back. Blood pooled on the floor.

Kathleen stared at the blood covering the girl's front. She stared until her eyes brought the dark-handled knife into focus.

The ceiling tilted. The walls swirled. Her knees buckled. Firm hands caught her, pulling her back into a warm, muscular body. Ed. He also held his little notebook and pencil. His grim face stared at the flapper on the floor.

Kathleen straightened and scanned the crowd for Chester.

Later, after the authorities removed the body, the band resumed playing and the crowd continued their own amusements. Just another ordinary night in Chicago.

Ed, Mac, and Brandy excluded all the others and sat in a quiet corner with Kathleen.

She needed a glass of water. Mac put one in front of her. Immobilized, she stared at it and listened to the three of them make plans. After a few minutes of being unable to concentrate, she sipped.

With raised voices dialed up by alcohol, they interrupted each other and did some finger pointing about Ed exposing Kathleen on the dance floor. He did some table smacking, and they all came up with outrageous speculations but no decent theories.

"What the hell?" Ed held his hands up. "You know the guy had to be standing near the bar to stab the girl."

"Bullshit." Mac finished off his gin Rickey and slammed his glass on the tabletop. "None of the regulars who drank at that bar tonight would murder anyone with a knife."

"How are we going to keep Kathleen safe?" Brandy backhanded Mac's biceps. "That's what's important. Answer me that, will ya."

Ed looked around the room. His gaze came back to Kathleen. "You okay, babe?"

She wasn't okay. Maybe the murderer was sitting at the table next to them or waiting outside the door.

Mac studied Kathleen's face too. "Hey, don't worry. He thinks he's stabbed you. You're safe for now."

Brandy put an arm around Kathleen.

Kathleen straightened and said, "Brandy, let's leave."

"Sure kid, but you're staying at my place tonight. And throw that dress away. I sure as hell won't ever wear it again."

They all stood and left the bar.

Ed placed his hand on Kathleen's back. "She can't stay at your place, Brandy. The guy must have followed us tonight."

"Where will I go?" Kathleen glanced behind them. Everything looked normal . . . lots of people coming and going . . . no one she recognized.

Brandy pointed to her left. "I have a friend who lives in a neighborhood west of here. It's a walk, but let's see if she'll put Kathleen up for the night."

"What about my things, and what about tomorrow?" Kathleen scrutinized each street they crossed.

"You're packed. That new apartment is close to mine. We'll make arrangements to get you to work."

Mac took over. "At nine thirty I'll escort this sweet thing all the way to her rehearsal at Friar's."

Ed took Kathleen's hand. "I'll find Martin. He spent the evening at the bar."

"What did he tell the police?" Brandy pointed down another street, indicating her friend's apartment would be in that direction.

Ed squeezed Kathleen's hand. "He probably saw something, but when the two of us started dancing, he left."

Outside noisy. Inside empty.

—CHINESE PROVERB

29

Kathleen woke the next morning swearing she'd been bowled over by a train. Not a single part of her cooperated. The light hurt her eyes, her fingers tingled, the pain banding the top of her head squeezed tighter and tighter, and the few fluids left in her stomach wouldn't quiet.

She refused the breakfast offered her but swigged down some of the black coffee in the china cup, dabbed her lips, and excused herself to sit in the parlor and wait for Mac.

This house belonged to a pleasant, older woman, a grandmother type. She'd been kind when Brandy knocked on her door in the early-morning hours last night. She invited them in, clutching her robe around her trim form. She listened to their tale, clucked her tongue a few times, assured them she'd find some suitable clothes for Kathleen to wear to dance practice the next morning, and escorted Kathleen to a narrow bed in the corner of her sewing room.

Kathleen wiggled her toes, unsuccessfully encouraging them to find more room in Brandy's dance shoes.

Until this morning her body had never experienced such widespread physical pain stabbing at her toes and spreading up to the crown of her head. If Chester hadn't murdered the girl, then Kathleen couldn't guess who did. She'd find no safety in Chicago. Dolly had given the murderer the equivalent of a road map to his prey.

Blast it all, with the murderer in Chicago she'd be safer back in Minneapolis, at home, sleeping in her own bed.

Mac knocked on the door at nine-thirty. He screwed up one side of his face when he saw her, but he kindly kept his opinions to himself about the longish gray skirt and billowy white blouse.

"You ready, kid?"

She nodded and called back a thank-you to the charitable woman who had housed her.

They left the whitewashed porch and hurried down the sidewalk. Mac jabbered. Kathleen couldn't find the energy or the words to hold up her end of the conversation. Each step pinched and jarred. She didn't know where she was or, for that matter, how to get to Friar's.

Mac stopped beside a parked automobile and opened the door for her. She climbed in. He went around to the driver's side and started the engine. The calmness that accompanies gratefulness spread over her.

"I've checked out Brandy's street," he said. "It's clean. Got two men posted around key points there."

"I don't want men—"

"Ed told me you'd say that. Forget it, will ya." He looked over at her. "Figured you'd want your own things to wear. Right?"

She found herself laughing and smoothing down the ruffles on the blouse. Maybe she should talk to him about Chester's watch. But she had stolen it from Crystal. Yet Crystal had stolen it first, so maybe that didn't matter.

"You'll have to hurry or you'll be late. Got it?" He sped down a backstreet, screeched to a halt, let the automobile pitch forward, then sped down another street.

"Irene will kick me off the line in a snap." She clutched the seat and braced herself against the door.

"Hey, don't lean against the door. Sometimes it flies open."

Kathleen lurched over and grabbed the dashboard.

He slammed to a stop in front of Brandy's apartment. "Hurry. You can change at Friar's."

She flew up the stairs and started to shove her key into the lock when the door opened. Brandy stood there, holding out her valise and a paper sack full of other belongings, including a pair of shoes. Kathleen tore back down and out onto the street. Mac, the gentleman, helped her into the car and returned to the driver's side.

They arrived at Friar's with minutes to spare. She changed. The throbbing in her head seemed less intense, and now that her feet had some breathing room she might actually live through the day.

Freddy started playing music, a cue for the girls to be on stage. Irene pulled a chair next to the piano. She interrupted Freddy's playing, sat, and penciled in a few last-minute modifications.

When practice started Kathleen's own comfortable dance shoes argued with the blisters from Brandy's shoes. This would be a long day.

They stopped and restarted the routine for Saturday night many times. Finally Irene let them break for a two-hour lunch.

Kathleen grabbed a bar towel to wipe her face, while kicking off her shoes. Mac and Ed sat over by the door in conversation. Then she saw Sophie at a table in the far corner, beckoning her over.

Kathleen couldn't cross the room fast enough. They hugged and slid into chairs next to each other. Seeing Sophie put her world back into order.

Kathleen lit up a cigarette. "How long have you been here?"

"Only a few minutes." Sophie pushed a blonde lock away from her eyes. "Do you have any free time?"

"Two hours. There's so much we should talk about, but first, before I forget, Pritchard told me to tell you something urgent. He said you have to leave the Southside immediately. He didn't say why, but he insisted."

"Golly, why would he say that?" Sophie's eyes widened.

"Don't know, but you know how he is. The message came as a command."

Sophie shrugged. "What's with Pritchard anyway?"

"This time I think he knows something, and you should do as he says." A tingle of truth slid through Kathleen.

"Horsefeathers. He's a busybody. Why should we listen to Pritchard? He's someone we don't even like. Besides, I've got me a beau." She grinned and pulled out a photo torn from some newspaper.

Kathleen sank deeper into her chair and studied the photo of a guy, all sharp angles with dark, slicked-back, greasy hair, big ears, a dimpled chin, and tiny rat eyes. She let the smoke slide from her lips. Tiredness flooded through her. She'd escaped being stabbed, hadn't slept, was still fighting the ills of all those gin Rickeys, and her toes and heels stung with broken blisters.

She closed her eyes and said, "I don't like Pritchard, but Sophie, he's always right." She handed Sophie back the photo. "Please, for Pete's sake, leave the Southside."

"Aw, Kath, I've never had a beau before. He's sweet and treats me like a lady."

"Hey, girls, over here," Ed called from the other side of the room.

Mac patted some skinny fellow on the shoulder. The guy passed him a piece of paper.

"Girls, come on—" Ed waved to get their attention. "Kathleen, Sophie, you too. We've got a huge surprise for you."

Kathleen pushed back from their table. Sophie grabbed her arm, looking puzzled. Kathleen cocked an eyebrow and shrugged. She retrieved her shoes from the bar area and slipped into them.

She and Sophie sauntered over to join the other dancers. Ed and Mac continued a quiet but enthusiastic discussion with the skinny fellow.

The men's excitement became infectious, causing the dancers to chat and giggle louder. Ed pulled away from the other two with his eyes full of amusement. He held his hand up to quiet them.

"You dolls, gather around. Wait until you see what we've got planned for you."

Gain cannot be made without some other person's loss.
—PUBLILIUS SYRUS

30

Mac said something else to the skinny man, who then nodded and loped out the door. Kathleen stood behind all of them, yawning and shifting her weight from one sore foot to the other. Instead of Ed's games, she could go for a long nap.

Ed sketched out walking directions on the paper map and held it up for the girls to see.

"We're all going over to this warehouse. It's easy to miss because the main entrance is around the corner. You'll be going through this doorway here, but none of you will be allowed inside until Mac comes out and tells us it's okay. Or just stick with me. You'll not have problems finding it. Let's go."

Ed went around and grabbed Kathleen's hand, but she pulled it away.

"What?"

"I can't go out there—because—you know. Besides, what about Sophie?"

"You'll be fine," Mac called over his shoulder, "and hell, there's enough for twenty others. Come on, kid."

"Let's go see." Sophie squirmed around her. "A surprise." She headed out behind Mac.

"Dammit." But Kathleen let Ed take her hand, and they followed the parade of exuberant flappers led by the ex-cop. She doubted her feet would survive through the yet-to-happen afternoon dance practice.

Ed told the group to keep quiet when they arrived outside the peeling, red-painted door. The dancers ignored him and continued to babble.

Sophie twisted up her face into a big question. Ed kept scanning the street, up and down.

Kathleen leaned against the building. "Ed, my good man, what's all this secrecy about?" Her blisters screamed. She didn't want to stand on the sidewalk in the sun. The intense light and heat added to her hangover.

The door opened, and Mac poked his head out.

"Deed is done." He winked at them. "Come on in, my sweet ladies."

The dark interior blinded them after the brightness of the day outside. They all quieted in the blackness and stood inside the door. Then Kathleen recognized an outline of a truck and stacked boxes. A sliver of sunlight appeared through a widening crack near the floor of the adjacent wall to Kathleen's right. In seconds the crack turned into a large rectangle and light flooded the room. The huge garage door stood open, and the truck started up. It rumbled out into traffic and disappeared. The door grumbled closed again.

Everyone talked at once. Ed shushed them and invited them over to the boxes. Kathleen's eyes adjusted to the dimness of the warehouse lights.

Mac opened one box and removed a full-length, cinnamon-colored mink coat. He handed it to Ed, who draped it over Kathleen's shoulders. She gasped and fingered the luxuriant fur.

"Ladies, you may each select one to call your own." Ed turned and grinned at Kathleen, who nestled her cheek deep into the soft collar. She saw him watching. She couldn't help but return his grin.

The following few minutes became frenzied as the girls tore into boxes looking for just the right size, color, and length. Sophie pranced over wearing a chocolate-colored mink with large cuffs.

"Kath, have you ever seen anything like this? Whole coats of mink, not just the collar and cuffs, not just wraps, but full-length coats—"

"Are these from France?" Kathleen looked up at Ed. "I bet these were created by Jeanne Paquin. Were they?"

Ed shrugged.

Sophie twirled around and around and wrapped her coat tight and hugged herself.

"Answer me, Ed." Kathleen sniffed at the fur. "Where did these come from?" She pushed her hands deep into the pockets and swished the bottom of her coat around her ankles.

"From the back of that truck." Ed waved toward the garage door.

"That's not what I mean. Are these for us? Are they ours?"

He nodded, grinning.

She closed her eyes and reveled in the safety and beauty of this moment.

"Ed, we gotta go." Mac's voice. "They'll be here in fifteen."

Mac clapped his hands, then whistled. The giggling stopped.

"Ladies, decide now or never. Pick your coats. We gotta go."

"Ed, I can't take this. Brandy would feel left out and—jealous." Kathleen couldn't do that to a friend.

"She must have at least three minks by now. Don't give her another thought." Ed moved Sophie and Kathleen back toward the door where they had entered.

They understood they needed to stay put while he joined Mac in rounding up the other excited flappers. Finally, all of them gathered by the door, judging each other's coats and vamping like they were Theda Bara.

Ed and Mac stuffed discarded coats back into empty cartons and closed each one. They surveyed their work.

"Have to leave." Ed darted back to the girls and opened the door for them. They trooped into the bright summer sunlight wearing their new minks. Kathleen didn't care about the eighty-five degree temperature. Evidently the others didn't either. They pranced their way down the sidewalk toward Friar's, flaunting their prizes with wide smiles.

Kathleen had swallowed her questions long enough.

"Okay, Ed. What happened back there?"

He laughed and shook his head.

"Dammit, Ed, give it to me straight."

"It's time for the summer coat shows when the furriers do their fall buying. Moran and his guys intercept the trucks, help themselves, transfer theirs to their own trucks, and offer them out to all of us newspaper guys."

"Wait a minute." Kathleen stopped walking. "How can you say they transfer what's theirs to their trucks? It's not theirs."

"Sure it is. Once Moran's guys take them off the trucks, the coats belong to Moran. See, Moran offers protection to the buyers. The sellers out of gratitude give him his choice of coats. He's earned them."

"Are you sure?" Kathleen started walking, wishing her muddled brain would clear.

She sweltered under her new luscious fur. Since she'd arrived in Chicago her world had turned into an outrageous circus. One thing, she'd never touch another gin Rickey. Still, Ed's words about the coats sounded logical.

She continued to mull it over.

Finally Kathleen said, "Why'd we have to rush out of there if it's not stealing?"

"We didn't want the rest of the reporters to get huffed because I got in there first. That's the only reason we needed to leave. It's a courtesy thing."

"Courtesy? Come on, I'm not stupid, you know."

He didn't respond.

"How'd you know about this before the other reporters?" Kathleen slowed her pace.

"Mac arranges the deal between Moran and the reporters."

Then the question she needed to ask came to her. "Why is he giving reporters mink coats—women's mink coats?"

Ed grinned again. "Moran knows we all have women in our lives. He helps us keep our women happy. In return, we give him breaks when it comes to headlines and news."

Our women? This new information stewed in Kathleen's brain. *Chicago makes everyone crazy, including me.*

If you have built castles in the air, your work need not be lost; there is where they should be. Now put foundations under them.

—HENRY DAVID THOREAU

31

When they entered Friar's, Ed went over to talk to Freddy. Kathleen pulled Sophie away from the others.

"Soph, don't ignore Pritchard's warning. You'll find another gig. Don't worry."

"I told you, I've got a beau."

Kathleen sighed. "You'll have plenty of beaus wherever you go. Don't settle for someone just because he shows an interest in you."

"Listen to what you said." Sophie put her hands on her hips. "You and Dolly slept around with a married guy. You can't deny me the comfort of a respectable man. If I didn't know you, I'd say you sound mean."

"Wait a sec. I never *slept* with him. Besides, this guy who showed an interest in me turned out to be a loser—a first-class bastard." Kathleen bit her lip before saying, "Please listen to me—and Pritchard."

"It's not only Hymie." Sophie slid her fingers over the fur. "They pay me way better than most places would, the guys in the band are terrific, and the hours aren't bad either. I like it there."

"What about Pritchard? He knows things we don't."

Sophie, snuggled in her coat, smiled. "Aw, Kath, look at us. Our lives couldn't be better."

"Would Dolly agree? How's her life?"

"Probably not." Sophie looked at the clock on the wall. "She's convinced her employer to give her the oddest work hours. She comes and goes from the boardinghouse when you'd least expect it. Sometimes she even calls a taxi if she can't find anyone to walk with her."

"Still nervous and scared." Kathleen examined the inside lining of her coat and ran her hand over the lapel to smooth the fur.

Sophie held her arms out to her side, fingers splayed, to check the sleeve length of her coat. She nodded in agreement about Dolly's condition.

"At least she has money now," Sophie said. "She called her parents and let them know she's safe. She'll hate not having a fur coat, but I didn't think I should ask for one for her."

"Did she tell her parents where she lives and about us?"

"I don't know. What if she did? I have to go."

"Keep in touch." Kathleen wrote down her new apartment address. "I don't have a telephone there. It's in the hallway outside my apartment. Here's the number. If you let it ring long enough, I'll answer. You can call me here, too, and leave a message. But please, please, please don't give Mrs. Taylor or Dolly my address."

"Why are you so secretive?" Sophie looked at the address and stuck it in her pocket. "You can trust them. Mrs. Taylor does her best to keep Dolly safe."

If Sophie knew about last night's murdered girl, she'd be hysterical. Kathleen searched for another answer. "I don't want my parents to know I've moved out of the all-woman's boardinghouse. If you tell Mrs. Taylor, and they call, she might tell them where I am."

"I've got to run." Sophie started toward the door, stopped, went over, and thanked Ed and Mac.

Ed kept staring at Kathleen and grinning. His fur-coat giveaway must have tickled him silly. Kathleen moved over to him.

"Thank you for the coat, Ed." She buried her cheek again in the collar. "But I can't accept this." She slipped it off and held it out to him.

All his grins vanished. Ed stepped back with his palms out toward her, and a wounded look spread over his face.

"But seriously, guy, it's been a world of fun," Kathleen continued. "I've not been this happy since I came to Chicago."

He refused to touch the coat.

"Come on, Ed, take it. I'm not willing to belong to anyone—even at the price of this expensive fur."

He shook his head and backed up another step. She gave up and draped it over a chair, and as she moved away, she said, "You're generous and kind. Again, thank you for the dream."

"Dammit, Kathleen." He reached for her and forced her to look at him. "I'm not trying to buy you." His eyes darkened. "I'm giving you a gift. Take the damn coat. I owe you heaps, but you don't owe me anything."

He seemed so dejected. An uneasiness of misjudgment spread through her. She lowered her eyelashes, regretting her ungratefulness. What could she do? He obviously liked her—a lot. She'd pretty much ignored his advances and often distanced herself from him.

She stepped in close. "Ed." She tilted her chin up and gave him a sweet little kiss right on his surprised lips.

His grin reappeared, full blown.

She picked up *her* coat and hugged it.

"Ed, you've been attentive and exceptionally kind. I may act indifferent, but that's not it. It's just that I'm unsure about everything." He listened without expression. "Things haven't gone well for me in many ways. I need to figure out my life. Everything feels confused and . . . please understand."

He started grinning again.

He could make a profession out of grinning. What a sweet guy.

He actually blushed, picked up his hat, and said, "I've got to get back to the office. Mac has his guys all over and around your new place, but we can't be too careful."

"No need. Tell them to go home. I'll be fine. Besides, I can't afford to pay them." Kathleen sighed.

"Don't worry. These guys owe him big favors. I'll stop over at your new place tonight with Mac and Brandy."

Kathleen needed sleep.

Fingering the brim, he said, "Martin may have seen something. I've asked him to come over tonight too. "

Martin, the man with the sad eyes, coming to my apartment. Her heart quickened.

Ed donned his hat and whistled as he went out the door.

Freddy jogged up to Kathleen. "Miss Kathleen, a Mrs. Taylor called. I wrote her number down."

"Thanks." She went over to the wall, but before picking up the receiver she glanced at the clock. Fifteen minutes before practice started. She placed the call with the operator.

Mrs. Taylor, polite and proper, said Kathleen's mother had called this morning and wished to speak to her. Mrs. Taylor assured her she didn't say anything about Kathleen's moving out or about where Kathleen worked. But she did think maybe Kathleen should return her mother's call soon.

Now what? Maybe her father had a heart attack, or maybe Mary had fallen ill with something torturous or incurable. She'd not be able to concentrate on the dance routine if she didn't find out.

"Something else," Mrs. Taylor said. "A woman stopped by several days ago and said your mother had given her a message for you. I try not to be judgmental, but this woman seemed strange. She kept muttering to herself. That made the hairs on my arms stand up."

"A woman—someone who knows my mother?"

"I told her to leave the message with me. She refused." Mrs. Taylor finished by saying, "Later, someone kept calling for you. Finally I mentioned you didn't live here any longer. I hope you don't mind I made that decision.

She thanked Mrs. Taylor and hung up.

Irene forbade them from making long-distance telephone calls. Kathleen could place a collect call, but then her parents would think she didn't have any money. She'd leave the money with Freddy to give to Mr. Fritzel.

She placed the call and asked the operator to give her the time and charges after she hung up. She listened to the telephone ringing in the hallway at the other end of the line. Her mother's voice came on.

"Hello? McPherson's residence."

"Mother—Kathleen. I'm returning your telephone call." Her heart pounded so hard she feared her mother could hear it.

"Hello dear. Are you well?"

"Yes." Kathleen held her breath.

Silence.

Then her mother's voice came through. "We're doing very well here too, thank you."

Kathleen should have asked. Her cheeks grew warm.

"Your father and I worry you may need some more money about now."

What the—? Kathleen set her jaw and held her tongue. Her mother's statement seemed a twisted way of showing concern and caring, but it hit Kathleen more as a chastisement of her own lack of ability to be independent.

"Kathleen, are you still there?"

"Yes, Mother." She knew her words sounded tight.

"Your father and I have discussed this matter until we've wrung every word dry of all meaning."

This matter?

"We've come to no other conclusion except to invite you to return home. We miss you, dear. We hope this pleases you."

It didn't. Last night, as frightened as she was, knowing she could go home would have pleased her. This morning, finding out her stalker wasn't in Minnesota anymore, she actually wanted to be home—but not now. Her mother's words became hard lumps to digest, causing her to bristle at their invitation to *allow* her to return to *her* home.

Their confidence in Kathleen's ability to make good decisions, to support herself, and to take responsibility for her life didn't exist. If she returned home, she'd be admitting a failure, and she hadn't failed at all.

"I'm curious, Mother. Why would you think I would care to come back?"

"We assumed by now you would have had enough of *that* life. We're sure you've run out of money because we know you didn't touch your savings account . . . your babysitting money wouldn't last long, and . . ." Her mother floundered for more words.

For the second time today, a jagged edge of shame from her lack of gratitude bothered Kathleen. They did care about her. Still, she couldn't keep the anger down from her parents' lack of faith.

"Mother, I have respectable work as a dancer and actress. I now own a mink coat, and you may tell Mrs. Dagget that Sophie's found happiness, too. I'm very pleased to hear you are all well. Give my regards to Father and to Mary. I appreciate your offer, but I have no need to be returning to Minneapolis any time soon."

The line held silence.

"Mother, one question. Did you ask someone to deliver a message to me?"

"Heavens no."

Her mother always took care of her own business. Kathleen should acknowledge her mother's veiled generosity with a little more charity. "Thank you for calling. I need to get back to my work." Kathleen murmured a quiet good-bye.

She returned the receiver to the telephone box. Her heart pounded in her ears. She stifled senseless tears. The telephone rang. The operator gave her the time and charges. Kathleen counted out the money and carried it over to Freddy, explaining to him the cost of her long-distance call.

Irene clapped her hands for the girls to assemble. They grumbled, but they removed their minks, stepped into their assigned positions, and practiced for several more hours. Then Irene dismissed them for the day.

"Hold back, Kathleen." Irene motioned for her to come away from the others.

Kathleen's heart sank—more conflict. Irene worked them hard and demanded more than any of them could give.

Irene cocked her head then said, "Sometimes I think your mind isn't with us, but when you're on stage, you outperform everyone. You're exacting and don't give up until you've mastered the routines. I've watched you practice long after the others have left. But I'm worried about you. You seem preoccupied while everyone else is having fun."

Kathleen searched for something to say, then said, "I didn't sleep well—but I'm fine. Thanks."

"I'm not talking just about today." Irene studied her. "I'm here for you, kid. You're a true professional."

She watched Irene leave. A warmth enveloped Kathleen, like sunshine. She couldn't help her stupid, Ed-like grin.

Don't play for safety—it's the most dangerous thing in the world.

—HUGE WALPOLE

32

After practice, Mac took Kathleen to neighborhood stores where she picked up incidentals for her new apartment. He helped her carry her valise and purchases up the two flights of stairs, gave her the key, and she turned it in the lock.

The door swung open into a large room where a chintz-covered divan sat under a window. A padded oak chair shared space on one side of the sofa. An oak table holding a walnut-based lamp functioned as an end table for the divan and also a bedside table. The single bed, partially hidden by an oriental screen, took over a back corner. The other back corner held an ice box on a stand next to a short counter with a hot plate and a sink. Above were a few cupboards. A white table and two chairs stood sandwiched between the counter and the living area.

No one would be dancing in this room.

"You okay with this?" Mac set the food on the tiny white table. "Your landlord said the real stove would be here next week."

Kathleen couldn't imagine where they'd install it. She put the groceries away and found places for her other purchases.

"As long as I don't sleepwalk, I'll be fine." She moved between the living-room furniture into the bed area. She set her valise on the floor, took off her coat, and smoothed it out on top of the bed. She stood and looked around.

"Where's the bathroom?"

"List of rules on the table says the bathroom is at the end of the hallway."

She sighed. Her mother would make some patronizing remark if she knew. At least Kathleen could afford the rent.

She patted Mac on the arm. "It's clean. I need to ask you something."

"Shoot." He leaned on the doorway and pulled out a cigarette.

"The badger scam where the debutante died—has anyone found out the identity of the man she took back to Mrs. Everstone's that night?"

"Never did find out."

"Ed said she went to some speakeasy in or by the Rex Hotel." Kathleen started to mention the pocket watch, but then he'd confiscate it. She wanted to keep it a little longer, but not because of any residual feeling she concealed toward the bastard.

"Not a nice neighborhood. Why?"

"Guess I'm looking for some type of conclusion."

"Well, thanks to you two, Crystal Everstone won't be playing her game again for a long, long time."

Someone knocked on the door. Mac opened it, and Brandy came in carrying a huge salami with a brick of cheese. Ed stood behind her with a loaf of French bread and a bottle of whisky.

Kathleen gestured toward the kitchen area.

Everyone talked at once. They shuffled around each other slicing the cheese, salami, and bread. Then Ed opened the hooch. In the cupboards, Kathleen found a small assortment of mismatched dishes and cups, two juice glasses, and three water glasses. Ed poured everyone whisky with water.

Kathleen went to the window, studied the street below, pulled the shade, and turned on the light. She heard her mother's voice sing out—*Dear, tell us about your glamourous apartment.*

She plopped down on the couch and kicked off her shoes and tucked her long legs under her. Ed handed Kathleen her drink. The others found places to sit, and Brandy passed out sandwiches.

Mac chewed and said, "We're working blind here, Kathleen. You must have some idea of who's after you. At least give us descriptions of possible people."

"Get off it, Mac," Brandy said. "She don't know nuttin' from nut-tin'." Brandy's affected street talk seemed to pop out of nowhere.

"She has to know something." He turned to Kathleen. "I'd think the murderer would be covered in blood."

"There'd be no blood on the killer if he threw the knife." Kathleen picked at her sandwich.

Ed shook his head. "Ribs protect the heart. Someone would have to be highly skilled."

"If we knew who wanted to kill you," Mac said, "then we'd know the murderer."

Brandy asked, "Did anyone talk to Martin?"

"Only for a moment." Ed set his glass on the floor and looked around for something to wipe his hands on.

"Don't keep us guessing. Did he see something or not?" Brandy drank from her juice glass.

"What about the guys at the bar?" Now Mac tilted his head.

"Mugsy came in for a beer, then disappeared. Martin thinks he came in to scan the place. Probably to pass on information."

"Mugsy." Mac gave a huff.

"Who's that?" Kathleen lifted an eyebrow.

Brandy stood, stretched, and said, "No one to worry about, but he's a machine gun when angered. He works for a guy who works for Screwy. Wonder why he stopped in when it's not his territory."

"Wait a minute." Kathleen held her hand up. "Here's an idea. What if we're wrong about this whole thing? What if whoever killed that girl wanted to kill *her*, not me?"

Everyone seemed to avoid looking at Kathleen.

Kathleen's face grew warm.

No one said anything.

So Kathleen said, "Mac, you need to look into who might have been after *her*—that other girl."

Brandy leaned against Kathleen, draped her arm around her shoulder, and said, "Buttercup, no one around here throws knives. They use Tommys or sawed-off shotguns."

Kathleen blinked several times and then studied the grain in the wooden floor.

"We know how much you want this to go away." Brandy picked up the glass. "I'll fix you another."

Ed intervened by taking Kathleen's glass. He took Mac's empty glass too.

"Did Martin see when the creep left?" Mac asked Ed.

"Who knows if Mugsy even left. Martin should be here any minute now. You can ask him."

Kathleen needed answers, and this conversation was going nowhere. "My friend Sophie has a singing gig in the Southside. Someone said to get her out of there. Do you know why?"

Mac asked, "Where exactly?"

"I don't remember. Somewhere around the twenty thousand block near Wabash."

Everyone exchanged looks.

"Come on, guys. Why?"

Mac said, "Do you know which club?"

"I didn't pay attention. She indicated she worked someplace, like, maybe in a hotel."

Mac said, "A rooming house—the Four Deuces?"

"Damn. Let's hope not." Ed slapped his knee.

Brandy, eyes wide, said, "The Metropole Hotel. I bet that's where."

"Guys, I don't like your reactions. Tell me." Prickles ran up Kathleen's spine.

"Lots of prostitution going on down that way," Mac said. "Rough group."

Ed spoke softly. "They'll draw her in, make her think she's in the best place on earth, and she'll be in way over her head before she knows what's going on. When that happens they won't let her leave. Kathleen, get her out of there now."

You are only what you are when no one is looking.
—ROBERT C. EDWARDS

33

A knock on the door brought Kathleen to her feet. Mac opened the door.

"Hi, Marty." Brandy popped up, blew him a kiss, and went to the kitchen area. "I'll fix you some giggle water."

"Rum and Coca-Cola?" He glanced around the room.

Kathleen's heart skipped beats. His presence commanded attention like her father's, but beneath his sophisticated, old-world ruggedness, his eyes nurtured something hopeless.

Ed stood and said, "Martin, this is Miss Kathleen McPherson. Kathleen, our friend from the east coast, Martin Davies."

Their eyes locked for a moment until Mac slapped him on the back.

"You're lucky to meet this young lady. Some guy tried to kill her last night."

"Can't think of a more dreadful loss. How can I be of help?"

Brandy interrupted, "Sorry, only whisky and water."

"Water will do."

Ed moved a kitchen chair over for Martin, and Brandy handed him a glass of water.

"Want a sandwich?"

"Thanks, but I dined a bit earlier with a client."

"So you honor prohibition, Mr. Davies." Kathleen glanced his way, held up her drink, and sipped.

"And well should you."

"And why should I, Mr. Davies?" She sent him her over-the-shoulder look.

"Because, sweet lass, my sober friends call me Martin."

The guys howled.

"What brings you to Chicago?" Kathleen sat, pulled out a cigarette, and willed her out-of-control beating heart to calm.

"Shipping business—lining up contracts and such."

He leaned in to light her cigarette, and again she held his gaze a touch too long. Her cheeks grew warm. She searched for somewhere else to look.

"We've got great salami." Ed's voice.

Martin shook his head, leaned back, sipped his water, and said, "Actually, I'm in and out of Chicago quite often. About last night's trouble—"

Ed cleared his throat. "Someone with a shiv plunged it into a Kathleen look-alike outside the powder room. He'd followed her here all the way from Minneapolis."

"Seriously?"

Ed continued, "Kathleen didn't recognize anyone. Gin Rickeys may have had something to do with that, but still . . . Who do you remember at the bar?"

"'Tis a long shot there, m'boy." Martin shrugged.

"Don't believe him." Mac took out a cigar and sucked on one end.

"Aw—don't start." Martin glanced at the ceiling. "You're wrong."

"About what?" Kathleen leaned forward.

Martin grinned. "They blame me for a faultless memory."

Brandy held her finger up. "How about when Fritzel decided to hire that scar-faced piano player. Marty took one look at the guy and told Fritzel he'd seen him making deals with a Southside thug months earlier. Martin remembered the exact date and the place he'd watched them. Fritzel hired Freddy instead."

Ed held up his hand. "Start with a description of the first person you saw when you went over to the bar."

Martin didn't miss a beat. "His cheeks and nose glowed from too much alcohol. His girth measured the same as his height, and he wore a white apron around his middle. Though I must say, his hands held quiet steady as he made my Cuba Libre."

Everyone except Ed chuckled.

"Let's move on." Ed interrupted the laughter.

Martin took a sip before answering. "A lanky young man, all hot-headed, accused the bartender of watering down his drink. His pointed nose, slicked-back rusty hair, and bloodshot eyes made him look like a rooster."

"What'd the bartender do?" Mac asked.

"He poured a fresh drink, gave it to him, and said it was on the house." Martin shrugged. "Cocky rooster went away. I didn't see him again."

Ed said, "Good thing he didn't start a fight with you there."

"Let me run down a list." Martin spoke directly to Kathleen. "Three giggly lasses stood around me most of the time. All three seemed about your age. Would they be a threat to you?"

Ed interrupted, "Of course not."

Kathleen shook her head.

"Several businessmen sat to my left. Since the powder-room entrance was over on the right behind the bar area in that little alcove, I don't see how they could be involved."

Ed tapped his notebook. "Who's next?"

"Martin?" Kathleen tingled with warmth, just saying his name. "What about the barstools on your right?"

He shook his head. "People stood, making it difficult to see."

"Take your time." Mac sucked on his cigar.

Martin looked at the ceiling again. "Those young lasses flitted around the men. I remember a tall man with an affected voice standing by one stool on my right. He—"

"He wore a bright window-pane suit—" Kathleen hadn't seen Pritchard there, but he could have been.

"Not at all . . . a dark suit, with a white tie and dark vest. My guess, about fifty because of the silver streaks in his hair. The auburn-haired lass tried to sit in his lap. Do you know him?"

Again, Kathleen shook her head.

"Anyone else?" Ed didn't hide his disappointment.

"Two others. Another shorter man, probably Irish, with a wonderful baritone speaking voice. His voice caught my attention. He argued with another woman because she said he took her drink."

Brandy said, "How could you hear? With the music, noise, and all—"

"He sat close to me. She yelled at him."

"How'd that one end?" Mac finished off his drink. Kathleen waited for Martin's response.

"The Irishman's words sounded like melted chocolate. He moved his drink in front of her and said something. I couldn't hear, but I bet it equaled, 'Lovely lady, if it upsets you, it would be my honor to leave this beverage in your care.'"

"What did she do?" Kathleen asked.

"I couldn't hear her words, but she seemed to be mumbling to herself and arguing with the man at the same time. She smiled, thanked him, shook her head, and waved her fingers while talking. Seemed she discussed the whole matter with someone who didn't exist. You've seen those batty people wandering down the sidewalk talking to their imaginary friends. She moved off into the crowd, taking the drink with her."

Mumbling to herself? This is the second time today someone mentioned a woman mumbling to herself.

Kathleen untangled her legs and lowered her bare feet to the floor.

"Martin, what did she look like?"

"Average, with dark hair under her ugly hat. My God, some of these outrageous hats women wear nowadays make pigeons look glamorous."

Outrageous Mrs. Schrader—Mrs. Schrader could have been the one telling Mrs. Taylor she had a note from Mother. Mrs. Schrader would have no problem being in a nightclub by herself. Maybe Pritchard escorted her there and hung around somewhere close. Maybe he didn't take a train after all.

"Did she sit with anyone?" Kathleen leaned in closer to Martin.

He shrugged.

Ed picked up Kathleen's hand and held it. "You know this woman, don't you?"

Kathleen laughed. "Ed, it could be a number of women. I do know someone who fits the description, but she lives in Minneapolis." She pulled her hand back and picked up her drink. "I don't know why she'd be here."

She murdered her child and husband, but why would she want to kill me?

Kathleen wanted them all to leave, except Martin. Underneath his congenial façade, he seemed pervasively sad.

Now their conversation made no sense. She yawned, closed her

[172]

eyes to rest for a moment, and thought of how to make Martin smile. Someone shook her arm.

Brandy stood with her face close to hers.

"We're going now, but you need to lock up after we leave."

Kathleen followed them to the door. Ed stood aside for Martin to go through, then gave her a peck on the cheek and grinned. Brandy and Mac scooted down the stairway, but Martin hung back. Ed glared at him and waited, but Martin didn't move.

"Come on, Martin, the lady's exhausted." Ed headed down the stairs.

Martin took her hand, held it tight, and filled her with his warmth and the deepest blue-green eyes she'd ever fallen into.

"Be safe, lass. Here's the number where I'm staying." He pressed a matchbook cover into her hand.

She pulled her eyes from his and glanced down—the Drake Hotel.

"If you think of another question, call me." He released her hand and disappeared down the stairway behind the others. She leaned over the railing. He stopped, looked up at her, and left.

Her heart raced after him.

A day to come seems longer than a year that's gone.
—A SCOTTISH PROVERB

34

Kathleen secured the door and headed to the bed area. She left her clothes on, crawled on top of her bed, and covered herself with the mink coat.

Martin's face appeared when she closed her eyes. The Drake Hotel floated in and out, while Chester's damned watch ticked in her ears.

Her exhausted mind wouldn't shut down. In the muddle, she sought to come up with at least one impressive question for Martin.

~

The early morning milkman, clanking milk bottles into the box on the porch down below her window, woke her. She stretched, looked at the matchbook cover on her pillow, and leaped out of bed to get ready for the day. When dressed, she shoved last night's food out of the way, rinsed out a cup, and started the coffee. She waited, studying the treasured matchbook.

When Kathleen left for Friar's, she still hadn't thought of a question worthy of the call she desperately wanted to make.

Later, during dance practice, her mind took a break from Martin. Only the intricate moves, the steps, and the rhythm mattered.

When they broke for lunch, Anita suggested they hop over to the luncheonette down the street. Kathleen begged off.

Anticipation drove her to the telephone. She touched the receiver. Maybe she shouldn't. Her stomach filled with jitters. She couldn't stand it. With the receiver in her hand, she listened to the operator place her call to the Drake Hotel. Next, she listened to the telephone in Martin's room ring and ring.

"Sorry, ma'am, there's no answer. Would you care to leave a message?"

Message—what message—?

"Tell him the damsel in distress will be at home this evening waiting for answers to her questions."

She hung up and clutched the matchbook. He wouldn't call her back. He'd come over.

Kathleen wished Brandy didn't sleep so late, but she placed a call to her anyway.

"I'm the wickedest for waking you, dear girl, but I have a colossal favor. I need to borrow some fancy rags from you before tonight. A friend might come over, and you know how frumpy my clothes are." She held her breath.

"No problem, sugar cakes. I'll drop a couple off on my way to work this evening. Take your pick but promise no more look-alike stabbings."

~

Brandy delivered a bundle of dresses with accessories. Kathleen selected a figure-clinging black silk with tiny pearls on the long trailing fringe.

"Why black?" Brandy held up a red one. "I thought you'd want more color."

"Black feels sophisticated, and besides, this goes with my clutch and my one pair of dress shoes." Brandy handed her a black headband embellished with pearls and feathers. When she went to the door, she paused and looked back at Kathleen.

"Can't stand it, kid. Tell me, who's the guy?"

Kathleen pulled her lips in tight.

"Ed?"

"Good God, no. I'll tell you later." She grinned and closed the door.

Kathleen slipped off her clothes, wrapped up in her robe, and gathered her bag of toiletries. She headed down the hall to the community bathroom, locked the door, and filled the tub with steamy hot water. She swished in some gardenia bubble bath and soaked in some delicious thoughts about Martin.

Someone banged on the door.

"Give me a few." She picked up her razor and carefully shaved her legs, then managed a quick pedicure. She wrapped her hair in a towel, gathered her things, and started to leave.

Oops, rule four. She went back and wiped out the sink and tub.

Back in her apartment, Kathleen applied makeup, straightened the seams on her nylons, and slipped into the dress. She checked her image in the mirror, grinned, and poured a whisky with water. She watched out the window for Martin's motorcar.

After a glance at the clock—nine thirty—and another drink, she knew he wasn't going to show. She'd misread his expression, his words, his interest in her. Her childish message had turned him cold. When did this nonsense about older men disappear? But then, Martin wasn't old.

When an automobile turned the corner, its lights flashed on her building. She held her breath. It drove down the street and turned another corner.

Dammit.

Kathleen locked her apartment, stormed out to the telephone in the hallway, and called a taxi. She bounded down the stairs to wait inside the front door. Some guy climbed out of an automobile, strode up the walk, and pulled open the door.

"You okay, Miss?"

One of Mac's guys. "Didn't Mac cancel this protection thing?" Kathleen flushed. "Honestly, in this new apartment I'm fine. I've called a taxi. You can go on home because I'll be out late."

"Where you're off to?"

"I thought I'd check out the Green Mill."

The guy shuffled back and forth a second, then looked at her. "You know you can't get in without knowing someone or having the password."

Crap. Disappointment must have showed on her face.

He pulled out a pencil. "Have something I can write on?"

She opened her clutch and took out Martin's matchbook cover. He opened it and wrote "Jackson" and "Ain't behavin'." He handed it back to her.

Her taxi pulled up. He escorted her down to the curb. She settled back and smoked. This silliness over Martin needed to end.

Even before the taxi stopped Kathleen could see a crowd of young people gathered at the corner of Broadway and Lawrence. She hopped out, paid, and tossed her cigarette butt into a metal trash can. The throng vied for entry into the nightclub, shoving and nudging each other under the fancy awnings. She heard snatches of conversation as she approached.

"Have you seen the garden?"

"Did you know Bea Palmer—?"

"Shimmy Queen performed here a while back."

Kathleen finagled her way up through the line before someone yelled, "Hey—"

Strong hands shoved her. "Take your turn."

Others cussed her out. She retreated back to the street corner and fumed. She'd dressed to knock everyone's eyes out, but no one cared.

Dammit anyway, Martin.

Maybe she had made a fool of herself by calling him. But being here, and not getting in, and—*To hell with it all.*

Kathleen tapped out another cigarette and walked around to find a side entry. None. She struck a match, but instead of lighting her cigarette, she watched it burn. When it got to her fingers, she shook it out and grinned.

Let the others stand in line.

She moved back to the trash can and nudged it with her foot. It moved. She struck a match, looked off into the distance, and dropped it into the can. She scratched another one and, with its flame, lit her cigarette. She flicked the still burning match into the can with the other match and watched it disappear between crumpled newspapers and other rubbish. She watched, blew out a smoke ring, and waited.

Little embers flickered, licked paper edges into flames, and made smoke that crept up the sides of the trash can. Right before the flames reached the top, she shoved the can over, kicked it hard, and watched it spill burning papers as it rolled across the sidewalk toward the entrance of the Green Mill.

She shouted, "Fire!"

The night-life crowd looked up, darted here and there, and joined in a chorus of "Fire! Fire!"

A commotion, much of it from curiosity, let Kathleen dart around the dispersed partygoers and up to the door of the Green Mill. She caught her breath, knocked, and a small window slid open. She told the faceless doorkeeper Jackson had sent her, and when asked for the password, she whispered, "Ain't behavin'."

Danger and delight grow on one stalk.

—SCOTTISH PROVERB

35

The wooden door opened. Kathleen stepped into a lobby where a doorman held open another door and beckoned her into a new world. Electricity surged through her.

She marveled at it all. Soul-tearing jazz poured from polished instruments. Della Robbia statues guarded the band on the stage. Sculptured light fixtures illuminated beautifully clad patrons moving in time to the rhythm.

Someone jostled her. She moved away from the crowded entrance and maneuvered between patrons toward the long, curving bar.

"Cut a rug, doll?" A hand slipped into hers.

A pleasant guy about her age winked at her. "I'll buy you a drink."

A lock of blond hair fell across his forehead, reminding her of someone.

"Or maybe two," she said and crinkled her nose.

Before they stepped onto the dance floor, Kathleen caught the rhythm and her toes took over. Once on the floor, her legs and arms responded to the rapid pace of "Yes, We have No Bananas" and, without stopping, the music slid into the Charleston.

His eyes sparkled. She beamed. The music paused. Breathing hard, he said, "Let's get those drinks and catch our breath."

The band started playing "Ain't We Got Fun?" and she couldn't help but do her imitation of Bea Palmer's shoulder shimmy. He hooted.

Others clapped and spread out to give her room. She glanced around and saw their desire—they were clapping for her to continue. They wanted to see those magic moves of this often forbidden dance, the Shimmy.

Kathleen ramped up her smiles and movements. The band pushed up their tempo, encouraging more from her. She felt it. They loved her. When the band stopped, Kathleen soaked in the applause. Out of breath, she smiled, grabbed the handsome blond man's arm, and headed to the bar.

At the bar, he moved in close and lit her cigarette.

She lowered her lashes and said, "Guess no one *here* wants the Shimmy banned."

"You're good." His raised eyebrow made her laugh.

He lit his own cigarette, took a long drag, and slowly let it slide out the side of his mouth.

"Tell the bartender I'm thirsty."

"I love to see you shimmy."

She gave him her over the shoulder look.

He waved to the bartender and ordered two of something.

"Give me a private show." He slipped an arm around her and pressed her next to him.

His boldness made her uneasy. "You're a fast mover." She took her drink from the bartender.

"To you and me, babe." He held his glass up for her to clink.

Kathleen shrugged and touched her glass to his. She sipped. *Absinthe.*

"Absinthe does not make this heart grow fonder." She slammed the glass down and turned away.

"Hell, lady, it's hot stuff—and expensive."

She heard a soprano voice next to her say, "If she's too good for it, I'll drink with you."

A sultry brunette in a beaded green dress sidled up to him.

Kathleen shoved away from the bar and moved through the crowd. *Damn Martin.*

"Hold on, lovely." A Northwood lumberjack–looking guy disguised in evening clothes touched her arm. "Anyone who dances like you should be happy."

"And you should be felling trees somewhere up north, not down here flirting." Something about his eyes reminded her of Martin.

"What's your pleasure?" He gave a slight bow.

"Bourbon and water."

"Meet my friends." He escorted her to a booth of young men and cooing flappers. "I'll be right back."

They made room for her, and Lumberjack guy left. No one bothered to introduce themselves, but they included Kathleen as if she belonged. She soon caught the thread of their conversation.

One of them said, "Can you believe—Johnson's 100th shutout—"

Kathleen smirked. "Three to zero—poor Yanks."

"Hey, you listened to the game." One of the guys cocked his head.

Lumberjack guy reappeared with her drink and one for himself. He slipped in beside her and joined the merriment. She snuggled back into the soft leather, enjoying the conversations and music.

Occasionally Lumberjack guy would whisper something naughty in her ear about one of the others.

"If she's about to get it on with him, he's in real trouble."

"Why?" Kathleen raised her eyebrow.

"He slammed the little fella in the automobile door today. It's all bandaged."

The two of them howled with laughter. No one seemed to notice.

She wiped her eyes and looked beyond their happy group. Someone familiar stood at the far end of the long bar, watching her. She couldn't place him. A twinge of uncertainty shot through her. She sat up straighter. She'd seen him—where? Not tall, not good looking, but not bad looking.

It's the bodyguard who gave me the code to get in this place—he had no right to follow me.

Someone behind him leaned in and said something to him.

Martin?

She nudged Lumberjack guy. "Excuse me, please. I need to get out. And thanks, you're all the cat's pajamas, and thanks for the drink."

She thought she'd have to climb over him, but he stood. She scooted out and stared at Martin.

Martin watched her and said something else to the bodyguard. He crossed the room toward her. Her heart raced.

Lumberjack guy leaned down and whispered in her ear. "Is he someone special?"

"Quite."

Martin stopped and studied the two of them.

"My loss." Lumberjack guy motioned to Martin by holding his open palm out toward Kathleen, then he slipped back into the booth.

Martin reached for her hand. She gave it to him. His warm fingers wrapped around hers. He led her onto the dance floor and pulled her in close. With his arms around her, she savored the warmth of his firm hand pressing on the small of her back.

They moved to the music in her heart.

A thread will tie an honest man better than a chain a rogue.
—SCOTTISH PROVERB

36

Kathleen lost the time, the crowd, the world. With Martin holding her, she glided with him to the sounds of the music. When the band jazzed up, they stepped, twirled, and blended into the beat.

"You're the smoothest dancer." She snuggled into him when the band finally stopped. "Your feet never touch the floor."

He took her to a small table, indicating he'd be right back.

She freshened her lipstick, wishing she had some sweet-smelling powder for her underarms, and waited. He returned with two drinks.

He squeezed the quarter lime from the rim of his glass into his drink and dropped it in.

Kathleen did the same. He held his glass up, they clinked, and he swallowed.

She cast a doubting look at the lime-fruited dark drink and took a sip. Kathleen looked up into his eyes and smiled. "My goodness, this is heaven. What is it?"

"Cuba Libre"

"We're drinking to Cuba?"

"Ah, but you do like it." Martin sipped and held his glass high. "When Spain lost to the United States in the war with Cuba, one of the captains of the victorious US Army Corp ordered everyone a mixture of Cuban rum with Coca-Cola and a slice of lime and yelled a toast. 'Por Cuba Libre!'"

"Liberty for Cuba!" She sipped more.

"I've never found a more satisfying beverage." He took a large swallow. "I drink no other."

"As will I."

He rubbed the back of her neck and whispered, "Let's get out of here."

She finished her drink. He guided her toward the door, but he stopped next to Mac's appointed bodyguard, who still sat at the bar.

"Good man, go kick up your heels." He slipped the guard some bills. "I'll take care of her."

"Dammit, I don't need a knight to slay my dragons." She pulled back.

Martin chuckled, grabbed her hand, and trotted out the door and down the block to his automobile.

"Have to be careful around here." He opened the car door for her.

"Take care of yourself." She smirked. "I'll take care of me."

"My dear lovely lass, this area is full of pyromaniacs. I saw a lady start a fire right over there." He got in and started the engine.

Kathleen's face grew hot. He'd seen it all. Her with the two guys—the shimmy—

Before he shifted into gear, he drew her close. Kathleen's ears filled with the sound of her heart beating. He tilted her chin up. She opened her mouth in surprise. He smiled and let his finger stroke her lips. Quick little currents of energy swallowed up all her awkward moments.

Sadness returned to his eyes. He lowered his hands, returning them to the steering wheel and the gearshift. He accelerated and drove out into the traffic.

"Have I done something?" She heard her words falter.

"Of course not." He glanced at her. "Tell me, why the bodyguard?"

She fiddled with the chain on her evening bag. "After the speakeasy stabbing, Mac and Ed said they at least owed me this."

"What's behind all the fear?"

She wrapped the chain tight around one finger. This decent, honest, and solid man had come into her life. No more Chesters, and no more relationships built on dishonesty.

"Several months ago I became friends with a man, a married

man—only friends. Someone stabbed one of my classmates and appears to be stalking another classmate. Both of them were involved with the man."

Martin's jaw set. He watched the road and didn't glance at her.

Kathleen glanced down. "I thought I'd be safer here in Chicago."

"You've been threatened?"

"Someone threw a knife at me. I stumbled at the right moment, or I'd be dead now."

He remained quiet.

"This all happened when I lived in Minneapolis."

"What about the lass who got murdered in the nightclub?"

She sighed.

"I don't know. I do know I can't have those friends of Ed and Mac's sitting outside my apartment for the rest of my life. I want them gone."

"Aren't you pleased they care?"

"They make me feel guilty, and they make me doubt myself."

"I believe a strong woman sits next to me, not some brainless lass."

"Brainless enough to find herself in jeopardy because of some married man. Never again."

He glanced at her, then stared at the oncoming traffic and didn't speak.

When his automobile pulled up in front of her apartment building, she asked, "Will you come in?"

"Na, time to call the evening quits."

Her heart sank.

"I've been in business meetings all day and way into the evening. I'm off to sea tomorrow—have to be at the airport by five in the morning."

"You're upset with me."

He picked up her hand, stroked it. "If only life gave me different choices—"

"Tell me. You seem so sad."

He squeezed her hand, moved his gaze to her face, and stared deep into her eyes.

"Please." Kathleen's breath disappeared.

Martin stayed quiet for a moment. He released her hand, putting both of his on the steering wheel. He looked out the front windshield, and said, "My heart says to sweep you away to my hotel where we'd spend the hours away, locked in each other's arms."

Her heart warmed into melted butter.

"Tonight," he said, "with you, I—I almost forget my responsibilities, my troubles."

"Stay tonight—here."

In the glow of the lamplight she saw his sad eyes change into despair.

"What? Tell me." The coldness in his mood made her clutch his arm.

He pulled her close and nuzzled his face in her hair, then held her away from him at arm's length.

"Dear—dear Kathleen." He touched her cheek. "I—I am a married man."

Kathleen pulled away. She expected him to laugh at his joke.

He turned his face from hers. She caught the sadness in his eyes again.

He's telling the truth.

She grabbed the door handle, her whole body shaking. She started to get out but stopped and slammed the door shut.

"You ass. How dare you—? Any decent man would have told me when we first met." She swelled with angry heat, and then swung her small evening bag, hitting him on the arm. Tears filled her eyes. She didn't know how to stop the shaking, or what to do.

Martin held out his linen handkerchief. "Everyone else knows. I thought someone would have—"

"You *thought*? Well, they didn't. I'm always the fool." She snatched his handkerchief and dabbed at her eyes, ruining her makeup. "Worse yet, you let me go on. I hate you, Martin Davies. I hate you."

She threw his handkerchief back at him, opened the door, and dashed into the apartment building. She ran up the stairs, entered her own apartment, and didn't turn on the light. She went to the window, watching and sobbing. His motorcar didn't drive away.

Why didn't he leave?

Minutes later, he stepped out of his car and entered the apartment building. Her heart pounded wildly. She couldn't think. She heard the tapping on her door.

Kathleen wiped at her eyes, held her breath, and wondered if she should open it.

She opened it.

He stood there, hat shaking in his hand. "I have no right to say this, but I can't leave until I do. You've enchanted me from the first time I saw you." He paused and swallowed. "When I'm with you, I forget everything except how lovely you are, and how much I desire to be your companion. Please find a way to forgive me."

Kathleen watched as he put on his hat and disappeared down the stairs—and from her life.

Beggars cannot be choosers

—SCOTTISH PROVERB

37

Kathleen trudged up the hot sidewalk after dance practice. The late August heat with its mugginess sucked the joy from everything. Even though no one could convince Sophie to leave the Southside, it was Martin who had left Kathleen emotionally empty.

When she'd confessed to Brandy how she felt, Brandy hunted for ways to lift Kathleen's spirits. She'd suggested that since Kathleen could afford higher rent, an improved living space might help her mood.

Thanks, Pops, for teaching me the value of saving. Yet her resentment toward him made her decide to never put money into any damned bank. Kathleen expected her new apartment and having money to spend would erase the dull ache of wanting Martin. Nothing much helped.

Ed wore her out with his incessant night-clubbing, and Brandy introduced her to every handsome man available. Most of these jerks had their own agenda. She hated being pawed.

She should have known better when one of them took her to an opium den. He said she'd meet celebrities who would advance her career, but he only advanced his own crudeness. He had pointed to some Asian women and said, "Look, you could throw a cat between their legs." She'd never forget that crazy night of floor pillows, smoke-laden air, groping, and lies.

Whenever Martin returned to Chicago, he made sure their evenings together included at least Ed and Brandy. When he wasn't around, no one spoke of him. And that seemed to make Ed ecstatic. He obviously didn't want to share her with anyone.

Dammit, Martin.

Kathleen dipped her hand into her skirt pocket. *Crap.* Still carrying around Chester's watch wasn't helping.

She never had made that trip to the Rex Hotel where she bet he had found the debutante. Kathleen could afford a taxi now.

Why not go there this afternoon? Afterward, I'll check in on Sophie.

The debutante murder happened back in April. Memories became fuzzy over time, and she might lose her chance to find out about Chester if she didn't hurry.

Kathleen quickened her step and planned her questions.

She strode up the block near a warehouse and started to cross the street. A black sedan sped around the far corner. She moved back out of sight and peeked around. This extra ten-minute walk to her new apartment took her through a neighborhood she detested.

The automobile's brakes screech. It pulled into a parking space in front of a mom and pop bakery. Another black sedan came from the other direction and took the last parking space on the other side of the street.

Chicago living had taught her things. When black cars speed and skid to a stop, everyone needs to move far away. She slipped back around the corner of the warehouse.

Damned gangsters, such bullies. They act like they own everything. Car doors slammed. *They take anything whenever they want, and no one stops them. Someone should treat them way they treat everyone else.*

The two cars sat empty, but four men dashed into the bakery carrying Tommy guns.

She held her breath and watched. *Must be a front for a speakeasy.*

Another black limousine hurled up the street, slammed on its brakes, and double-parked. Two more men leaped out and sauntered through the front door of the bakery.

If she wanted to avoid this street, she'd have to walk an extra five blocks. She set her jaws and sprinted up the bakery street, heart pounding.

The police would shut traffic down when the murders started. Kathleen skirted wide around the bakery. If she owned an automobile she'd not have to worry about these things or about calling taxis to take her to the Rex.

When she neared the double-parked vehicle, she slowed. *What the—? They left the motor running.*

Kathleen fingered the pocket watch. *To hell them and this crappy summer.*

She lunged to the idling vehicle and jerked open the door. *And to hell with taxis.*

Her left foot landed on the running board and the other plunged inside the car. Kathleen, heart racing, threw her pocketbook on the seat. It flew open and contents spilled on the floor. She jerked the door shut, pushed the clutch in, shifted the automobile into first, lurched forward, shifted into second, and, pitching ahead faster, moved into third. She floor boarded it down the street, howling in delight, taking the corner on two wheels.

Giddy with adrenaline, she forced herself to slow and use extreme care while weaving her way over to State Street. If an officer stopped her she'd get more than a ticket for reckless driving. After a few blocks Kathleen lit up a cigarette and reveled in her ride. This luxurious limousine, smaller than most, reeked of real leather.

She slowed, absorbing the experience, and promised herself one day she'd drive her own luxury motorcar. She might even drive it from New York all the way to California. She drove down State Street.

Hello, Mother. Want to go to California? I'll drive you there in my new automobile. Somewhere, deep inside, an empty spot held a longing to be with her mother.

Kathleen rubbed her hand over the soft leather seat. When she finished at the Rex, she'd drive around and check out where Sophie worked. Her face hurt from grinning.

Those gangsters stole from everyone. It's their turn.

She laughed out loud.

But when they saw their automobile missing, they'd be wildcats let out of a cage. They'd hunt her down and—and—no one would be laughing then.

Damn.

Kathleen drove past Twenty-First Street. *How do you get rid of a hot automobile?*

She found a parking spot on Twenty-Second Street next to the Rex. An unshaven guy about her age leaned against the lamppost and gave her the once-over.

Kathleen's skin crawled.

She crushed her cigarette in the ashtray and leaned over to pick up her lipstick and the other spilled contents. Some indistinguishable noise nearby gave her the heebie-jeebies.

Ignoring it, Kathleen continued to stuff everything back into her handbag. She smelled something rank and saw movement out of the corner of her eye. She glanced at the window.

An unshaved face leered at her. She yelped.

Rolling up the window, Kathleen shouted at him to go away. He laughed and sauntered off. She climbed out and slipped the car key in her pocket next to Chester's watch.

Most of the buildings looked overused. Signage seemed skimpy, tasteless, and old. An elderly woman carried a bundle of laundry up a flight of stairs. Some men stood on the corner chewing tobacco. The vibrancy of this area felt lacking. It didn't measure up to the neighborhoods farther north.

She pushed through the doors of the Rex and went over to the bored-looking desk clerk.

"Excuse me, who worked this desk last spring?"

"Not answerin' any questions."

"My brother, he's missing, and the police closed his case." Kathleen pouted and batted her eyelashes. "They won't reopen it because they say he's choosing to stay 'missing.'" She leaned in closer to him. "I'm desperate to find him. Mother's dying and—"

"Don't want trouble, miss."

"My brother's scared. He doesn't know the police solved the case. He's not a suspect anymore."

He wrote something in a ledger, ignoring her. The elderly desk clerk seemed entrenched behind the counter.

"You worked here then, didn't you?"

"What case you talkin' about?" The desk clerk shifted on his stool and glanced around. No one seemed to pay any attention.

"Remember the debutante who drowned in the river? She left here with a man." Kathleen wrapped her fingers around the watch.

"Nope, don't remember. I remember the story, but don't remember her leavin' with any man. The police questioned me. I had nothin' to say."

Chester and the girl probably left from the speakeasy, not the hotel.

"Here's a photo." Kathleen cracked a winning smile. "He's ten to fifteen years older now and taller than I am. He's quite annoying. Did you notice him cracking his knuckles? Bet you'd never do that."

The desk clerk looked around again and picked up a newspaper. He shook it out, held it up, and prepared to read.

Kathleen's heart sank.

"This guy, who could be your brother, I'm not saying he is, checked out right after he saw the photo of the dead girl in the morning's newspaper. I remember because he broke out in a sweat, threw his room key at the cash register, and yelled at me to hurry—he wanted his change back. Who killed the girl?"

"Some woman badger. Do you know where he went?"

"Sure. Murder suspects always say, 'Hey, Jasper, I'm out of here—on my way to Tennessee 'cause I killed someone.'"

"Right. Thanks for your help anyway." She stared at him for a response. She didn't get it, so she started to leave.

He called to her, "Miss."

She looked back.

"I heard him on that phone over there asking what time the next bus left. Said he didn't care where."

She thanked him and walked out into the hot sun and over to the limousine. Kathleen needed to find the nearest bus station, ditch the automobile somewhere, and call a taxi. She opened the driver's door, pulled out the key, and stepped up on the running board.

Something hard jabbed into her ribs. She jumped and gasped. The object bit deeper into her side.

The smelly bastard from the lamppost stood next to her.

"Don't make a sound, babe. Me and you is going for a ride."

She stiffened. *Don't panic.* But her heart flew around her ribcage.

She'd never expected a gun, only a knife in her ribs. He shoved it even harder.

"Oow. Stop that."

"Shut up."

What a little creep. Kathleen's summer of disappointment resurfaced in one big rush. Her internal temperature soared. *If I'm going to be murdered, it sure as hell won't be by this idiot.*

He moved in close to her ear and said, "Climb in nice and slow. You'll drive your beautiful motorcar to wherever I say."

His breath smelled of stale blood from rotting teeth. The angry furnace roared within her. She slammed her other foot into the car, watching him. He opened the back door behind the driver's seat, keeping the pistol leveled at her temple.

She stopped moving and glared at him.

How dare he.

He wagged the gun at her.

"I don't need reminding. I'm not stupid." She clamped her teeth. "Get in."

Kathleen edged forward—she hated being bossed. He wiped at the sweat dripping off his forehead then leaned into the back seat.

"Bastard!" She flung the ignition key into traffic and threw herself on the floorboards.

"What the fuck—?"

He lunged into the street. Car's honked and swerved. Kathleen scrambled out the passenger's door, then bolted back into the hotel.

"Jasper, someone's after me."

He yanked her behind his desk and ran to the window. "Don't see nothin' out there except some bum drivin' away in one of Big Al's deputies' limousines."

Kathleen stopped breathing. "Big Al?"

"The deputy who drives it comes in here all the time."

She burst out laughing. "The bum's in for one hell of a surprise when he finds out it's not *my* car."

Jasper looked down at the wooden floor planks. He didn't join in her laughter.

"What's going on?" Kathleen touched the elderly man's shoulder.

"Didn't think I had any business telling you, but I like you." He sat back on his stool. "That brother of yours, he's pretty worthless. I didn't much like him the few days he stayed here."

Kathleen remained silent.

"I don't think he left town. I saw him going into one of those flop houses down the street about a month ago."

He that won't be counseled can't be helped.

—BENJAMIN FRANKLIN

38

Her little sister ran down the stairway, slapping a stick against the balustrades. The noise filled the air with an awful rat-a-tat-rat-a-tat sound.

Why didn't mother make her stop?

Kathleen snuggled deeper under her winter comforter. Someone knocked again and again on her apartment door. Kathleen opened her eyes to darkness.

She didn't move. The knocking continued. She'd open the door all right, if nothing more than to strangle the person.

Kathleen flipped on her bedroom lamp and tiptoed, shivering, through the living room. She plastered her ear against the door but quickly straightened. What had she expected to come of that?

More knocking. Dolly called out, "Kathleen, it's me."

Kathleen unlocked the door, and Dolly pushed through, wearing a white cotton jumpsuit with her hair tucked under a cap bearing the words *Bowman*.

"You're delivering milk now?"

"I wanted a disguise. That's how I got here." Dolly hugged herself. "It's cold out there."

"Where's your milk?" Kathleen looked around for her cigarettes.

"Stop it, Kathleen." Dolly flopped on the couch. "You'll be glad I came when I tell you."

"Did you walk here in the dark looking like that?" Kathleen flipped on the kitchen light and glanced around the counter tops.

"I swear you're worse than a toothache."

"Why are you still sneaking around?" Kathleen found her cigarettes behind some books. "No one's after you."

"You don't know that. A couple of months ago, you said Chester still lived in Chicago."

"I said he might be here. That's all." She found her matches nearby.

"But we can't be sure he didn't kill Lillian."

Kathleen slid down into the chair, pulled the mink off its back, and snuggled into her coat.

Dolly's eyes widened. "I didn't know you got a mink too."

"Maybe next spring we'll get you one, if no one's murdered you by then." She lit her cigarette.

"I have two things to tell you. Sophie left to go to work tonight, but she never came back. I know because I listen for her to come in."

"Is she always home before morning?"

"Always. And I overheard Mrs. Taylor talking to someone about you. I stayed at the top of the stairs—didn't want to be seen, but I needed to go because Mabel and I walk to work together. Still, I had to know what Mrs. Taylor would say."

"Male or female?" Kathleen blew out a smoke ring.

"Don't know. They talked over the telephone."

"Hold it." Kathleen's stomach flipped. Being fully awake made her fully aware. "How did you know where to find me?"

"Sophie told us all about your new apartment." Dolly removed her cap and shook out her hair. She'd cut off her long curls. She'd probably done the butchering herself.

Kathleen prickled. She'd pleaded with Sophie not to tell anyone. If Sophie couldn't figure out a consequence for telling something, she'd spill everything.

Dolly yawned. "When I heard the milkman in his truck clanging bottles up the block, I waited downstairs. When he delivered bottles to Mrs. Taylor's, I asked if I could bum a ride. He'd already made his deliveries over here, but I got him to agree. He even let me wear his extra coveralls and hat."

Kathleen wondered what to do with her.

"If Sophie's home, now she'll be worried about me." Dolly chewed her lip. "I don't know what to do."

"Makes two of us. When it's a reasonable hour, use my telephone and call Mrs. Taylor, ask if Sophie is there, and tell her you're with me." Kathleen's patience had drained away.

"Sophie said you had a bodyguard. Is that true?"

"I'm going to bed." Kathleen stubbed out her cigarette.

Dolly pouted. Kathleen pointed to the sofa.

"You can sleep there. And when you call Mrs. Taylor," Kathleen couldn't help her gruff voice, "don't give her my telephone number or my address. Got it?"

Part of her ill mood came from worrying about Sophie.

"Will your bodyguards take me to work?" Dolly's eyes lit up.

"Criminetly, girl. This isn't some game. Call your work, tell them you're sick, and hang out here for the day."

"Are you staying home too?"

"I've got to go to practice. After you talk with Mrs. Taylor, call me at work and tell me what you know."

Dolly pulled her lips in.

"Let's catch a few more winks, then you make the call to Mrs. Taylor. I bet Sophie will be home by then. If not, we'll think of something."

"Stay home so we can figure this out." Dolly's forehead crinkled.

"Nope, I'm leaving here at eight-thirty." A new roommate was the last thing Kathleen wanted. "Please don't spend time looking out the window, don't go anywhere, don't let anyone in, and don't tell anyone where this place is."

"You're awfully bossy."

This truth caused Kathleen to suck in a breath. "I'm upset about Sophie. Guess I'm taking it out on you."

"That's okay. Aren't you even curious about that telephone call?"

"At this point I'm too exhausted to care. Sophie's another matter." She'd talk with Mrs. Taylor about the telephone person.

"Remember how mad you were at me over Chester? Maybe there's another woman who has a reason to be even madder at both of us—and Lillian. I suspect his wife."

"You obviously don't know her. She's a kind and decent lady."

Kathleen studied the girl. It wasn't the Chester thing that caused her to dislike Dolly. She wasn't a dumb Dora, and she seemed friendly to everyone, especially the guys, but she managed to be a big pain in the derriere.

Dolly sighed. "This is all so balled up. It's the only reason I came here tonight. I thought you would want to know about Sophie and the telephone call."

"I'll be off work by four-thirty, and I'll get something for dinner. Early tomorrow morning you can catch a ride with your favorite milkman." Kathleen plopped down on the couch next to Dolly and lit a cigarette.

Dolly nodded toward the cigarettes. "Who do you think killed Lillian?"

"My theory?" Kathleen tossed the cigarettes to her. "Lillian didn't see the knife because she trusted someone and let them close to her. Maybe they threw it at her like that person threw one at me."

"You know, if Chester's still around, he could have killed the flapper who looked like you."

"But he wouldn't need to cut your photo, or Lillian's, out of the school's book." Kathleen blew out a smoke ring. "What woman would hone knife-throwing skills to murder someone? Women seem more inclined to use poison, don't you think?"

"I'd want to pick something less messy." Dolly looked pale. "Even a gun."

Kathleen flicked ash into a tray. "I know a woman who may have drowned her child in the bathtub. The authorities called it an accident because they couldn't prove otherwise. This same woman kicked the ladder out from under her husband, causing him to fall to his death. Again they couldn't prove anything. If this woman kills people, I can't imagine her using something as messy as a knife to bloody her so-called stylish clothes."

"Does this woman live in Minneapolis?" Dolly tilted her head, waiting.

"She does."

"Do you know her?"

"I do, but only because my mother knows her." Kathleen stubbed out the cigarette. She promised herself she'd not smoke anymore until lunch break.

Dolly picked at the embroidery on her cap and didn't look up. "Do you think that woman is here in Chicago now?"

39

Irene started with warm-up exercises, and then Freddy played a lead-in to a new routine.

Crap. They had just mastered one new routine, and now Irene would push them into another series of unfamiliar of moves. Lunch couldn't come soon enough.

"Miss McPherson, are you with us this morning? Saturday night one of you will be the standby in case someone actually breaks a leg or something equally stupid."

This threat sent enough fear to create a visible zing in everyone's kicks and turns. Kathleen would not be anyone's standby. She gave Irene and her dance instructions full attention until they stopped for lunch.

Kathleen grabbed a bar towel, wiped her face and neck, and saw Sophie wrapped in her fur, sitting at a back table in the darkest corner of the room. She sprinted over and gasped.

Sophie's face looked old. Dark circles showed under her eyes. She'd split her lip and her eye was swollen. The rest of her face, in contrast, seemed pale, as if she'd powdered it with flour.

"Soph, what's wrong? How long have you been here?"

Sophie stared at Kathleen, swallowed, but didn't speak.

"Come on, Sophie, tell me . . . tell me something."

She shook her head. "I'm fine. I came to see how you are." She smiled, burst into tears, and covered her face.

Kathleen slipped down beside her and held on until Sophie quieted. Sophie pulled back, found her hanky, and dabbed her eyes.

"Sorry."

"I'm listening."

"Pritchard said I should find another place to work. But he hasn't seen my bank account. Now I can pay for Dolly's room and mine. I've never been able to buy fancy clothes. I even send money home to mom. When I sing, everyone applauds, calls for more, and once someone even threw me a bouquet. Remember? Last spring you said they would. They treat me well—or at least they did until the boss heard I might leave—"

"Pritchard said you had to—how long ago was that?"

"This guy came up to me after rehearsal . . . he slapped me and yelled, waving some papers at me. I guess I signed a contract. He said I'm theirs for the next twenty-four months. He shoved me hard, and when I fell he walked out. Everyone just stood around. I thought they were my friends."

Kathleen slid an arm around her.

"No one did anything . . . I'm so embarrassed." She flushed and tears trickled down her cheeks.

"You're not going back."

"I have to . . . I don't remember signing any contract. Did you sign a contract to work here?"

"There are no contracts. Stay with me. We'll find you another place to work."

"I have to go back, Kathleen. I only came here to ask about the contracts."

"How can you even think about returning? You're a mess."

"When Hymie came through the door and saw me, he screamed at everyone and hollered for ice. He's good to me. Said he'd take care of the matter. Said no one would ever lay a hand on me again."

"Baloney. You can't trust him." They had set her up. The guy smacked her, making her afraid, and then Hymie ran in to rescue her, making her feel safe.

"When he came in and yelled, everybody jumped and did what he asked. He's got power. He's nice to me. Look at this locket." She tugged an impressive gold chain with a heart-shaped locket out from under her collar.

"Did you spend last night with him?" Kathleen's stomach soured.

Sophie tucked the locket back down her blouse. "We went to his place where he called a nurse to tend to my lip and eye. Then he ordered a steak dinner with champagne sent up to his suite. We talked and talked."

"That does it." Kathleen scowled. "Dolly and I fretted for hours wondering what happened to you."

"Kath, I didn't sleep with him or anything like that. He's a kind and good man."

"You're going to my apartment now. You stay there until I get home. We'll figure this out." She hated sounding like her mother.

"I won't hide out like Dolly." She stood.

"I'm not letting you go back, Soph. Pritchard's right."

Sophie stared at Kathleen then said, "I understand you want to keep me safe. But—"

"And even Ed and Mac say bad things happen on the Southside." Kathleen.grabbed her arms. "You wouldn't let me go back if this situation were reversed."

Sophie's eyes glazed over. "Considering what could happen, Hymie's my best choice."

"He's a terrible choice. He's using you. You're young and good looking—with talent. But you're naïve, Sophie. Just because someone's nice to you doesn't mean these are good people. They must be making lots of money off your talent. They have to keep you. Hymie's their tool for doing that because they can't keep smacking you around. They can't have you appear on stage with split lips and blackened eyes."

"I have to stay for twenty-four months. I am afraid of that other guy."

"Mac and his friends will protect you."

"I won't live my life in hiding." Sophie stared at the floor and said, "Hymie will protect me."

"He won't. Can't you see? Oh, Sophie. How can I make you understand? This world isn't a kind place. You're such a gentle, innocent person." Kathleen's heart beat crazily. "Sit with me. We'll come up with something better."

Sophie shook her head. "Neither of us knows what to do about this, do we?"

Kathleen watched her as she walked out the door. She'd never seen Sophie look totally hopeless before. Kathleen should have run away by herself, not foisted all these troubles onto Sophie.

Her stomach churned. She called Dolly and told her she'd seen Sophie.

Mac came over and waited for her to hang up. "Doesn't your friend work somewhere down on the Southside?"

"She does."

"Why's she headed toward the lake on a cold, miserable day like today?"

They that know no evil will suspect none.
—BEN JONSON

40

Kathleen grabbed her coat, tore out the door and down the walk, waited until the traffic cleared, crossed over to the park, and ran toward the lake. The chilly autumn wind sent most of the park people elsewhere. She didn't see Sophie.

Kathleen's breath was coming in heaves by the time she stepped onto the boards of the pier.

Sophie stood halfway down between Kathleen and the end of the dock, her blonde hair flying above her brown fur coat.

Kathleen shouted her name, but her words were lost into the wind. *Oh crap, Sophie, don't do this.*

When she could be heard, Kathleen called out again. "Sophie, I've something to tell you."

"Go away." Sophie pulled a brown bottle up to her lips and took a swig.

Panting, and holding her side, Kathleen slowed and walked carefully up to her friend.

"Lovely day for a little nip of hooch on the dock." Kathleen gave her a big smile.

Sophie didn't look up. She seemed to be staring down at the churning water, watching the dock-tied boats bump into each other.

"Aren't you going to share?" Kathleen held out her hand.

Sophie shook her head and took another long swig.

"This isn't you. What's going on?" She should have spent less time with Brandy and more with Sophie.

"Leave me—alone." Her words were slurred.

"Come on back, Soph. Let's get out of this wind." She put her arms around Sophie's shoulders.

"You go." She drained the bottle and slung it far out into the water.

Kathleen looked down at the cold, black waves sloshing against the pylons. She pulled Sophie around to face her and said, "I'm not going to have any drownings on my conscience. Forget it."

Sophie stumbled back. "You don't know what it's like, and you haven't seen what I've seen, and you don't even know how they operate." Her words slopped over her tongue. "We—you and I and these other girls—they *own* us."

Kathleen grabbed Sophie and shook her. "Listen to me—look at me."

"Go, Kath, I have to figure things out. It's about me and Hymie against those others." She made tiny whimpering sounds.

"Hymie won't care. He'll find some other innocent girl. You can't trust him."

"You're wrong. He said he loves me, but he has to make sure I'm not one of those two-timers." She found her fingernail to chew.

Kathleen looked out across the lake. "He'll always be suspicious. We've seen movies like that. Ugly stuff."

"It doesn't make any difference anyhow." Sophie lowered her chin and closed her eyes.

Kathleen's own teeth chattered. "I'm freezing. Let's go."

She didn't respond.

"Think of what this news would do to your mother. 'Blonde singer in full-mink coat pulled from Lake Michigan. Foul play suspected because of various bruises on face and torso.' For heaven's sake, you can't have your mother read that about her little girl."

She knew Sophie had listened because the whimpering sounds stopped. She removed strands of Sophie's hair from her face. The wind whipped them back.

"She'll think you were whoring to get a mink coat. She'd never understand otherwise. You, being dead as a mackerel, wouldn't have the opportunity to tell her the truth. Come on."

Kathleen reached for Sophie's arm.

"I'm not going." Sophie shoved Kathleen hard with both hands.

Kathleen stepped back to catch her balance, but there was nothing under her heel. Only air. She grabbed for something, anything . . . nothing . . .

Before the dark waves consumed her, she saw Sophie's mouth opening and her blue eyes—wide—peering down from above.

On down through cold-shocking-wet darkness, deeper she plunged, buffeted one way by swells and then the other, but constantly going deeper into the wet and cold. Shoes off—gone—purse caught—nose bumped—frozen—hurt—rocks scraping—pieces of wood—wonderful soft wood in her hands—darkness—black crawling into her thoughts—in the corners of her head—erasing cold—erasing everything—erasing.

Then tingling, thoughts emerging, distant sounds, warm hands on her.

"Kath?" Sophie's voice and sobs.

Kathleen's confused mind couldn't sort it out. All she saw was wetness—wet grains in wood with embedded sand. She raised her head to better see the wooden planks of the pier beneath her. Sophie's chocolate-brown mink covered her.

"You fell—over the edge—the ladder—you could have frozen to death."

"The ladder?"

"Golly, don't you remember? Let's get out of this wind. I'm freezing."

"You pulled me up the ladder? How could you do that?" Kathleen shivered hard enough to break her bones.

"Hurry," Sophie said. "This wind cuts worse than razor blades." She helped Kathleen to her feet. "Where're your shoes? Oh, right. Walking will help keep you warm."

Kathleen took a step and stumbled. She caught herself and stood looking down the pier all the way to the park.

"Can't you hurry?" Sophie leaned her head in close to the fur of the coat. "I can't feel my fingers."

Kathleen stopped and lifted one foot. She brushed at the bottom of it. "Crap—boards full of splinters. My feet—the cold—my toes will fall off." She limped down the pier with Sophie holding on to her elbow.

"We're almost there." Sophie's teeth chattered. She moved her hand farther down Kathleen's wrist and buried it under the sleeves of her fur. Sophie had no coat.

"Wait," Kathleen stopped. "Where's *my* fur coat?"

"I threw it in the lake. Hurry, Kath. We'll both die of hypothermia."

"My mink . . ." Now Kathleen wanted to cry. "Sophie, how could you?"

"Have you ever seen a drowned bear?"

Kathleen groaned. "But you're not strong enough to pull me out of the water." Even though Kathleen wore the coat, her teeth chattered "You couldn't climb down the ladder and pull me out."

"I didn't."

"But I felt your hands."

"Rubbed your hands—to get them warm. Covered you with my coat. Can we talk about this when we get someplace warm? I'm about to die here."

"How'd I get up the ladder?" It hurt to walk. She couldn't take another step, but she did.

"You climbed it. Don't you remember anything? Golly, Kath, your nose is bleeding. You must have hit it on something."

Kathleen didn't remember the park being this wide. She couldn't help limping. Her hair stuck to her skin, plastered tight. She touched it. *Ice?* She shoved her numb fingers down into the coat pockets.

Sophie shivered uncontrollably.

They arrived at the street. "Kath, do you want to go to the Congress Hotel instead of Friar's Inn? It's right here." Sophie's teeth chattered.

"Let's. Give me a cigarette. We'll call Ed. He'll take us home."

When we remember we are all mad, the mysteries disappear, and life stands explained.

—MARK TWAIN

41

When Kathleen, Ed, and Sophie entered Kathleen's apartment, Dolly jumped up and stood, staring, her mouth open. Kathleen dripped water everywhere.

"Dolly, what are you—a cracked milkman?" Sophie said. "Why are you here?"

"Why is Kathleen's all wet?" Dolly cocked her head. "And your eye—"

"Later." Sophie slipped the coat off Kathleen.

"I'm at a loss." Ed plopped down in the chair. "Don't know how to help."

"You could put the kettle on for tea," Sophie said. "We need to warm up."

"I'll do it." Dolly skittered into the kitchen and put the kettle under the faucet. "I know where everything is in this place." She set it on the stove, lit the burner, and turned the knob to high.

Ed, looking quite uncomfortable, watched the girls. Sophie guided Kathleen to the bedroom and helped her out of her wet clothes and into a nighty. Dolly took a blanket out of the closet to put on the bed and went back to her tea assignment.

Sophie tucked Kathleen in. "I need a Band-Aid."

Dolly called out, "You won't find medical supplies of any kind in this place."

Kathleen bristled at Dolly's snooping, then she remembered Irene's break-a-leg and standby comment. She let out a soft groan.

"What's wrong?" Sophie darted back to the bed.

"I'm missing practice. I'll end up being the standby for Saturday's performance."

Sophie looked down at Kathleen. "You're quite battered. There's no way you could dance today, and probably not tomorrow either."

Ed stuck his head in the doorway. "I'll stop by the club and tell them you'll be off for a few days."

"Are you leaving now?" Sophie's voice sounded distressed.

"I shouldn't?"

"I wanted to stay a little longer, warm up, be sure Kath's okay. I'd hoped you'd drive me to work." Sophie bit her lip and looked at the floor.

Kathleen reached up and touched her. "Sophie, stay here. Dolly will leave early in the morning and you and I can spend the day together. We'll figure this out."

Sophie shook her head. "Go on, I'll call a taxi. I can't have Hymie see me drive up in an automobile with a good-looking guy."

"Good looking?" He positioned his hat on his head, touched the brim in a pseudo salute, and left.

"Tea's ready." Dolly carried a cup to Kathleen and handed one to Sophie.

"I'm so cold my bones feel brittle." Sophie reached for her coat, then spread it out. "It's wet. Wait, what's this?" She held up the sleeve. "Dammit, Kathleen, you burned a cigarette hole in the fur—right here!"

Kathleen set her cup down and squinted. "Where? Oh poop, Sophie, you can barely see it."

"I see it. My coat's ruined."

"You're overly sensitive about everything right now." Kathleen patted Sophie's hand. "No one will even know."

"But I know it's there."

Dolly leaned over and touched the coat. "Where did all the water come from?"

"I'll tell you." Sophie took a swallow of her tea then said, "After you tell me why you're dressed as some crazed milkman with a bad haircut."

Kathleen interrupted. "What can I say to keep you from going back there?"

"What choice do I have? It's four o'clock. I'll call a taxi."

"Will you keep in touch?" Kathleen grabbed Sophie's hand.

"Of course."

"I hate the thought of you being with Hymie." Kathleen let loose of Sophie's hand. "I'm worried sick."

Dolly held out Sophie's mink. "Goes double for me."

Sophie draped the wet mink over her shoulders. "I'll be back at Mrs. Taylor's right after my show."

"But last night—Hymie might expect you—" Kathleen heard Dolly gasp.

"You slept with a man last night?"

Sophie's face reddened. "How dare you. He only comforted me, that's all. *I'm* not seeing some married man. I've got to hurry. I'll need lots of makeup tonight."

Kathleen hated not knowing how to persuade Sophie.

Sophie hesitated then said, "After today on the pier, I've decided this is my best choice. They'll never let me work anywhere else."

She headed toward the door with Dolly following.

When Dolly returned she picked up the tea cups and said, "I'm sorry about what happened to you. Is there anything else I can do?"

I'm losing my mind—I almost like this girl.

"Thanks, but I can't keep my eyes open. I promised I'd make dinner, but—"

"Oh don't give it a thought. I'll fix myself a cheese sandwich. Unless you want to go to sleep, I'll fix you one too."

Believe nothing and be on your guard against everything.
—LATIN PROVERB

42

"Kathleen?" Sophie called from the other side of the door. "Kath? Are you awake?"

"Of course," Kathleen rasped. She had no voice. She turned toward the window. *Dark outside.*

"Unlock the door."

Kathleen struggled out of bed, turned on the light, let Sophie in, and relocked the door.

"How're you feeling?" Sophie, with a small jar of something and a sack, headed to the kitchen area.

"I'll live. Where's Dolly?" Kathleen slipped back into bed.

"Dolly caught her ride back to Mrs. Taylor's this morning. Someone needed to care for you, and she shouldn't miss any more work." Sophie carried in a cup and a plate, set them on the bedside table, and handed the cup to Kathleen.

Kathleen sniffed but couldn't smell anything.

"Beef broth. Mrs. Taylor made it for you. It's supposed to be healing. Here's some crackers too."

Kathleen sipped. Sophie still looked miserable.

"Kath, I have to tell you something. I'm going to work in a few minutes, but it's getting more difficult."

"Because . . . ?"

"Lots of things. The guy who slapped me around stood right off stage last night the whole time I sang and watched everything I did."

"What about Hymie, your protector?" The warm broth slid down her throat, soothing out the roughness.

"He came in as I finished. He wanted me to come upstairs to his suite, but I told him I had to go. I said my best friend needed help, being sick and all. I'm not ready to spend the night with him. I haven't figured this out yet—like how I feel about him and where this is going."

Kathleen set the cup down, not looking at Sophie. Her insides felt twisted because she couldn't come up with anything to say.

"I hate being trapped, Kath." Sophie chewed her fingernail.

Kathleen took Sophie's hand away from her mouth and held it. "You will be if you go back."

"We've had this discussion." Sophie picked up the cup and took it to the kitchen. When she returned, she bent over Kathleen, gave her a peck on the cheek, and said, "I'll stop in tomorrow evening before I go to work. Feel better, okay?"

"Take this." Kathleen handed Sophie a key. "If you need to hide out, come here."

Someone knocked on the door.

"Who's there?" Kathleen rose. Color drained from Sophie's face.

"The most handsome Ed comes knocking at your door with important news for the ladies."

Sophie unlocked the door. Ed stepped in, removed his hat, and nodded at the two of them. His somber face didn't match his jovial greeting from the other side of the door.

"Something's wrong, isn't it?" Kathleen fumbled for her robe. Pulling it around her, she crumpled on the couch and tucked her bare feet under herself to keep them warm.

"Afraid so." Ed watched Kathleen get situated, and he motioned for Sophie to sit.

"I've got to leave, Ed. I'll be late if I don't go now."

"You better stay put." Ed pointed again at the sofa.

"But . . ." Sophie shrugged and perched on the arm of the couch.

"Some big guy with a neck thick as a rhino came into Friar's looking for you. He told Freddy you were Kathleen's blonde singer friend. He demanded to know if you'd been there. Freddy told him you hadn't been in today, but you might be at Kathleen's."

"That's the guy who slapped me around." Her eyes widened. She looked toward the door, stood, then sat again.

Kathleen groaned. "Please say Freddy didn't tell him where I live." She dreaded what Ed would say next.

"I don't understand why he'd be looking for me."

Kathleen sighed. "Because Hymie probably thinks you're running around with some guy and not really taking care of a sick friend." She looked up at Ed. "What did Freddy tell him?"

"Nothing. Just that you weren't there. You were sick."

"What a relief." Kathleen relaxed.

"When the big guy started smacking little Freddy around, Wart came in and shot the big guy. Left quite a mess over by the piano."

"Good God. Now what?" Kathleen jumped up. "Is Freddy okay?"

Sophie's voice shook. "I've probably lost my job." She stood and began pacing to the kitchen and back.

"Freddy's kind of messed up, but he'll be fine," Ed said. "Everyone's nervous. They thought maybe this was another turf war starting." Ed sat. "Wart used the excuse to shoot the big jerk because he slapped Freddy around. But Wart didn't care about Freddy, he actually wanted to settle some score for one of Moran's guys."

"How bad is this?" Kathleen read the worry on Ed's face.

"Fritzel will get some of their guys to be diplomats. They'll use their contacts to straighten it all out. Let's just say I'm glad you're staying out of there for a few days."

"If Hymie finds me he'll be really angry." Sophie clouded up. "I'll never be able to hide from him and still work anywhere."

"Sophie, go home." Kathleen studied her fingernail. She couldn't bring herself to look at Sophie.

"What—back to Mrs. Taylors?"

"Minnesota."

Sophie gasped and shook her head.

"Ed and Mac will help. We can't let him find you." Kathleen felt a coughing spell starting up again.

Sophie sat, tears streaming down her cheeks. She put her hands over her face and cried softly like an exhausted child.

"You'll be safe. Go on back to your mother's, Soph. Enjoy your nice bank account. Think of the stories you can tell."

Sophie choked back a sob and said, "We've worked hard to get here. I'm scared, real scared. I've heard what Hymie does to people who double-cross him."

Kathleen put her arms around Sophie but didn't say anything. Her throat ached from more than being sick.

"He truly loves me." Sophie looked up at Kathleen. "He said so. I don't think he would ever hurt me. Not intentionally."

Kathleen nodded to Ed. "Call Mac."

A man cannot be too careful in the choice of his enemies.
—OSCAR WILDE

43

Sophie spent the night at Kathleen's, and Mac picked her up and took her to the bus station at dawn the next morning. He said at that time of day the terminal would be less crowded. He hoped to buy her ticket and get her on the bus to Minneapolis before most of Chicago woke.

After Sophie left with Mac, Kathleen crawled back into bed. At eight o'clock, Kathleen sprang awake. Someone was pounding on her door.

"All right already, hold your horses." She forgot to ask who it was.

She unlocked the door and jerked it open. Mac and Ed pushed in, closed her door, and locked it.

"Is she here?" Mac asked. Ed dashed over and looked in the bedroom.

"Who?"

"Your blonde friend. Where in the hell did she go?"

"You lost Sophie?" Kathleen's knees gave out. She fumbled for the chair. "I can't believe you—"

"We'll find her." Mac huffed and folded his arms.

"We've searched everywhere." Ed's face turned gray. "There's nowhere else left."

"You said she'd be safe." She clenched her fists. "How could you—"

"Calm down, Kathleen." Ed started to put his arm around her, but she broke away."

"How in the hell did this happen?" She caught herself yelling, then used a more controlled voice. "Tell me."

"We got to the bus station ten minutes before six. People were lined up to buy tickets at each of the windows, and, hell, the place looked like a zoo. Everyone going everywhere. School kids dressed in uniforms—running into everyone."

She didn't care. She wanted to know what had happened to Sophie.

"There we stood, behind a group of giddy guild ladies going to a rally. Naturally, each of them complained about something, mostly the price of their tickets. Your friend and I waited. Three nuns came up behind us. Before the guild ladies left, there was a line a mile long behind the nuns, waiting to buy tickets."

Kathleen smirked at his exaggeration then waved her hand, indicating he should speed up his story.

"When we finally got to the ticket counter, I told the man we wanted one ticket for Minneapolis on the six-fifteen bus. I handed him the money. He gave me the ticket and counted out my change. I turned around, and she'd vanished."

"Before you ask," Ed said, "we did look everywhere. We even had a woman check the powder room. She went poof—gone."

Kathleen shook her head. "With all those people standing around, someone would notice her leaving the ticket line."

Her irritation sounded in her voice. She couldn't figure out how Mac could lose a young girl standing right beside him.

"Honestly, Kathleen, when Mac called me we questioned everyone we could. No one saw anything."

"The guild ladies were so wrapped up in themselves, they didn't even know Sophie had been standing behind them for five long minutes."

"I'm making coffee." Kathleen went to the kitchen, filled the pot with water, dumped in coffee, and set it on the burner.

Ed and Mac continued rehashing each detail. Their voices became heavy with frustration.

"What did the nuns see?" Kathleen set three cups on the table.

"They'd left by the time we checked the powder room."

"Left? How long did it take you?" Kathleen poured the coffee.

"A couple of minutes." Mac took his cup and sipped. "I bought her ticket, and not knowing where she went, I checked the telephones. She'd wanted to call her mother."

"I don't understand," Kathleen said. "Weren't the nuns waiting to catch their bus?"

"The ticket master said he'd already pulled four tickets out when they changed their minds." Mac thought for a moment, then said, "But I only saw three."

Mac looked at Ed. Ed looked at Kathleen, and Kathleen stared at both of them.

Mac said it first. "They threw a habit over her."

"First they'd knock her out," Ed said. "Chloroform?"

"It's got a strong sweet smell." Mac slammed his fist into his palm. "Maybe a sucker punch."

Kathleen went to the window and looked down on the street. She didn't want them to see her anguish. They weren't to blame. It was rough out there. She didn't want to think of Sophie being pulled out of the river in a few days.

She began to shake. An ocean of thoughts flooded her. She had talked Sophie into coming to Chicago. But they had lost their close connection when she'd given up her side of the bed to Dolly.

Ed's arms encircled her. She turned and buried her head into his shoulder.

"This wouldn't have happened if I'd stayed closer and protected her." Kathleen took his hanky from his jacket pocket. "She's too vulnerable. She needed me, not Dolly."

Ed held her. "We'll find her."

"You won't. I can hear it in your voice, and it's written all over Mac's face."

"Truthfully, our chances aren't good," Mac said, "but that won't stop us from searching."

"For the first time, I believe I'm safe. No one seems to know where I am except my closest friends. Please, Mac, take all your guys, your contacts, and go get Sophie."

They mumbled good-byes and opened the door. Brandy, breathless, was standing on the other side about to knock.

"Good grief, Brandy, why are you up so early?"

She shoved through the doorway, nodded good-bye to the men, and grabbed Kathleen's arms.

"Big news about Friar's. Irene's taking a gig with the Ziegfeld

Follies from December through February. She's off to practice with them."

"Wait—who's taking her place?" Kathleen closed the door and locked it.

"You are."

It is a good thing to learn caution from the misfortunes of others.

—PUBLILIUS SYRUS

44

"Aren't you excited?" Brandy helped herself to coffee. Her grin faded when Kathleen sank down on the couch.

Kathleen didn't know what to feel or say or do.

"Hey, babycakes, what's wrong?" Brandy sat next to her. "Did those guys upset you?"

"It's Sophie." Kathleen sighed and sorted out her words.

When she'd finished, Brandy had nothing to say. Kathleen knew Brandy's silence verified the truth in the hopelessness she, Ed, and Mac felt.

"Listen," Brandy said, "you can sit around and feel miserable, and the misery won't go away. You might as well dance it out of your system. Come on, this is your chance."

"I couldn't." She needed to tell Dolly, and someone should call Sophie's mother. How long should she wait to do these things?

She looked up at Brandy's worried face. No, she wouldn't tell either of them. Not until someone found definite proof of what had happened. Besides, they could be wrong. Sophie might be having a glass of champagne with Hymie right now.

Kathleen sighed. *Who's kidding who?*

Brandy's brows furrowed. "I know you're distraught and all, but this—"

"I'm sick, stiff, and sore, and I can barely walk across the room. I'm emotionally devastated. I certainly can't dance."

"Nonsense." Brandy lit up a cigarette and handed the pack to Kathleen. "One of your dance mates, to impress her new boyfriend, decided to do the Charleston on the wall of a rooftop yesterday evening. The loony lamb fell off—five stories—tore through two awnings and landed in a flower garden."

"Did she die?"

"Nope, all the white lightening in her system kept her pretty loose. She's banged up with a broken leg and a terrific hangover. It's a wonder she didn't go blind." Brandy shook her head. "She won't be dancing for at least six weeks." She leaned back and blew out a perfect smoke ring. "Irene called me before my regular show last night. Begged me to come in early."

"Bet Irene was ready to chew glass over that one." Kathleen cocked her head and studied Brandy. "Why did she want you in early?"

"Your dance group was bungling around with only three dancers. Irene did some adjustments and decided I should sing and add a few steps with them during the second show. Turned out not too bad."

"Did she know about Ziegfeld then?"

"She got the call before I got there. Here's the best part—Irene said to get you out of bed and over there this afternoon. She knows you're a quick learner. With your agility, high kicks, and all the extra practicing you did this summer, you make the other dancers look like a bunch of camels on poppy fumes."

"Damn." Kathleen felt a grin hiding down somewhere too deep to show.

"Irene said to do that third routine from back in August. If you're in the lead maybe the other girls will keep it together."

Sparks of emotions flew through Kathleen. She'd been waiting for this. But her nose and her muscles and Sophie.

"Look at me. I'm a physical wreck."

"I'll help you with your makeup, cover up the bruises. You don't have to be there until two o'clock. Go back to bed and sleep. I'll pick you up at one. You'll be fine."

"Maybe by then they'll have found Sophie."

"Right." Brandy stood and headed to the door. "Get some sleep." Brandy stood.

Kathleen walked her to the door. When Brandy started down the stairs, Kathleen called, "Brandy, all the guys are out looking for Sophie. I shouldn't leave my apartment."

"Call the newspaper office and leave a message for Ed." Brandy waved back at her and skittered down the stairs.

~

After Fritzel approved her as the new choreographer, Kathleen searched the dressing room. She couldn't find where she'd put the August instructions. She knew the moves, but since she didn't have music for most of her own rehearsing, she needed to review the music's transition time.

She checked her handbag. No luck. She searched her pockets, then she remembered she had put it in her purse.

The new piano player stuck his head in the dressing room doorway. "Looking for something, doll?"

"An intelligent man, Earl. Know where to find one?"

"I'd be yours 'cept I'm taken." He held out the folded instructions.

"Where'd you find these?"

"Some Southside creep came in earlier. Asked for you and then Freddy."

Kathleen wrinkled her forehead and unfolded her notes. In the top left corner, she'd written, *Check with Freddy.*

"How'd he get this?" Then she remembered—the stolen car purse incident.

"He wanted to know what time you dance."

"For Pete's sake, you didn't tell him?"

Earl smiled. "Told him you got a better-paying gig down at the Four Deuces. Like I said, I'd be your man, but—"

She kissed the old guy on the cheek.

~

Before the night's performance, Kathleen did what she always did. She peeked out at the evening crowd from behind the curtain. Couples sitting at their tables, a small party of mixed couples at the rear, some singles standing around, and another group—no one looked familiar and no one looked suspicious. Everyone seemed to be loving the new band and Earl's playing.

[219]

Sophie's disappearance kept raking through Kathleen's emotions. *Ed, please call.*

She let go of the curtain and made her way down the darkened hall to the dressing rooms. The vanity lights flooded the narrow area, and all the flappers sat on stools staring at their mirrors. Different floral fragrances tickled her nose. Each flapper seemed to have her own favorite smelling lotions and powders.

She slipped out of her dress and into her dance costume then sat at her vanity.

"Brandy, are you wearing my heels?" Kathleen had to yell over the latest jazz coming from Anita's radio. She leaned across her vanity to look at Brandy three down from hers.

"The purple taffeta ones with green heels are under your stool," Sylvia said and stooped to pick them up. "Are these the ones?"

She slipped them on and wiggled her toes.

And I worried about missing a practice—what a joke.

Excitement combined with her distress about Sophie made her queasy. She took a second to breathe and watch Brandy put on a thick layer of plum-colored lipstick. Kathleen squinted at her bruised nose and wished she looked more glamorous.

She dusted her face, neck, and upper chest with a light powder and stood.

"Is everyone ready? Remember, our canary sings first. When she throws her feather boa around her neck and takes three steps back, we come out. I'll be on the left with Anita. Sylvia, watch for us to move in, and then you and Clare move in from the right . . . and for Pete's sake keep your chins up. This is a new band playing for us tonight. It's not like they know what we're doing. Count each step, but I'll kill you if I see any lips moving."

Kathleen watched as they filed out of the dressing room. She threw her cigarette in the waste can and gulped several swigs of her whisky and honey concoction to prevent a coughing jag. She stowed the bottle in her vanity.

Sophie, Sophie, where are you?

She took one last look at her makeup in the mirror and joined the rest.

In the hall the sounds of Anita's radio were replaced with live jazz coming from clarinets, saxophones, and trumpets. When her eyes adjusted to the dark, Kathleen saw that everyone stood rock still in their places. Brandy held her feathered boa away from her sides with both arms fully extended. The music changed, and Brandy pranced out in front of the band to sing. Kathleen's plugged-up ears made it all sounded tinny. Two minutes later the four dancers appeared behind Brandy, and all of them executed their routine perfectly.

After their number, they quietly scurried off the stage. In the hallway, Kathleen whispered congratulations to them on their performance, announcing to each of them, "You're true professionals."

She glanced down the darkened hall and saw two men enter. Her heart leaped when she recognized them—Ed and Mac.

An idea that is not dangerous is unworthy of being called an idea at all.

—ELBERT HUBBARD

45

The two men waited by the dressing-room door.

"Why aren't you out in front?" Kathleen couldn't force a smile.

"Thought you'd be home in bed." Ed frowned.

"Get your coat. We need you," Mac said.

"It's Sophie, isn't it?" Her heart moved into her throat.

"We've got to go," Ed said.

"Tell me . . ." Her ears started ringing.

"If it is, she's fine, but we don't know." Ed moved her along down the hall.

Kathleen shoved open the door to the dressing room and stepped in. She grabbed her pocketbook and her coat. "Brandy, I've got an emergency. Figure out how to do the eleven o'clock without me." Before anyone could ask her questions, she left.

The men ushered her out the back door and up the steps to the sidewalk. Mac nodded toward his car. Ed hurried to open the door.

She climbed in the back seat of Mac's Ford and Ed shut the door. He went around and got into the passenger's side next to Mac.

"I wish to hell someone would tell me what's going on."

"We're not sure," Ed said. "We got word that a canary matching

Sophie's description is singing at the Anton Hotel. We thought we should check it out."

"Why aren't you there?"

"Hey," Mac said, "the big guy knows me. That's his headquarters sometimes. I'm not going in there looking for one of his dames."

"Sophie isn't 'one of his dames.'" Her head didn't have enough space for all of this. "She hangs around with one of his mules, Hymie. Hymie's a nothing—a creep."

"They don't know you. You can slip in and see what's what without being noticed," Mac said. "After all, you're dressed like an entertainer."

"Ed, this is dangerous stuff." Kathleen touched his shoulder.

Neither man said anything.

"I see." Kathleen coughed then said, "Your plan—two big-muscle men hide out in the car while I go in and get my brains blown out."

"You're wrong," Mac said. "We love you, babe. We'd never put you at risk without being sure you're protected."

She stifled another little series of coughs under her breath.

"Here's our plan. Ed and I drive up and stop three blocks away. Those bodyguards watch the cars coming and going, so we don't want to get too close."

"Yeah, right."

"Kathleen," Ed said, "there's risk, but we don't think there'll be problems. We'll drop you off on the corner of . . ."

"Hold on, you're not dropping me off on any corner in a Cicero neighborhood. Even if I wasn't dressed like this I wouldn't want to be alone there during the day or night. I've heard stories about what goes on. Figure out another plan, Eddie boy." Kathleen settled back, lit up, and took a long drag on her cigarette.

"It's not like that," Mac said. "This guy will be your escort."

"What?" Her anger boiled up from deep inside. She dropped ash on the back seat when she scooted up to lean between the two of them. "Where in the hell do you two come up with this stuff? I refuse to be some target's escort. Think of something else."

"Calm down, Kathleen," Ed said. "Hey. You're spilling ash all over my coat. Look, when we get to the drop-off point, Sullie will be waiting. He's a nice guy. He'll look out for you."

"No one's nice in that neighborhood." Kathleen mumbled and

took several short puffs while brushing ash off of Ed's shoulder. "Who's Sullie?"

"Good man." Mac sounded like he wanted to convince himself. "Known him for about four years. He did some time for heisting steaks from restaurants in the North. No big deal. It was one of those, 'I'm gonna put a thorn in you guys' side.' What they didn't get him for was the racketeering down around South Clark or Roosevelt somewhere. Running numbers. Anyhow, he knew I knew, so when he got out he's been doing quiet favors for me. I'm careful what I use him for because he's playing both sides. That can get him a ticket to the bottom of the river."

"Swell. I get an ex-con as an escort into one of the roughest districts."

"Listen," Ed said. "We're almost there. Sullie will be on the corner. We'll drop you off, and the two of you act like you're doing the town—next stop, the Anton. Sullie knows the words to get you where the action is. When they let you in, you find a table, have a drink, and look around for Sophie. Sullie says she's scheduled to sing at eleven. We're calling it close. The lights will be down except for the stage. She won't be able to see you. If it is Sophie, or even if it isn't, you two leave. We'll pick you up at this same place. Don't do anything. Mac will call his guys in, and they'll handle it."

"What choices do I have?"

"This is for Sophie." Ed nudged her. "There's Sullie standing in that doorway over there."

Sullie appeared to be quite tall and well dressed in his dark topcoat, white silk scarf, and top hat. She'd expected some little weasel, a scumbag. *Dammit, Martin.*

"Ed, give me your cigarettes."

She dropped them in her pocketbook as the car stopped. She climbed out and Sullie sauntered over to greet her.

She heard Mac's automobile pull away. She and Sullie headed down the sidewalk toward the hotel with a cold night breeze nipping at her face. Neither talked. When they entered the hotel, Sullie escorted her through the crimson-carpeted lobby toward the marble stairway. They went down the stairs, around the corner, and Sullie knocked on a heavy-paneled door. One of the smaller panels slid back and Sullie said, "Deuce of Clubs."

The door opened into a hallway leading to another door. A man opened it and motioned them into a large, smoke-filled dining room packed with nightlife seekers from a variety of backgrounds. The trumpet solo echoed off the walls, drowning out any hopes of hearing the accompanying piano music.

The trumpet tones sent chills down her spine. This was one of those black-and-tan clubs. Terrific playing. She glanced around to see if Chester might be there. *Silly.*

Sullie took her elbow and moved her toward a table for two on the far side of the room.

"We don't want to be too close to the stage," he shouted in her ear. "Sometimes these canaries work the crowd."

A waiter poured her something. She didn't know what, nor did she dare to ask.

Sullie nodded at her drink. "I'm a regular in here and always order the same thing. They do this automatically."

Kathleen pretended to sip, then smiled at him. Too many flappers died from wood alcohol poisoning. She watched the stage. When the musician finished his solo the band started a quieter number.

"Hang on. She'll be out now," Sullie said.

Kathleen slumped in her chair as a buxom, bleached blonde strolled out to the microphone. She was wearing a low-cut, black, silk-crepe gown with gold beads and silver threads. Kathleen looked at Sullie and shook her head.

He motioned for her to drink up. As soon as the song was over they'd leave.

She pushed her glass away, and they stood. Sullie tossed some bills on the table. Kathleen saw Hymie come across the room with some redhead on his arm. *Where's Sophie?*

"Sullie. Do you know him?"

"He's one of the Big Guy's men. Don't know his name. Why?"

"That's Sophie's boyfriend. His name's Hymie." Kathleen stood. "Creepers—I think she's wearing Sophie's mink."

"There are lots of minks, can't tell one from another. Let's get out of here."

"I wore her coat. She had a shit fit because I burned a hole in her sleeve with a cigarette. It's a small one, I told her no one would notice." Kathleen popped up and maneuvered through the maze of people sitting at their tables.

"Kathleen, wait." Sullie hurried after her.

The performer was singing something about "her man," and the audience was captivated. Hymie and the redhead were a few feet from Kathleen when they stopped at a table to talk to someone. Kathleen scooted up but couldn't get a good view.

Someone behind her said, "Down in front, please."

Hymie and the girl moved on to an empty table. She followed. Hymie, ever the gentleman, helped remove the coat, and he slid it over the back of the girl's chair before she sat.

He was about to sit when Kathleen said, "Excuse me, don't I know you?"

Hymie, stood back up. "Naw, I don't think so."

"Pardon me, but I don't mean you, I mean your lovely escort. I could swear we've met. Didn't we audition together a few months back?"

"Maybe." The puzzled look on the girl's face let Kathleen know the girl didn't have a clue. The redhead said, "What's it you do? Sing or dance?"

"It doesn't matter, does it? Just so we get one of these Northside mink coats, right?" Kathleen smiled and held up the sleeve. Sullie cleared his throat somewhere close behind her.

"Hey, wait a minute." Hymie balled his fists. "That's no Northside coat. I gave that to her myself." Hymie moved into her face. "We don't like nothing from the Northside and that means you. I bet you're one of those charity cases."

Sullie stepped forward and in his deep, low voice said, "Don't call my girl a prostitute if you want to live much longer. Come on, sweetheart, let's get out of here." Sullie grabbed her arm and jerked her hard. The tables around Hymie were telling them to quiet down. She glanced back. Hymie didn't follow.

"You're uncontrollable, lady." Sullie gritted the words through his teeth. "You don't know what you're messing with there." He maneuvered her up and out of the hotel and started down the sidewalk.

She stopped. The limousine she'd stolen sat parked under the streetlamp. Soft-yellow light gleamed off its black, waxed body. She jerked her arm away from Sullie and walked around it. One neat bullet hole pierced the driver's side window. One hole two months later—still not repaired. Someone must be pissed.

Her knees went rubbery. Her dance instructions had been in her purse when the contents spilled on the floor, connecting her to this car.

Sullie took her arm. "Lady, get away from there."

"Hymie's dame had Sophie's coat." Kathleen looked behind her. No one followed.

"You couldn't see a cigarette burn in that poor lighting."

"You're wrong. It's Sophie's coat. Hymie admitted he gave it to Miss Redhead. He took it from Sophie."

"There's Mac's automobile." He waved them over and pushed her across the street. When Mac drove up and stopped, Sullie opened the car door for Kathleen and pretty much shoved her in. He said, "You two have your hands full with this one. I'm gone."

He backed away and started to close the door. Kathleen caught the door before he closed it.

"What do you mean by that?" Kathleen shouted after him. Sullie walked away.

"What *does* he mean by that?" Ed asked.

"I don't know." Kathleen fumed. She lit another cigarette and ignored Ed, who was chastising her for something he knew nothing about.

"He's furious about something."

"Dammit, Ed. Not now."

She smoldered in silence.

"Tell us what happened." Mac sped up.

"I'm worried sick about Sophie and all you do is chew on me." Kathleen looked out the side window. She couldn't see anything.

Mac honked his horn at a drunk pedestrian.

Kathleen glanced up and saw Ed staring straight ahead. She had hurt his feelings. After all, he did care, and he was worried about Sophie too.

"It's Hymie," she said. "I think he's done something to Sophie, and he gave her coat to some redhead. Sullie's mad because I talked to them."

"You what?" the two men said in unison.

"I confronted them about the redhead wearing a Northside coat."

The two men groaned in unison. Ed said, "No wonder Sullie flew."

"What was I supposed to do? Dammit. There's Sophie's boyfriend with this dame, and the dame's wearing Sophie's mink. I couldn't let that one pass. You wouldn't either."

"Damn it to hell, lady." Mac slapped the steering wheel. "You don't *know* it's her coat. How could you? They all look the same. Hymie's gonna be watching for anyone who looks like you. He doesn't forgive, and he'll find you. Do you know why? Because in your job you can't hide. Now we have to worry about you up on stage, Sophie, Hymie, and some stalker with a knife. Sweetie, you're making my life hell."

They turned down the street toward Friar's.

"Would you take me home? I've got a splitting headache."

"We'll keep looking for her," Ed said. "There's only so many places she could be, and we're uncovering them one by one."

"I doubt if you'll uncover them all, because you haven't searched the bottom of the river or the lake," Kathleen mumbled.

Ed turned and leaned toward her. "Don't give up. We'll find her. Want me to come up for a while?"

Mac pulled the automobile in front of her apartment and waited.

"Thanks anyway." Kathleen, irritable and tired, wanted to go to bed. She needed more of her cough medicine, and she seemed to be developing an earache. She patted Ed's arm. As an afterthought, she said, "Mac."

He looked at her.

"I do appreciate you taking this on. Sullie's a solid guy. I hope I didn't cause him any trouble."

"I'll tell him what you said," Mac shrugged. "I can't use him anymore though. Hymie will be watching for him now."

"I screwed this one up, huh?" When Mac didn't answer, she opened the door and slipped out.

As they drove away, she looked up and saw a light on in her apartment. She hadn't left a light on.

Only Sophie had her key. Sophie was back.

Kathleen scrambled up the stairs and opened the door. "Sophie!"

"Sorry, kid." Brandy sat on the couch reading a magazine.

"Brandy?" Kathleen's mind couldn't put the information together. "Why aren't you at the Inn?"

"We had something strange happen. Thought you needed to know, but it might be nothing. Hope you don't mind me making myself at home." Brandy opened her purse.

"How did you get in?" Kathleen slipped off her coat and went into the kitchen.

"The old guy downstairs was changing the hallway lightbulb. I figured he was the super, so I told him I needed to wait for you and didn't want to sit on the steps this hour of the night. Since I'm still in my stage clothes, he believed me when I said we worked together. I slipped him a fiver and convinced him I wasn't going to steal anything."

Kathleen poured herself an inch of whisky in a small juice glass and spooned in honey for her cough. After she let it slide down her throat, she made two rum and Coca-Colas.

Brandy stood in the doorway and waved a piece of paper. "Found it." She took her drink and sat back on the couch. "Don't know what to make of it."

Kathleen plopped down next to her.

Brandy said, "We finished our last number, stumbling in the wrong places. When we came off, one of the guys who works the lights, Gus, handed me this note. You know how dark it is. I had to wait until I got to the dressing room to see. What do you think?" Brandy handed Kathleen a small piece of folded paper.

Kathleen took the torn piece of stationary. She unfolded it. The stationary heading said Metropole Hotel. Under the heading, neatly penned in Sophie's writing, were three words:

Kath, 442 Hurry.

"Who gave this to Gus?" Kathleen's energy level skyrocketed.

"All Gus could tell me was that Hal said an elderly lady in a black hotel maid's uniform had handed the note to Joey. Joey's the one who delivers chops and steaks to Friar's. Joey gave it to Hal. Hal figured you were backstage, so he handed—"

"Good grief, I can't follow that, but this *is* Sophie's writing." A wave of relief fueled Kathleen's excitement. "Let's go get her."

"Hold your horses. The only worse place I can think is the Four Deuces. We're talking gambling, prostitution, murders, and the big boss lives there somewhere. You can't go to that neighborhood. It's bad news."

Kathleen glared at Brandy. "We're talking about Sophie's life." Then quietly, she said, "Sophie's alive. She needs help. I'm calling a cab."

To live is so startling, it leaves but little room for other occupations.

—EMILY DICKINSON

46

Brandy stood with her hands on her hips, watching while Kathleen called for a cab. "We should wait for Ed or Mac."

Kathleen grabbed her coat. "We're going back to Friar's."

"Ed and Mac won't be there. It's after one."

"Don't care." Kathleen tossed Brandy her coat.

"You're nuts, kid." Brandy put it on.

Kathleen hesitated at the door. "Remember when we did that hotel skit for the lunch crowd the other day? We wore a maid's uniform and a waitress's outfit. Let's go, the taxi's probably downstairs by now."

"Why do I hang around with you?" They scuttled down the stairs and out onto the sidewalk. The taxi driver sprinted around, opened the backseat door, and helped them in.

When the taxi drove down the street close to Friar's, Brandy touched Kathleen and pointed. She told the driver to pull to the curb and stop. He did.

Three police cars were parked in the front, and people scurried in and out of Friar's.

"Are they raiding Friar's?" Kathleen asked.

Brandy nodded. "They do this periodically. Some rich dame

probably thinks she's been cheated. Never mind the booze she brings to put in her drink, she whines about bootleg liquor being served. So far Fritzel's been clever enough not to get busted. Let's go back to your apartment and call the guys."

"You can get out and call another cab. I'm not letting Sophie stay at that hotel any longer." She dripped perspiration. The cool evening didn't matter.

Silence. Then Brandy said, "I'm with you, whatever."

"Driver, take us to the Metropole Hotel. It's somewhere on South Michigan."

"You dames sure you want to go there?"

"Please." She kept her voice steady, but her heart jittered.

"Kathleen, we can't just waltz in there and . . ."

Kathleen shook her head and nodded toward the driver. "Driver, we have a few minutes worth of business, it won't take us very long, but we will need a ride back. Could I interest you in remaining at the side door while we talk to these people? If you take us back to where you picked us up we'll double the whole fare."

"I'm not supposed to do that."

"We don't mind calling another taxi."

Brandy chirped in, "Another cab certainly would be cheaper."

Kathleen added, "I'd prefer the convenience of your waiting out-side for us, but she's right. Another taxi would be cheaper."

"Naw, ladies, I'll wait. This time of morning not much is going on. Lots of drunks going home. They get sick all over the back. I'll wait if you're quick. Five—ten minutes?"

"Probably fifteen or twenty. If you can't, don't worry."

The driver pulled up to the side entrance and parked. Kathleen paid their fare and added a fat tip. He settled back, cocked his cap to the front, and prepared to snooze.

When they were out of his hearing range, Brandy said, "What do we do? The desk clerk isn't going to give us a room key. Do you plan to play a little hoochy-coochy with him while I steal his keys?"

Kathleen smirked. "Hardly."

Brandy stopped. She grabbed Kathleen to keep her from going farther. Her eyes flared.

Kathleen sighed. "Let's see what happens." She jerked her arm away and picked up her pace. She headed around to the main entrance and didn't want to think about answering Brandy's questions.

"Smart. No plan. Honestly, Kathleen, why do I even like you?" Brandy caught up with her and kept in step.

Kathleen put her arm around Brandy's shoulders and gave her a little squeeze. "Because we are so much alike, and we both love excitement?"

"I don't want to get killed."

"If you worry about bad things, bad things happen." Kathleen stopped. "So far tonight we've been quite lucky. It's timing . . . Luck's on our side."

"You were scared out of your wits in my apartment last spring. After the girl who dressed like you wore a knife in her bra, you were a tiger trapped in Jell-O." Brandy peered toward the glass doors going into the lobby. "You're not counting on luck. This goes deeper."

Heat prickled Kathleen's cheeks, and she laughed.

Brandy stared at her.

Kathleen's inept bodyguards couldn't save her, so why bother? Her heart hurt from her parents' rejection. Martin brought her to a whole new realm of despair. All her pent-up anger struggled to burst out and needed to be directed somewhere.

Kathleen had felt a thrill when she stole the limousine and again when she had zeroed in on Hymie the Sleaze and Miss Redhead. It surfaced now with her wanting to infiltrate the Metropole.

"Since you're not answering me, I guess crossing my fingers won't help."

Brandy moved toward the entrance.

"To hell with them all." Kathleen stared at Brandy. "Maybe I've lived with heartbreak and terror so long I'm sick of being bullied by others. Tonight, I'm doing something about my life."

Brandy nodded and bowed toward the door. They entered the hotel, walking with purpose across the marble floor of the lobby.

At the reception desk the bellman was talking excitedly to the desk clerk. Kathleen took a deep breath, walked over, and cleared her throat. The men quieted and gave her their attention.

She let her gaze glide around the hotel lobby before turning back to them and saying, "Sorry to disturb you, Mrs. Williams asked me to check for an important message she's expecting."

"Williams, Williams, we don't have a Williams staying here, miss," The clerk said.

"Could it be under another name?" She nodded to Brandy.

"Try Thompson." Brandy raised her eyebrow. "It's quite important."

The clerk studied his ledger, then he went to the row of wooden boxes behind him and ran his finger down until he came to a number. He went back to the desk and pointed to the ledger.

"We do have a Mr. and Mrs. Thompson, but there isn't a message."

"I guess we'll have to tell them the deal fell through. This won't make them happy." Kathleen frowned. "But the message could still come in. If it does, would you ring up right away? I'll run down and get it."

Kathleen and Sophie strode to the elevators as the bellman said, "Like I said, the police raided all these joints and locked up all these people when they found liquor on the tables. Lots of guests will spend the night in the pokey."

"Did you hear?" Brandy whispered.

Kathleen nodded. "Look, elevator's self-operated. Are you game?"

After they closed the elevator doors, Kathleen said, "Maybe they locked up Hymie and Miss Redhead." Kathleen moved the lever to the fifth floor.

"Why did you do that? The note said 442?"

"542 should be right over 442. I'd like to see where it is first before we decide what to do."

The elevator stopped, they opened the doors, and the two of them stepped out into a hallway with white wainscoting and blue, maroon, gold, and white striped wallpaper. The carpet was a diamond pattern of purples, reds, and grays, and the hall was empty.

They followed the numbers to one end. Brandy nudged Kathleen. "Here it is."

"It's a suite, maybe three or four rooms." As they walked back to the elevator, Kathleen grabbed Brandy's arm and whispered, "Let's take the exit stairs."

The sign for the stairs pointed them down another hall. Before they got to the back stairwell they saw light coming from a partially opened door. Kathleen put her finger to her lips.

She peered into the lit room, pushed the door open, and motioned Brandy inside the maid's closet. Three carts stood to one side. One had a big ring over the handle that held a pass key. The night maid must have been counting out towels and wash cloths on the table. Sheets, towels, ashtrays, soaps, and various items filled two of the carts. The cart with the key had all the items except for the towels.

"Bet she had to go to the bathroom," Brandy said.

"Let's go." Kathleen slipped the key off the ring. They opened the door and stepped out into the hall as the housekeeper came around the far corner.

"Excuse me, ladies," the housekeeper said. "You can't go in there."

"We need some towels." Kathleen pushed the key down into her pocket. Thought maybe we could help ourselves."

The gray-haired housekeeper scowled. "We have to account for each towel. Everyone steals them. What's your room number?"

Brandy said, "We're staying on the top floor—guests. We didn't want to disturb our host."

"Top floor, is it? Wait here." The woman went into the room and then handed them two bath towels, wash cloths, and hand towels. "If you're Mr. Alphonse's guests, that's good enough for me."

"We appreciate this," Kathleen said to the woman's back. She and Brandy scurried to the stairwell, stifling giggles. "I'm proud of you," Kathleen whispered. Their dance heels echoed off each descending step. She slowed and mouthed, "Shhh."

"What about Sophie?" Brandy whispered. "If Hymie's there, or one of his stooges, we've got problems."

Kathleen stopped at the door to the fourth floor. "If anyone is there, I bet they're sleeping."

Brandy pulled the door open. "In this town, people are just getting started. We can't bet on anything."

They stepped out into a hallway identical to the one above.

Glancing down the hallway in both directions, they took the one leading to suite 442. Kathleen stopped and grabbed Brandy.

"Wait," Kathleen whispered. "Let's go back." She stifled a cough. Her ears felt plugged.

"What's the matter?"

"Have an idea." Kathleen headed back around the corner. Brandy followed.

Kathleen used the pass key on the maid's closet. The key opened it. She pulled Brandy inside and closed the door.

She felt overhead for the light. After a few seconds, her hand touched its chain. She pulled. Light from the bulb blinded them. This closet, identical to the one on the fifth floor, contained dirty laundry bins, some full of towels and sheets. They didn't see evidence of anyone sorting or doing work in this room. Kathleen went over to one of the laundry bins. She pulled out a black dress with a white collar and cuffs, a maid's uniform.

"How do you feel about putting on someone else's dirty clothes?"

"Disgusting," Brandy said.

"That's what I thought. I'll do it. Hold my coat and towels." Kathleen stripped down to her undies and sorted through more rumpled black dresses in the bin. She held one up for size, put it back, and fished out another, holding it up for inspection. She slipped it over her head, buttoned it, and went to the bin with the white aprons. She slipped a reasonably clean one over her head and tied it around her waist.

"How do I look?"

"Ridiculous with purple and green dance shoes."

Kathleen shrugged. She picked up her clothes and handed them to Brandy with her coat. "Hang on to these and wait here. How long have we been gone?"

"About ten or fifteen minutes."

"The taxi driver—better hurry." Kathleen grabbed both sets of clean towels and headed toward room 442. Walking down the hall, passing all the closed doors, she started to feel weak-kneed. *What if Hymie is in there?*

Kathleen stopped at room 442 and pressed her ear to the wood. She heard a faint vibrating hum from something mechanical. Nothing else. She knelt down and peered through the keyhole. Everything was dark. She slipped the pass key into the keyhole and turned it, listening for the soft click. She squeezed the handle and inched it down, opening the door enough to allow her to slip inside. She eased the door closed to the point where it wouldn't latch. The vibrating hum was louder and came from somewhere to the left. She paused, letting her eyes adjust. An outside sign flashed red, orange, and dark, producing a pulsating, fiery glow in the room.

Kathleen stood in a living area. Off to the left she saw a closed door. To her right there was a kitchen-bar area, and behind it stood an open door. She waited until the red sequence of light came. Through the open door she could see a neatly made bed.

The closed door to the left next to the couch caught her attention. She moved toward the door, hoping not to trip over any lamp cords or bump into any tables. The humming sound, louder now, came from near the couch. Because of backlighting from the window, she couldn't figure out what made the couch look lumpy.

The sound stopped. The lump grew larger.

"Hey, who the hell are you?" A man rose to a sitting position then jumped to stand inches from her.

Snores—damn—my stuffed up ears. "Maid service." She said in a chirpy, high voice. "Someone called for fresh towels. I didn't want to wake you. I'll put them here."

"No one called for towels. What the—it's two thirty. We're asleep for Christ's sake."

"We never mind, sir. Our service is here to please no matter what the time." She backed to the door. "Oh, maybe I have the wrong room. I'll check my notes. Sorry to have disturbed you." She closed the door.

We're asleep . . . that means someone else is there with him. Kathleen sprinted down the hallway to the maid's closet. Out of breath, she told Brandy what had happened.

"I'm not waiting alone anymore." Brandy sounded grouchy. "If we don't get to that side door soon, we lose our ride, if we haven't already."

"I'm not leaving without Sophie. I know she's there. Think, will you?" Kathleen struggled out of the too-tight maid's dress. She picked her rhinestone-adorned purple chemise with green fringe off the floor and slithered into it.

Brandy stubbed out her cigarette, "You have to get Mr. Whoever out of there. It wasn't Hymie was it?"

"Haven't a clue who it was, but he's not Hymie. I'd recognize his smarmy voice anywhere. We could incapacitate him some way." Kathleen grabbed the key out of the maid's dress pocket and, with her other hand, fluffed her hair.

"I'm not into matches of brute strength. Whatever we do, we have to do it now," Brandy said. "We've run out of time."

"Let's go."

"And do what?"

"I don't know, Brandy. We'll do something." Kathleen clicked off the light. They hurried down the hall to suite 442.

This time Kathleen didn't use the key. "Hymie!" She knocked and called out loud enough to wake everyone in the surrounding rooms.

Brandy joined in, "Hymie, hurry."

Kathleen tugged up on her dance dress to show her knees, and she motioned for Brandy to do the same. She hoped the guy in there wouldn't recognize her as the maid. But then she hadn't turned on any lights.

[236]

"Hymie," they both shouted.

Kathleen heard the key in the lock and the door jerked opened. "What the hell are you yelling about?"

"Hymie, we have an urgent message for Hymie. It's an emergency." Kathleen said as breathlessly as she could manage. A tickle in her throat announced another cursed coughing attack approaching.

"He ain't here. Go away."

Brandy stuck her foot, showing her silk-stockinged knee, in the doorway and said, "Wait a minute, who are you?"

"I'm Seymour, why?"

Brandy looked at Kathleen, and both of them choked back giggles.

"Hey, don't you snigger at my name. It's a good name," Seymour said.

"No, no, we're surprised. My brother's name is Seymour, after my grandfather, you know." Kathleen opened her eyes wide.

"And another coincidence," Brandy batted her eyelashes as she said, "Mr. Alphonse, up in the penthouse, said if we were to run into 'Seymour' while we were getting Hymie, to tell Seymour to come too." She put one hand on his shoulder, smiling broadly. "So big old you are Seymour. I would not have guessed." She squeezed his biceps.

"Where might we find Hymie?" Kathleen interrupted.

"Hymie's out."

"Not good." Kathleen shook her head. "Mr. Alphonse won't like hearing this. He specifically said he had to talk to Hymie right away."

"About what?"

"We don't know," Brandy said. "He never talks to us about business, but it's something about the cops and the raids on places tonight and hundreds of people being locked up. He said you were to get upstairs to his penthouse with Hymie right this moment."

"Can't leave here. I've got someone to look after."

"He's going to be angry," Brandy sang. "Hymie won't want to be left out, and you're his man. Do you have a choice?"

"What the hell, how long can it take?" Kathleen said. "You go ahead and rush up to the penthouse. See what's going on, and the two of us will wait here. You won't have to worry about not doing what you're supposed to do."

"Should we give the person medicine or something?" Brandy asked. "What's the problem?"

"She's asleep. Guess it's okay. You mind?"

"Not at all." Brandy sounded irritated. "But hurry. We do have plans, and Mr. Alphonse wants us back upstairs when his meeting is over."

Seymour rushed to the elevator and waited for the incredibly slow-moving cage of brass and wood to reach the fourth floor.

Brandy and Kathleen sprinted to the closed bedroom door. It was locked. Brandy's shoulders slumped. Kathleen shoved the pass key in the lock. She fumbled, tried again, and the door opened into a very dark, but sweetly fragrant, bedroom. Draperies were shut. No outside light came in.

Brandy found a lamp on the dresser and turned it on. A huge bouquet of white roses and lilies stood on the bedside table. Kathleen gasped when she saw Sophie.

Sophie silently watched them with her one good eye. Someone had blackened her other. It was swollen shut and turned various shades of blue and green. Her jaw looked broken too. She wore an expensive-looking lace nightgown, and evidently someone had brushed her hair and tied it back with a white satin ribbon.

"Oh, Sophie," Kathleen's words barely came out. "Can you walk?"

Brandy moved close to one side and helped Sophie stand. Sophie didn't say anything or make any sounds. Kathleen found Sophie's shoes and grabbed the quilt off the bed.

"Let's go, sweetie." Kathleen put the quilt around Sophie's shoulders. Brandy stood on one side of her and Kathleen on the other. They navigated Sophie down the hallway.

"Kathleen, we can't use the elevator. He'll be coming back down any second now."

"You're right. Back to the maid's closet." When they got there Kathleen left the light off and locked the door. They sat Sophie on a pile of laundry on the floor and waited in silence.

"We've missed our ride," Brandy whispered.

"I'm sure." Kathleen muffled some little coughs by placing her hands over her mouth.

Kathleen heard Brandy shuffling through clothes.

"My turn to play maid. I hope I don't have it on inside out. I'll be back. Unlock the door, please."

She did, and Brandy opened the door and left. Kathleen heard her go through the stairwell door.

"Sophie, I'm sorry. We'll get you out of this mess," Kathleen crooned to her as she stroked her hair. Sophie didn't even whimper.

She had no idea how long Brandy had been gone, but she jumped when she heard a soft tapping on the door.

"Hey, it's me," Brandy whispered.

Kathleen unlocked the door. Brandy pushed in and closed it. "We have a ride. The taxi driver fell asleep and I woke him. Told him I was also a maid here at night, that's why I was wearing this outfit, but we needed him to take us back to your place. He wasn't happy because we've been gone so long, but he was even madder that he had slept so hard. He said it was going to cost us, but he is waiting."

"Did you see anyone?"

"No, but the door to 442 is closed. We'd left it open. Seymour knows by now."

"He's probably on the telephone to other goons," Kathleen whispered. "They'll search this whole place. Help me. Sophie, we have no choice but to take the stairwell down four flights. It comes out close to the side door where a taxi is waiting. Let's put your shoes on and go."

Sophie let Kathleen slip them on, and they helped her to her feet. Kathleen checked to be sure the hallway stayed empty. They made it to the stairwell and moved down the stairs. When they reached the first floor, Brandy opened the door and scanned the hallway.

"Clear."

The three of them moved to the side door, out onto the sidewalk, and into the waiting taxi. The driver said, "Wait a minute. What's wrong with her?" pointing toward Sophie wrapped up in the quilt.

"She's fine," Kathleen said.

He couldn't see her face; they had made sure of that. "I don't want no sick person in my cab. That's not part of our deal. Out."

"She's not sick, she's with child." Brandy shoved him on his shoulder. "The midwife's waiting at my apartment."

Kathleen added, "If you don't hurry, you'll end up being this baby's godfather."

Not he who has much is rich, but he who gives much.
—ERICH FROMM

47

Kathleen and Brandy gave the taxi driver an outrageous tip. Then they helped Sophie up the stairs.

"You call Mac while I get Sophie into bed." Kathleen unlocked her apartment door and helped settled Sophie. "Can I get you anything?"

Sophie beckoned for Kathleen to lean closer. She whispered, "If they find me, they'll kill me."

"We won't let them find you this time. Promise."

Brandy stuck her head in the bedroom door and motioned for Kathleen to come over. "I can't get Mac or Ed. The only other person who we can totally trust is Martin."

"Martin?" Kathleen's emotions skittered everywhere. "But he's gone."

"If he's not out to sea, he might be home or even here."

Kathleen shook her head and swallowed hard.

"Come on, kiddo. He's our only hope."

"He doesn't even know Sophie. Why should he bother?"

"Because that's who Martin is. He hates these thugs who dominate Chicago. This isn't his first clash with them. But his anger comes from a different level. His concerns are financial, you know, something to do with trade. Besides, he's probably making amends for past sins or something, but I think he's subconsciously destined to help injured women in distress."

Kathleen hated the thought of being indebted to Martin. But Sophie needed more help than she could give. She gestured to the telephone.

"His home's a long-distance call."

Kathleen blinked. "How far?"

"Oyster Bay."

"Long Island? Like the—the—" Now Kathleen couldn't think of even one old-money name.

"Yep, like the Rockefellers. Didn't you know? He's unbelievably rich." Brandy sighed. "Hear he has another home in the Caribbean somewhere."

"He's too far away to be of help to us." Her heart slumped.

Poor Sophie. What could they do? The familiar fluttering deep down inside started, then a longing to be with Martin hit her full force.

"Not if he flies. He could be here by noon." Brandy looked beyond Kathleen over toward the bedroom. "He's had some bad breaks. But I see there's electricity between the two of you. If he thinks he can be of help, he'll come running."

Here by noon—Kathleen doubted this. She cared too much, he too little.

"Gawd, what a night we've had." Brandy stretched. "I'll make the calls, but the time and charges will show up on your next month's rent, okay? Fix us one of your limey rum and Coca-Colas."

Sophie seemed deep in sleep, so Kathleen puttered around the kitchen while Brandy made the telephone call.

Kathleen handed Brandy a Cuba Libre and sat, saying, "Thought I'd make us pancakes, but I don't have any milk. My last milkman didn't deliver any. Totally incompetent." She needed to tell Dolly about Sophie because Dolly's worrying might send her off masquerading as who knows what again.

"Kid, this won't be over when she leaves. You know that, don't you?" Brandy picked imaginary lint off her dress.

Kathleen refused to let her mind go there. A chill swept through her.

"Hymie's not going to like what we did."

"He doesn't know we took her." Kathleen wished she believed her words.

"He and Sophie had long talks. He knows where we work. Remember, someone came to Friar's looking for Sophie. He knows we're the ones who care about her." Brandy took a large swallow of her drink, set her glass down, and folded her hands in resignation. "If two flappers steal her from under his nose, guess who those two flappers must be?"

"Good God, Brandy." The stolen car and the dance instructions, confronting him about Sophie's fur coat, and now this. She hadn't thought about the long-term jeopardy her actions created.

Brandy picked up a pack of Kathleen's cigarettes, shook one out, and handed the pack to Kathleen.

"Look, kid, Hymie and his lovely may be locked up because of the raid, but if not, it will only be a short time before he puts all the pieces together and shows up at Friar's." She struck a match.

Kathleen watched the match flare while a circus romped in her head. She leaned over for Brandy to light her cigarette.

Brandy didn't say any more, and Kathleen understood. She figured they'd just ended their careers at Friar's Inn. She watched the patterns of smoke twist and rise and found meager comfort in the cool, sweet warmth of her Cuba Libre.

Both Brandy and Kathleen jumped when someone tapped on the apartment door.

Kathleen scooted over to the door and put her ear next to it. "Who's there?"

"Martin."

Kathleen looked at the door, then mouthed to Brandy. "How—?"

Brandy shrugged. "Forgot to tell you. He arrived in Chicago this morning—er, yesterday morning."

Kathleen unlocked the door, bracing herself for a flood of emotions.

After all these months, he stood there now—in her open doorway—and stared at her. Heat rose up her neck into her cheeks. He smelled of sea, and woodlands, and fine cognac. She held her arms behind her back to keep from throwing them around his neck. But he wasn't here for her. Her throat ached.

She stepped aside and let him enter.

His mouth moved to say something, but then he closed it.

His nearness caused her heart to thud uncontrollably.

Martin moved a few steps into the apartment and in a quiet voice said, "Let me see your friend."

Kathleen measured her movements as she showed him to the bedroom. Still she stood close enough to feel the warmth of him.

Sophie opened her eyes. She didn't move.

"Hi there, lass." Martin's voice, deep and strong, sounded like Kathleen's father's. "I'm Martin Davies. You'll never be mistreated again. Are you able to walk?"

Sophie managed a weak "Yes" without moving her lips.

"Good. Can you trust me?"

Sophie looked from Kathleen to Brandy and back to him. She nodded.

"You and I are going down those stairs and into my limousine. I'll take you to my hotel. There you'll have your own room with an armed guard. A doctor and a nurse will be waiting when we arrive. The nurse will stay with you for as long as needed, six hours or six weeks. I'll come back to get you after my business meeting ends later this morning."

Sophie closed her eyes.

Kathleen took Sophie's hand and said, "It's okay, Soph, you're safe."

Sophie pulled Kathleen close and mumbled, "They know— Minneapolis—I can't—"

Martin caught the meaning. "You won't be going back to Minneapolis until you've mended and decided it's safe. Tomorrow, if you can talk, call your mother and tell her you're taking a vacation. You get to decide when to go home."

Admiration and comfort settled over Kathleen. "Where?"

"We'll fly to the gulf to one of my ships. Sophie, I have a small villa on St. Thomas in the Caribbean. You'll recuperate in paradise."

It is the dim haze of mystery that adds enchantment to pursuit.

—ANTOINE RIVEROL

48

Kathleen and Brandy helped Sophie into Martin's car. Kathleen ached to go along, but Brandy eased her agony by chattering away the rest of the dark hours of the night.

When the sun rose, and Kathleen knew Mrs. Taylor would be fixing breakfast, she called the boardinghouse and spoke with Dolly.

"Kathleen," Dolly said, "thank goodness. I'm worried out of my mind."

Hearing Dolly's worried voice, Kathleen decided not to discuss this over the telephone. "I've been with Sophie. Let's talk. Would you meet me at Friar's over the lunch break?"

Dolly didn't answer. Kathleen waited.

Kathleen sighed. "You haven't seen anyone suspicious since you arrived in Chicago months ago. No one's ever bothered you."

"Only because I'm super careful and very clever, Miss Know It All."

"Goodness, you're testy." Kathleen took a long puff on her cigarette and stared off into space. The girl sounded so defensive.

"I guess being careful is a bad habit now. I'll take a circuitous route, but I do believe the murderer is more interested in you."

"What makes you say that?"

"You were upset about those telephone calls, thinking I'd called you back when I hadn't. Then the mysterious woman showed up at

Mrs. Taylor's asking for you. Sophie knows there's more you haven't told us."

Kathleen stayed silent.

Dolly said, "I'll be there. I'm tired of this cat-and-mouse game. Besides, I'm bursting to tell someone, anyone, what's happened, and you've helped me make my decision. See you around noon."

"My turn." Brandy held her hand out for the telephone. She called Mac. "Are some of your biggest guys free to hang around Friar's today?"

When Kathleen dismissed the troupe for lunch, she saw Dolly standing close to the piano. She was carrying on a hand-waving conversation with Freddy. Freddy's face, still bruised, glowed like a neon sign.

Kathleen beckoned Dolly to come sit on a barstool. Dolly pranced over and put a sack down. She opened it and pulled out two sandwiches, grinning ear to ear.

"Swell. I'll get us Coca-Colas." Kathleen went to the bar and put ice in two glasses and squirted in the beverage. She returned and said, "You're thoughtful, Dolly. Thanks. What's so exciting?"

Dolly unwrapped her sandwich and said, "You first. Tell me what's going on with Sophie."

When Kathleen finished the string of events, from Sophie being snatched from the bus station to Martin whisking her off on a plane to catch his ship and then to live in the Caribbean while she healed, Dolly sat silent.

Kathleen lit a cigarette, blew out a stream of smoke, and watched it for a few seconds.

"What makes me feel terrible," Kathleen said, "is I should have watched over her more carefully. I shouldn't have let her take whatever job she thought without helping her check it out first."

"There you go." Dolly actually shook her finger at Kathleen. "You always think you know it all, and that you're the only one who makes good decisions. You need to get over that. People won't want to be around you if you keep being bossy."

Good grief. Kathleen didn't know if she should laugh or accept the chastisement.

[245]

"Think about it, Kathleen. Compare your life with Sophie's. She's flying away to some exotic place with a very rich man, and you don't even have your fur coat anymore. They'll fall in love, and she'll live like a princess ever after. Aren't you happy for her?"

Kathleen's stomach flipped. When Martin stood next to her, or talked with her, her heart pounded, and a fire started deep inside. She ached to touch him. She swallowed hard

"Okay, here's my news." Dolly sat up and clasped her hands together. "I received a message from someone we both know." She fumbled around in her pocketbook and pulled a note out and waved it in front of Kathleen. "This person is evidently romantically interested in me. He's asked me to go sailing with him today."

"You're being coy." Kathleen took a drag. "Who?"

"Pritchard." Dolly beamed.

"Dolly, what is it with you and older men?" Kathleen swigged the last of her Coca-Cola and stubbed out her cigarette.

"He's rich and oh so debonair, not unlike my other beau. Delivering milk doesn't pay much." Dolly played with her newly bobbed spit curls. "I'm convinced the murderer is after you, and you've convinced me I'm safe. Like you said, it's been months."

"Criminetly, Pritchard . . ." Kathleen took the note and read it.

"You're jealous because he asked *me* to go sailing."

"Hardly. He gives me the creeps." Kathleen stood, straightening her dance-practice skirt. "If you ask me, there's something off about him. "Why else would he leave you this note instead of calling?"

"Bye, Kathleen. I've spent too much time hiding. Even you can't make me unhappy on this beautiful day. I meet him in a half hour, so I'm off to surprise him with a little thank-you gift—maybe a silk sailing scarf." Dolly slipped on her sweater, pulled on her gloves, and snatched up the typed note, inviting her to a day on the lake. "I'll see you around—on the arms of my new sugar daddy."

Kathleen watched Dolly glide out of Friars and, through the multi-paned windows, saw her tuck into a shop down the street. The little blonde piece of fluff did look rather hotsy-totsy. But Kathleen would die before she let another middy blouse hang in her closet. Let little Mary and her friends have them all. With Dolly, no one would guess that under her navy and white blouse and pleated skirt lived a mindless gold digger.

"McPherson." Jake, one of the stage managers, came out from the back room. "Someone's here to see you back by the dressing rooms."

Before she reached the back hallway, she saw Pritchard talking to some actors. He must have heard her heels clicking on the wood, because he swirled around.

"Miss McPherson, may we talk now, or should I return?"

"Now's fine. I'll buy you a Coca-Cola." Kathleen glanced at the front door. *Wasn't Dolly off to the docks to meet him?*

"This isn't social." He strode into the Inn and ignored the bar. He picked a table and remained standing until Kathleen sat.

"You appear to be settling in well in your new apartment. I'm pleased to hear your singing friend found a safe refuge. Regardless, whether you remain in Chicago or not, it's most unpleasant to have this rift with your parents. Would you appreciate my speaking to them on your behalf?"

"How on earth do you know these things?" He made her want a cigarette. "Who told you about Sophie?"

"Chicago has layers of webs and vines of communication. One must be knowledgeable enough to use only secure connections pertaining to whatever current business is at hand. To give you a hint, I know something about precious cargo being shipped to distant places."

Something else brought him here to see her.

"You come from a fine family, a loving family, and you've benefited much from their watchful and protective nature. Many women flee from their families for different reasons. Your vigor for this life on stage comes from somewhere deep within, not from your desire to escape. Mrs. Davidson and I have had many an argument on your behalf about your work here. I've told her to relax and celebrate your new promotion."

Mrs. Davidson?

"I hate seeing talent wasted. I believe I could be influential on your behalf."

Someone actually understood her passion for dancing and acting. Of course, his explanation didn't account for the homicidal knife thrower. Her mind snapped back to the fact that he was sitting across the table from her, he'd told Mrs. Davidson about her, and he'd denounced this visit as social.

"Pritchard, I haven't a clue why you're here. I seriously doubt if you care enough about my feelings to try to right this situation with my parents."

"You're wrong. It saddens me to see you and your parents at odds." He leaned back and studied the ceiling a moment, then faced her. "You don't much like me, and I understand why. You're smart. You sense things. You don't appreciate not knowing what it is you don't know." His gaze lowered, he spread his hands on the table, and waited.

Was he waiting for her to speak?

"Why aren't you down at the dock preparing for your day of sailing?"

"Miss McPherson?" He sat straight, knitting his brows.

"Dolly showed me your note, inviting her to sail with you." Kathleen now felt foolish. Had Dolly typed the note herself? "She left a few minutes ago to shop for a sailing gift before joining you on the dock."

"I would never ask any young lady to go sailing. What's this about?"

She shrugged. Pritchard bothered her by confusing her thoughts— she couldn't get her mind to untangle them. She sighed, took out her cigarettes, and pulled the ashtray closer.

"Why would she say I wrote her a note?" He actually flushed. "Does she engage in that new social device called treating? Totally absurd. I detest the thought of young women flitting about, expecting men to shower them with gifts and good times, all for payment of romantic encounters. Deplorable."

Oh, what the hell. "She's quite infatuated, Pritchard. I think she's too young for you, but what I think doesn't matter."

Kathleen thought of him with Mrs. Schrader hanging on to his arm at the Davidsons'. Then the woman on the train—that woman ranged closer to his age than Dolly's.

Pritchard, jaw set, stared at her.

At last he leaned back in his chair and closed his eyes. After a moment he opened them and spoke softly to Kathleen.

"I am Pritchard. I am not Mr. Pritchard, nor am I Miss or Mrs. Pritchard. I am Pritchard. I have no desire whatsoever to have any type of romantic encounter with any man and especially not with a woman." His usually dramatic voice fell into a monotone. "As a child, a young teen, my parents left me to figure life's difficulties out on my own. They clothed and fed me. They saw to it I received a decent education. They did not give me the care a young person must have. No one watched over me. When the young are not guided or protected, evil happens. The consequences erupt in different forms depending on the psychological verve of the child."

Ice slivers cut through Kathleen. She remembered an ugly story concerning children.

"All three of us held on, determined to survive. As adults we each sought solace and justice in our own way." He closed his eyes again.

"Who—what happened?" But Kathleen knew what had happened the moment the words left her lips. Her stomach soured. "Mrs. Schrader and Mrs. Davidson—you're all friends, aren't you? This is about Mr. Temple and his perverted behaviors with three young girls, isn't it?"

He nodded. Kathleen studied him.

She opened her eyes wide and whispered, "You're a—*woman*."

Pritchard's face sagged. He nodded.

She stifled a gasp, transforming it into a deep breath.

"What's this façade about?"

"After they locked Mr. Temple up, the adults ignored his victims. They treated us like nothing had happened. We were discouraged to ever talk about the *incidences*. For years the three of us struggled to find a normalcy. I decided if I embodied a man, no man would ever hurt me again. The longer I lived the part, the more I enjoyed playing the part of being other people. The stage became my salvation."

"What about Mrs. Schrader?" Kathleen had never thought about the reason provoking the woman's murderous and outrageous behaviors.

"We all felt rage and helplessness. Her helplessness came out as anger and meanness. They became her shield. She's doing better now, probably because of her healing charity works."

He's probably told her and Mrs. Davidson about me. Poor Mrs. Davidson. After a rotten childhood, she put up with Chester's inappropriate behaviors with other young ladies. She had to have loved Chester deeply. Kathleen couldn't imagine Mrs. Davidson's despair, believing her husband had drowned in the Mississippi River.

"Mrs. Davidson," he said, "never seemed to find a way to feel secure, or protect herself. I'm meeting her at the Congress Hotel for dinner tonight."

She's in Chicago? "You care about both of them, don't you?"

"I do." He looked at his watch. "Vivian, or Vi, whichever, does worry me the most. She can't find herself. She doesn't know who she is, or what she wants. She switches from kind and compassionate to angry, hostile, and vindictive. I'm sure it's from the damage left when her father killed her beloved dog. His teaching us those magical skills often left her wilted like a flower in the desert."

"Magical?"

"Ah, some would say not magical at all, just a heightened sense of awareness. He taught us how to read meaning from words not said, how to blend into shadows and appear when least expected, and we all learned the fine art of knife-throwing. We practiced relentlessly until we were proficient, then we practiced more in his backyard."

They all threw knives. She couldn't breathe because Pritchard had used up all the air.

"Horrifying as it seems now, we'd throw knives at each other. Vivian's dark moment came when he used her and her dog as impalers—the targets for his vaudeville act. Since then, one never knows if she'll be amenable or explode. When I speak to her, I always couch my words in magnificent spun sugar."

There's no place like home.

—DOROTHY, WIZARD OF OZ

49

Pritchard's information about his childhood made Kathleen dizzy. She appreciated Pritchard's intentions as far as she and her parents were concerned, but her parents' stubbornness would never waver.

She stared out the window, watching him walk away.

Pritchard gives what he never received. Protection.

She stubbed out her cigarette. *Dolly. Why would the silly girl type up a note and lie?* Kathleen needed to get ready for rehearsal.

But her stomach jittered and twisted into twinges. A warning—danger.

For months now, Dolly had refused to leave Mrs. Taylor's except to go to work and home again. Had someone really left the note at the boardinghouse? Dolly worked odd hours and not every day. To know when she came and went, someone would need to watch the boardinghouse for hours, maybe even days.

But if someone enticed Dolly to wait on the dock . . .

A day on the lake with Pritchard would be one way to draw Dolly from the safety of Mrs. Taylor's home.

Safety? Little girls in a backyard throwing knives at each other.

Mrs. Davidson's in Chicago.

And so is Chester.

She jumped up and yelled to Jake, who was busy arranging props on the stage.

"Jake, tell Brandy it's an emergency and have Mac meet me where the private boats are moored—hurry."

She dashed out the door.

The knife thrower couldn't be Mr. Temple, the father. He'd still be locked up or dead. But Vivian Davidson knew this skill, Pritchard had discussed Chicago things with her, and she had the motive to murder Chester's young women.

Kathleen sprinted across the wide park. Mrs. Davidson seemed terribly depressed, but even in her sadness she reached out to Kathleen, wanting to help her, guide her, and encourage her not to throw away her college chances. Gentle and fragile, Mrs. Davidson couldn't be a murderer.

Pritchard said she often exploded into anger and vindictiveness. And Kathleen's father and mother described her as someone hard, difficult, and much different than who Kathleen knew.

Venders dotted the shore, and sightseers milled around the park and the dock. Kathleen wove her way through the languid groups and trotted down the pier, looking for Dolly. Fishermen with tackle boxes dangled their lines over the edges. Some stood chatting, baiting their hooks, comparing the morning's catches, and enjoying the cold autumn sunshine.

Children ran past with red and blue balloons held by strings tied to their coat buttons. Kathleen danced around a cluster of people bundled in sweaters. They selected flavors from an ice-cream vendor.

Way down the pier, away from everyone, Dolly sat on one of the pier pilings. She filed her nails. Only a lone fisherman occupied her end of the dock.

Kathleen waved her arm. Dolly glanced up then focused back on a nail.

"Hurry." Kathleen sucked in air. "Got to get off this pier. We're in danger."

"Horsefeathers. You're jealous." She started on another nail. "Save it for someone else."

"You're right. It is Mrs. Davidson. She's out to kill us both, like she did Lillian." Kathleen swiveled around and scanned the pier.

"I'm waiting for Pritchard. Mrs. Davidson may kill whomever she pleases. It doesn't concern me." Dolly stood and bent over, looking down at the small boats tied to the dock. "I wonder which one of these we'll take sailing."

The ice-cream vendor pushed his cart closer to their end of the dock. The crowd meandered along behind him. The balloons bounced up and down over the heads of the children.

Mrs. Davidson might appear at any moment now. She could walk up to Dolly, chat, and nonchalantly stab her. But then people would see. She might stay as part of the crowd and just throw the knife.

"Pritchard didn't write that note." Kathleen grabbed Dolly's arms, making the girl face her. "He's not who you think he is."

"Get your hands off of me, Kathleen McPherson." Dolly jerked away, moving to the other side of the dock. "Leave. You're not wanted here."

"Hello, young ladies. I'm pleased to see you." Mrs. Davidson came around the ice-cream cart and continued along the pier as if nothing but the beautiful day concerned her.

Kathleen's heart pounded. The woman's expertise in knife throwing ensured she wouldn't miss her target. Kathleen glanced over at Dolly. She stood on the other side of the pier. *Good. Mrs. Davidson would face two targets.*

Kathleen snapped her attention back to Mrs. Davidson.

"Hello, Mrs. Davidson," Kathleen shouted. "I'm pleased to see you too. My parents said we needed to talk about scholarships."

Mrs. Davidson's step faltered, but she regained her composure and continued moving closer.

She waved and called back, "I actually have something for you from Stephens." Her voice deepened and growled. "You mustn't— you idiot. All you young pretty things think you can do whatever you want."

Dolly gasped and started toward Kathleen. Kathleen waved her back. They had to stay apart. Kathleen's stomach felt twisted into knots. She trotted down the dock a few feet to narrow the space between her and Mrs. Davidson.

"You do believe Stephens is the right college for me, Mrs. Davidson?" Kathleen caught her breath and stopped an arm's length behind the last fisherman sitting on the pier. He stared at his dangled line cutting fast away through the water, apparently uninterested in the fact that a killer approached.

Mrs. Davidson's face softened before she spoke again.

"Your mother is quite distraught about your leaving school."

Mrs. Davidson looked down at her hand, which held her pocketbook. It seemed to shake without purpose. She put her other hand over it.

"I do wish I could make my mother happy. Do you have any suggestions for me?"

Mrs. Davidson, a lilt in her voice, said, "I've written some letters, and now I have something to show you." Her face knotted up again. "Your mother has no idea what an ugly bitch you and your little blonde trollop friend are."

Dolly started toward Mrs. Davidson. "I'm not a trollop." Her fists clenched.

"Stop, Dolly," Kathleen's words fired out. "Go back."

Dolly evidently obeyed, because Kathleen didn't hear footsteps on the wooden planks.

Kathleen, her eyes locked on Mrs. Davidson, said, "Mrs. Davidson, are you feeling all right?"

The woman shifted her purse to her other hand and stared at nothing. She looked around like she didn't know where she was.

"Here." Kathleen pointed to the piling next to the fisherman. "Sit for a moment. I'll get us some ice cream."

"All that water." Mrs. Davidson moved closer to the fisherman and looked down. "My husband drowned. Did you know? I wonder how it feels. It's a form of suffocation."

The fisherman ignored them. He leaned in now, reeling in his fishing line. Kathleen glanced at him and saw he'd worn out the fighting fish.

"You need to rest," Kathleen said softly to Mrs. Davidson. "What flavor do you want?"

"Flavor? Favor? Free flavors—you're too free with your favors, Kathleen." The older woman's voice changed again as her face darkened. "You're worse than a trollop. Your parents are delighted to have you gone."

Mrs. Davidson fumbled opening her pocketbook, moving in close. Her whole body now shook. Mumbling, she slipped her hand into her purse.

Dolly screeched.

Kathleen skidded sideways into the fisherman. She thrust the man out of the way, snagged his pole, and whipped the shortened line with the huge bass at Mrs. Davidson.

It smacked Mrs. Davidson in the face. She shrieked, twisted, and

[254]

flailed, dropping her purse. Kathleen flung the fishing pole aside and launched herself toward Mrs. Davidson, pinning the woman's arms against her side.

Kathleen willed herself to breathe. Mrs. Davidson's shrieking turned into wailing.

Dolly's hysterical screams continued.

The fisherman blubbered unintelligible words and stumbled away. The fish flopped around on the pier, opening and closing its mouth like it too wanted to say something.

The crowd gathered, pointing and jabbering about things they knew nothing about.

Kathleen's vision blurred. Mrs. Davidson mentioned an invitation to a tea held in the parlor at the college. Kathleen swallowed, repositioned herself, and whispered soft words of comfort to the woman.

Quivering from strain, Kathleen couldn't remain standing behind Mrs. Davidson, holding this crazy woman. Her search for help caused her to gasp.

Down the pier, a woman wearing an orange and black feathered hat bobbed away through the crowd.

Mrs. Schrader?

Kathleen closed her eyes and listened as Dolly's screams subsided into gulping air and Mrs. Davidson rambled about not wanting to do tatting for the guild's doilies. A large hand closed around Kathleen's. She opened her eyes and saw Mac. She didn't know how to unlock her death grip on Mrs. Davidson. Mac gently removed Kathleen's hands, one at a time. He took Mrs. Davidson from her.

The woman shrieked and thrashed. "Get your filthy hands off of me, you pervert. Don't touch me." She melted into sobbing. "One horrid young trollop after another."

Kathleen's wanted to slump down onto the wooden planks next to the flopping fish. She watched Mac's gentle brute strength come into action as he handcuffed Mrs. Davidson.

"I'm rid of you." Mrs. Davidson hit Mac with her forehead. "You've drowned. It's the crazy one who stabbed. I'd drown all of them, one at a time." She jerked her cuffed hands around and screamed for all to hear. "Carve his finagling heart out."

Kathleen knelt to collect the few spilled contents of Mrs. Davidson's pocketbook. She stopped, looked inside, and pulled out an envelope. *No Knife?*

Kathleen blanched. *Did Mrs. Davidson's mixed-up talk implicate Chester?*

Mrs. Davidson stared at Kathleen and, in a childish voice, said, "The envelope is for you. Stephens College will grant you admission even though you didn't graduate. Send them your test scores."

Dolly sidled over to Kathleen and stood transfixed. The fisherman, with his tackle, retrieved his fish, grunted something as he unhooked it, and tossed it back into the lake. He sauntered off down the pier, shaking his head.

"Let's get you some help." Mac nudged Mrs. Davidson.

Mrs. Davidson studied Kathleen before she spoke. "Do you know I loved Chester?"

Mac pushed her forward a few more steps. She stopped and looked over at the ice-cream wagon. "Ice cream. When you return home, please stop by for tea. There's this lovely all-women's college in Missouri. I believe it would suit you. Promise you'll visit."

Kathleen watched Mac lead Mrs. Davidson down the pier.

"Golly, Kathleen, you put those great dance muscles to good use."

"Dolly, go." Kathleen closed her eyes. "Pritchard isn't coming."

"But, we—"

"Not now, please." She looked at Dolly.

Kathleen's face must have looked murderous, or strange, because Dolly backed away and stood. Dolly looked down the pier toward Mac and Mrs. Davidson. She glanced back at Kathleen, shrugged, and trotted after them.

No knife. Does that mean she isn't the murderer? If not, it has to be Chester or Mrs. Schrader.

Kathleen watched the blonde bit of sweet fluff disappear into the crowd and then stared as the crowd dispersed. She saw no sign of the woman with the orange, plumed hat.

She knew Ed would arrive in a few minutes. He would have his tiny notebook and pencil, and he would ask her questions, hoping for a front-page scoop.

She gazed out over Lake Michigan. A lump grew in her throat.

Chicago: they'd make the big time here. They'd dance and sing, like one big party, and the world would magically turn into a happy place.

She swept her gaze across the blue, cloudless sky. *Sophie's up there, winging her way to the ship and then on to paradise, with Martin.*

She swallowed and watched the people farther down the dock. There was Ed, striding around everyone. Behind him, way across the park, stood the Congress Hotel where she'd called her parents that first weekend in Chicago. Something unsettling shifted inside.

In addition to the knifer Kathleen still had to deal with Hymie.

Pay him in his own coin.
—SCOTTISH PROVERB

50

Kathleen hated walking to work through this neighborhood of alleys full of trash, vacant lots with kids and yippy dogs, and sidewalks needing repair. She turned down the street where she'd stolen the gangster's automobile from in front of the bakery.

If Kathleen stayed on as choreographer at Friar's she could save enough in her shoebox for an automobile next year. No, she and Brandy had to leave—soon.

Everything looked normal, except now this city felt too small. Hymie, Mrs. Davidson, and Mrs. Schrader knew she worked at Friar's. *Would they release Mrs. Davidson or send her to a treatment facility?*

A woman came out of the bakery, carrying a loaf of Italian bread. Kathleen hurried past, turned the corner by the warehouse, and headed over toward the theater district. A shiny, black automobile drove slowly toward her. *Crap.* She ducked her head and turned to look in a shop window and watched its reflection move by.

She sprinted down the walk for several blocks. Then she took deep breaths and slowed to a brisk pace. Still blocks from Friar's, she caught a glimpse of the automobile again, or one like it. She cringed, stepping into a doorway. *Paranoia, once inside, is difficult to eradicate.*

The automobile turned up a side street but then appeared a few minutes later from another side street, now driving in her direction. *Dammit.*

She ducked into an alley and jogged toward the other end. Kathleen stopped halfway down and crouched behind some large trash bins. She peered around at the motorcars passing on the street. A noise—she jumped and glanced behind her.

An alley cat chased something through a stack of trash and flattened cardboard boxes.

She looked back at the street in time to see the black automobile moving past.

She relaxed.

It stopped, backed up, and maneuvered into the alley.

Her heart pounded. She swept her gaze around, darted over to the pile of trash, and burrowed under the cardboard. Seconds later she heard and felt the vibrations of the vehicle moving past and out the other end of the alley. She bolted in the opposite direction and sped around the corner. Kathleen pulled on an office door then another until she found an unlocked one, and she jerked it open. As she yanked the glass door shut behind her, she caught the reflection of a black automobile.

Had she been seen?

Dashing down the dark hallway, turning corners, and checking for other unlocked doors, she heard the outside door open and shut.

Kathleen ducked into a doorway leading to a steep stairwell. The scary thought of being chased and trapped on a roof terrified her, but someone like Hymie, who probably had a gun, scared her more.

She sprinted up the stairs two at a time. At the landing, she pulled a door open and stepped into the dark. Before the door closed behind her, the dim lightbulb on the landing gave her a glimpse of the interior. She stood on something narrow with railings on both sides. All her senses told her to move. Kathleen crept along the passage, clutching to the railings.

When her eyes adjusted, she shuddered. She stood high above some auditorium on a catwalk. Her muscles tightened. Geesh, she hated heights.

She felt around wooden belaying pins set in the railings and shuffled down the narrow lane. It intersected at a right angle with another. She stepped into an adjoining aisle and kept moving deeper into the catwalk maze of paths above the theater.

A flash of light stopped her movement. Someone had opened the door. Rhythmic vibrations announced someone else now maneuvered these catwalks too.

She inched, now stepping lightly, past hanging ropes and around electrical cords.

She couldn't see, but she felt vertical electrical cables attached to lighting canisters and railings with ropes tied to belaying pins. They lined most of the walks, but not all. She pressed into a dense curtain of ropes, hoping to keep her position hidden. Below her would be the fly space. The stage hands used these ropes, tied to belaying pins, to pull the curtains and scenery up out of view. They'd untie the ropes to lower them back onto the stage.

Old cigar smoke. She could hear him panting, coming nearer from the left. She pulled in tight against the ropes and held her breath. To her right would be another intersection going two different directions. They'd control the center-stage lighting.

Out of her peripheral vision in the dark, she saw movement. Maybe an arm—a hand stretched out in front of someone—only a few feet away. She leaped out, snapping her left leg into her strongest and highest kick ever. Her foot connected, probably with his arm. He yelped. Something metallic clanked and skittered—followed by a second of silence—before it clunked down onto the stage below.

Kathleen ran, rounded the ninety-degree turn, and kept going. She may have knocked a gun out of his hand, but these guys always carried a backup. If he didn't have another pistol, he'd be carrying a stiletto blade somewhere. She put her fingers out to assure herself of a protective curtain of ropes or electrical cables.

Nothing?

Chills flooded her body. She halted and dropped to her knees, grabbing the catwalk floor.

She stretched her fingers up, feeling for the railings on this catwalk.

Nothing.

Nausea washed over her. She curled into a ball. His footsteps pounded on the metal walkway, then stopped.

She'd rather walk through cockroaches than be up here. She took a deep breath, got to her knees, and forced herself to stand. Sweat poured from her neck and underarms.

He must have turned the other way. She could hear him moving again. This time he was coming in her direction. She cursed the darkness and slid her feet straight ahead along the catwalk, her arms and fingers stretched out. Her hand connected with a railing and something metallic. She took a deep breath.

Exploring it with both hands, she wondered if the electricity was still connected to this spotlight canister. She angled the direction of the canister from its stage target below so it pointed along the catwalk where she'd been. With her hand on the switch, she'd wait until—*cigar smoke mixed with sweaty body odor.*

Her fingers clicked the switch. Hymie, in a blaze of spotlight, lunged back. His hands shielded his eyes. He stumbled and grabbed for the railing that wasn't there.

She held her breath, shut her eyes, and clung to the canister. His scream stopped when the stage floor silenced him. She vaguely remembered the auditorium lights clicking on, people shouting to each other, then someone snapped off the spotlight and took her hand.

All life is just a progression toward, and then a recessions from, one phrase—"I love you."

—F. SCOTT FITZGERALD

51

"I still don't understand why you and Brandy want to go to Detroit." Ed sat on the edge of the window and watched Kathleen fold clothes. She packed each in a trunk to be shipped.

"Detroit's wide open." Kathleen didn't want to go to Detroit. She wanted to go to the Caribbean. "Their Mayor supports speakeasies and cabarets instead of raiding them. Friar's and its ilk are done for." She held up a long, sapphire-colored velvet opera coat and folded it with the upmost care. She picked up a black turban covered with blue-green bugle beads and placed it in the trunk on top of the opera coat.

"Kid, this town won't be the same without you." He got up and headed toward the kitchen. "I need a drink."

A few minutes later he came back carrying two glasses. "You don't have much to choose from. Do you know your counter top is all sticky? What is that stuff?"

"Honey. I take it for my cough."

"Surprise, here's a rum and Coca-Cola." He handed her a glass.

"I keep thinking about Sophie."

"Martin's a good guy to let her hide out and recuperate in that

[262]

mansion of his." He glanced away, then back, and looked her in the eyes.

Kathleen took a large swallow of her drink. "It's not a mansion, it's a villa." Kathleen put her cigarette in the ashtray and started to sort clothes into piles.

Ed stood from his perch on the windowsill, pulled the chintz-covered vanity stool close to the bedside, and sat to watch.

"Why didn't Hymie do away with Sophie? Why beat her up, buy her flowers, and keep her a prisoner?" Ed started crunching on his ice.

"Christ, Ed. That sets my teeth on edge."

"Sorry. I'm going to get another, how about you?"

She finished off hers and handed it to him.

"The way I see it," her voice was loud, "Hymie owns things. Sophie was his property." Kathleen took the fresh drink, set it on the nightstand, and lit another cigarette.

"You've already got one burning." He nodded toward the ashtray. "Let's go somewhere. Leave this mess."

"Got to finish. Brandy and I leave tomorrow." Kathleen stubbed out the cigarette in the ashtray.

"But why?

"You've asked that, and I've explained it."

"You don't even have a job there, and Detroit is a tough place."

"Maybe."

"No maybe. It's true. They pipe that Canada stuff directly in under that lake, and I hear there are turf wars all the time."

"I don't believe that, about the pipe under the lake. They couldn't do that. And the turf wars can't be any worse than the ones here." Kathleen started her folding project again.

Ed stood and, taking hold of Kathleen's hands, he turned her toward him. "Look at me, Kathleen. I care about you." He sighed. "There's more to this, isn't there?"

"What makes you think that?" Kathleen glanced around the room. "Oh, I almost forgot." She pulled away and picked up her white satin mules from under her vanity.

"You're frightened."

"Don't be silly. I understand they have an opening for a choreographer at Luigi's, and I'm going to be that person. Brandy will get on because no one can resist her voice. That's all." Kathleen examined her bedroom for more hidden clothing.

"Hymie's not a problem for you. You don't need to run away." Ed loosened his tie.

"I'm going, Ed. You may not like it, but I am." Kathleen finished her drink and handed it to him. He took their glasses into the kitchen. She stared at the mess of clothes still unpacked.

"I'm feeling so goddamned awful about everything."

When Ed returned with another Cuba Libre, she still hadn't moved.

"How could Hymie do something like that?" The tears slid down her cheeks. She took a big drink, stared at him, and started to giggle.

"What?"

Kathleen laughed harder until she spilled her drink. She set it down and collapsed on her bed, her laughter uncontrollable.

"What's so funny—?"

"Your—" she gasped for air and pointed at the floor—"Your shoes."

Ed glanced down. Toilet tissues Kathleen had used when she coughed and then thrown on the floor were stuck to the underside of his shoes.

"What the hell?"

"It's the honey." Kathleen cackled but tears were streaming down her face. "I feel lousy about Sophie."

"I know." Ed sat on the edge of the bed and pulled bits of tissue off his soles. The tissue stuck to his fingers. He picked up his glass and downed it in one gulp. "Dammit anyway." Bits of tissue now stuck to the glass. "Oh, for . . ." Then he broke into his classic Ed grin.

She stared at him.

"You're a good guy." She slid over and helped pick the tissue off his fingers, making his eyes twinkle. He erupted into tiny chuckles of delight, melting all her fears.

He pulled her into the warmth of his arms, and she closed her eyes, remembering Martin's firm hand on the small of her back when they danced.

Youth doesn't need friends—it only needs crowds.

—ZELDA FITGERALD

52   Detroit, Ten Years Later

"Ed, dammit, it's like old times." Kathleen called to the kid behind the bar, "Hey, Richie, set us up, okay? Now, fill me in on all the news . . . How's Friar's?"

Ed slid onto a barstool and grinned. She took the one next to him.

"Still smoking Camels." She lit one of her Pall Malls. "It's been—what?—years."

"This market crash hurt." Ed tapped his cigarette on the rim of the ashtray.

"Are you okay?"

"I count myself lucky," Ed said, "but good people went down. One day you're up there—next day, soup lines."

"Russian factories seem to be doing well."

"Possibly. With no European goods coming in, how's Martin's shipping business?"

"We still need oil and other imports." Kathleen picked at her red nail polish. "He's clever. My parents were hit hard—Pop being in the banking business and all."

"I forgot. Sorry."

"They almost lost their house. Mother loves that home." Kathleen let ashes drop onto the bar.

Ed shoved the ashtray closer.

"For God's sake, Richie." She pointed at the bartender.

"Hold your horses." Richie scurried the length of the bar. He'd been carrying on with a perky little brunette.

"Rich, you're worthless. You should be fired." Kathleen gave a lopsided smile.

"I know. Tell dad." He set Cuba Libres in front of them and rushed back to finish his conversation.

"Dad?"

"Luigi's boy."

"Do you like this place?"

"It's a blast. We take the show on the road a couple of times a year." She looked at Ed through her long lashes.

"You're kidding?" Ed took her hand.

"It's not that big of a thing." But it was. Not many chorus lines performed professionally enough to book gigs in other cities. "A friend— you remember Pritchard—he lined up a gig for us in St. Louis. Luigi gave us two weeks off. Word spread. Now we also do a few shows a year on the road."

Ed smirked. "Pritchard. You've got some crazy Minnesota friends. Is the woman on the pier still in some sanitarium?"

"I don't know." Kathleen should ask Pritchard. She often confided in him. He swore not to tell anyone about her being in Detroit and said he'd alert Kathleen if Chester appeared.

"How does big-time entertainment survive while everything else struggles?" Ed took a big swallow with ice.

"Ed, please don't start chewing that."

He shrugged with a grin, then said, "I heard what happened to Dolly."

"Poor kid." Kathleen rested her chin on the back of her hand. "She thought if she gave up looking for sugar daddies, and settled with her milkman lover, she'd be safe."

"I'd have put my money on her just being paranoid." Ed raised his eyebrow.

Kathleen sighed. "Pritchard visited her in the hospital. He said she couldn't identify the woman who poisoned her. I told him who I suspected, but he and the police didn't agree."

"Why not?" Ed pushed his glass away.

"She's a friend of Pritchard's, and the police said she was in Minneapolis when it happened."

"Well, there you have it."

"Not really. Since childhood, she's been a master of deception. I'm surprised the authorities didn't hold the restaurant responsible."

"It's a high-volume lunch crowd." He shook his head. "Great reputation."

Kathleen took a drag, let the smoke slip out, and said, "The message is if you share a table with a stranger, don't leave your drink unguarded."

"And Sophie?"

"Back in Minneapolis teaching piano and giving singing lessons."

"You've gone to see her?"

"Staying away." Kathleen picked a piece of tobacco off her lower lip. "I didn't even attend Mary's wedding. Mary's my little sister."

Ed studied her. She knew he wanted to know why.

"Everyone knows my parents disapprove of my work. If I attended, then I'd be the focus of attention. Mary deserved to be the main attraction, not me."

Richie brought fresh drinks and a dish of peanuts.

She took a handful, then said, "I loved those years in Chicago, Ed."

"You didn't think so on that catwalk."

"I could get a high-paying job as a wing walker." She winked.

"Kathleen, have you thought of settling down—getting married?"

"Sometimes . . . Then I get over it."

"Aren't you lonely?"

"Aw, Ed, those wrestling matches or ball games on your press passes, then dinners, staying up all night getting drunk, listening to the big bands—Gawd, I do miss it." Kathleen stared into her drink.

"Have you been to the Big Red Barn yet?"

"Hockey?" Kathleen spilled some of her drink on her sweater.

"Mitch, with the Detroit Free Press, writes up the hockey games," he said.

She felt him watch her brush at the liquid with her thumb.

He continued, "Told me to invite whomever I wanted. Are you and Brandy free tonight?"

"If we charged we'd be prostitutes."

Ed pulled out another Camel and stared at it.

She raised her eyebrow. "You've got something on your mind."

He shifted on the stool and looked around the bar.

"Dammit, what's up?"

"I don't know how to—" He lit his cigarette and took a puff. "Is it over with you and Martin?" He picked up his drink and stirred the ice with his finger.

"It'll never be over." Kathleen finished off the last peanut. She shoved the dish aside.

"You still care?"

"I will always care. We see each other. Talk about something else."

"He hasn't left his wife."

"You could say that."

She set the glass down hard on the bar and watched the quartet set up to play.

They started with the new Jerome Kern song, "Smoke Gets in Your Eyes."

Ed sipped his drink in silence. When the song finished, Kathleen said, "I need to powder my nose."

An instrumental piece, rather loud and unruly, blared as Kathleen left the ladies' room. Brandy was sitting with Ed.

"Brandy, what's this? First you steal my barstool, then you make time with my guy?"

"Ladies," Ed said, "let's get a table. I'll call Mitch." He winked at Kathleen.

"Whatever your heart desires, sweety. Rich, another now." Richie looked her way. She snapped her fingers and pointed at a table in the corner away from the stage.

Ed left to call Mitch.

Brandy grabbed her wrist. "Is there something going on between you two?"

"Some things a lady should never tell." Kathleen went over and slid into a chair. She lit a cigarette, fluffed her hair, and looked around the room.

"Dammit, Kathleen."

Richie set three drinks down and another bowl of peanuts.

"Good boy." Kathleen gave him a pat on his rear end.

Richie hooted.

"Brandy, you sit next to this Mitch guy, okay? Eddie and I want to catch up."

"You never call him Eddie."

Ed sprinted back to the table.

"Dear heart, what did Mitch say?" Kathleen patted the chair next to hers and crinkled her nose.

He gazed into her eyes and said, "Who?"

Brandy swatted at Ed. "All right. I don't buy this for a minute."

"Hey, kid, relax." Ed pushed her glass closer. "Life's too unpredictable and way too short to get all your feathers fluffed." He slid an arm around Kathleen's shoulders.

When Mitch joined them, Kathleen said, "Mitch, what do you think about your friend here talking about getting married again?"

"I won't have him marry the wrong type of gal."

"Yeah, who you gonna marry, Ed?" Brandy asked. She downed her drink.

"The only woman I've ever loved." He squeezed Kathleen's shoulder.

"Your own true love is the only one you should ever marry."

Dammit, Martin.

[Growing up] is a terribly hard thing to do. It is much easier to skip it and go from one childhood to another.

—F. SCOTT FITZGERALD

53 St. Thomas

"Life's unpredictable and way too short . . ."
Beyond the roar of the airplane's engine, Ed's words echoed in Kathleen's ear. She stared past her own reflection in the window and focused her eyes on the approaching runway.

A couple of months ago, back in Detroit, they'd pretended. It had all been a joke—a game. After hockey and speakeasies, at five minutes before midnight, the Justice of the Peace declared Ed and Kathleen to be Mr. and Mrs. Edward Thornton. Brandy and Mitch, the witnesses, cheered. Then they all headed out the door and tromped up the block to the nightclub where they'd left their last round of drinks.

The next day, Ed flew back to Chicago.

A few weeks later Richie called Kathleen to the telephone.

"Is this Kathleen?"

"It is." She couldn't place the voice.

"I'm Ed's eldest daughter." Seconds of silence filled the line. "He always talked about you."

"Is something wrong?" Kathleen's heart quickened. This woman sounded distraught.

"My father passed . . . a heart attack this morning. Your photos are all over his house. He—you need to come for the reading of the will."

His daughters had welcomed her. They both had Ed's sweet personality. Signing her inheritance back to Ed's daughters felt right. Hell, she didn't deserve it.

Brandy, Mac, and his guys helped make arrangements. Fritzel asked his current Friar's musicians to play a special tribute. Martin came rushing to her side. After the funeral he stayed with her. So Martin-like—always comforting and ready to rescue.

After Ed's death, her desire to dance and entertain disappeared. Her mind couldn't make her heart go there.

Martin convinced her she needed a change of scenery. She finally agreed to join him in the Caribbean.

~

When the Stewardess opened the door to the plane, Kathleen stubbed out her cigarette and waited her turn to join the people in single-file movement down the aisle.

Her mood changed. Joining Martin filled her with lightness.

At the cabin door, she straightened her lemon-yellow skirt and smoothed down her jacket then stepped smartly out onto the stairway platform.

"Kathleen," Martin waved as he called, "over here."

She tingled all over as she hurried down the steps onto the tarmac. *Life is too unpredictable. I'm so, so sorry, Ed.*

"Oh, Martin, I've missed you so much." She blinked back tears.

He held her hands and gazed at her. "After all these years, now I am finally in paradise."

"Do we have a long drive?"

"Only a few miles. Wait until you see the view. After you freshen up, we'll have drinks by the pool."

~

Benje Ange accompanied Kathleen into her bedroom. "I opened the doors and shutters to let in the sunlight. Do you like this room?"

Kathleen felt the sea breeze on her face. She crossed the tile floor and stood on the balcony, where she soaked in the spectacular view of the glittering-turquoise Caribbean Ocean below. A dewy-glass pitcher of something with limes sat on a coral-colored placemat. Tall goblets stood beside it along with a small plate of butter cookies.

"Did you do all of this for me?" Kathleen asked.

"Oh, no, missy, that would be Curline. She fixes all the food." Benje Ange's brilliant white teeth broke into a smile and welcomed her.

Nahalia carried Kathleen's luggage into the room.

Kathleen took a deep breath of the damp, salty air before she pulled herself away from the ocean view and went back into the bedroom. Nahalia was unpacking and hanging Kathleen's dresses in the closet.

"Nahalia, I can do that. Please."

"Mr. Martin tells us we are to take very good care of you. We always do what he asks." Nahalia held up a long, white, sleeveless cotton dress. A small pattern of red Hibiscus decorated the left shoulder and cascaded down below the neckline. "This is lovely. You wear this tonight. I will press the wrinkles out." She carefully placed it on the circular bed and pulled out some red and white sandals with stacked heels. "Now all you need is a bright flower for your dark hair. I'll go pick one."

Before Kathleen could respond Nahalia was gone.

"What time am I supposed to be at the pool?" The thought of butter cookies made her stomach gurgle.

"He has cocktails when the sun sets over the yardarm." Benje Ange drew hot bathwater into the tub, put something oily in, and swished it around with her hands. "Probably in about an hour."

Then Benje Ange put two fluffy white towels on the little stool next to the bathtub.

"I help you with your bath." She held up a chunk of natural sponge in one hand and a bar of soap in another.

"Go—do what you do. I'll be fine." Kathleen took the sponge and soap while ushering the maid toward the door. "Thanks."

Kathleen dropped the sponge and soap on the bed, rushed to the balcony, and grabbed a cookie. The door opened again. She popped the cookie into her mouth and turned. Nahalia stood right next to her.

"Geesh," Kathleen mumbled, "you're a quick one."

"See the flowers. Which one do you like?"

Kathleen sniffed them and shrugged.

"I like the Hibiscus, to match your dress. But the white one would look beautiful too. After you bathe, I'll fix your hair, and we'll see."

I'll never be alone.

"Would you care for a cookie? I'm starving." Kathleen picked up the plate and held it out to Nahalia.

"I eat later."

Nahalia filled one of the goblets with water and placed her collection of flowers in the glass as she talked. "You'll be sailing with friends all tomorrow. Mr. Martin said he wants you to know some people because he's gone so much."

～

An hour later, Kathleen started down the circular stairs and heard Martin's voice.

"You're an angel." He stood below in the doorway.

"You're dreaming." She hurried down the steps.

"It's good to be home." He watched her descend and nuzzled her neck.

"Do you think of this as your home, not New York?" Kathleen pulled back, searching deep into his eyes for the truth.

"I do now that you live here." He held her hand and pressed it to his heart. His eyes never left hers.

"I don't get it. How can you have two of us? How can you ever be happy being pulled in different directions?" She placed her finger over his mouth to quiet his protest. "Seriously, I've resigned myself to sharing you with her. But then again, I can be one big fool."

"Kathleen, look at what we have . . . paradise . . . each other . . . anything your heart desires. Please let that be enough."

She loved him, and for the first time in years, she didn't need to live in fear. No one would find her here. Maybe this could be enough.

Positive anything is better than negative nothing.
—ELBERT HUBBARD

54

"I felt you watching me," Martin rolled over to face her.

"How could you? You don't read minds, too, do you?" Kathleen pushed her pillow up under her cheek so she could see him better in the dark.

"Sometimes I think I do."

"What am I thinking right now?"

"You're thinking, 'I wish to hell he'd be quiet and make love to me again.'"

"Oh, for Pete's sake. You're not even close . . . I long for a man with magical powers. What a shame you aren't that man." Kathleen leaned over and kissed him on the forehead. "All these months on this island doesn't feel real. Sometimes I think I'm in a dream. What's on for tomorrow?"

"Greg and Helen have a new sloop and want to see how she runs. They asked if we would like to go with them. They're leaving for the Bahamas next week. Are you game?" Martin asked.

"Sounds like a day of sun and fun."

"I told them we'd need to be back by early evening. You know I have to leave, don't you?" He was propped up on one elbow, looking at her, studying her face.

"Martin, I love you. When I'm alone, I think about every little thing we do—picnics on your yacht and cocktails at that cute little hotel on the hillside—Hotel 1829. I love sitting in that bar or on the veranda, looking out over the harbor. And the best are those enchanting nights we build bonfires on the beach with your friends and dance until dawn."

He kissed her gently on the lips. "You left out exploring other islands, and what about when we read to each other by the pool. And you love it when I finish your crossword puzzles."

She hit him with a pillow. He grabbed her wrists, held her down, and touched his lips to hers. She let the pillow fall. He chuckled.

"I love our life, Martin. It's only when we aren't together that it gets bad for me."

"I do have to pay for all of this," he murmured in her ear, holding her tight. "Is Fernando about finished with your portrait?"

"He needs me to pose for one more sitting. Why?"

"I'm anxious to see it."

Kathleen frowned. "Seriously, what on earth are you going to do with a life-size portrait?"

"Hang it above the landing in the stairwell."

"You've gone to extremes with that one." Then she feigned an exaggerated pout. "Do you realize you're away more than you are here?"

"You need more to do. I could arrange for a flight to—"

"I need *you*. That's all. Could I go with you sometime? I've never been on one of your ships."

"My sweet lass, business and pleasure never mix." He nuzzled her neck. "It's time to quit talking business and enjoy this pleasure."

The next morning, when the sun filtered through the open veranda doors and splashed on Kathleen's eyelids, she woke. Tonight he would leave again—for another six weeks. She looked over at him. He slept. While waves crashed on the rocks below and birds sang to each other from the trees, she laid there and watched him, wanting the moment to go on forever.

~

"Miss Kathleen, what I can do to make you feel better?" Nahalia opened the doors to the veranda, letting the morning sea breeze fill the room. She fluffed Kathleen's pillows and smoothed the sheets.

Kathleen wiped her mouth with a tissue and washed her face in cool water. Talking was too much of an effort. Nahalia held the sheet up while Kathleen climbed back into bed.

"It's been over a week now. Maybe you have the flu. Mr. Martin wouldn't like it if he knew you were sick. Benje Ange will call the physician."

"Please, don't." Kathleen closed her eyes. A few minutes later she felt a cold, wet cloth on her forehead. She wanted to be left alone. These busy little hummingbirds always hovered over her, not letting her do anything for herself. She started to drift off to sleep again when another wave of nausea hit her.

She leapt from the bed, ran to the toilet, and lost the rest of the buttered toast Curline had insisted she eat. Nahalia handed her the wet wash cloth to wipe her face.

Someone's poisoned me.

"Nahalia, I need to be alone." She said with as much conviction as she could muster.

"But Mr. Martin said—"

"It's all right, Nahalia, I'll take full responsibility. Give me an hour." She slept.

Somewhere off in the distance Kathleen heard voices.

High tide. Maybe she didn't hear voices but only the waves. She opened her eyes. The morning light still poured through the open doors.

Nahalia and Benje Ange were huddled on her veranda in conversation. Their words didn't make any sense.

"He'll . . ."

"She's made it clear."

"We can't let this happen."

"Should we wait until tomorrow?"

"It isn't her decision."

Kathleen got up and went to the doorway.

"Miss Kathleen, you shouldn't be up. We're calling the physician now." Benje Ange waved her back.

"Nonsense. I feel splendid."

If they poisoned me they wouldn't want to call a doctor. "Something I ate didn't agree with me. I'm ready for some tea and an English muffin with blackberry jam. I also want a soft-boiled egg." Kathleen went to the vanity and peered in the mirror.

"Geesh, my hair looks awful."

"Do you want to eat here or downstairs?" Nahalia asked.

"Downstairs, of course." Kathleen started brushing her hair, hoping to hide her irritation. "Oh, Benje Ange, do you know if Grace and Dorthea will be coming to play bridge this afternoon? If so, we'll need a fourth since Helen's still in the Bahamas. Any suggestions?"

"Mr. Hendrix's wife, Ruth, plays bridge. You met her at the party several weeks ago. Shall I call her?"

"Leave her number by the phone, and when I come downstairs I'll give her a ring." Kathleen made certain that Nahalia had left. She went over to the other maid.

"Benje Ange, before you leave, tell me what you talked about on my veranda."

"We're worried about you."

"What is it you can't let happen?" Kathleen slipped into her robe. *Had someone else died from poisoning before?*

"Do you like me to draw you a bath?"

"You know something that I should know. What is it?" She tied her sash.

"I have no answers for you, Miss Kathleen." Benje Ange lowered her head and would not meet Kathleen's eyes.

"We're friends. You take such good care of me." Kathleen walked closer to the woman and said in a soft voice, "If you know something about Mr. Martin I should know, please tell me."

"I know nothing you should know. I must see if Curline has your breakfast ready." Benje Ange scurried from the room, closing the door behind her.

The trouble with our times is the future is not what it used to be.

—PAUL VALERY

55

For the sake of coolness, the four bridge players wore shorts and sandals, which none of them would dare do in the states. Back in the forty-eight all the women would be decked out with hats, gloves, dresses, hose, and heels.

Island life favored the slow and casual.

Dorthea shuffled the deck and dealt the cards. She started the bidding. When the bidding was finished, Kathleen ended up with the dummy hand.

"While you all play, I'm off to check on something in the kitchen." Kathleen went in search of Curline. She found her filling a tray high with tiny, rich tasties.

"Beautiful. I'll take them out."

"I do this. You visit with your guests." Curline picked up the tray, skirted around Kathleen, went down the kitchen steps, and headed toward the living room.

Powerless, Kathleen decided to freshen her makeup. She kept extra lipstick and her silver powder compact in a guest bathroom across from the living room.

The women's conversation, drifting in and out, touched on doctors and female problems. Kathleen smiled at their restraint compared to her risqué discussions with her flapper friends. She censored everything coming out of her mouth when around these ladies.

Their conversation fell into hushed tones. Kathleen strained to hear. Something about Martin's wife—a horse-jumping accident—a spinal injury.

The compact slipped from her fingers and clattered on the marble floor. The talking silenced. Then Ruth mumbled something. Grace emitted some artificial chatter, and a feigned semblance of polite conversation ensued.

Kathleen left the powder on the floor and cleared her throat to announce her entrance.

"Did I take too long?" She hadn't.

Grace smiled and played one of her two remaining cards.

Kathleen stole a cookie. "These cookies melt like butter."

"Well, that ends that." Grace picked up the cards. "We love the tea sandwiches, too. I must have Curline's recipes."

"Come play at my place next Wednesday." Dorthea plucked a cigarette from a gold case.

"Ruth," Grace said, "I can't wait to hear how the lamb special turns out."

Everyone but Kathleen laughed.

Kathleen crossed her legs and, without thinking, furiously jiggled her foot.

"I'm sorry." Grace pursed her lips. "How rude of us. You were in the kitchen when we talked about this."

Ruth leaned over. "It's my fault. Somehow we got on about doctors and I told this sad story concerning my sister-in-law's best friend." Ruth took several more cookies. "I don't know her name, but she's almost fifty with six children, all boys ranging from two years to thirty."

"Lordy," Grace said, "I'm exhausted to think about it." She fanned herself with her napkin. "I can't wait until this woman stuff is over."

Kathleen sipped her rum punch and waited. She couldn't taste any rum.

"Go on, Ruth," Dorthea said.

"This friend's husband works away from home for long periods of time. You can count back nine months from each of the boys' birthdays, and you'll know when hubby came home."

Grace shuddered. "Just kill me."

"Here's the sad thing. She thought her baby-making days were over. She felt miserable—hot spells, restless, couldn't sleep at night, and all those other symptoms. Then hubby comes home for several weeks. One morning she wakes up nauseated. She can't keep anything down."

"He's goddamned knocked her up again." Kathleen said flatly, then bit her lip.

"You say it quite well." Ruth smiled.

"Tell Kathleen about the lamb special part." Grace picked up the deck, tapped to square the cards, and dealt.

"This woman raised a half a dozen children by herself," Ruth continued. "She's worn out. Now who would want a baby to care for when you're fifty?" She sorted her cards. "That's why she's going to get the lamb special next Monday."

"Men," Grace said. "They have it easy."

"This lamb special is code for . . ." Kathleen paused to select the socially correct terminology.

"Right. Wicked, but necessary." Dorthea studied her cards.

"I knew this woman who was fifty-two years old. The baby wasn't right. It's in one of those state institutions." Grace dabbed her temples with her hanky. "I think I'd just kill myself. I'd walk out that door over there and jump off that cliff." Then she added, "I bid one heart."

Kathleen planned how to respond to Grace's bid.

Dorthea bid one spade. Now it was Kathleen's turn.

"Three hearts. Why call it a lamb special? Seems rather macabre."

"I agree . . . lambs to the slaughter," Dorthea said.

"Here's the story," Ruth said. "Dr. Mondragon, who practiced OB-GYN in a hospital in Jamaica, did something medically wrong. They took away his license. His wife's father had a business in Puerto Rico, so they moved there." She tapped her cards with her long, tangerine-colored fingernail. "I'll pass. Mondragon worked for his father-in-law until the elder man died of a heart condition. He left his business to Mondragon."

Grace said, "Four hearts." Everyone else passed.

Kathleen held the dummy hand again. "What business did this doctor inherit?"

"It sounds awful," Ruth said. "It is a meat market down in the old part of San Juan."

"Close to the convent." Dorthea played her card.

"To end this story, any woman who goes into the meat market and asks Mondragon—they never call him doctor anymore—for the lamb special, he'll tell them there isn't one today. He writes a date and time on a piece of white butcher paper and tells them to come back then." Ruth glanced around the table. "Whose turn is it?"

What loneliness is more lonely than distrust?
—GEORGE ELLIOT

56

"Miss Kathleen." The maid shook Kathleen's shoulder.

Kathleen stretched, turned onto her side, and curled up in a fetal position. She opened her eyes to the late afternoon sun and started. Benji Ange's face was right next to hers.

"Mr. Martin called from the airport. He'll be here in about twenty minutes."

"He isn't due back until next week." Kathleen sat up and swung her feet over the edge of the bed. A wave of nausea hit her. She stood and started toward the bathroom.

Benji Ange remained silent. She smoothed the covers on the bed and fluffed the pillow.

"Did you tell him I've been sick?"

"I tell him what he needs to know."

"Dammit. It isn't your job to stick your nose into my private business." Kathleen covered her mouth with her hands as she loped to the bathroom. *What in the hell is wrong with me?* She bent over the toilet and heaved until nothing but bile appeared. *I've never taken naps before.* She ran cold water over her hands and then splashed some on her face. She looked in the mirror. *I look like hell. Maybe it's a slow poison. I do need a doctor.*

She brushed her teeth. She stopped and said to the maid, "I'm sorry. I know you want to help."

"We worry about you, Miss Kathleen. If something bad happened to you, Mr. Martin will know what to do."

"Why do you think he'll know any more than you?"

"He would be angry if we didn't tell him." Benji Ange finished straightening the bed.

"What do you think a doctor would say?" Kathleen continued to brush her hair.

"I don't know if I should say."

"Go on." Kathleen selected a strawberry-colored lipstick and started to apply it.

"I think the doctor would say you are with child."

Kathleen's hand jerked, smearing lipstick across her cheek. She whirled around and faced the trembling maid. When she saw how worried the maid appeared, Kathleen took a quick, deep breath. "What do you know of these matters?"

"I've delivered two of my sisters and a couple of cousins." The family calls me because I've had experience."

Kathleen couldn't respond.

"Sometimes when the mother is carrying the child she's quite sick to her stomach for weeks and always very tired. Miss Kathleen, you have lipstick on your cheek."

Kathleen turned back to the mirror. She took a tissue with cold cream and removed the streak and then ran her finger along her lips to smooth out what remained.

"You must have morning sickness."

"You can't tell Martin this." A wildfire of panic swept through her. She hurried to the veranda and turned her face to the ocean breeze. *She can't tell him, she just can't.* Whirling around she saw Benji Ange about to leave the bedroom.

"Stop. Goddamn it to hell, Benji Ange." Kathleen squeezed her eyes shut. "I can't let you tell him."

"I'm sorry, Miss Kathleen."

"What do you mean?" Her eyes filled with moisture.

The maid stood still, facing the doorway.

"Good God. You've already told him."

Benji Ange's shoulders shook. Kathleen rushed over to her.

"Don't cry." Kathleen held her hand. "Please." *What a Goddamned splendid mess.*

The maid whimpered, then said, "What am I to do? We can't let it happen again."

"What can't you let happen again?"

"We only wanted to help." Benje Ange twisted her apron and wiped her eyes with it. "After the fall," she caught her breath a couple of times before continuing, "we thought if we moved her," she took two more short intakes of breath, "into the house . . ."

She started sobbing again.

"What fall?"

"We came here because her parents couldn't stand us around. They blamed us and the horse." Her apron was twisted in a knot and soaked from her tears. "I called Mr. Martin. He needs to know before we do anything."

"This is about," she selected her words carefully before she said, "Mr. Martin's wife back in the states."

"I'm not supposed to say." Benji Ange bolted from the room. Kathleen could hear her sobbing all the way down the stairs.

Then she heard the massive front door open and Martin call, "Wait, what's wrong?"

She went to the banister and peered down. Benji Ange had disappeared.

"What's wrong with Benji?"

"A misunderstanding." Kathleen descended the stairway with all the grace she could muster and put her arms around his neck. "You're full of surprises. I didn't expect you back until next week."

His lips met hers and lingered a deliciously few seconds. Then he wound his fingers into her hair and buried his face in her neck.

"You tickle." She took his hand and led him out to the swimming pool. "Do you want to change into something cooler? Would you like a snack?"

"How many questions can I answer at once?"

"I'm so happy I can't contain myself. Why are you back so soon?" Kathleen sat in the chair with her back to the afternoon sun. Martin sat next to her where the umbrella would shade his eyes.

Curline appeared. "I made some fresh limeade and pecan cookies." She smiled at Kathleen and placed the tray with the pitcher, napkins, glasses, and cookies in front of them. Then she disappeared.

"I'd rather have my Cuba Libre. I don't think Curline even put any gin or vodka in this. Here, take a sip and tell me what you think," Martin said.

Kathleen refused his glass and took her own. "I know she didn't. She doesn't think I should have any alcohol."

"Why?"

"They've already told you." Kathleen took a long drink.

"They told me you've been sick."

"They tell you everything."

"I'm certain they don't tell me everything." Martin reached over and patted her leg. "But I insist they take care of you." He leaned in and kissed her cheek.

"Like what happened to your wife?"

He stiffened.

"Your wife was in some sort of an accident."

"Who've you been talking to?" He sat rigid.

"I don't have spies like you." Kathleen averted her eyes toward the ocean. *Why did I say that?* She didn't want the maids in trouble. "I hear things, bridge-table talk, and I put pieces together."

Martin remained quiet.

"You feel guilty about what happened to her, whatever it was, and you feel honor bound to take care of her for the rest of her life. You will never marry me no matter what."

"Kathleen . . ."

"I know why you are here," Kathleen said. She shoved the plate of cookies to the far side of the table. "Benji Ange said she told you I was carrying your child."

"As a matter of fact, those were exactly her words. I couldn't be happier." He handed her a small package wrapped in white paper and tied with a green grosgrain ribbon adorned with fresh heather.

She unwrapped it, opened the leather box, and lifted out a gold watch. The inscription on the back read, *For where thou art there is the world itself.* Kathleen looked up, puzzled.

Martin, with a goofy smile, stuck the heather in her hair. "Shakespeare—how I feel about you and our child. Let's get to the doctor—he's one of the finest."

"Will you divorce her?"

"Kathleen . . . we're going to be parents. We live in paradise. We love each other. What more could we want?"

"To be married."

He looked crestfallen.

"I know," Kathleen said. She shoved her chair away from the table and stood.

He quickly rose from his chair and went to her side. "What?"

"They're wrong."

"Who?"

"Your maids." Kathleen forced herself to look at him.

"About what?"

"Me being pregnant. I went to a doctor several years ago in Detroit about some female problems. I can never be pregnant. We're not going to have a child."

Martin's face darkened. He shook his head. "The morning sickness, Benji was certain—"

"She's wrong. I have an undiagnosed food allergy."

"I don't believe you."

"It runs in my family. Mother is allergic to pineapple, Father to . . . to celery, and my little sister is allergic to shellfish. They only found out about these allergies after years of each one being sick." Kathleen looked out to the sea, then glanced back at Martin. "They were always sick in the morning after eating whatever they were allergic to the night before."

"You're making this up."

"I have a food allergy." Kathleen stared out over the rolling waves and toward the pinkish clouds along the horizon. "I haven't the foggiest idea which foods are causing it. I'll be fine once I know."

Martin put his hand to his temple.

"You seem disappointed."

He pulled her in close, holding her tight. "I hadn't thought about a family with children until Benji put the idea into my head. After that, I couldn't stop thinking about our future. I am more than disappointed." He sighed. "At least I still have you."

"We need to talk about that."

What you do speaks so loudly that I cannot hear what you say.
—RALPH WALDO EMMERSON

57

Mornings on the island were all the same. This one was like the day before, and the day before that, and Kathleen knew it would be like the one tomorrow. She wouldn't be there to experience it. If she hadn't been horridly nauseated, she'd have cherished her last breakfast on the veranda.

"Kathleen, you can't do this to us." They stood on the front steps of his villa.

"I can't live this life." A tingling started way back on the inside of her jaws. She might throw up at any minute.

"You know I love you."

"And I you, Martin. But I find this unbearable. You can't be loyal to two women. I'll let the maids know where to ship my trunks." She motioned for the driver to put her bags in the car. She dreaded the twisting turns down the hillside.

"If you go, we'll both be miserable." Martin clung to her arm.

"It's time for both of us to let go." Kathleen checked her purse for crackers. "I won't change my mind. Will you come with me to the airport?"

He shook his head and released her arm.

This powerful business man is about to cry? Men don't cry. "Martin—Martin, you are my one true love." Kathleen moved in against him and pressed her mouth to his. Her heart had ripped. She didn't dare let him see her tears. "I'm a prisoner here. And my jailers aren't allowed to be my friends."

Kathleen pulled back and stared at him. He closed his eyes. She hugged him tight.

"I must go back to my world and leave this beautiful dream. I'm sure after all these years away from Chicago I'll be safe. Come with me to the airport."

"I hate good-byes." His face lost all muscle tone.

She stooped to climb into the car, paused, and blew him a kiss. "Until next time, love." She tried to smile, but she couldn't make it happen. Her chin trembled too much. She couldn't look back at him. He would be standing there, holding her heart.

~

An hour later Kathleen settled into her seat in the small aircraft as it winged its way to San Juan, Puerto Rico—back into her world of danger. She'd assured Martin she'd be safe, but her crazy knife thrower had seemed terribly obsessed. She calmed herself by eating crackers and watching the miniature ships far below.

Kathleen had called her parents and asked if she could visit. After Minneapolis she'd go back to Detroit to see Brandy, maybe make a trip to visit her sister. Mary lived somewhere close to Denver. If Kathleen liked Denver, maybe she would stay. She'd be safe there.

Martin had appointed her to the board of some wholesale company based in Colorado. She tried to refuse, but he insisted. She had no idea if what he had given her, or what Ed's daughters insisted she keep, would be worth anything. She didn't care. Shoeboxes had saved her from the ills of the stock-market crash, leaving her financially comfortable.

When the airplane landed in San Juan, the cabdriver took her to a quaint hotel within walking distance of El Convento. Kathleen unpacked and went down to the front desk. "I'm going to be here a few days." She handed him a tip. "Where can I shop for fruits and necessities? I need them to be close by—walking distance."

She wrote down the information, stuffed it in her purse, then strolled out into the sun. Several blocks away, she stood outside of Louie's and Son's Better Butcher Shop. Kathleen glanced up and down the street. She didn't see any other meat markets. She went inside. Raw meat smells assaulted her nose. Her stomach lurched. She charged back out onto the sidewalk. *It's twelve o'clock. What's this morning sickness crap?*

She took crackers from her purse, ate two, then went back inside.

"A lamb special, please."

"Señorita, no lamb special here. You go down the street to the harbor. You see Mondragon's Meats." The butcher handed a package to a dark-eyed woman. They gave Kathleen broad smiles.

Next I'll find a sign that says "Deli and Abortions."

Relieved to be outside, Kathleen headed down the cobblestone walk toward the harbor. She scanned the shop signs, looking for Mondragon's Meats.

"Oh, Miss McPherson." Someone tugged on her blouse.

Kathleen whipped around. *Who on earth?*

Mrs. Schrader, wearing unusually thick glasses, said, "I've been looking for you."

How in the hell? Kathleen didn't remember her wearing glasses.

"I'm glad you're still gangly, or I'd never have spotted you." She waved her red and yellow purse.

"You're quite easy to spot, Mrs. Schrader."

She straightened her orange and purple feathered hat. "Let's have lunch. You have to be careful in these islands. Cleanliness, bad water, food poisoning, you know. There's a sidewalk café around this corner. You'll pay for your own, of course."

Kathleen stood blinking at the woman. What reason would this woman have to murder her? Had she poisoned Dolly? If she was also the knife thrower, why didn't Kathleen have a knife sticking out of her back right now?

"How did you find me?" Kathleen followed her out of curiosity.

"You've been an embarrassment to your parents, you know. Please call me Ivy."

"Did they tell you I'd be here?"

"Your mother said you'd be flying from San Juan to Minneapolis sometime this week to spend a night." Ivy Schrader faltered along on the cobblestones, then grabbed Kathleen. "Here, we'll eat here."

The sidewalk café had a clear view of the harbor below. Ivy Schrader pulled out a chair, sat, and started to read the menu.

"I knew I'd find you." Ivy giggled. "It worked, even with my eyesight.

[289]

But I had to make sure it was you. I didn't want to make that mistake again."

"Why do you care?" Some inner voice told Kathleen to leave, but this weird woman looked pretty harmless. Kathleen pulled out the other chair and sat.

"The only friend you have is Pritchard. And even Pritchard refuses to discuss you. Everyone must hate you. Where have you been all these months?"

"With friends who don't hate me." Kathleen sat.

"Menu print's small." Ivy removed her glasses, rubbed her eyes, and adjusted them back on her nose. "Let's have their fruity drink. It's quite good." She ordered two and then waved the waiter away.

"Why were you so desperate to find me?"

Ivy's lunch idea seemed to have disappeared. She ran her fingers along the feathers sticking out of her hat. "Don't you care about Vivian Davidson? She continually asks about you." Ivy opened her purse, turning and shielding it so Kathleen couldn't see. "The medication helps Vivian."

The hairs on Kathleen's neck bristled. Ivy might look frail, but she concealed a strong dark side.

The waiter set a creamy-pink fruit drink by each of them.

Mrs. Schrader took a good deal of time to slip off her gloves. Then she arranged them in a neat fold beside her placemat.

"I need to go." Kathleen moved her chair back. Mrs. Schrader put a hand on Kathleen's.

"Please stay. I need your advice." She pointed down toward the bay. "See those lovely sailing ships? I plan to take a trip on one. Would you suggest the large clipper there or the smaller ship?"

Kathleen stared at Ivy, but Ivy kept nodding and pointing toward the bay. Kathleen turned and looked. Elegant sailing ships, with sails unfurled on their tall masts, glided on the calm turquoise waters. Several others were moored in the bay. Sounds of a faint rustle sent shivers through Kathleen. She glanced back at Ivy Schrader.

"Which one?" Ivy played with her gloves and smiled.

"You've spent years stalking me." Kathleen looked at their drinks, then back at Ivy's face. "Why?"

Ivy laughed. "You can be quite silly, can't you? Drink up. You'll love the taste." She held her glass in a toast and took a large sip, covering her top lip with foam. She set her glass down and leaned back. "Go on, it's marvelous."

"I'm not stupid, you know." Kathleen jumped up. She studied the throng of people on the street behind Ivy.

"What's happening?" Ivy cocked her head.

We'll see who wins this game.

Kathleen waved. "It's Pritchard. See him crossing the street over there with those people?" She called out, "Pritchard, come join us."

Ivy stood. "Pritchard?"

Kathleen switched their fruit drinks, picked up her purse, and said, "You see him, don't you?"

Ivy took off her glasses and rubbed her eyes again.

"I don't think he sees us," Kathleen said. "I'll catch him." She snatched Ivy's glasses, sprinted up the walk, tossed the glasses to a young boy, and darted around the corner.

Dammit. Now I crave a creamy-pink fruit drink.

Exhausted, physically and emotionally, Kathleen returned to her hotel. She'd take a short nap, then find Mondragon's Meat Market. She entered and went up the dark, cool stairway to her room. She checked her purse for her room key. It wasn't there.

She patted her pockets, then checked her purse again. Her usual contents and packets of crackers remained, but not the key. *Impossible.*

She went back to the desk, and the clerk gave her another. He said she'd be billed for the lost key if she didn't return two when she checked out.

Once in her room, she relocked the door and pulled off her shoes and dress. With heavy eyelids, she climbed between the sheets to doze.

Her eyes popped opened. *Pritchard.* She sat up, pulled on her clothes, and washed her face. *Mr. Temple taught them magical things, how to appear and disappear into shadows, how to know things unspoken . . . and probably how to steal hotel keys from purses.*

Kathleen packed her clothes while imagining Ivy stabbing her in her sleep. She'd find another hotel. She closed her luggage and started to leave but stopped.

Enough. No more running or hiding.

After years of being stalked, this time she'd end it. She plopped into the chair by the window and waited. Kathleen filled her thoughts with the good times, Chicago, Detroit, and Martin.

When the sunlight grew faint and street noises amplified, she decided to keep her room dark. She opened her last package of crackers, ate, and wondered how she would stop Ivy. Kathleen's head throbbed, and her foggy brain needed sleep.

A soft scratch of metal against metal put her on alert. The door handle turned. Kathleen sucked in air, sprung across the room, and jerked the door open.

Ivy gasped, dropped the key, and stepped back.

Tonight all those years of anger from being stalked ignited something. Her tense muscles exploded, shoving Ivy back against the wall.

Stepping away and taking deep breaths, Kathleen watched. Ivy, red faced, straighten her hat, gather her skirt, then bent over. She slipped a thin dagger from her shoe.

Insanity! Kathleen kicked toward Ivy's face, but her foot connected with the silly hat, knocking it askew. Ivy, muttering nonsense, charged Kathleen, nicking her arm. Kathleen yelped, and Ivy gave Kathleen's shoulder a nasty slash. Kathleen spun away, clutching her wound. Ivy continued to sliced air, as Kathleen ducked and dodged. Ivy's hat slipped, flopping over her glasses. She faltered, stumbling nearer the stairwell.

Heat flooded over Kathleen. Ivy would never give up.

Enough of this murdering, crazy hat woman.

Kathleen lowered her head and bulldozed Ivy over the top of the stairs—and beyond. Ivy's screams chilled the air.

Kathleen turned away from the tumbling woman. She couldn't stomach the noise or the splatters of blood.

The family is one of nature's masterpieces.
—GEORGE SANTAYANA

58

The huge propellers slowed. Kathleen put her smoldering cigarette in the little armrest ashtray and closed the lid while the stewardess gave instructions. The buildings of Chicago loomed as the plane flew over. Then the wheels jounced on the ground.

Kathleen collected her luggage and took a taxi to the train station. She'd told Sophie to always keep enough money for their return tickets, so it simply seemed fitting to return to Minneapolis the way she'd left years ago. With luggage in hand, she paid the driver and walked up the sidewalk to the entrance of the station.

The taxi wars were over. Bums squatted or stood around the entrance, holding out their hands or maybe a cup full of pencils. Recovery from this recession took a long time to reach everyone.

Kathleen pulled a few bills from her purse as she neared the men. One leaned against the building cracking his knuckles. She sensed a familiarity. She studied him, his features, his greasy-yellow hair, his large hands, his build . . . she knew this bedraggled man, and a wave of nausea swept over her.

He held out his scarred and soiled palm, as if from some rehearsed routine now turned habit.

"Chester?"

Despondent, rheumy-brown eyes met hers.

"Good God. It *is* you."

He shifted his eyes toward his feet and lowered his hand.

"Oh, Chester." She had no words for him.

He shook his head—waved her on.

"I'm not leaving." She shook with disbelief. "Look at you. How did this happen?"

He coughed, wiped his mouth with his shirt sleeve, and squatted against the building, ignoring her.

Kathleen knelt too. She pulled a pack of Pall Malls out, took one, lit it, and put it in his mouth.

He inhaled deeply and, after a few seconds, let the smoke curl out around the stubble on his neck and chin. After several more drags, he muttered, "Thanks."

"Who murdered Lillian?" She handed him the rest of the pack and matches.

"Ivy Schrader. She's out to kill me, too."

"Why—what's wrong with her?"

He never looked at Kathleen, only mumbled, "Jealous. We were lovers."

"That explains nothing. She wanted to kill me. How would she know about us?"

"Vivian didn't care what I did. I told her everything." He shrugged. "Ivy found out who I was seeing because Vivian told her."

"You told Vivian about—what kind of cruel, selfish man are you?" Tears filled her eyes. "You coward, faking your own death."

He cleared his throat. "If the police knew about me and Lillian, they'd come after me."

"You left a wife who loved you, and you let Ivy go on killing. You're a bastard."

She shoved a bunch of bills into his hand, then fumbled back in her purse until her fingers wrapped around the gold chain. Kathleen pulled it out and slung his pocket watch at him.

"Enjoy your fucking life."

∿

When the train rolled into the station in Minneapolis that evening, Kathleen didn't expect her stomach to be overtaken by a brewing storm of nerves. She took in a deep breath of fresh air, signaled a taxi, and gave the directions to Fremont Street.

When the taxi pulled up, Kathleen stepped out and paid the driver. She looked up at the house and relief washed over her. Her mother and father waved from the porch, actually welcoming her.

She bounded up the steps, and her mother hugged her for long moments until her father cleared his throat.

"How are you, Kathleen?" He pecked her cheek, picked up her luggage, and carried it inside. He set it all at the foot of the stairs. Yeast and rosemary smells wafted from the kitchen.

"I smell Louisa's homemade rolls and my favorite butter-herb roasted chicken." Kathleen removed her gloves and hat, glanced around, and soaked in the multitude of fragrances and comforts she'd loved as a girl.

Her parents exchanged looks, then her mother gave a half-hearted smile. She nudged Kathleen into the living room to sit.

Her father asked, "What's your pleasure? Sorry, I don't have rum."

"I'm quite thirsty. I could do nicely with a plain glass of water right now."

He mixed drinks and handed her a glass of water with a slice of lime.

"Dear, we had to let Louisa go." Her mother pulled out a Pall Mall. "I'm doing all the cooking now."

"Why didn't you tell me? Poor woman—"

Her father handed a bourbon and water to her mother and picked up his own. He moved to the large picture window.

"Don't give it a thought." Her mother patted her knee. "We manage well."

Kathleen hated this. This ever-present pride—her parents always kept conversation at an impersonal level.

"What about Louisa? Where is she?"

Her father moved over and sat in his club chair. "Living with her son."

"Pops, I always thought of her as our family. Why didn't you tell me?"

"Couldn't." His face lost muscle tone. "Your saving this house was enough."

Her mother stood. "Kathleen, I've made your favorite triple-fudge cake. Now, come help me set the table, and I'll tell you all about Mary, her wedding, and her doctor husband. She loves Colorado."

After dinner, her father carried her luggage to her bedroom. Again, familiar smells, this time of furniture wax and laundry soap, flooded her with warmth. She slid her hand along her comforter.

Her father asked if she needed anything, then wished her a good night and closed the door.

Kathleen had told her parents she would be leaving the next day, after a visit with Sophie. She mentioned she'd be off then to follow her career as a choreographer with her friend Brandy. She didn't tell them where, and they didn't ask.

She'd go back to Chicago, at least for a few days—have dinner with Pritchard, visit with Dolly and meet her milkman husband. She should buy a gift for Dolly's toddler.

Chicago. The crazy things they did. Her wild ride in the stolen automobile . . . she'd always wanted one—a fancy one. She smiled. Her time had come.

Kathleen opened the window and looked at Lyndale Park. The evening breeze gently played with her draperies. She breathed in a different air, longing for the salt and sound of sea, and Martin's arms around her. A soft breeze caressed her face like Martin might have—*Martin.*

If he knew, he'd never forgive her. He'd never understand. After all she'd put her family through, she couldn't raise a child out of wedlock.

From the light of the streetlamp, she could see Mr. Field walking a large, white dog. So many years ago . . . *Lillian.*

Chester, so needy in so many ways.

Sophie, Dolly, Brandy. . . I miss our times together. And her little sister opening their home to everyone—feeding the world. When Kathleen handed out bills to street people, it came from knowing Mary's heart of gold—Mary's arms spread wide, ready to take care of anyone.

Mary.

Kathleen looked from the window to her desk. She pulled a fountain pen from her purse and sat. Then she removed a small, white square of stationary from the drawer and stared at it.

Could she do this?

You'll need your family someday—Father's words from so many years ago.

She pressed her palm on her abdomen, swallowed back the ache in her throat, and wrote.

My Dearest Sister,

Father always said never put anything personal in writing, but what I'm about to ask of you is most personal. I hope you will let me give you a secret gift, a gift you'll love forever.

I'm arriving in Denver by motorcar next week. I hear the Brown Palace Hotel is lovely, so I'll be staying there for a while. If you and your husband are willing to open your hearts and accept my gift, we should meet and make preparations.

Lovingly,
Your sister, Kathleen

DISCUSSION QUESTIONS

1. Compare the parenting style in the time of Angus and Elizabeth McPherson with your own parental figures.

2. Teenage slang changes from generation to generation. Criminetly, hooey, gold digger, and heebie-jeebies were common in the 1920s. What were some of the common expressive words during your high-school years?

3. Describe one lesson Kathleen learned from her impetuous behaviors.

4. What personality traits made Sophie more vulnerable than Dolly or Kathleen?

5. If your feeling toward Pritchard changed, tell why.

6. In many ways Vivian Davidson and Ivy Schrader had similar characteristics. In what ways did they differ?

7. Vivian Davidson, Elizabeth McPherson, Angus McPherson, Martin, and Dolly reacted at one time or another in surprising ways. Pick one and describe how it affected Kathleen.

8. Martin's refusal to divorce his wife compromised his relationship with Kathleen. Evaluate Kathleen's final decision regarding this.

9. What should Kathleen have done about Chester's watch?

10. Kathleen faced some difficult decisions toward the end of this story. Should she have made other choices?

CPSIA information can be obtained
at www.ICGtesting.com
Printed in the USA
LVHW111757071118
596308LV00002B/417/P